i

Anachron

Books

Camp Jane

Book Two
Double Trouble for Lizzy

To Mike,
who is,
against all odds,
verifiably nonfictional

Chapter One

*T*rouble wasted no time in coming to Camp Jane.

The trouble at the Regency Resort, the lush Jane Austen theme resort in upstate New York, began the day of the Meryton dance, if you can believe it, the very first event of the *Pride and Prejudice* storyline on the opening day of the tourist season.

Now, make no mistake, the event itself was a howling success. The essay winners playing Austen's characters displayed their training delightfully and everyone, even stiff Will Arlington playing Mr. Darcy, remembered the dance steps they had been taught the previous week.[1] Even more commendably, our favorite, Maggie Argyle, playing Elizabeth Bennet, managed to get through the evening without embedding her lovely dancing shoe too deeply into her own mouth, metaphorically speaking, or any other literal or figurative location it should not have gone, either.

As we said, by any definition, a howling success.

Yet, with the arrival of the Janeite guests in our narrative, an even quirkier bunch than the essay winners that arrived the previous week, we must pause and acknowledge truthfully (and universally, too, if you like) that Jane Austen, the author of the *original* Meryton dance, would likely have been entirely perplexed by the whole blooming lot of them.

We do not disparage the good Miss Austen's imagination. Far from it!

But Austen could hardly have imagined that she would have what we shall call *most ardent* fans (*rabid* having such negative connotations) gathering to celebrate her works

---

1   This week was detailed in Book One of the series, *Camp Jane: The Winners Rally Round.*

two centuries after her death, could she? Could any author anticipate that devoted readers would eagerly spend their vacations dressed in clothing from a bygone era and lodging in re-creations of the manor homes described in her novels? How could anyone have foreseen that highlights from her storylines would be re-enacted in two-week cycles by thrilled essay winners selected for their *real-life* personality similarities to her *imaginary* main characters?

Least of all, perhaps, could Ms. Austen have understood the *intense* popularity (again, eschewing words like *fanatical* that will have no place in this affectionate narrative) of something called the "Austen Canon Scavenger Hunt," or CanonScav, that Janeites from around the world traveled to Camp Jane to play.

The "Scavvers" at the Meryton dance, for example, were thrilled to:

a) overhear Mr. Darcy remark that he had found Miss Elizabeth Bennet 'tolerable' but not handsome enough to tempt him *(check)*,

b) see the jovial Mr. Bingley dancing with Miss Jane Bennet *twice* causing gossip throughout the room *(check)*, and

c) note that Miss Caroline Bingley had an 'air of decided fashion' in that she was wearing the tallest [fill in the blank] in the room (correct answer: *feathers*).

In short, the delighted resort guests had been able to tick off no less than three *Pride and Prejudice* elements from the paper lists that they carried either tied like dance cards on their wrists or tucked into coat pockets.

But our ardent Austen fans were but newly arrived in the 19th century, so they could not go long without the tender touch of their mobile phones. Since they were only permitted to use technology in private spaces at the resort, they dispersed rather quickly to their guesthouses after the dance and the four character players calling themselves

LaGGards emerged from the assembly hall a few minutes later to find themselves quite alone.[2]

Bingley spoke up first. "Let's go home the long way around the lake, y'all." The farm boy dialect that he used in his real life as fresh-faced Indiana naïf Casey Barmettler re-emerged for just a moment after staying mostly hidden throughout the dance where he felt obliged to "talk fancy." His suggested route would more than double the usually brief travel time between Meryton and Longbourn. But since this would give him more time to linger in the moonlight with his sweetheart, the stunning beauty playing Jane Bennet, this was absolutely fine with him.

"Yes!" Jane agreed happily. "*Emma* had some kind of singles mixer event tonight at the Highbury gazebo, Harriet Smith's Welcome Party or something. We can check it out if we go that way."

"Oo! They may still have food out," Maggie said, perking up and walking a bit faster. "If you bring your own box, they let staff take leftovers back to your room so they don't have to haul it back to the kitchen. But we need to get there before it's gone." She motioned for Darcy to walk faster but he seemed disinclined to do so.

"You have no box, Miss Elizabeth," Darcy observed peevishly.

"She has *pockets*, Darcy. Look, she'll never give you any peace if she doesn't get her rangoons," Jane reported factually. The lovely Jane, called Jerri Lyn Parker back home in Oklahoma, had a calm inner stillness that bespoke her Native American roots, but when she did speak up, she often cut right to the heart of the matter. In Maggie's case, the heart in question was filled with gooey cream cheese

---

2   These essay winning character players had met at LaGuardia airport and Maggie had dubbed them LaGGards. Again, see Book One, *Camp Jane: The Winners Rally Round,* for their origin story hijinks.

and surrounded by a crunchy fried wonton shell.

"I needs my wontons, Darcy," Maggie said, putting a hand on a hip, a slight warning edge in her voice. With the exuberance of her Scottish father and the organizational skills of her Black activist mother, Maggie often served as social director for her group of friends. We might also add that she was more than a trifle stubborn and, though we say it with love, frankly enjoyed getting her way.

"Remember what I told you about the sow," Bingley said pointedly to Darcy, under his breath.

"Believe me, I have no desire to stand between Miss Elizabeth and her rangoons," Darcy insisted loudly, raising his palms in surrender to the power of fried wontons. "But, I am not a cheetah inclined to out-sprint all comers to the buffet table. Bingley, Jane, you two run ahead to Highbury and snap up any spare rangoons before they disappear into someone else's pocket, all right? Wait for us there. Lizzy and I will be along shortly."

"Roger that, Darcy," Bingley said cheerfully, taking Jane by the hand and walking forward briskly. "Just remember what I told you," he called over his shoulder.

"Yes, yes, Bingley," Darcy said quickly, glancing toward Maggie. "Off you kids go now. See you soon."

Maggie looked sideways at Darcy as they continued their leisurely stroll. *Get this guy away from his richy rich family back at the winery in Napa and he's almost becoming a real boy,* she thought to herself. *At least he's trying to loosen up. But he still needs a good teasing now and then.* She smiled to herself. She was just the woman for that job. "So, what was Bingley going on about? Something about a sow?"

Darcy cleared his throat before replying. "Just an Indiana proverb about steering clear of danger in the farmyard."

"How delightful. What about the *sow*?" Maggie persisted.

An embarrassed cough. "It seems one never stands *between* a sow and the trough. Of food. Dangerous spot."

"Ah. And in this particular application, I am the sow?" Maggie asked pointedly.

"Bingley rarely thinks before he speaks," Darcy said uncomfortably, defending his chum as well as one might when your friend has just described a resemblance between your lady friend and a pig. "He has no future in the diplomatic corps, I'll grant you. But his heart's pure gold."

"I suppose," Maggie conceded reluctantly. It *was* true. Impulsive and scattered he might be, but Bingley would never intentionally hurt a soul. "He's not a bad sort but he speaks without thinking. Remember your saying, Darcy, that 'not every thought must be spoken aloud?' You've *got* to work with him on that."

"True enough, true enough. But, you know … " Darcy walked backward for a moment, then halted his tall frame in front of her. Maggie came to a stop, too, arms crossed, coolly gazing up at him. With her head tilted upward, the moonlight glinted off her tumbling auburn curls fetchingly, something not at all lost on Mr. Darcy.

"In some cases," he continued, "a free speaker's *honesty,*" he impishly drew a tiny circle on her forearm, "can be quite refreshing. At least I find it so." He smiled disarmingly and enjoyed her fine eyes for a long, long moment. Maggie's toes had grown suddenly warm and her skin tingled where he had touched her arm. Inevitably, her defensive ramparts crumbled into a disordered heap as she laughed aloud. She playfully guided Darcy back to her side and shook her head.

"Get over here and keep walking, crazy man." They resumed their stroll, with Maggie's heart beating faster than she wanted to admit and Darcy smiling smugly.

Maggie suddenly flashed back to a moment from her childhood when she had stood in the doorway of her mother's home office, listening to the quiet voices of her parents. Her father was urging his wife to take a break from writing on her latest grant project, rubbing her tired shoulders and murmuring to her in his soothing Scottish tones. Her mom had said she still had work to do. But Maggie had seen her gentle smile even as she issued the droll warning, "I am not trying to play with you, Hamish." Then, when her father nestled his red beard against his wife's ear and a private something passed between them, the glorious music of her mother's boisterous laugh burst out. It was one of the most beautiful sounds Maggie had ever known, the soundtrack of her childhood, two loving people sharing a laugh.

"Watch out for these crazy white boys, Maggie," her mother had called out to her young daughter as she leaned back into her husband's embrace. "They got no more sense than to make you laugh right while you're trying to be mad at 'em."

Sure enough, thought Maggie now, her own lips unconsciously mirroring her mother's soft smile. *These crazy white boys got no sense at all.*

"Tell you what, Will," Maggie said aloud. "You get me some rangoons and all will be forgiven with Bingley on this sow thing, okay?"

"Consider it done, Miss Elizabeth," Darcy readily agreed. "Though I would have fetched food for you anyway out of pure self-interest, I assure you."

"You're coming right along, Mr. Darcy," she acknowledged. "You *might* make good boyfriend material in time. Eventually."

"Such fulsome praise. I blush."

"Try not to swoon. I don't want to have to drag your big carcass back to Netherfield."

We can report with relief that there *were* leftover rangoons at the Highbury location (which Maggie happily stuffed into her pockets) and that the four players made it back to their respective lodgings with nary a swoon between them.

Finally, then, as a yawning Maggie crunched her rangoons before retiring, she checked in with her best buddy, the winner playing *Northanger Abbey's* Henry Tilney, on his JaneyApp account.[3]

LizzyB: Hey, Henry. How did your dance go in Bath?

Tilney: Smashing success. Catherine convincingly attracted by my charms, of course. CanonScavvers thrilled to see us introduced.

Henry was the fifth LaGGard, London actor Ian Henry Tidball. His early career success as a child spokesman for the Power Oats cereal company had contributed to his highly confident and cheeky personality. Even so, Maggie was a fair match for the clever lad and she never missed a chance to banter with her bestie.

LizzyB: Good, good. Did anyone faint? It seems last year's Henry made girls swoon.

Tilney: Last year's Henry, indeed! SO "last year". I believe everyone remained upright.

LizzyB: Hmm…perhaps the sexual appeal of Henry Tilney is fading?

Tilney: Not a jot, my dear! A girl stole my handkerchief! Brazen little thing reached into my pocket (!) asked if it was "muslin" and ran off with it.

LizzyB: Well, there ya go. You're still being objectified by women. Huzzah.

Tilney: I am a short and shaggy man, Lizzy. I shall take my adulation as it comes. I suppose Sir Darce-a-lot was appropriately un-tempted by you at Meryton?

---

3   JaneyApp: the internal communications app for the Regency Resort.

LizzyB: Of course.

Tilney: Arrogant fool. Thought I saw a moment between the two of you the other day at the swimming hole. Made me think our Will might be…warming a bit in the real world? Toward you in particular, perhaps?

LizzyB: Perhaps. We're trying to figure things out.

Tilney: I require no figuring at all, my Lizzy. I shall carry your bonnet til the sun grows cold if that tall beast turns out not to be to your liking.

LizzyB: Got my own bonnet for now, son. But thanks. Get some sleep.

Tilney: You as well. And if you see a young woman with my kerchief, wrestle it back for me, will you? I probably could have overpowered her but it's dashed hard to think when a woman has her hand in one's pocket, you see.

LizzyB: Oh, I see quite well. Go to bed, Henry. And tell Catherine we're happy her event went well despite the fact that she had to play it with you.

Catherine Morland was the final LaGGard player, a petite and shy Texan named Katie Morales who had gained the admiration of the group, not least among them Henry himself, with her adorable innocence and steady moral compass.

Tilney: Will do. Pleasant dreams.

LizzyB: Back atcha, Henry.

Climbing between the sheets in her cozy Longbourn room, Maggie realized that a decision was coming her way. *You've got to choose between these guys, chica,* she thought to herself firmly. *Mom would say "if you go flirting with two men, you're only making double trouble for yourself, little girl."*

Cuddling down into her bed, Maggie tried to weigh the merits of the two gentlemen objectively. *Sure, Darcy is sorta hot. Ish. Maybe.* She sighed. Well, that was a lie. *All right, fine. He's smokin' hot. The man is actual fire. And you know you like him.* She rolled over irritably and thumped her pillow, peeved with herself for that fact. *But Henry is your boy, Maggie, your sidekick, your ride-or-die,* she argued with herself. *Cheeky, funny, just like you, a real soulmate. But is he a friend zone guy or ... more?* She sighed deeply. *Whatever else happens this summer,* she resolved, *you have GOT to figure out which one is really best for YOU.*

Others at the resort were preparing for sleep, too. In her darkened bedroom at the elegant Rosings manor house, Edith Pelletucci, aka Austen's Lady Catherine de Bourgh, owner of the Regency Resort and one of the world's foremost Janeites, checked her laptop one last time for the day. Regency dance lessons were always a tough pre-sell package but sales usually would increase after the first dances ended. Janeites tended to be rather shy at first, eager to wear their new Regency outfits but hesitant to get up and dance about in them.

Edith sighed, remembering her own reluctance to dance during an awkward adolescence. She knew, however, that even the shyest Janeites could feel safe when they were with Austen's beloved characters just as it had happened for her. She vividly remembered the night, many years ago, when she had finally danced without fear. She smiled, recalling it now, utterly unaware, of course, that the events of that fateful evening would soon come back to haunt her.

For the moment, Edith knew only that here in Jane's world, a shy bookworm's wallflower tendencies could fall away like a cocoon no longer necessary. Given time to adjust, Janeites most certainly *would* want to "party like it's 1799," with "tall, dark and fictional men" as it read on the Etsy mugs from which they drank their sensible beverages every morning.

As Edith gazed into the soft glow of her computer screen,

sure enough, online dance lesson bookings were already beginning to rise. Edith knew her beloved Janeites well. The grand dame of Camp Jane closed her laptop and headed for bed, humming a little tune. All seemed well at the Regency Resort.

But that was just an illusion. Across the lake at the Barton Park location, home of the *Sense and Sensibility* cast, the trouble had already come, in a form that seemed utterly harmless at first, but in fact was nothing of the kind.

Chapter Two

The Dashwood sisters of Barton Cottage both got raging cases of poison ivy.

This was not from a light brush-by in the prettyish wilderness up the hill from the cottage. No. This was the miserable kind of itchy, puffy rash contracted when an impetuous sister playing the role of Marianne wanders off the marked path and a sensible sister, her Elinor, must tramp through a glade filled with the stuff to find her.

This is the kind of poison ivy rash that makes one not only willing but eager to sit in stinky vinegar baths, stagger around half-drunk on antihistamines or, frankly, sell any organ the doctor might demand for payment, anything at all, really, as long as it will make the itching stop.

Fortunately, Miss Judith, the Physician's Assistant at the Regency Resort, was not inclined to exact payment in human body parts. But if she had been, she could likely have stripped the poor girls as clean as twin '69 Mustangs parked too long in a sketchy neighborhood. Thus were the Dashwood sisters, played by identical twin sisters Garija and Vanaja Singh, found on Tuesday morning, too itchy for either sense *or* sensibility to reign, as their storyline events were supposed to begin.

By contrast, things were hopping at Longbourn as news about the Dashwoods began to spread. Lizzy was touring a newly-arrived family of guests, the Engelvardts, as she felt the phone in her pocket start to vibrate with notifications. Faithful to her training, however, she did not take out her phone in front of the guests.

"As you can see, you will have access to two sitting rooms here at Longbourn. One has a pianoforte *(buzz)* if you play.

11

If you want to borrow a book from Mr. Bennet's library, just use the sign out sheet on the desk *(buzz)*. Breakfast is served on the sideboard in the dining room between 7 and 9 a.m. Lunch *(buzz)* and dinner are served next door at Pemberley or if you attend an event at another location, your meal plan will follow you. Please make yourself *(buzz)* comfortable in your Longbourn home."

That has to be Henry, Maggie thought with irritation. *If he sends me one more photo of those stupid Northanger gargoyles, I'm blocking him.*

"Please, Mama, can we go see Netherfield now? Please, please, please?" begged the older daughter, Dahlia Engelvardt, spinning around in her new Regency dress.

"Well, I suppose so," said Mrs. Engelvardt, looking toward her husband.

"Whatever the girls want, Pamela," Mr. Engelvardt responded. Less enamored with his Regency outfit, he tugged at his high collar. "As long as they feed me, I'm fine."

"Oh, they feed us very well here, Mr. Engelvardt," said Maggie, proceeding to 'give her opinion very decidedly' as Lizzies tend to do. "These high-waisted dresses are really loose, but believe me, my Regency scanties are getting pretty tight under there!" She smiled and gave her belly a reassuring pat.

Not sure what to do with this overshare, the gentleman looked confused and cleared his throat. "Well, that's ... great. I guess. About the food. Not about your ..." He floundered and waved vaguely toward Maggie's midsection.

"My husband means to say how delightful everything is, Miss Lizzy," interjected Mrs. Engelvardt hastily. "We're so happy to be here, aren't we, girls?"

"Yes, Mama," replied the younger girl, Dora, with a solemn curtsy. She had recently discovered curtsies and sought to inject them into every possible interaction.

"Can we go to Netherfield *now*, Mama? You said there was croquet or something. Pleeease?" the older girl whined.

Mama Engelvardt quickly assented, and Maggie led the family to the front door. "Just go straight out this door to the main walkway and head east, to your right. Netherfield is the next house over. Can't miss it." The family walked out and with a final stiff curtsy from Dora, they were gone.

Maggie closed the door and carefully checked the sitting rooms before pulling her phone out of her pocket. The vibrant African kente design on her phone cover was hard to miss and she did not want to take any chances of being reported for using technology in front of the guests. Everyone except Longbourn staff was out at the moment, however, and in short order Maggie was able to confirm that it was, indeed, Henry exploding her phone.

Tilney: Lizzy! I have the very freshest gossip. Where are you?

Tilney: The Dashwood sisters got poison ivy. Both of them.

Tilney: Why are you not at my beck and call? I've becked, I've called. If you do not answer soon, I shall pout.

Tilney: Well, I'm pouting now. You have no one to blame but yourself.

LizzyB: Henry!!!

Tilney: Finally! Where were you??

LizzyB: Touring new visitors. Some of us work! That's sad, though. Poison ivy is yuck.

Tilney: Yuck, my dear?

LizzyB: An abomination.

Tilney: Ah. Have you ever had the stuff? I state with pride that in London we walk the streets without fear of our greenery.

LizzyB: Well, same in Chicago. But my Dad got into poison

ivy once at my grandma's house. Miserable stuff.

Tilney: Lays a person out, does it?

LizzyB: Depends. It can. We should go visit them. I'm free til noon. You?

Tilney: Free. Catherine is riding around Bath with the Thorpes today but I'm out of sight. I was actually playing billiards with the militia boys here at the Meryton bunkhouse.

LizzyB: Okay. Stay put. I'll be walking past Meryton in ten. We can walk over to Barton together.

Tilney: Righto.

LizzyB: And Henry, if you ever find out that I have a rash, consider NOT telling absolutely everyone, k?

Tilney: Of course. PS: Exactly where IS your rash? For science.

LizzyB: Darcy's right. You ARE a few scones short of a full tea tray.

Henry responded with an emoji of a smiley face wearing a halo. Muttering to herself, Maggie pulled the door shut behind her and headed out.

Back at Barton Cottage, fans of Sense and Sensibility will not be surprised to learn that true to character, Elinor was trying to suffer in silence but Marianne was ... well, was actually the opposite of silent.

"It's so hor-or-or-rible," Marianne blubbered as Elinor daubed the crown of her sister's head with calamine lotion. "We barely STARTED our storyline and now ...." She paused for more weeping. Mechanically, Elinor handed her another tissue.

Garija Singh had logged many hours tending to her younger sister Vanaja back home in New Delhi. Garija was the sensible one, not unlike the Elinor Dashwood character she was role-playing at the resort. And as to her sister, well, the girl *was* a bit of a Marianne Dashwood. More than a bit, if we're honest, with emotions that seemed constantly on the verge of driving her off a cliff. Like her Dashwood counterpart, however, nature had issued her an older sister who could usually steer her back to more sensible level ground.

"I am sure the resort has a plan for this sort of thing," Elinor said calmly. "Right now, I just want you to be comfortable enough to rest. Neither one of us slept well last night." She paused as she looked through her sister's thick hair to the inflamed scalp beneath. "How did you get this all over your *head*? Did you *roll* in it?"

Marianne wrung her handkerchief miserably. "I … I wanted to …" She sobbed again. "You are going to think I am very foolish."

"Speak freely, my dear. I *already* think you are very foolish," Elinor offered pragmatically.

"I wanted to learn how to make a garland of leaves for my hair," Marianne sniffled, wiping her nose. "For Willoughby's outdoor poetry reading. Now I probably can't even go-o-o …" The sobbing began again.

Elinor sighed deeply while she rearranged the cooling cloths on her own itchy feet. Then, with the dexterity born of many years of practice, she simultaneously handed Marianne another tissue while continuing to tend her sister's foolish head.

Chapter Three

Maggie met up with Henry outside of the Meryton militia bunkhouse just as the youngest Bennet sister, Lydia, and her paramour Wickham, apparently entering another "off again" phase of their turbulent affair, stepped outside the building to further their latest argument. Though the unwilling eavesdroppers walked away as briskly as possible, they were still subjected to another installment of LydWick's summer-long clinic on relationship dysfunction.

The argument *du jour* was over whether Wickham had shown excessive attention to a barmaid at the Meryton Distillery the previous evening.

"Look, I'm a friendly guy," Wickham was explaining. "Are you saying I can never hug a friend? Because if that's what you're saying, we need to have a very different kind of conversation."

Maggie rolled her eyes and glanced at Henry who motioned for them to walk faster. Maggie knew this discussion was not going to end well. Maggie's own Uncle Reggie was a "friendly guy," too, but her Aunty Denise had never found this argument compelling.

Nor did Lydia. "You weren't *hugging* her! You were *kissing* her!" she screeched.

"Same thing. It's a hug … but using your lips," Wickham elucidated, surprisingly able to keep a straight face.

"*Seriously?*" Lydia stared at him incredulously. "Did you just *say* that?"

"Again, if your view of friendship is this narrow," the handsome man said with a shrug, "then I don't even know how to *be* friends with you …"

Mercifully, their voices faded as Maggie and Henry progressed onward around the lake. They took a few silent steps.

"I know what you're going to say, Henry. Not all men are like that," Maggie remarked preemptively. "Very few, probably."

"Well, not many would live to see another day after that kind of statement, would they, dear girl? Rather sorts out the quick from the dead."

"Would in my family," Maggie agreed, nodding soberly.

They continued on past the sign marking the stairs leading up the hill to Northanger Abbey.

"Are you staying in the Abbey tonight or going back to Bath?" Maggie asked.

"Well, I thought I'd hang around the Abbey. They have one of those after-dark gothic tours tonight, the one where the curator fellow leads you through the garden maze with all the scary statuaries. It's very popular."

"Oh, right. Jane and Bingley wanted to see that. Darcy, too. Maybe we can slip over there tonight. We're all at Netherfield for Luncheon and Cards until about 3, but after that we're free."

"That would be wonderful, Lizzy girl. I've barely seen the old LaGGards since the storylines started. I wish you and the gang could have seen us at the dance in Bath last night. I mean, one hates to brag … "

"One does?" Maggie queried pleasantly. "One seems to love it."

"Well, one is devoted to speaking truth, my dear, always truth. And my Henry Tilney muslin-loving fangirls were out in force."

"How wonderful for you," Maggie observed drily.

"Bit of the old green-eyed monster popping up, Lizzy?" Henry inquired brightly. "Hope springs eternal that you'll throw Darcy over for me some day, you know."

Maggie laughed but had to admit to feeling a tiny jealous *ping* in her heart thinking of other girls chatting up Henry. *He's so ridiculous,* she thought with consternation. *That can't be a real LIKE like* ping, *can it? No way, right?* "Can't say what will happen with Darcy," she continued aloud, "but end up with you? That's a frying pan/fire situation right there, buddy."

"Absolutely. But oh, how we'd sizzle." Henry waggled his eyebrows.

Maggie gazed heavenward and pleaded, "*Please* give me the strength not to kill this man."

"Huzzah!" Henry exclaimed. "She doesn't want to kill me! Progress indeed."

The two friends bantered onward until Barton Cottage came into view.

They arrived, warm and slightly winded, just as the gentlemen playing Colonel Brandon (Lionel Bell, a very tall, richly dark and gallantly handsome retired military officer from downtown Detroit) and Edward Ferrars (Cal Falconer, a stocky, pale and allergy-prone wedding venue actor from remote Gretna Green, Scotland) were stepping out of the house.

"Ahoy, gentlemen," Maggie called. "I see you've visited the patients."

"Lizzy, old girl. Great to see you," Ferrars called. "Tilney. Staying out of trouble at Northanger, I hope." The gentlemen bowed all around while Maggie bobbed a curtsy.

"So, how are the girls doing?" Maggie asked. "We've heard it's bad but not much beyond that."

"They're as might be expected," Brandon said with a

shrug. "Elinor is keeping a cool head and Marianne is …
well …"

"Oh, let me, Brandon. I learnt some new American
slang from a tourist chappy this week," Ferrars said eagerly.
"Miss Marianne is … an emotional … railroad smash-up
or something, wasn't it?"

"Train wreck," said Colonel Brandon, a bit annoyed.
"But I say again, Ferrars, that one's *really* unkind."

"Dumpster fire, then?" Ferrars offered.

"No! Honestly!" Brandon responded irritably. "That's
even worse. Let's just say Miss Marianne is quite overwrought."

"Brandon *really* likes her, Lizzy," Ferrars said with a grin.
"Lacks only a cape in his attempts to rush in and try to save
her, most often from herself, I'd say."

Brandon responded coolly. "Miss Marianne is an absolutely lovely and very *spirited* young woman. Any decent
person would feel drawn to help her," he said a bit formally
as one does when one is called out on one's secret crush.
"It may interest you ladies to know that some of us," here
he bent his tall frame to look pointedly at Ferrars, "have
grown *quite* fond of her sister."

"Yes, well, Elinor is a different sort altogether, isn't she?
Not noisy at all but rather a take-charge girl, so she's a bit
… intimidating." Ferrar's pallid face broke into a revealing-
ly silly grin. "Rather attractive in its own way."

"Okay, okay, both of you have to stop talking immediately," Maggie said, curling a lip and raising a hand as a stop
sign. "Way too much information. Are they alone up there
or not?"

"Miss Judith just came to examine them," Brandon said,
"so that's when we left. But she probably won't be long.
Not much a Physician's Assistant can do for them, poor

things, besides steep them in oatmeal baths and tell them not to scratch."

Henry tilted his head and glanced around. "I say, do you hear something?"

The friends were standing on the stone pathway leading away from the lakeside Barton Cottage toward Delaford House just where it passed under the trees of a wooded glade inhabited mostly by squirrels and bunnies. Consequently, like many areas of the Regency Resort, it was a quiet place, usually devoid of the noises found in modern technology. But Henry was correct. There was an odd *whirring* noise coming from somewhere in the woods nearby and growing louder.

In fact, there was a dirt path in this woody area that ran parallel to the main rock sidewalk around the circumference of the lake. But aside from an occasional scamper by the previously mentioned woodland creatures, the rutted path seemed unused. Today, however, was a day of change.

An electric golf cart suddenly broke through the tree cover and braked to a dusty stop where the path intersected the Barton-to-Delaford walkway. The cast watched in frank wonder as the driver was revealed to be no less a person than Lady Catherine de Bourgh herself, dressed to the nines as always, alighting from the cart and briskly walking toward them. Since Lady Catherine almost *never* left the Rosings/Pemberley complex and was never seen with modern technology, the shock of the cast members might well be imagined.

"Lady Catherine! What are you doing here?" exclaimed Maggie as she reflexively curtsied, voicing aloud what everyone else was thinking but had the good grace not to shout.

The great lady nodded briefly. "Good day, everyone. Always the frankest girl on the lot, aren't you, Lizzy? Don't change a hair, my dear," she said, patting Maggie on the shoulder.

She turned to address the Dashwoods' gentlemen suitors. "Obviously, I've come about the sisters. What is your estimation, Colonel Brandon? Are they among the walking wounded? Or incapacitated altogether, *hors de combat*, as it were?"

"You'd have to ask Miss Judith for the particulars, ma'am," he replied, "but I do believe they are out of commission for the moment, yes."

"Hmm, as I feared," she murmured. "Lizzy, I'm heading upstairs. Will you accompany me, please?"

"Yes, ma'am," Maggie answered, glancing uncertainly at Henry.

"Don't worry about me, Lizzy girl," Henry said heartily. "No telling what state of undress the poor girls might be in. They don't need another chap hanging about. Pay your call. I'll head over to Delaford and see if I can't beat these fellows at billiards again."

Bidding the appropriate farewells, Maggie stepped aside to allow Lady Catherine to lead the way into the ivy-covered home of the itchy Dashwood sisters.

Chapter Four

As *Sense and Sensibility* fans know, the Spartan nature of Barton Cottage, a squatty and rustic stone box of a home, was due to the decidedly *unwelcome* "reduced circumstances"of the Dashwood women in Austen's novel after losing their home when their father died. But in the world of the Regency Resort, Barton Cottage served as a highly *welcome* option for Janeite guests in need of a budget package to live out their Austen fantasies.

As we shall see in this narrative, the Barton Cottage Regency Resort experience emphasizes lovely outdoor events, nature walks through the woods with Edward Ferrars or Colonel Brandon, outdoor poetry readings with the rakish villain Willoughby and even the imaginative addition of "bathing" in the lake with the *S&S* characters on the first Saturday of the storyline. But you may know that there are also fancy luncheons and a grand ball at London locations in the *S&S* storyline, too, even a wedding feast back at the Delaford mansion when the tale wrapped up, as ever Austen's stories must, in a blissfully happy wedding or two. So Barton Cottage guests *did* enjoy wonderful Regency experiences for a fraction of the cost paid by their counterparts at more plush lodgings across the lake at Pemberley or even up the path at Delaford.

But as Lady Catherine enters the low doorway, we must frankly own the facts of Barton Cottage. It's sparse in there.

"Let's go up, shall we?" Lady Catherine abruptly began to climb the stairs that lay directly in front of the entry. Maggie took an extra beat to realize they were moving, but then quickly mounted the staircase behind her, trying to keep up with the sprightly elderly woman.

Unlike the Bennet sisters' lovely adjoining studios at Longbourn, the Dashwood sisters shared one cramped apartment with the girls' twin beds currently pulled apart to accommodate a central table cluttered with medical accoutrements. Miss Judith and the Barton Park housekeeper further crowded the room, the former examining Elinor's feet, the latter fluffing a pillow at her bedside.

Maggie had only a brief moment to observe the ongoing actions in the room, however, before the grand entrance of Lady Catherine de Bourgh brought all activity therein to a screeching halt.

"Hello, everyone," the great lady announced, stepping briskly through the door. "Please don't let me distract you. I've come to check on the patients for myself."

The patients and their caregivers could hardly have been *more* distracted, however, by the stunning appearance of the notoriously reclusive woman. The ladies reacted rather like a bear had entered the room and begun a little dance on its hind paws. (A bear's dancing in such a circumstance may, in fact, be delightful but one really must concede that the fact of his arrival will significantly distract even the most enthusiastic devotee of *la danse*.)

"Lady Catherine!" exclaimed Miss Judith, startled upright from her examination crouch over Elinor's bed, unfortunately with one of Elinor's itchy ankles still clutched in her gloved hands. Abruptly rendered into a right angle with a pillow dropped by the stunned housekeeper onto her face, Elinor urgently sought to get Miss Judith's attention, her muffled cries and waving hands the only sound or motion for a long, frozen moment in the room. Eventually, a sudden reawakening occurred, of course, and when both of Miss Elinor's feet were restored to their previous positions of dignity on the foot of her bed, her head propped up against the headboard with numerous pillows and both caregivers' many apologies acknowledged, the purpose of

Lady Catherine's visit could be addressed at last.

"Well, first and foremost, how do you *feel,* my dears?" the good lady began.

"We have been given every kind attention, ma'am," Elinor said graciously. "I would describe the condition as uncomfortable but tolerable, especially during the day."

"Worse at night, then?" Lady Catherine inquired sharply.

"Perhaps a bit," Elinor acknowledged.

"We can hardly sleep at night, ma'am," Marianne inter-jected, weeping pitifully. "Poor Elinor has her own pain but she is also awake tending me half the night, too-oo-oo. My worry for her, in fact, is the worst of it for me—ee—ee!" The housekeeper patted her shoulder and muttered "There, there, dear."

"Well, this is the best of news, then," Elinor said drily, "because my situation is quite bearable. So my sister need worry no more about me." A moment passed. Another sob filled the silence. "I expect that this will not stop her, how-ever."

Marianne, swept by another wave of anguish, clutched the housekeeper's arm. "How brave she is, you see?" which led to another round of shoulder patting and maternal tending.

"I'll contact you by text every four hours, Miss Elinor," Miss Judith offered. "If you find we need to adjust your antihistamines in the evenings, we will. It can cause … drowsiness, you know. Knocks some people right out at a higher dose." She glanced toward Marianne's bed. "Right. Out. Just so you're aware," she added, looking pointedly at Elinor.

"Yes. We will be in touch," replied Elinor, returning the lady's gaze evenly.

"Well, my main concern is your health, of course, ladies,"

Lady Catherine said briskly, "but I must turn to the topic at hand. Miss Judith, can our Dashwood sisters carry out their character duties at this time?"

"Not for the moment, I'm afraid," Miss Judith said, shaking her head. "It's mainly about their feet. The rash will make it difficult for them to wear shoes for at least a few days."

The ladies all gazed downward at the sisters' feet and the truth of her words could not be denied. The blistered and inflamed blotches fiercely encircled Marianne's poor feet and it was clear that shoes were not in her immediate future. Elinor did not seem to have rash on the soles of her feet but the tops and ankles were blotchy and obviously too swollen for footwear. Their hands and arms had been affected, too, their lovely *café au lait* skin now darkened in patches that extended from fingers to upper arms.

"Any skin that touched the oil from the plant, I'm afraid," Miss Judith explained, "even oil that got on your clothing could, and in this case obviously did, cause a reaction."

"For the record, everyone," Elinor stated wearily, "I *did* put on shoes when I went out to search for my sister. I was not seeking a barefoot nature experience like she was. It's just that my stockings were hanging up in the bathroom to dry so I went out without them."

"Oh, no! That was my fault, too!" Marianne exclaimed. "I spilled hot tea on her feet while Willoughby was here yesterday practicing his poetry reading!"

"Not sure which was more painful," Elinor muttered as the sound of sobbing filled the room again. "Honestly, though, sister, it was spilled *tea* not a nuclear holocaust. You must get a sense of proportion about these things."

Marianne nodded dutifully and blew her nose, murmuring "so brave, so brave" while attempting to pull herself together.

"Please, I know we have caused a great deal of trouble, Lady Catherine," Elinor spoke up with sincere distress, "but will we be allowed to stay? Winning the essay contest and getting a chance to come here this summer and play Austen's characters, this has been the dream of our lives. We are only on Day 2 of the storyline and Miss Judith says we may be active again in only a few days, isn't that right?" She looked pleadingly at the Physician's Assistant.

Miss Judith nodded, slowly. "Yes, I believe so. Many people respond well, so that wouldn't be an unreasonable timeline, at least for initial healing. But at this stage, treatment involves medications that can cause considerable drowsiness. So it's likely they will be asleep or taking skin treatments during much of their recovery time. Just so you understand, Lady Catherine. They really need this time completely off until they've healed a bit. I'm afraid you should plan on using understudies at least until the weekend, probably Day 6 or so."

"All right," Lady Catherine said with finality. "Miss Judith, please keep me updated. Dear girls, please focus on your healing. We have a plan for this and will use our understudies for the first days of the cycle. Please do not worry and focus only on getting better."

"Yes, ma'am," Elinor responded gratefully. "Thank you."

"Of course, my dear," Lady Catherine said kindly. "Look, ladies. Miss Elizabeth Bennet came to call on you. Quite a thoughtful gesture, don't you agree?" Still in a bit of celebrity dancing-bear-in-my-bedroom shock, all heads nodded.

"Thanks, but it was nothing," Maggie acknowledged with a wave of the hand. "Henry came too. But of course, he was thinking about you girls being naked up here so he …"

"Yes, yes, thoughtful all around, my dear," Lady Catherine interrupted forcefully. "We'll take our leave now. Miss Elizabeth, I shall need to speak with you about your new responsibilities for the upcoming story cycle. Please follow me." After a brief wave, the dancing bear left the room and as if on a switch, regular conversation and movement re-started.

A few seconds later, with a brief curtsy, Maggie followed the lady down the stairs, mystified about what her "new responsibilities" might be. She was not suffered long to find out.

On the sidewalk in front of the cottage, Lady Catherine turned to her purposefully, causing an instant knot to appear in Maggie's belly.

"Lady Catherine," she began uneasily, "it's been a long time since I signed the essay winners' agreement but ... are you about to remind me of something?"

"Yes, indeed," the older lady admitted. "We rarely use it, but there is a clause that all winners agree to understudy other roles *temporarily* as needed. The *Pride and Prejudice* cast is assigned to understudy roles from *Sense and Sensibility*. And vice versa, for that matter."

"So I'm supposed to fill in as a Dashwood sister?" Maggie was incredulous. "But how could that even work? I've got my own storyline events with the *P&P* cast! Who would be Lizzy Bennet?"

"*You* would, my dear," Lady Catherine assured her. "We've written the schedules so that events in the two casts don't overlap. It will take a bit of scurrying around but it can be done."

"So, am I Elinor, then?" Maggie inquired. "And, what, Lydia or somebody plays Marianne? I mean, I can see it. Young. Immature character."

Lady Catherine gave a small cough and cleared her throat.

"Well, actually, my dear, the plan calls for Jane Bennet to understudy for Elinor."

"Okay, okay." Maggie nodded. "Quiet, sensible. I can see it. So that leaves me as ..." Realization dawned. "No!"

Lady Catherine's head, however, nodded in the affirmative. "I'm afraid so."

"No!! You can't mean it!" insisted Maggie.

"But I do, my dear. Elizabeth Bennet understudies for Marianne Dashwood."

"What? The woman's an emotional train wreck, a complete hysteric! How am I supposed to play *that*?" Maggie cried hysterically.

"I'm sure you can muster up a bit of emotion when necessary," Lady Catherine said, suppressing a smile. "Anyway, I hate to mention it but the event here at Barton, the Nature Walk, begins in an hour so there is some urgency here. Shall I notify Jane Bennet or will you?"

"I can go get her but ..." Maggie paused to consider. "Can I get a ride back to Longbourn in your cart? We're going to be pressed for time to get back here by 10 o'clock."

"Absolutely," Lady Catherine agreed, "but *tempis fugit*, my dear. We must make haste." She headed without delay toward the golf cart.

"Oh! Henry!" Maggie cried, suddenly remembering him as they reached the cart. Lady Catherine sat down and regarded Maggie impatiently from the driver's seat.

"I am not inclined to wait, Miss Elizabeth."

"No. I understand. I'll just text him that we're leaving." She took a seat in the rear of the cart as it lurched into motion. Maggie managed to text Henry the essentials of the news, albeit with many typos, in the bumpy cart, and promised to return with Jane to join Ferrars and the others for the Nature Walk. (Well, it was "naturrewalj" as she texted it, but Henry got the idea.)

In a relatively short time, the cart stopped abruptly in the woods just behind the Longbourn orchard as Lady Catherine pulled the brake handle noisily.

"I'll walk to Pemberley from here," the good lady announced, handing Maggie the key. "I'm leaving the cart here for your use, Miss Elizabeth. You and Jane will need to travel back and forth between locations so it seems practical. And now I must run. I have a meeting with the county sheriff. We've had some petty thievery at Northanger. Nasty business but hopefully he can help us resolve it."

"Oh, dear," Maggie said, looking worried. "Nothing related to the incident last week, is it?"[4]

"No, no, nothing of that scale," Lady Catherine assured her. "A couple of bottles of wine and some other mischief at Northanger. More of a nuisance, really. Anyway, we'll talk later. I must go now, my dear."

"I appreciate the golf cart so much, Lady Catherine," Maggie said, both touched and alarmed at the same time, "but I still have so many questions. How will we know what to do during the Dashwood events?"

"You've read the book, haven't you?" the great lady asked testily. "*Sense and Sensibility*. Or … seen the movie?" There was a twinge of disdain in the question.

"Well, I suppose, but …"

"Well, just follow along, girl, follow along! Ferrars or one of the other gentlemen lead the outdoor events. Just act like Dashwoods and follow their lead. Take a hanky, act emotional like Marianne, get Jane to look worried like Elinor. You're Kate Winslet, she's Emma Thompson, and hallelujah, everybody's happy nowadays. At this point, my dear, the CanonScavvers only need to recognize you as 'Dashwood sisters at Barton Cottage' so they can mark you

4   To see the full story of the mystery that unfolded during the Winners' training week, see Book One, *Camp Jane: The Winners Rally Round.*

off their lists. You'll be fine." Lady Catherine nodded and turned to leave.

"But …" Maggie didn't even know where to begin. "What about clothes?"

"Wear them!" Lady Catherine called over her shoulder.

Maggie stood for a helpless minute. She stared at the golf cart. It stared back at her, silent as the Sphinx and similarly reluctant to give up its secrets.

"I don't know how to drive a golf cart!" Maggie shouted into the woods desperately.

But the good lady was gone. Maggie was on her own.

The key told no tales as she turned it over in her hand. "Don't you snicker at me," she muttered to the object, probably unnecessarily. "My people are bowlers, not golfers."

"Golfers," she mused, deep in thought. Biting her lip, she pulled out her phone and quickly tapped out a text.

LizzyB: Darcy, do you golf?

Darcy: Good morning to you, too, Miss Elizabeth. Occasionally. To what do I owe this sudden interest in my sporting life?

LizzyB: No time to explain. I'm in the woods behind Longbourn and I need a favor.

Darcy: Why am I not surprised?

Chapter Five

Mr. and Mrs. Bennet, the senior members of the *Pride and Prejudice* cast, were played by the jovial Dalrymples from Australia, who had won in the "Over 35" division of the essay contest. The couple had discovered a pleasant bench in the Longbourn garden where they often enjoyed a cup of tea in the mornings and other soothing elixirs in the evenings. Enjoying their perch this particular morning, they were the first to see Maggie approaching the house through the fruit trees out back of the Longbourn veggie garden.

"Crikey, Gert," the grinning Mr. Bennet said loudly to his wife. "There's an old tramp coming up our orchard, love. Should I call the constabulary?"

"Might should, love," Mrs. Bennet responded with equal volume. "That one has a rugged look. Oh, hang on a tick! That's our *daughter*, Mr. Bennet!"

"Bless me if it isn't!" Mr. Bennet chuckled. "G'day, Lizzy! Taken to walking through the bush for your morning constitutional, have you?"

Maggie arrived at the bench looking frazzled but with enough good humor left to smile at the Bennets as she caught her breath.

"There's a path back there, believe it or not. Goes all the way around the perimeter of the lake. I've been over visiting the Dashwood sisters."

"Ah, yes, poor dears," Mr. Bennet nodded. "Poison ivy is it?"

"Afraid so," Maggie confirmed. "Should heal soon but they're laid up for now. How did you know about it, Papá?"

she asked, feeling oh-so-posh as she accented the second syllable.

Mr. Bennet smiled. "Your Mr. Tilney is a marvel, isn't he?"

"Marvelous gossip," she said, shaking her head. "And he's not 'my' Mr. Tilney, by the way. We're just friends."

"Well, the summer's young, dear," Mrs. Bennet said, sliding her eyes toward her husband. "Mr. Bennet and I think you've got *two* admirers. We've got a case of beer bet on whoever gets to Lizzy's heart first, Darcy or Tilney. I'm for the tall and handsome bloke, just like my Colin Firth."

"Chatty and cheeky is my man, that Tilney boy," said Mr. Bennet. "Always like pulling for the long odds, I do."

"Well, I think you're both wrong," Maggie insisted. "Darcy probably won't have me once he gets to know me and Henry's got eyes for Catherine Morland. I'm a friend zone girl, can't you tell?" she asked, drawing up her hem to strike a pose, highlighting scratched leather walking boots ugly enough to make even an ardent admirer recoil. She had a point.

"No, no, my dear, the summer does strange things to a young man's heart," Mr. Bennet said, waving his hand airily, unconvinced. "I'll 'wish you joy' with one of 'em yet, I think."

"Just count up your *pings,* love," said Mrs. Bennet confidently. "Count up which one makes your heart go *ping* the most. That's how you'll know which one is for you. Don't settle for anything less than maximum *pings!*"

"Well, thanks for the advice. And the vote of confidence," Maggie offered gratefully. "But I've honestly got to run. Is Jane inside?"

"No, she's gone over to Netherfield," said Mrs. Bennet. "Darcy's giving remedial card lessons before your event this afternoon."

"Dang it," Maggie said, disappointed. "We've been called into service, Jane and I. We have to understudy the Dashwoods over at *S&S* for a few days while the girls are down. Did you know the *P&P* cast understudies for *S&S* if somebody gets sick? It's in the winners' contract."

"What? Do you remember that, pet?" Mr. Bennet asked his wife.

"Couldn't prove it by me," Mrs. Bennet admitted. "Fifteen pages, that contract was. Can't pretend we read it when we got the news we'd won. Signed it and popped a cork or three that night, didn't we, Mr. Bennet?" The two laughed, relishing whatever vague memories had survived the celebratory evening.

"Well, I didn't read it either but here we are." Maggie shrugged. "Jane and I have an event that starts in less than 30 minutes so … I guess I'll just text her. Cheers, folks." She walked toward the orchard for a few paces, texting, then turned back. "Sorry, but she's not answering. Do either of you happen to remember what Jane was wearing? Especially her shoes."

Mr. Bennet wrinkled his brow and looked upward. "Shoes? Was she wearing shoes, Gert? The dark-haired one. When she left."

Mrs. Bennet stared at her husband incredulously and shook her head before turning to Maggie. "She had on that pretty cream-colored dress with the roses on it. Probably had on her little ivory heels or something dressy for the Netherfield luncheon."

"Hmm. Okay, thanks." *Well, that's no good for an outdoor event,* Maggie thought to herself. She raced into the house and up the stairs. Fortunately, the ladies had left the door between their adjoining rooms unlocked and Maggie quickly fetched a set of walking shoes from her sister's closet.

Mrs. Bennet was still haranguing her beleaguered husband when Maggie sprinted down the stairs and back out the rear door.

"Of course, the girl was *wearing* shoes, ya daft old drongo, there's no question about that. She wanted to know what *kind* of shoes. Blimey, twenty-eight years I've put up with this. They ought to hand out a pin for that kind of service."

Maggie rushed past with a quick goodbye and loped back into the orchard, leaving the perplexed Bennets to speculate about why Lizzy preferred whacking through the rustic bush instead of taking the paved front walkway to Netherfield.

They were barely three minutes older and no wiser at all, however, when the housekeeper, Mrs. Hill, appeared at the back door.

"Mr. Darcy is here, sir," she announced with a quick curtsy.

Darcy walked out the back door, looking confused, before greeting the Bennets with two brief nods.

"Good morning, sir. Madam. It seems that Miss Elizabeth is … " he began, uncertain exactly *what* Miss Elizabeth was. "In need of help. Somewhere in the woods."

"That way, good sir," Mr. Bennet said, pointing. "Just past the orchard, I believe."

"Ah. Yes. Um … any idea of why she might want me to meet her in the woods?" Darcy queried cautiously.

"Well, any girl might want that, don't ya think?" Mrs. Bennet said, alarming Darcy with a flirtatious wink. "And our Lizzy's so adorable, isn't she?"

"Bit of trouble, though." Mr. Bennet spoke up quickly,

not taking Mrs. Bennet's pro-Darcy electioneering lying down. "Cheeky girl, you know. Not everyone's cup of tea," he added, wrinkling his nose before looking at his wife smugly.

Darcy pondered the enigma of this human conversation with his usual lack of success. He found himself longing for the quiet of trees. "Yes. Well. I'm off, then." He backed away, heading treeward and nattering inanely. "Woods await. Dark and deep. Miles to go before I sleep, all that."

"Fare thee well, good fellow, fare thee well!" Mr. Bennet called out, waving pleasantly as Mrs. Bennet sent another chill down Darcy's spine by twiddling her fingers at him with a saucy wink. Motivated afresh, Darcy turned on his heel and sprinted away energetically.

"So like my Colin," Mrs. Bennet sighed as the gentleman's tall form disappeared into the trees.

"Well, he's hardly *your* Colin, is he now, Gert?" Mr. Bennet argued sensibly, lifting his teacup. "Millions of women in the Colin Firth fan club, old girl. Oo, tea's cold."

"I'll take me chances," Mrs. Bennet intoned with a quiet confidence before leaning her head back and braying toward the back door. "HIIIILL!! HIILLLLL!!! Bring us a warmup, will you, love?"

In the woods, Darcy froze for a moment and crouched low, startled by the baying and eager to establish that it did not emanate from a woodland beast ravenous for a haunch of fancy boy. Hyperalert, the gentleman resumed his walk forward on tiptoe, scanning the forest for danger. But in the end, of course, he found only Maggie, circling a golf cart and muttering to herself, a sight that brought immediate relief and a playful smile to his lips. Straightening his waistcoat and his posture, the suddenly-fearless Darcy then strode, nay, swaggered into the clearing before addressing the young lady much louder than necessary.

"May I be of assistance?" he boomed, pleased to see Lizzy jump in surprise.

"Good Lord, Darcy!" Maggie exclaimed, clutching her heart. "You can't go scaring people like that!"

"I'm all astonishment," he replied, innocently. "You called for my help and of course, here I am."

"Well, good for you," said Maggie, still ruffled. "But ... don't do that. You could get hurt. Chicago girls will cut you first, ask questions later." She resettled the lace around her collar. "But ... thank you for coming," she added belatedly.

Darcy nodded in acknowledgment and stepped forward eyeing the golf cart. "So, where did you get this thing?"

"It's Lady Catherine's. She lent it to me so Jane and I could get around. We have to understudy for the Dashwood sisters this week."

"Really? *You're* the understudies? I heard the originals are down with poison ivy."

Maggie nodded. "Yeah. Henry is a wellspring of resort gossip, I see."

"He is," Darcy agreed, "And Bingley is the thirstiest consumer at Netherfield."

"Oh, lordy, Netherfield! I texted Jane I'd be there ten minutes ago! How do you start this stupid thing, Darcy? I've turned the key in the ignition ..." she reached in from the passenger side and did so " ... but see? Nothing starts."

"It's electric," Darcy said delicately. "It doesn't make a noise when it starts up."

Ignoring Maggie's tirade against "secret" golf cart technology, which is apparently not only "stupid" but also "counterintuitive" and "used by elites to keep down the masses," Darcy continued his tutorial after Maggie had stomped around the cart and slid into the driver's seat.

"Once it's on, release the hand brake. Then, press the accelerator for go," he continued, "and press the brake for stop. It's not rocket …"

The cart lurched forward a few feet before braking to a dusty stop.

"Science," Darcy added with a dry cough. "Press lightly, though. Smoothly."

"This thing is lurchy," Maggie complained, bucking forward like a rodeo bronc.

"Golf carts are like that," Darcy agreed, jogging alongside. "But accelerate gently, like you're stepping on a marshmallow."

Maggie pressed the pedal again with undiminished zeal and the cart burst forward another ten yards before jerking to a stop.

She turned and waved to Darcy happily. "I think I've got it."

"Do you, though?" Darcy murmured, brushing the dust from his sleeves and walking toward her.

"Now. How do I turn this thing around? Where's reverse?"

Darcy sat down in the passenger seat and toggled a switch on the dashboard. "Here. Reverse, forward, reverse, forward."

Duly edified, Maggie managed to accomplish a jerky thirteen-point turn that made Darcy vaguely nauseous but undeniably ended with the cart pointing in the opposite direction toward Netherfield.

"Yay!" Maggie gloated triumphantly. "Score one for the masses!"

"Huzzah," Darcy said grimly, swallowing hard and prying his hand from the armrest to return the fist bump she offered.

"Forward ho!" she called out, pointing toward Nether-field. "Hang on, Darcy!"

Refreshing his grip on the armrest, he reassured her, "With you at the wheel, *always*, Miss Elizabeth."

With her customary lack of subtlety, Maggie lunged the two of them forward.

Chapter Six

Maggie had finally reached Bingley by text. At the moment, he was dutifully sitting with Jane on the bench where Maggie had told them to wait, near the woods out back of Netherfield. What Maggie had not anticipated, however, was the presence of guests, swarms of women, mostly, all exuberantly playing a Regency-era croquet variation called Pall Mall on the spacious Netherfield lawn. The Engelvardts of Longbourn were in the crowd, too, with Mr. E pressed into service as something of a referee for a game he clearly did not know how to play.

"What on earth?" Maggie exclaimed, peering through the trees as she set the hand brake on the golf cart. "They can't all be staying at Netherfield, can they? There must be forty women out there. I can't be seen at Netherfield until I come in later, you know, with the muddy hem. I'll have to text Janie." Glancing around, she pulled out her colorful phone and started tapping.

"Netherfield only got the overflow, thank God," Darcy explained. "It's a school librarians' club from Nebraska. They rent out all the singles rooms at the Highbury *Emma* location for a sort of girls' bacchanal at the end of every school year. Rather famous for going a bit wild."

Maggie walked closer and peered out through the trees. The ladies seemed to be having a grand time indeed, many with at least one mimosa glass in hand. A ragged cheerleading squad was standing near Jane and Bingley's bench, for example, shouting aggressively and taking cues from a *de facto* head cheerleader.

"That's their queen, a woman named Laura Vranes from Omaha," Darcy whispered, pointing at the leader. The dark-haired lady's dress was exquisitely decorated with lines from Austen's works printed along the hem.

"That headband in her hair ... is it made out of donuts?" Maggie asked, tilting her head. "I love it. Eccentric, but also delicious, right?"

"Yummy," Darcy said glumly.

Under Ms. Vranes' tutelage, the cheerleaders were now performing a coordinated routine with lots of hip shaking and finger-wagging directed toward the opposing players.

"We're librarians ... so ...

We'll catalogue you ... yeah ...

Before we crush you ... uh huh...

That's how we rollllllllllll ... YEAH!"

"Well," Maggie observed, "they don't seem *too* wild."

"Maybe not yet," Darcy replied dubiously. "But they stole a gnome last year, you know."

Maggie looked at him uncertainly. "I'm sorry, they did what?"

"Stole ... a ... gnome," Darcy enunciated clearly. "A three-foot-tall statue from the garden maze over at Northanger. Said it's their mascot. Put a top hat on it, took it to the Meryton Distillery and bought it drinks all night, which of course, they had to consume. Lady Catherine was not amused."

Maggie snickered. "I like 'em already. But I've got to get Jane and get going, like, *now,* and she's not hearing her texts." She waved her phone at him in frustration. "Please, Darcy, go get her for me."

"What, in that mob?" Darcy said with alarm. "Do you know what they named their pet gnome? My Little Darcy! Can you imagine what they'd do to the original? No, thank you!"

"Look, you've got to mingle with the guests. That's part of your role. You don't have to like it, you know. The real Darcy would have hated it. So, hey. Show your disdain or whatever but *go get Janie.* Please, Will. We're *so* late."

"It's not safe!" Darcy remonstrated. "Look at the sheer numbers!"

Maggie inhaled to tell Darcy what a complete wimp he was being but just then a heavy ball clunked noisily into the golf cart behind them and rolled onto the ground with a muffled thump. The younger Engelvardt daughter Dora, she of the many curtsies, entered the woods a few seconds later, awkwardly lugging a mallet with a handle taller than she was, clearly looking for something.

"Uh-oh," Maggie murmured. "You and I are *not* supposed to be here but I think we're busted." She stepped forward a few paces. "Hello, there," she called out.

"Hey! Put your phone away!" Darcy whispered urgently.

"Oops," Maggie said, slipping her bright phone into her pocket quickly and moving forward a few more steps. "It's, Dahlia, isn't it? From Longbourn? Or was it Dora?"

"Dora," the girl replied flatly. "Dahlia is my sister. She just likes dresses. But I remember things. I'm a pro-gi-dy." She wiped her nose on her sleeve and continued. "You're Miss Elizabeth Bennet, the next to oldest Bennet sister." She glanced over at Darcy. "Is that Mr. Darcy?"

"Yes," Maggie confirmed. "He's staying here at Netherfield. Mr. Darcy, please allow me to present Miss Dora Engelvardt, a guest at Longbourn."

"Pleasure," Darcy said with a stiff bow, receiving a sober curtsy in return.

"Mr. Darcy was just about to take a secret message for me out to my sister Jane, out there on that bench. But he's afraid the ladies will be a bit mean to him. Personally, I think they will like him very much, don't you, Dora?" Darcy rolled his eyes and leaned back against a tree, crossing his arms and sending a variety of "stop talking" signals to Maggie.

"They like Mr. Darcy a lot," Dora confirmed. "A LOT, a lot. But, I don't know." She sighed and shook her head. "It's a *weird* kind of like, Miss Elizabeth."

Darcy shot a triumphant look toward Maggie and leapt forward from the tree pointing at Dora. "A-ha!! It's a *weird* kind of like, Miss Elizabeth! And *this* girl's a *pro-gi-dy!*"

Maggie persisted. "Well, sure, but they're not going to hurt him. I mean, it's not *dangerous* for him to go out there, right?" She laughed at the thought, encouraging Dora to join her levity.

Dora looked upward, however, and considered the question very seriously while absently scratching her hip. "I'll have to get back to you on that, Miss Elizabeth," she finally answered.

"I'm sorry, what now?" Maggie asked, leaning forward.

"It's what I'm supposed to say if I don't know the answer to a hard social question. 'I'll have to get back to you on that.' Social questions can be very confusing for pro-gi-dies."

"Ha! I'm stealing that one," Darcy said enthusiastically. "It's a problem for a lot of us, Miss Dora."

"I can take your message to your sister," Dora offered pragmatically. "No one notices me. I mean, I'm an eight-year-old wandering around in the woods and no one even knows I'm gone, right?"

It was true. Her father was extremely distracted trying to resolve a dispute between two players, her sister was flirting with a groundskeeper and her mother was helping herself to another beverage at the mimosa tent.

"Well, okay," Maggie said, warming to the idea. "Just please go tell Miss Jane to come over here where I am. But it's a secret so none of the other ladies can know." Maggie put her finger to her lips.

Dora nodded conspiratorially and returned the gesture. She headed out of the woods dragging her long mallet and made a direct line for Jane's bench, passing the rowdy cheerleaders just as the opposing team made a score. Undeterred, the librarian cheerleaders nearby began to scream in unison, more or less, along with more finger-wagging:

"It don't matter ... no

How well you play ...yeah

Cuz your estate is ... uh huh

Entailed away ...yeah!

Well into her third mimosa, Mrs. Engelvardt was heard to shout across the pitch, "Yeah! And all of your uncles were in TRADE!" This provoked a series of whoops by the cheerleaders and some staggering high-fives directed near, if not exactly onto, the good lady's extended palm.

Meanwhile, Dora arrived at the bench where Bingley and Jane were seated and, it will not surprise you to learn, curtsied. "Excuse me, but ... I need Miss Jane to help me find my ball. In the woods."

"Really, sweetie?" Bingley said, ever the gentleman, rising to assist. "I can help you if you like. Miss Bennet is waiting here to meet someone."

"I know," Dora said with a shade of irritation. "That person ... told me to come *here* and have Miss Bennet come *there*," she pointed, "into the woods." Dora glanced toward the line of cheerleaders, but they heeded not since they were now attempting to form a *very* unstable human pyramid. "The person she's waiting for told me that. That person. In the woods." Dora added, turning back to Jane and raising her eyebrows significantly.

"Oh!" Jane exclaimed, rising suddenly. "That ... person ... is in the woods? Oh, my. Lizzy's here Bingley. Okay, then. I'll be back for cards."

"Okay, then," Bingley said, smiling. Contented at the thought of her return, he sat back on the bench and waved as the two young ladies hurried away. With the sudden return of his sensory perception after Jane's departure, however, Bingley realized that he was absolutely parched and headed forthwith to the mimosa tent.

Meanwhile, in the woods, after a minimal greeting, that is, one squealing of names and one quick hug, Maggie bustled Jane into the golf cart passenger seat and ran to the other side. "No time, girl. We have to go *now.*"

"Lizzy, seriously, what are we *doing* over there?" asked a confused Jane. "I know we're understudies but what does that even mean?"

Maggie slid into the driver's seat and released the hand brake. "I'll tell you on the way over. Your walking shoes are on the floor, chica. Put 'em on, okay?" And with one of Maggie's signature lurch starts, they were off to Barton Cottage.

Darcy stood in the woods gazing after them, feeling a bit at loose ends with time to kill before the Luncheon and Cards events. He longed for his quiet chair in the Nether-field library but despaired of getting there without wading through the noisy field of women covering the lawn in front of him. He glanced around looking for an alternate exit and realized with a start that Dora was still there, staring up at him.

"You're Mr. Fitzwilliam Darcy from *Pride and Prejudice,*" Dora stated.

"That's right," Darcy answered with a nod. Oddly, he

didn't mind interactions with Dora. He actually found her frank statements of fact rather soothing.

"Mr. Darcy, are you socially awkward or proud?" she asked, looking at him unblinking. "My mom says Jane Austen didn't make it clear so that everyone could make their own guess."

Amused, Darcy pondered for a moment. "Hmm. A bit of both, I suppose."

Dora nodded solemnly. "That was *my* guess. I'm socially awkward. But I think I'm kind of proud, too. People can be both."

"They can," Darcy agreed. "Here's your ball, by the way." He handed it to her.

"Thank you," she said, taking the ball and adding a curtsy just in case. "Mr. Darcy, do you like Miss Elizabeth?" she asked directly. "I mean LIKE like. In a romance way."

Darcy looked upward for a few seconds.

"I'll have to get back to you on that," he finally answered with a small grin. "That's a very confusing social question."

"It's okay," she said politely. "I think you're supposed to like her. In the book. But Mom says things don't always work out like they're supposed to in real life, especially romance."

"Your mother is very wise," Darcy acknowledged, nodding slowly.

"Sometimes. But when she's with silly people, she can be pretty silly, too." She looked unhappily toward the crowded lawn where her mother, bosom lace askew and much of her decolletage exposed to the outdoors, was currently on her hands and knees as part of the extremely ill-advised human pyramid.

"Being silly isn't terrible, you know," Darcy said, thoughtfully. "Especially if it's just an occasional thing. It's just … not for everybody."

"Yeah," sighed Dora. "It's not for me."

"Yeah," Darcy replied with a sigh of his own. "I understand." *More than you know, little one.*

"You know," Dora said cautiously, "if someone went into Netherfield and unlocked the big bay window in the library, I think you could go through the carriage house and get into the library through that window without anyone seeing you." Dora blinked a time or two, gazing impassively up at Darcy.

Darcy considered the plan, a smile slowly bending his lips. The carriage house was on the side of the house that came very near the woods. It was probably true that the few steps from the carriage house to the bay window could be covered without being observed. It was genius.

"I believe you may be my favorite pro-gi-dy of all time, Miss Dora."

"Better than Mozart?" Dora asked, with a derisive snort. "He's really the best one," she stated with a whiff of condescension, doubtful of the man's judgment if he couldn't make that out. "Sheldon Cooper is fictional but Mozart was *real*."

"If you can get your father's permission to wait for him in the library, then get inside and unlock that bay window, I will name you One that is Even Better than Mozart."

This, finally, made Dora break into a smile, her first of the morning.

"Well, it's still a pretty weird opinion but that's exactly what I'll do."

And in fact, that was exactly what she did.

And so it was that aside from the admittedly silly sight

of Darcy catching his trailing foot on the sill of the library window and tumbling headlong onto the hardwood floor, both parties were able thereafter to enjoy a welcome morning of silent literary communion in the Netherfield library with virtually no silliness at all.

Chapter Seven

The newly minted Dashwood sister understudies arrived at the *S&S* venue about twenty minutes after the Nature Walk had begun. Groundskeepers directed them to a red-painted hitching post at the entrance to a wooded path with a small sign noting in scrolled lettering "Nature Walks Begin Here, 10 o'clock."

The path began flat enough but soon began to inch upward onto the landform called "Delaford Ridge" on resort maps, yet still called "Vermicelli Ridge" by resort old-timers in honor of the name given to it by old Mr. Pelletucci, Edith's father, in the Bellisimo Resort days. The rise was imperceptible at first but in time, the sisters began to huff as they hastily climbed upward through the trees.

"Do you hear voices?" Maggie asked finally, pausing to catch her breath.

"Just ahead," Jane whispered back, nodding and gulping for air. "I think there's a little clearing up there. So, do we say anything or just slip in?"

Maggie considered. "Well, I think Elinor would be embarrassed by being late."

"Right," Jane agreed. "I mean, *I* would be, personally. I will be now, even."

"Ha!" said Maggie. "*Both* of those characters are like your real personality. Way too nice. So maybe you should give an apology to Ferrars or whoever is leading the talk?"

"Sounds right," Jane replied.

"But Marianne's probably the *reason* we're late, right?" Maggie suggested with a giggle. "So that's on me. Lady Catherine said all we need to do is be recognizable as

Dashwoods for CanonScav, no specific actions necessary. So, we can wing it."

"Got it. Okay, come on, Marianne. You've made us late enough, dear sister," said Jane with a wink.

"Oh, so *sorry*, my dear Elinor. How difficult for you," said Maggie, placing the back of her hand on her forehead.

As the ladies walked into the clearing, Ferrars was pointing out a particular type of ivy entwined around a large tree. There were benches placed in convenient shady areas around the clearing and visitors were fanning themselves as they listened to his explanations. Henry Tilney was seated on the farthest bench in the back with Colonel Brandon and he beckoned the ladies toward the empty settee next to them. The ladies wiggled their fingers in thanks and sat down quietly as the talk went on.

"Now, this type of English ivy is often seen on cottages in the English countryside," Ferrars continued, "just as you see it on the wall at the Dashwoods' home, Barton Cottage here. It's quaint and beautiful, of course, and quite prolific. But gardeners must be a bit careful as it can be a naughty little vine that bullies and takes over other plants if not made to behave properly in its youth. But couldn't that be said of us all?"

His audience tittered appreciatively. The usually shy Ferrars was in his element here among the flora he loved so well, despite the allergic sniffles he always suffered outdoors.

"Ah, and speaking of our Dashwoods, here they are," he said as he caught sight of the sisters. Clearly, Ferrars had been prepared to encounter Dashwoods with significantly altered appearances since he had seen them at Barton Cottage that morning. "Welcome, ladies. Say hello to our little group here as I take a moment with my hankersniff, eh?" He pulled out his kerchief and issued a resounding blow.

"Thank you, Mr. Ferrars," Jane said smoothly. "So sorry to be late. We were delayed."

"That's *my* fault, I'm afraid," said Maggie, waving her hand conspicuously as though signaling a rescue helicopter. "Me. Over here. I'm Marianne Dashwood and, well, I spilled tea on my stockings," she extemporized, lifting her hem and miming the action of spilling tea as though playing to the back row of a five-thousand seat auditorium. "And I had to change, you see. My stockings." She gave a huge sweeping gesture toward her feet. Her sister looked at her incredulously, sending the nonverbal message: *What are you doing?*

Being Marianne! Maggie sent back with a significant look. "I'm such a flutter-pate!" she said aloud, pounding her head and continuing to emote to the cheap seats in an amphitheater only she could see. "How trialsome I must be for my dear sister!" she continued with emphatic gestures so large that Jane had to duck and weave so she would not be hit. "When dear, dear *Elinor*," another weave "is so *punctual*" a near miss to Jane's face "and *organized* and I am so very, very …"

"There, there, sister," Jane interrupted, corralling Maggie's flinging hands while surreptitiously stepping on the toes of her foot. "I think we have commandeered the conversation long enough. Please, Mr. Ferrars. Continue with your enlightening talk." Still smiling, she muttered to Maggie, "Zip it, missy."

"All right, then, let's have a look at this sturdy oak," Ferrars continued, drawing the attention of the audience back to the matter at hand by gesturing with his handkerchief. "But, ah! What *kind* of oak could it be? Any guesses?"

"Get off my foot!" Maggie murmured to her sister *sotto voce* while keeping her lips in a frozen smile and working to free her pinioned wrists. "And let me go!"

"Not on your life, drama queen," replied Jane from behind her own fake smile as she tightened her grip. "You're dangerous!" Their struggle escalated as Ferrars' talk continued.

"So, here's a riddle," he posited cheerily. "If our Longbourn neighbor, Mrs. Bennet heard of her daughter Lizzy marrying someone very rich, say, Mr. Darcy, for example," adding a theatrical wink, "she might rejoice to think that Lizzy would have a very large allowance of ... what type of money? Anyone?"

This provoked considerable chatter among the gathered crowd. The speculation elevated noisily as people shouted out—"Allowance?" "House money?" "Egg money?"—and the general conversational din increased in volume.

Suddenly, an ear-piercing whistle silenced everyone in the glade, including, briefly, Maggie and Jane. A tiny red-headed lady standing near the front bench with her pinky fingers stuck into both sides of her mouth seemed to be the unlikely originator of the deafening sound.

"Hey! People!" the small woman barked commandingly. "Jen here has the answer. Listen up." She sat down and motioned to her bench mate. "Go ahead, Jen."

"Thanks, Jen." The woman sitting next to her was a similarly petite brunette and spoke up confidently. "It's me, Mr. Ferrars. Jen Dowdy, well, they call me Jen One since we've teamed up. This is Jen Nissen. They call her Jen Two." She motioned toward her friend.

"Ah, yes, Miss ... erm, Miss One," said Ferrars, awkwardly. "Good to see you again. And good to see you again, Miss ... Two." The petite red-head bowed her head genteelly. "So, ladies, what is the answer, then? A housewife's allowance might be called ... what?"

"Pin money!" Jen One shouted exuberantly.

"Brilliant, Miss Jen!" commended Ferrars. "Spot on!"

Jen Two looked around the silent glade pointedly. "Hey! Let's show some Janeite spirit, people. Let's hear it for Jen One," she called out, leading the group in a vigorous applause—"Come on, clap it up, people!"—which the giggling group, given permission to depart from usual lecture decorum, joined enthusiastically as Jen Two added another whistle for effect.

Jen One retired behind her fan quite pleased at the support. She turned her gaze toward Ferrars and batted her eyes at the puffy man.

Ferrars paused for a beat to enjoy the unaccustomed fawning as any shy and doughy man might. "Yes. Excellent indeed."

From across the clearing, Colonel Brandon was heard to cough meaningfully a time or two before giving a subtle hand motion for Ferrars to move things along. On the bench next to Brandon, the ersatz Dashwood sisters' whispered argument/wrestling match was growing in intensity again— *"You're not the boss of me!" "Oh, yeah? Well, you are certainly not the boss of ME!"*—and would soon be observed by all in the glade if Ferrars did not recapture the attention of the audience.

"Yes!" Ferrars called out loudly, turning all heads his way. "Yes, yes, YES! Pin money! So, let's use our clue and get back to our tree. It's a type of oak. A _blank_ oak. What type is it, friends?"

"A pin oak!" shouted Jen Two. The Two Jens high-fived and this time the Janeites in the glade burst into applause quite spontaneously.

"Yes, indeed! Very good. A pin oak. The pin oak is sturdier than it sounds, friends, and is frequently used in landscaping, so let's give it a very, *very* close look," Ferrars continued, intent on keeping the focus on his tree rather than the back bench where the wrestling women had begun asserting in dangerous gutterals that things were about to "*get real*."

"*Psst.* Ladies! I say! *Ladies!*" This was Henry Tilney's voice. With considerable stealth, he had risen from the neighboring bench and was now squatting behind them, addressing them in an angry whisper. "*Stop it!* Stop it this *instant!* Austen never wrote a rugby scrum!" The ladies remembered themselves and turned away from each other, assuming postures that still evidenced hostility but were, at least, more Regency-appropriate.

"Come with me," Henry said tersely, rising and moving briskly into the woods behind the bench. The sisters sat for a moment, arms folded and unmoving, glaring. From the next bench, the oversized military man Colonel Brandon hissed tight-lipped at them and jerked his long thumb toward the trees in a way that commanded compliance. Still staring at each other, the ladies rose and reluctantly dragged their feet into the forest.

"Honestly, Jane, ... or Elinor, or ... whoever you are," Henry began as they arrived.

"Her name is little Miss Perfect," Maggie said petulantly, kneeling to wipe the dust from the top of her shoe.

"Well, regardless, my dear, you can't just wrestle another character into submission onstage. Heaven knows, I understand the impulse. I did a benefit performance with John Cleese once, the man was *literally* chewing up the scenery, not a metaphor, mind you, chewing with his *teeth*. But you cannot physically restrain them, you know. It isn't done."

"Whatever. You saw what she was doing," Jane said testily, rearranging her sleeves.

"Well, I *did*, yes," Henry acknowledged, turning to Maggie. "Not sure if you're playing vaudeville or kabuki, old thing, but I'm pretty sure those gestures were visible from space. Love the energy but you've *got* to dial it back to about a 7, hmm?"

"Marianne is a very big character," Maggie said thickly, reluctant to give any ground.

"Well, she *is* and I think we can all agree that she should be played with spirit," Henry conceded. "But you were dashed close to taking out your sister's eye, my dear. Mustn't blind the other performers, right? Especially not our Janie. Fellow LaGGard and all that?"

Jane's eyes were looking at Maggie reproachfully at the moment and Maggie felt a pang of guilt for unwittingly putting the lovely orbs in peril.

"Oh, all right. I'm sorry, Janie. I didn't even realize. Carried away, I guess."

"Oh, it's … it's okay," Jane said, shaking her head and relaxing her shoulders. "And *I'm* sorry, too. I saw that hand coming at me and all of a sudden I was wrestling you like a rodeo steer. Don't know what got into me."

The ladies moved into a healing hug as Henry cooed happily.

"Aw. Now that's a pretty sight. I must say, though …" he began.

"Must you?" Maggie asked wearily. "We're only *just* now all friends again."

"Well, just a bit of a director's note, my dear. You've both got a week of this ahead and the Dashwood characters seem to bring out the worst in you. You've spent many days as Bennet sisters with never a cross word. Five minutes as Dashwoods and you were at each other's throats."

"Well, as soon as I'm Elinor Dashwood," Jane complained, "I immediately feel stressed, like *I'm* responsible for whatever my crazy sister does. I never feel that playing Jane Bennet."

"Yeah, and Lizzy Bennet has her faults but at least she's sensible," Maggie added. "Marianne Dashwood, on the other hand, spends about half of her story melting down."

"Yes," Henry acknowledged thoughtfully. "Bit of a dog's breakfast, that one is. Hard to play because she's hard to like. Well, the Singh sisters figured out a way to play Dashwoods without fisticuffs, probably from all their years as real sisters and the fact that they do, actually, love each other. You love each other, ladies. So, play it like you *are* Garija and Vanaja. You'll be close enough to Dashwoods *and* probably not kill each other."

There was a silent moment as the ladies pondered this advice. "Occasionally, Henry, you say intelligent things," Maggie acknowledged. "Credit where it's due. If your good looks fail you onstage, you could always direct."

"Thanks, old girl. Every actor's dream," Henry said, with a saucy wink that made Maggie register a heart *ping* in spite of herself.

At that point, Colonel Brandon cautiously approached, stooping under a few low-hanging branches to join the three players. "Everybody all right back here? It seemed to have gotten a bit ... quiet," he said, glancing from face to face and assessing the threat level.

"Ah! Good man, Brandon. Kind of you to check on my well-being. But we've all had a good hug and the world is rosy once again," Henry reported.

"Excellent," Brandon said, visibly relieved. "The Nature Walk is heading for the top of the ridge now."

"Oh. Well, I guess we should rejoin the group," Maggie said unenthusiastically.

"Well, actually, um, no," Brandon observed with some embarrassment. "Ferrars asked me, very kindly, mind you, if you would consider ... perhaps ... *not* rejoining the group today. Just until you've settled things, of course."

"Well, that *is* awkward," Henry observed impishly. "Kicked out of class, you naughty girls. Well, trust me as one quite experienced in this paradigm, we shall have a great deal more fun on our own."

"Did you have something else in mind, Henry?" Maggie inquired. "We don't have to be at Netherfield until three."

"Well, I did, truthfully, but I hated to be a bad influence on the rest of you," Henry said gleefully. "Now, that you've been expelled, however, I can hatch my plot with impunity. Brandon, you don't have any further responsibilities here?"

"No, I just had to be present for it, actually, so CanonScavvers can check me off as present. Isn't that so for you ladies also?" Brandon asked.

"Yes, same for us," Maggie confirmed. "Just here so people can see us."

"Well, I think everyone *saw* you ladies, there's hardly any question of that," Henry ventured carefully. "Brandon, don't you concur?"

"Yes. Absolutely," he agreed. "I saw several visitors reaching for their lists during the skirm … um, well, earlier." He cleared his throat and restarted. "Anyway, as for me, Ferrars called me by name several times. And … well, let's be realistic. I'm a 6-foot-4-inch-tall Black man wearing a top hat in the woods. If they *didn't* see me, they're just not trying!"

This brought a laugh. "Hear, hear!" exclaimed Henry. "If they've missed you, old chap, they don't deserve to win a scavenger hunt!" All nodded in cheerful accord.

"So, what mischief did you have in mind, Henry?" Maggie asked.

"Well, I've heard a story this morning from one of the older staff members, a groundskeeper fellow named Gary over at Northanger, who was here back in the old

Bellissimo days. He says some workmen built a charming little chapel up in the woods, somewhere between Northanger and Delaford, back when the two sites were being built in the early 1960s. Supposedly, they blazed a trail to it about halfway up the Ridge and I was thinking of trying to find it. Can't be too far from where we're standing."

"Would the trail blazes still be visible?" Maggie asked, glancing around.

"Quite possibly," Brandon replied, examining the nearby trees. "The WPA blazed a lot of trails in the 1930s that are still visible today. If this was in the '60s, some marks might still be here. Look for a blotch of paint or a carved arrow on a tree."

Brandon organized the company into a search line arranged vertically along the hillside, walking a few paces apart. The cry came after only a few minutes.

"Hey, everyone!" Brandon called out. "I think I've got something." The group assembled around the tree in question, confirming that there was, indeed, a faint yellow circle of paint.

"That's gotta be it, right?" Maggie said, excitedly. With the shape and location of the markings discovered, it was the work of only a few moments to find the next one and the one beyond that.

"So, why do workmen build a chapel in a forest that no one knows about?" Jane asked thoughtfully as the group proceeded through the woods.

"Well, it's quite a tale, actually," Henry began.

And so it was, a rather *tall* tale, in fact, as the reader will soon discover.

Chapter Eight

The chapel origin story that Henry heard had undergone significant cosmetic surgery over the years to make it more pleasing to staff as well as visitors. But here we shall provide an expanded truth, a truer truth, if you will, around it as Henry tells his version.

"Business was booming here at the resort in the early 1960s," Henry began, with fair accuracy up to that point. *"All the guest houses were filled to brimming and booked out months in advance. So, being quite the clever businessman, Benny Pelletucci decided he wanted to build more guest houses and started construction on the Northanger Abbey and Delaford Manor guesthouses in 1962."*

Well … yes. Construction began in 1962. We can agree there.

Despite the resort's success, however, that year was not entirely a bowl of cherries, or *pasta fagioli* if you prefer, for *all* the members of the New York Pelletucci family. Benny's grandfather, the venerable mob boss Nicky "Bones" Pelletucci, after handing over the funds for Benny to build his resort in the late 1940s, had returned to his own business interests in the City. The resort idea had prospered and aside from routinely turning down Benny's requests for new project money, Nicky had mostly left Benny and his modest legitimate profits alone.

Grandpa Nicky Bones' city business was, to the casual observer, much smaller in scale. He ran a rather rundown Italian social club that was incredibly successful, (and by that we mean successful beyond *all* credibility) in its financial reach. Some of the richest businessmen in New York

City had been observed entering the club's cheap metal door with the grate over the window, apparently just to chat and play cards in a dimly lit space with Nicky. In fact, the inexplicably vast influence of Nicky Bones' humble club had strained the credulity of more than one law enforcement agency on both state and federal levels by the spring of 1962. While grandson Benny was happy making legit money and dancing the night away at his fancy resort in upstate New York, his grandfather was dealing with an unwelcome scrutiny that made him nervous and frankly had taken a significant edge off his gin rummy game.

This all came to a head at midnight on a cool April evening, just before tax time, in 1962 when Nicky arrived at the resort. He had a truck filled with cash, ironically stashed in literal laundry bags since the universe does, indeed, have a sense of humor, along with a new set of instructions for his grandson.

It was time to expand the business, Nicky announced. Benny was to build new guest houses, buy new property, hire new staff, put "all-a them ideas" into practice that Nicky had previously refused. Immediately. Suddenly, nothing was too silly, too expensive, too impractical. Nicky would send a smart accountant named Larry—"Barry Tedesco's boy who just got out of NYU, some kind of genius with numbers"—and Benny was to spend freely until all of Nicky's bounteous cash infusion had disappeared into the infrastructure of the resort itself, far from prying eyes in the city.

"With my love, Benny. Got a little present from your father in there, too," Nicky said, tenderly cupping Benny's cheek in parting, an enigmatic statement at best. (Benny's father Carlo, a man who rarely had a pocketful of cash, much less a truckful, was distinctly and specifically *not* in the family business, instead following an artistic bent by running a struggling Arthur Murray dance studio.) Benny, however, was not inclined to quibble. He hugged his gramps, unloaded the bags and dutifully promised to start spending it right away.

So, yes. Construction began in 1962. In earnest.

"The place was swarming with work crews that summer, staying in tents at first. Naturally, the first place they built was the bunkhouse so the work crews would have some place to stay."

The dormitory that now housed the Meryton militia had been a rough piece of work from the very beginning both in its rapid unvarnished construction and in the activities that went on inside its walls. Benny's work crews included many city men who were accustomed to having the entertainments of urban life available to them during their off hours so they quickly brought those favored activities to the bunkhouse. The gambling and drinking inside the workers' lounge area soon expanded to epic proportions and frequently spilled out into the street, disturbing the peace of the lovely pastoral resort. Late night disagreements were frequent and outright brawls not unknown. Benny started to get noise complaints from visitors at the nearby guesthouses.

"Benny decided that dozens of men rooming in crowded spaces away from their families needed a place to go for a bit of wholesome recreation. He had fond memories of going to dances and playing table tennis at a neighborhood church when he was a young man. So he had a crew build a smaller version of it here in the woods for the workers. Chapel, recreation room, that sort of thing. Bit of spiritual contemplation and a round of table tennis to keep them occupied on the weekends."

Well. It's creative. Mostly fictional, but creative.

Benny did have fond memories of the "mixer" dances held in the basement of his old neighborhood church

St. Ignatius, which lived in his mind as "St. Pugnacious." (Benny was never good with names. He misremembered his wife Patsy's school, for example, as Our Lady of the Perpetual Laundromat, what with "Lamentation" being such a big word and all.)

Fast-forwarding to his adult problem, however, Benny was tired of apologizing for his noisy work crews. He had called his youngest brother Vincenzo, also the foreman of his construction crew, to his office and informed him in no uncertain terms to move all the shenanigans, booze, cards and whatever else the boys were up to "O-U-T out" of the bunkhouse and further into the woods. Benny didn't care where, but it had to be far away from the guesthouses.

"I don't want to hear nothing, I don't want to see nothing. Build it like one-a them underground bunkers for all I care, Vinny. Like on TV, them ones for if the Russians start shooting. Listen, I had some of the best times of my life in a church basement and Ma said she couldn't even hear the radio playing when us kids was down there, even when the ladies was meeting upstairs. St. Pug's was built outta brick and concrete, buddy boy, and that old girl's still standing to this day. Build something like that and them boys won't bother nobody."

Benny's foreman scratched his head. "You want me to build a brick church out in the woods, Benny? Cuz I know what them boys want and believe me, it ain't no church."

"But it's not a bad idea." Benny jumped involuntarily at the voice coming from the wingback chair in the corner. He had forgotten that his accountant was in the room. Larry Tedesco was a good man with the books but quiet in a way that reminded Benny of his wife's cat. He looked like a cat, too, Benny always said, with a mustache that shot out unruly whisker hairs and two cowlicks that stood up at the back of his head looking for all the world like pointed ears.

Patsy's cat had always hated Benny and he suspected that his accountant harbored similar feelings. "I'm speaking tax-wise, Mr. Pelletucci," the man clarified, straightening his horn-rimmed glasses before refolding his thin hands. "A church or chapel structure won't be taxed the same as your guesthouses, you see."

"Ah, yeah. Sure, sure. That makes sense," Benny replied, affecting a slow nod and rubbing his chin, like Bogart did in the movies, to convey a brightening dawn of understanding. (In Benny's long, dark night of cognition, however, the roosters slept on. Soundly.)

"And if you construct a basement area, oh my, Mr. Pelletucci." A dreamy look came into Larry's myopic eyes as visions of deductions danced and swirled. "If you make the walls thick enough to qualify as a fallout shelter, the incentives would double. The government is offering tax incentives quite generously to anyone who builds a fallout shelter just now, Mr. Pelletucci. Quite, quite generously." An actual grin appeared on the accountant's face. Benny half-expected him to purr and lick his paws.

"You mean ... the government will give me money to build a church and even more money if I put a bunker thingee under it?" Benny asked, narrowing his eyes.

"Well, in a manner of speaking," Larry stated carefully. "They don't hand it to you in bags." Benny seemed disappointed. Money in bags was his favorite kind. "But they give it to you in tax breaks," the accountant pressed on. "That means there's more money you can keep instead of giving it to the government in taxes. You can think of it as the government scratching your back, so to speak, if they feel you're scratching theirs. You're doing them a kind of favor."

This was helpful. Benny understood this dynamic well.

"You see, the more square footage that is in a nuclear

fallout shelter, Mr. Pelletucci, the more people the fallout shelter will hold. The more citizens that can, theoretically, be protected in a nuclear war, the better it is for the United States. So, the bigger the shelter, the bigger the tax break you get from the government."

Benny suddenly sat upright and pounded both palms on his desk. "Vinny, build them boys a fallout shelter, a big one, with lots of that footage business. Them boys can play cards 'til the cows come home down there and I'm doing the government a favor!" Benny beamed with pride. "Oh, and put a little church on the top!"

"Watch for a natural spring nearby," Henry instructed his search party. *"They put a bench outside of the chapel by a little stream for contemplation and such."*

Contemplation? Well, the workers in 1962 had often contemplated how wonderfully cool their beers stayed when they tied a canvas bag full of them to the leg of the bench and dropped it into the little stream, if that counts.

Back in Benny's office, however, a frustrated Vincenzo had responded to his instructions by throwing up his beefy hands and sinking into a chair. "Benny, you don't even know what you're asking! We're killing ourselves just to dig out a foundation under that Lombardy Lodge site up the hill." (This was the gothic castle-like guesthouse that in later years would be called Northanger Abbey.) "There are patches of bedrock underneath this whole property, Benny. Now, that is great for building *up* on, I'll grant ya that. But it's terrible for trying to dig *down*. I wouldn't even know where to start to dig to make a whole underground bunker."

"*I* know where." The slick accountant's voice cut through the silence in the room. The burly foreman glanced around to where the delicate fellow in the wingback chair was smugly straightening his little mustache, as if picking the last canary feather out of it.

"Oh, yeah?" challenged Vincenzo. "Where's that?"

"Enos Stook's root cellar," the accountant enunciated with perfect calm.

Vincenzo looked at his brother in confusion. "Benny, I know the kid's talking English but I have no idea what he's saying."

Benny, however, for one shining moment in his life, understood perfectly.

"Stook is the guy that owned this property before me. He died and left it to his grandson. That's the kid who sold it to me back in '47. The only building on this property then was a little fishing shack back up in the woods. The Stook kid showed it to me when I bought it. So, how do you know Enos Stook had a root cellar, Larry?"

"I did a very thorough inspection of this property, Mr. Pelletucci, when your grandfather sent me to work here," the accountant said primly. "That fishing shack was near a natural spring. Apparently, Mr. Stook built his shack there so he could use the spring as a source of drinking water. And it seems he also dug out an underground storage area, a root cellar, near the shack to keep food from spoiling. I saw it myself during my inspection."

"So there's a cellar. So what?" Benny asked, confused.

"Nah, nah I get it, Benny," interjected Vincenzo, raising his hand. "There's a root cellar up there. So we know we can dig a hole *there* because somebody already *did*."

"Precisely," said the younger man, looking pleased with himself and turning his cool gaze back to Benny. Benny wondered briefly what the man would do if rewarded with a saucer of warm milk. It worked with Patsy's cat sometimes. Temporarily. Before it returned to its usual pattern of clawing and hissing at him.

Nah. Sometimes ya just walk a wide berth around 'em, thought Benny. *And this guy looks like a hisser.*

"Okay, then, Vinny. You heard the man. Dig there. Give them noisy boys a rec hall before I lose all my swanky customers," said Benny firmly.

Vincenzo sighed and stood, putting his work cap back on. "Okay, Benny. I'll take a few guys from each crew for a few weeks. We'll build them boys a rec hall and you'll never hear a peep from 'em again. And we'll get you a nice tax break from Uncle Sam," he said, glancing toward the preening Larry Tedesco. (This turned out to be truer than the gentlemen could imagine. Well into the 21st century, the United States government continues to offer tax breaks for eligible shelters that were built during that bygone era.)

"And put a church on top, Vinny," said Benny brightly, thinking of St. Pug's nostalgically.

"Sure, Benny, sure," said Vincenzo, abandoning all reason as he walked out the door, shaking his head. "A church with a bomb shelter underneath it in the middle of the woods. Why not?"

Why not, indeed? Time alone would answer that question.

But let's not get ahead of ourselves. The chapel search party is about to find something.

Chapter Nine

"I hear water," Maggie said suddenly. "Listen."

The group stopped moving and tilted their heads like a pack of bird dogs on the alert. Sure enough, there was a liquid *whoosh* gurgling beneath the ambient forest noise.

"This way," Brandon said, taking the lead and motioning the others to follow. The terrain had gradually become more uneven and Brandon encouraged everyone to stay closer together. The trees grew denser and the shade deeper as the group advanced while the path itself became more conceptual and less factual with every step. The players began to struggle along steep drops and vertical climbs, navigating around or over roots and fallen branches as they continued forward. Their pace slowed and their uncertainty grew.

"Has anyone seen a yellow blaze lately?" Jane finally asked with some concern. "I mean, I don't think we can be really lost but …"

"You'd like a better idea of where we are," Maggie added, speaking for everyone in that moment as she paused and wiped her hands after traversing hand-over-hand up a steep and jagged stairwell made of roots. "Yeah, me too."

Just then Henry slipped a few feet downhill on some loose rocks and saved himself from falling further with an awkward grab of a cedar sapling branch. "I'm fine, all," he called up the hill reassuringly. "Just doesn't feel very path-ish at the moment, does it?" He picked a few cedar needles out of his palm. "Brandon, are you confident that we're still on the trail?"

"Well, not completely, no," Brandon admitted finally. He stopped and looked around. "The thing is, we can still hear the water running. And the chapel is supposed to be near the stream. So if we can find the stream, we should be able to find the chapel. Can everyone push on for a little bit?"

"I guess so, but mostly because I don't think we'd be any better off turning around," Maggie replied with her usual candor. "I'm not sure we could find our way back if we tried. So, yeah, we should go forward but ..." She bit her lip, reluctant to sound wimpy. "Look, it's hard to climb in this kind of dress without tripping over the hem and I ... I need a hand on some of the steep spots."

Brandon and Tilney both sprang forward reflexively, jolted into gentlemanly action by the emergence of a damsel in distress.

"Of course, dear girl, of course," Henry said, struggling to find a purchase for the slick soles of his boots on the small escarpment he had just slid down. "Should have been more aware."

He continued to chatter as he found a better climbing line several feet away where he managed to pull himself up to the previous level. "Foolish to have missed your troubles, Maggie old chum. Sorry about that." He arrived in front of Maggie with his friendly smile at the ready and offered his arm to her, thereupon becoming the final member of the group to notice that Maggie had already taken Brandon's arm about half a minute earlier.

An awkward moment passed.

"Ah!" observed Henry before belatedly lowering his extended wing. "Good show, Brandon! Johnny on the spot to help our girl. Well done, well done." He smiled toward Brandon with more enthusiasm than he felt.

"Well, of course," the shy Colonel murmured, glancing downward with some embarrassment. "A Brandon has to step up for his Marianne, doesn't he?"

"Well, I should say so!" Henry replied cordially.

"Listen, if you're offering, I think Janie could use a hand, too," Maggie contributed, feeling a bit awkward on behalf of Henry. He was her absolute ride-or-die guy and it felt bad to leave him hanging. But Brandon's thickly-muscled arm inspired confidence in a way that Henry's dear but bony appendage did not and she was reluctant to make the trade in the middle of a scary woods.

Jane spoke up. "I really could use a hand over here, Henry, if you can see your way clear." She smiled her angel's smile at him and its effect was immediate. Henry leapt toward her as if on winged feet.

"Say no more, Janie. I'm daft for not offering sooner. This terrain wasn't what we thought it would be at all," Henry said, pleased to help Jane to stable ground nearer the others so they all could confer.

"Well, it does seem that we've lost the path, that's true enough," Brandon summarized calmly. "Maybe a blazed tree had fallen or we just missed it. Doesn't matter. But remember, we still know our general directions and we know that the stream will always run downhill and take us toward the lake if it comes to that."

"In other words, we're not *lost* lost," Maggie interjected. "Like, lost-in-the-woods-all-night, *scary* lost. Because this city girl ain't down with all *that*."

"No, no, of course," Brandon said quickly. "This isn't even close. This is just an inconvenient kind of lost. Think of it like taking the wrong subway line in city terms."

Maggie shrugged. "Okay, then. I've done that. It's a pain to correct it but not scary. Well, maybe a little, depending on the part of town. But yeah. I got it."

"Well, I feel quite the fool for suggesting this adventure," Henry said ruefully. "Thought it would be a lark, not an all-terrain march. The groundskeeper fellow made it sound like the place was easily accessible, at least back in his younger days. Which admittedly was a number of years ago."

"What about our cell phones?" Jane asked. The group checked for signal.

"Not bad," Brandon observed. "Got a few bars of service. But it hasn't come to that, has it?"

Maggie spoke up quickly. "What would we even say? 'Hi there, we don't know where we are, but come and get us?' No, come on, people. That's lame. Let's just find the water and go from there."

"Yes, brilliant," Henry agreed. "Can't be far."

And indeed, it wasn't. Five minutes of persistent forward motion later, the group was standing at the side of a small stream.

"Huzzah! Here we are!" pronounced Henry, sharing a high five with Jane. He gazed about for a moment. "Now. Where are we?"

Brandon peered into the dense growth beyond the bubbling water. "Is that … a building? Just there. Beyond that big spruce tree," he said, pointing forward.

"By jove, I believe it is," Henry agreed cheerily. "If we can get across this little trickle here, we're practically home free."

"Here! Come up here," Brandon called out, heading uphill toward a section where the stream narrowed to about twelve feet across and passed over a number of rocks. "It's a natural ford, more or less. Just across those rocks."

Maggie followed but dawdled behind the group reluctantly. Her city girl sensibilities were drawing the line at wading across a raging river, even though the ten-inch-deep rivulet before them was hardly "raging" and in fact, could barely be thought of as "miffed."

Henry stepped across the line of rocks with admirable agility, however, and extended his hand for the next contestant. Jane readily bundled up her skirt into a bulky wad and spoke reassuringly to Maggie. "As kids we used to wade across an old dam fifty feet across all the time back home, Lizzy. Just put down each foot carefully and go slowly." Managing her dress with one hand and navigating with even, deliberate steps, Jane was quickly across, though she did lose her balance once and suffered one soggy shoe in the process.

"Now your turn, Miss Elizabeth," the Colonel said kindly but unequivocally. Maggie sighed deeply and stepped forward.

"I don't think I can do this," she pleaded softly, looking up into Brandon's kind eyes as she felt an embarrassed flush move up her neck. "I don't do well standing on one foot. I have, like, no balance. Seriously." Her heart was pounding as she admitted her weakness.

"Of course you can," Brandon said gently. "You are the most intrepid character here, our own unsinkable Lizzy."

"I've seen you hop out on the dance floor, Lizzy," Henry shouted from across the stream. "You're a master on one foot, my girl! Put Darcy and me to shame with your mad hopping skills."

"Yeah, but we weren't balancing on slippery rocks at the time, Henry," Maggie responded nervously, stalling as long as she could. "Honestly, my balance is really bad."

"Look, Henry and I will be your hand railing for most of the trip across," Brandon said, extending his long arm reassuringly. "Navigate those few rocks in the middle and you're home free."

Imitating Jane, Maggie bunched up her skirt and petticoat, slung it over her arm and side-stepped out onto the first few rocks, cautiously moving her steely grip from joint to joint along Brandon's tree limb of an arm, all the way down to his fingertips.

"Well done, Lizzy," called Henry. "Now just a few steps on those middle rocks and you'll be right to my hand over here." Henry stretched out his hand out as far as he could from the shoreline.

Maggie unhappily inched her feet forward on the flat rock in the middle of the stream but when it was time to step to the next one, her feet refused to budge, her central nervous system calling an abrupt halt to the proceedings.

"Right here, Lizzy," said Henry in a soothing voice while stretching his thin arm out with perilous instability.

"I tried to tell you, I am not a dang mountain goat, people," Maggie said loudly, embarrassed and stressed but nonetheless standing as though welded to the center rock.

"Just reach out, Lizzy," Henry urged, stepping out toward her on a round rock near the shoreline. "I'll come and get you."

"Tilney!" Brandon shouted urgently. "The rocks on your side aren't stable. Just stand still and let her come to you!" Jane and Henry's suggestions got lost in the muddle of what happened next, but everyone was shouting at once when the inevitable finally occurred.

Maggie lifted a foot and placed it squarely in the wrong location on the next big rock, sliding her body weight forward and causing her to flail with both arms to regain her balance. One hand caught hold of Henry's fingers just as he was stretched toward her at full wingspan, which tipped him into the stream face first, legs upstream and torso downstream. His buttocks, meanwhile, formed a new set of meaty steps on the pathway which Maggie promptly slid into, landing knees first on Henry's derrière, her arms elbow deep in the water, her dress and petticoat hems drifting gently down the stream to rest over Henry's submerged head.

"Henry!" Maggie shrieked, grasping at his waistcoat and managing to pull his head out of the water momentarily. Henry, unseen under the cover of her frilly undergarment, was heard to gasp for air and cry out something like "eeeees" before Maggie's grip failed, casting him again into the water.

"Oh, what did he say? What did he say, Janie?" Maggie cried, desperately clawing at Henry's collar and managing to bend him backwards again briefly.

"Eeeeees!" came the muffled syllable once more as Henry's linen-covered head slipped again from Maggie's unreliable grasp and pitched forward a second time.

"Is it keys?" Maggie looked frantically into the water on both sides from her perch atop Henry's posterior. "Did he lose his keys?"

"Sounded like 'bees' to me," Jane shouted, glancing around the shoreline. "But I don't see any."

"It's "KNEES!" Brandon shouted urgently, sloshing rapidly through the water toward Maggie's position. "KNEES, Miss Elizabeth! The poor man needs you to get your KNEES off his back!"

Eschewing all Regency protocol, Brandon straddled Henry's body and abruptly hauled Maggie up into the air by her armpits, placing her on the flat rock in the middle of the stream. Henry surfaced with a huge gasp, bracing himself with both hands to hold his head above water. Brandon then dismounted from his awkward pose and extended a hand toward the soggy Henry to assist him back to dry land. Heedless of his own soaked clothing, Brandon then waded back to Maggie and said firmly, "Grab hold of my neck." Not inclined to argue, Maggie did as instructed whereupon Brandon scooped her up under her knees, inadvertently recreating a dramatic Brandon/Marianne carry similar to the one in *Sense and Sensibility*. Thus encumbered, the Colonel carefully made his way across the bed of the stream to the shoreline. He deposited Maggie into Jane's waiting arms before accepting Henry's proffered hand and climbing to *terra firma* himself.

As might be imagined, everyone tried to talk at once after that. There was much apologizing and a great deal of checking and rechecking the well-being of each member of the group before any plans about moving forward could be made. In the end, however, it was firmly established that Maggie was extremely sorry for her deficient stream-crossing skills, Brandon was similarly sorry for pushing her to attempt the feat, Jane was sorry that everybody was feeling sorry and above all, Henry was passionately and unequivocally sorry for suggesting the whole silly hike. Once these apologies were spoken and accepted all around, finally Jane's clear and reasonable voice could be heard and considered.

"I think we need to get home as soon as possible. Everybody's wet and it's time to go home. We can look for the chapel another time."

"Agreed, Miss Bennet," Brandon said with a sigh. "Should have turned us back as soon as we lost the trail. Again, so sorry everyone." This set off another round of apologies as each member of the group tried to assume a measure of responsibility while simultaneously assuring the others that unexpected things happen and that no one was to blame.

Henry piped up from his seat on a tree stump where he was dumping a load of river rocks out of his boot. "I know we could follow the stream downhill from here but let's check out the building over there before we do any more scrambling through the brush. It's obviously not a chapel but there might be someone there who can direct us toward the main path." Henry's bushy hair was dripping into his collar and made Maggie remember the first time she had met him, similarly soaking, in the downpour at the LaGuardia airport when they were all just beginning their Camp Jane adventure. She smiled at the memory and Henry noticed.

"Something else, old girl? You're ever so much better at planning than I am," Henry asked, smiling up at her brightly as he emptied his second boot. Maggie felt her heart go *ping,* again. It wasn't quite a this-guy's-cute *ping* but it was a very warm *ping* nonetheless. *He's such a scramble head,* Maggie thought to herself affectionately, *but so wonderfully attentive to his friends. Best bestie ever, really. I literally try to drown the man but he comes up nothing but friendly.*

"Just agreeing with you, Henry," Maggie said supportively.

"Off we go, then," Henry said cheerfully, pulling on his boot and standing.

Though squishy of boot and muddy of hem, the group was much lighter of heart as they approached the structure. Not only was the forest less dense and easier to navigate on this side of the stream, but the building they were approaching was clearly a modern metal-sided maintenance shed of some type. Electrical lines ran into it and at least two clear paths, one heading downhill and one stretching laterally across the hillside, originated at the door of the building.

"Huzzah!" said Henry with obvious relief. "Civilization is nigh!"

"I wonder if there's somebody in there," murmured Jane as she tried to smooth out the wrinkles from her dress self-consciously. "I doubt if these workers ever see character players tramping around up here. I wonder what they'll think of us showing up looking like this."

Jane was not destined to wonder long, however, because just then the front door of the building swung open, surprising everyone, including the new arrival.

"What are *you* doing here?" asked a stunned Colonel Brandon.

"I might ask you the same thing," said the man in the doorway with some astonishment.

In the doorway stood *Sense & Sensibility's* handsome villain, the essay winner known as John Willoughby.

Chapter Ten

Mr. Willoughby was pale and visibly nervous, glancing over his shoulder before stepping forward and closing the door with a hasty *clunk*. Though usually quite meticulously dressed, the man looked disheveled today, shaggy, unshaven and not at all dressed to character. Willoughby's usual wardrobe was that of a gold-digging dandy but today he looked more like Willoughby's gardener in a set of ill-fitting breeches and a rough workman's shirt.

"Just ... up here getting my phone looked at," he stammered. "Day off, you know." After a pause, he rattled on. "They run all the communications from up here, keep the wifi running, that kind of thing. That tallest tree hides a cell tower, believe it or not. Figured the guys up here could help me with a JaneyApp problem and, um, well, they did." The thin man lifted the hand containing his cell phone briefly before slipping it quickly into his pocket. He coughed uncomfortably and glanced around at the group.

"Huzzah, then," said Henry pleasantly. "Glad you got it cleared up."

"Yes, yes. Me too," Willoughby replied distractedly. His car salesmen instincts seemed to kick in just then because he suddenly smiled broadly and deftly turned the conversation. "Anyway, enough about me. It looks like you folks had to swim the lake to get here. Is everything going all right today?"

And what do I need to do to put you in a car this afternoon? Maggie finished up to herself mentally. *He's just like the man who sold me my Honda. Do they make all of these guys in a lab somewhere?*

"We got a bit closer than planned to the stream, but

no harm done," Henry offered succinctly, detouring any further questions with a follow-up question of his own. "I say, Willoughby, we haven't seen much of you since the Pemberley dance last week. Where have you been keeping yourself?"

"Yes, I'd wondered that myself," Brandon chimed in. "Your room is just down the hall from Ferrars and me over at Delaford House. I heard you moving around in there this morning, even saw your laundry outside the door. But we've barely seen you downstairs at all."

"Well … that's on purpose," Willoughby answered, a bit unevenly at first but warming as he continued. "See, Willoughby wants Marianne, right? But so does Brandon. They're rivals, see, and he hates me from stuff in the past. And Delaford is Brandon's house, so, yeah. I can't be seen, like, at breakfast at that guy's house."

"At *my* house?" Brandon asked for clarification. There was a pause. "I'm Colonel Brandon."

Willoughby looked embarrassed. "Right, right. Sorry, I can't believe I forgot that."

"Yeah, me neither." Perplexed, Brandon looked at Henry. "Tell me honestly, Tilney. Black man in Jane Austen clothes. Six-foot-four. Am I seriously just *forgettable* at Regency events now? Dime a dozen?"

"My dear fellow, after *Bridgerton,* who can say?" Henry shrugged.

Brandon returned his attention to Willoughby. "Well, I guess it's true that you can't exactly come downstairs and hang around. If the real Willoughby showed up to breakfast with me at Delaford, then I probably would have to call you out to a duel."

"Might cast a pall on the old egg and b, that," Henry chimed in. "Best avoided all around, I'd say."

"Yeah, that's right!" Willoughby agreed, looking relieved. "Anyway, nobody can see me until the third day of the storyline thingee, which is tomorrow afternoon. That's when I come running out of the woods to pick up Marianne when she falls and hurts her ankle. That's during the Nature Walk. There's a path to that site just a little bit uphill from here." He pointed up the hill behind the shed toward the trailhead. "Goes across a bridge over that stream, past an outdoor chapel."

The drenched chapel-seekers exchanged glances with each other. "You don't say?" managed Maggie, her wit still dry despite her swampy petticoat. "Well, another day we might like to see that."

There was a general mumbling of agreement that indeed, another day might be best.

"I say, Willoughby. Speaking of tomorrow. You've heard that the original Dashwood sisters have been replaced for the week, haven't you?" Henry inquired. "It was on JaneyApp this morning."

"Ah, no, I hadn't heard, actually," Willoughby replied. "JaneyApp problem." He knocked on his cell phone through the pocket of his breeches.

"Oh, right, right, sorry," Henry acknowledged. "Anyway, the original Dashwoods are laid up with poison ivy and the resort has called in the understudies. Your Elinor stands there and your Marianne Dashwood is here, dear sir." He gave introductory hand gestures toward Jane and Maggie.

"Really?" Willoughby looked frankly displeased. "You're the new Marianne? The other one was the little gal from India, right? You're kind of … a healthy gal."

Maggie's frayed patience snapped abruptly.

"Well, regardless of who's playing Marianne, *your* part is not exactly rocket science, is it, Willoughby?" Maggie said sharply. "You just rush in and pick up whatever 'gal' is on the ground, right?"

Willoughby stared at Maggie coldly as an awkward beat passed. Henry broke the tension with a collegial stage whisper and an elbow to the ribs. "When she puts it that way, it does sound like one can sort it out, eh, old man?"

A lesser version of Willoughby's smile returned with a generous side order of snark. "Right you are, Tilney. Hopefully, in this case the understudy's extra weight won't throw me off balance too much when I pick her up."

Maggie could only sputter and make scoffing noises in reply but Brandon leapt into the breach gallantly. "I can vouch for the fact that this woman is light as a feather, Willoughby. I have personally had the privilege of carrying Miss Marianne recently and I assure you, I had no troubles at all in that area. If you find yourself incapable of ... performing ... with a fully-formed woman, please let me know and I'll be happy to step in for you."

Maggie smiled up at the Colonel admiringly. *Well, that was one of the prettiest lies I've ever heard. These hips are wearing every fried wonton I've ever eaten and you were grunting plenty when you were carrying me across that stream. But dang, B. That felt good.*

Willoughby bucked up instinctively at the implied insult to his masculinity. He straightened to his full height, only to find himself looking Brandon squarely in the shoulder and discovering in that instant his sincere desire for peace with the man.

"No, I'm ... I'm sure I'll manage. No worries." The sugary smile returned with an extra dollop of friendly sauce added for Brandon's benefit.

"Yes," Brandon replied coolly. "Now that we've discussed it, I'm quite sure you will manage."

"There's a trick to lifting, you know," Henry interjected. "If I may add a practical staging note here. Come to the downhill side, for one thing, Willoughby. Or position her up off the ground on a stump or something before you do the big lift. Let gravity work *for* you, not *against* you. And Lizzy, don't be just dead weight. Hold tight to his neck and help by subtly pushing up with your foot. Here, we can … no, wait. Lizzy you're a bit wet but Janie, do you mind demonstrating what I mean?" Henry maneuvered Willoughby and Jane into position and helped them block out a respectable looking stage lift as Lizzy and Brandon observed.

"Thanks for stepping up, Brandon," Maggie said quietly. "You stood up for thick girls everywhere. I kinda had you down as someone who liked the little wispy girls best."

Brandon shook his head at her. "Why? Since I enjoy the writings of Jane Austen I *must* be into skinny pale women, I suppose? Girl, please."

Maggie smiled and held up her hands playfully. "Hey, *I* have no idea what 'type' you're into. You might be stuck in the past with some old paradigms for all I know, B, just because you are so *old*."

"Really? That was an *old* man carrying you across that stream, then?" Brandon asked, jerking his thumb over his shoulder in mock surprise.

"Little bit, yeah," Maggie allowed with a twinkle in her eye. "But, you know. An old man with his own charms, I guess, especially since he's got such … broad viewpoints about women."

"Uh-huh. I see how it is. Well, that's so *kind* of you to see past my decrepitude, Miss Elizabeth," Brandon returned, shaking his head wryly. "To be clear, though," he said, more seriously, "I don't think I have a 'type' like you're talking about. What *I* look for is a lively *spirit*. Period. And that can come in any color or configuration, believe me, or at any age. It's true, I *am* kind of a Brandon type. I accept that. I know I can be a bit grim. But … I do love *spirited* women." He grinned at Maggie and shrugged, helpless before his truth.

"I can understand that," she said, nodding slowly and returning his grin. "Listen, along those lines, B," she paused to clear her throat. "I wanted to ask you about somebody. Did you ever meet …"

"Damianne? From *Black Girl Loves Jane?*" Brandon interrupted irritably. "Why does everybody keep asking me that? Like all the Black Janeites in the Midwest are supposed to know each other? That's pretty funny coming from you, Miss Maggie Argyle of Chicago!"

"No, no, no," Maggie said backpedaling rapidly. "It wasn't that at all." Brandon exhaled wearily. "Okay, yeah, it was that, but really, I was asking because she's cool, you know. Loves Jane. And really rocks her little fascinator hats so … hey. Spirited." A moment passed and Maggie slid her eyes over toward Brandon suspiciously. "You *did* meet her, didn't you? Don't lie."

The large man sighed deeply and closed his eyes. "It's possible that we've chatted online. A bit. In the past."

"Aha!" Maggie exulted. "Y'all got history. I knew it. I *knew* it!"

"Life is complex, Lizzy. Not everything works out like an Austen novel," Brandon murmured with quiet exasperation. "All of you little Emmas, you little Austen matchmakers, you need to stop asking me about her. Y'all are *all* so young. *So* young."

"Whatever you say, B," Maggie answered with a shrug. "But she is cool, though."

"Give it up, Lizzy."

"Okay, then."

They stood for a quiet moment watching Willoughby sink lower and lower each time Jane leapt into his slender arms. "You know," Maggie said matter-of-factly, "I'm probably going to just about kill that little man when he tries to carry me tomorrow."

"I know," Brandon said with a sly smile. "But you'll never hear him say a word about it, now."

And at this, the two shared both a hearty laugh and a satisfied fist bump.

"Hey, let's go down, people," Maggie called out to the other players. "Jane and I have a luncheon coming up at Netherfield."

Willoughby bid farewell and departed along the lateral path toward Northanger. The rest of the group descended along the downhill path, making good time on the well-groomed terrain, and soon intersected the main walkway.

Henry said he would go with Brandon to Delaford and bring the cart back for the ladies. The plan was readily agreed to and the men headed off quickly.

"So?" Jane asked confidentially as the men disappeared out of earshot. "Has he met Damianne?"

"Oh, come on, Janie," Maggie said, scoffing with new-found piety. "It's not like all Black Midwestern Janeites know each other."

A beat passed as Jane looked at Maggie with narrowed eyes. "He *did* meet her, didn't he?"

"Apparently so," Maggie said, relaxing into a smile. "Probably DM'ed her like a fanboy. 'Good day, dear lady. I find the portrait of you in your yellow *chapeau* quite "fascinating" indeed.'"

"Would you care to share a few *bon mots* via this quaint

textual method?" suggested Jane.

And thus the ladies amused themselves with Austen-inspired modern pick-up lines—"I say, let us take a turn about the chat room, it's so refreshing"—until Henry reappeared with the golf cart.

Chapter Eleven

Maggie and Jane were ironically well-prepared for the Luncheon and Cards event at Netherfield after their unfortunate encounter at, or rather *in*, the hillside stream since they arrived muddy and sneezy respectively. Of course, this is how one expects a muddy Lizzy and rain-soaked Jane Bennet to show up in that section of the *Pride and Prejudice* storyline, where they manage to simultaneously intrigue their suitors Darcy and Bingley as well as horrify their hostesses, Bingley's snobby sisters, in equal measure.

It must be said, however, that in the original text, Lizzy's petticoat hem at Netherfield was described as 'six inches deep in mud,' but our Maggie had exceeded Austen's imagery by adding a great many extra damp inches of her own. In addition, our modern role-playing Jane had not exactly caught cold, like her character had done, but her soaked left foot *did* make her prone to sneeze. Perceiving that these were real sneezes, an alarmed Mr. Bingley fussed over her a great deal, burying Jane in so many layers of shawls that she had to protest, ever-so-sweetly, just to maintain an open airway.

Aside from these variations, however, our young women played their roles with excellent verisimilitude. The happy CanonScavvers were thrilled to observe the damp young women, mark these items off in their canon lists and whisper explanations to their puzzled husbands as luncheon was served.

After the meal, the attendees were shown into the sitting room so that the assembled characters and visitors could play the card game "Loo" just as Austen's characters had done. As card tables were being assigned, an enthusiastic fangirl named Amelia Woodley was particularly zealous in trying to engage Mr. Darcy in conversation, following him to every corner of the room where he tried to find solitude. Darcy gave Maggie several earnest *I-told-you-so* looks from across the parlor as this played out and Maggie began to feel a pang of sympathy for him.

That little Dora's right. These fangirls do have a 'weird kind of like' for their Mr. Darcy, she thought. *I could almost feel jealous. Almost,* she thought smugly, proving once again that "denial" is not *just* a river in Egypt since our Maggie was, in truth, *madly* jealous every time someone looked Darcy's way.

To the great disappointment of the ardent Amelia Woodley, however, she was not assigned to a card table with Mr. Darcy but rather to one with her chief rival for Darcy's attentions, Caroline Bingley. For the rest of the afternoon, therefore, Miss Woodley had to content herself by making increasingly pointed observations to the table in general, and Miss Bingley in particular, about how terribly unbecoming it was for young women nowadays to throw themselves at men.

Lizzy had not been assigned to a card table at all because in the original story, her character had opted to read a book rather than play Loo. Thus, accompanied by many sets of eyes and a general rustling of #CanonScav cards, Maggie had dutifully walked toward a stack of books placed on a nearby table and selected one. Under the noise and bustle of the card table setup, Darcy approached her as she made her choice so he could discreetly ask the burning questions of the day in the guise of discussing her book.

"What on earth happened to you and Jane?" he queried urgently. "Why are you so wet?"

"Just prepping for my role, Darcy," Maggie replied, pointing to the book cover to further the illusion of literary chat. "I arrive at Netherfield with a muddy hem, remember?"

"Yes, but you've vastly overshot the mark, haven't you?" he persisted. "It was 'six inches of petticoat' not a dress soaked all the way up your back side, cute though that back side may be."

Though she had planned a saucy retort, Darcy's last comment drove it completely out of her head and produced instead an incoherent lip sputter. Darcy watched this with considerable amusement but maintained his solemn countenance and made do with one subtle wink.

"Well, I'd hardly say ... I mean, leaving my back side out of it for the moment ..." Maggie began, doggedly trying to recapture her composure.

"Oh, let's not," Darcy interrupted pleasantly.

"Leaving it out for the *moment,*" she insisted, whereupon Darcy sighed and motioned for her to continue, "a few of us fell into a stream coming back from the Nature Walk today."

Darcy pursed his lips and tried to keep from laughing. "You and Tilney, I suppose, cooked up some impulsive off-road adventure and got Janie sucked into it, too, poor girl."

"Sort of," Maggie admitted unhappily. "But we had Colonel Brandon along, a *bona fide* military escort with real outdoor survival training. So it seemed safe, you know? It just ... didn't work out like we planned."

"It never quite does for you and Tilney, does it?" Darcy asked wryly.

"Oh, hush," Maggie said, not intending to smile at the man but failing utterly in this. "Go play your cards."

"Go read your book, you vixen. Enticing me with your huge, knobby brains," Darcy said, tapping on the book cover and widening his eyes at her seductively.

She lifted the book sideways as if to backhand Darcy and the gentleman hastily retreated to the Loo table. He sent one more wink toward Maggie for good measure as he was seated. However, she shook her head resolutely and buried her face in her book. In fact, probably much like Austen's Lizzy, she pretended to ignore the handsome man all afternoon even though his eyes kept drifting her way. If we're honest, her eyes wandered toward Darcy several times, too, and each time she felt it in her toes. *These aren't even pings,* Maggie realized that afternoon. *This is like when they hit you with those electric paddles in the ER. I don't know what this feeling is, but it ain't no* ping.

The hour passed agreeably with an extra dose of laughter since Mrs. Engelvardt's first name, by happy chance, was Pamela. In Loo, the highest possible card is a jack of spades trump referred to as "Pam." To the card players' delight, one of the rules of Loo is that in cases when play of "Pam" is restricted, this is signaled by one player making the stern injunction, "Pam, be civil." Since Pam Engelvardt was fresh off a morning of bounteous mimosa consumption, it will not surprise the reader that she carried on quite uncivilly all afternoon, too, stealing cookies and reciting bawdy limericks without restraint, until the rebuke would inevitably come. The card players roared anew each time trump "Pam" received the admonition to "be civil" because it usually caught the human Pam greatly in need of the reprimand, too.

Young Dora Engelvardt, who had been assigned to Mr. Darcy's table by the gentleman's special request, glanced disapprovingly at her mother at these times but Mr. Darcy whispered kind reminders that a *little* silliness can be acceptable and non-sillies like themselves did well to overlook it. In the end, it was agreed all around that the *P&P* Luncheon and Cards event had exceeded all expectations.

True to her role in canon, Jane had made her exit upstairs before the card game began, displaying symptoms of her "cold" and staggering out under the weight of her many shawls. Therefore, when cards ended, it was quite natural for Lizzy and Bingley to slip upstairs, too, mentioning how eager they were to check on Jane's health. Darcy ascended, too, under the ruse of returning to his own room. This is how the four LaGGards escaped the crowds (with Darcy just steps ahead of the persistent Amelia Woodley) and gathered moments later behind the door of the small lounge where Jane was waiting. Though a restless Darcy kept checking the inner latch nervously, the quartet was able to relax a bit and congratulate themselves on another successful event for the *Pride & Prejudice* storyline.

"We rock, y'all!" Bingley exulted, seeking and receiving high-fives all around. "Who knew 'Pam' could be *so* uncivil, right?" he added, drawing a chuckle from Darcy and a confused look from Jane. This, in turn, launched Bingley into a jumbled explanation of uncivil Pams that was utterly incomprehensible to his beloved Jane but made her smile just the same.

Meanwhile, Maggie walked toward the window to plan out the rest of the day by addressing the missing LaGGards on their group text.

LizzyB: Hey, LaGGards, what's up? Gothic Night Tour at Northanger starts at 8:30 tonight. Who's going?

Catherine: Hopefully, me. I'm coming over later. Right now I'm in Bath with the main storyline. In a couple of minutes we're leaving so John Thorpe can drive me around in his carriage. *rolls eyes*

LizzyB: Yikes. Hang on tight.

Catherine: Thanks. Pray for me. Where's Henry, anyway? Is he with you all?

LizzyB: Nope. Probably over at the Abbey. He's supposed to meet us over there tonight.

Catherine: Everyone else is coming?

Darcy: I certainly am. Lizzy?

LizzyB: I'm standing right here, Darcy. You know I am. Let me ask the others.

Darcy: They'll just say yes. They say yes to everything.

Maggie verbally polled the ever-distracted Bingley and Jane. "Hey, are you guys going to the Night Tour at Northanger tonight?" The lovers nodded in the affirmative while continuing to stare at each other and whisper.

LizzyB: OK. They said yes.

Darcy: Do tell. Who could have seen that coming?

LizzyB: I kind of hate you right now.

Catherine: You guys are hilarious. Are you literally standing in the same room?

Darcy: Literally. I can smell the fragrance of her river mud from here.

LizzyB: Trust me, he's no bed of roses. We'll see you tonight, Catherine.

Catherine: Great! See you then!

And so they did.

All six LaGGards, after a good scrubbing and a change into blissfully bone dry clothing, were finally able to share a meal together once again at their favorite table on the Pemberley terrace. Afterward, they were in a warm and jovial humor as they walked under the stars along the lake shore toward Northanger. Their laughter and good spirits lifted the mood of all Janeites they passed on the promenade. More than one visiting couple, enjoying an after-dinner stroll of their own, glanced at one another with renewed affection after passing the happy players, grouped as proper Regency couples with ladies on the arms of their suitors.

"Say, Tilney," Darcy asked the man in front of him. "Why didn't you answer the group texts today? I reassured the ladies repeatedly that you would always find your way to the supper table but your absence worried them no end. Bingley and I had to hear about it all afternoon."

"Sorry, lads. It's my phone, I'm afraid," Henry replied over his shoulder with a sigh. "Got wet when I took that tumble and has refused to do anything since then. It's currently sitting in a bowl of rice in my room drying out. I've given it a stern talking to so I'm sure it will come around in time."

"Oh, dear," said Maggie with a side glance toward Darcy. "However will you live, Henry, without blowing up the group texts every day?"

"It's been difficult," Henry acknowledged, "though worse for you lot, doing without my brilliant insights, I'm sure."

"Oh, I imagine we'll soldier on," Darcy murmured, shaking his head. He glanced toward Northanger and tilted his head. "Listen, is it my imagination or is some type of lighting system coming on? Just there. On the stairway to the Abbey."

Indeed, where the rock stairway had been hidden in darkness as the group approached, a subtle glow had begun to illuminate it. Slowly, more features became visible, including the sturdy hand railing. Then the garden maze on the broad terrace lawn in front of the Abbey gradually became visible, too, its tall hedges showing up as long shadows set among pools of orange light.

Lights within the Abbey brightened, too, casting a matrix of confusing new shadows but also allowing glimpses of the interior walls and furnishings through the narrow windows.

"Oo, it looks so cool lit that way," Jane said, eyes shining up at Bingley. He nodded and gave her hand an affectionate squeeze where it rested on his forearm.

"I know, right?" Catherine echoed in wonder. "The safety system on the stairway comes on every night at dusk but this is the first time I've seen it from this angle. Looks cool but a little creepy, right?"

"Oh, absolutely creepy, my dear, no question," Henry replied, shivering with delight.

"Henry, who's at the Abbey tonight?" Maggie queried, squinting upward into the darkness. "I thought all the guests were over in Bath for this part of the storyline but just now I saw someone standing upstairs in one of the guest rooms."

"Really?" Henry replied, peering toward the castle. "As you say, everyone else is gone to the other apartments in Bath, except for Catherine and myself. I suppose the care-taker and kitchen staff are still onsite but they have their own apartments on the ground floor, not upstairs."

"No, he was up in that third story tower room, the one with the balcony." Maggie pointed toward it. "I could have sworn I saw a man in the double doorway there." She sighed and lowered her eyes. "Gone now, though, whatever it was. Maybe some shadow is set up to appear and disappear for these gothic Night Tours."

"Probably so. I've heard there is an eerie pre-recorded track of lights and sounds. But if I see a strange man wandering around the Abbey tonight, I'll speak to him in the strongest possible terms and send him your way for a good dressing down, dear girl," Henry declared. "The man owes our Lizzy an explanation. And if he turns out to be an old coat hanging on a rack, well, I shall berate the tatty thing anyway, just for scaring you."

"Thanks, Henry," Maggie said sardonically. "You're far too kind."

"Isn't he though," Darcy muttered, patting Maggie's hand on his arm and rolling his eyes.

At his touch, Maggie's toes felt the electric tingle again and she found herself smiling in spite of herself. *Margaret Nichelle Argyle,* she exhorted silently, her internal voice sounding alarmingly like her mother's, *don't you make fun of those Nebraska librarians-gone-wild when YOU are the most ridiculous fangirl in this whole place! Hanging on Darcy's arm, grinning like a fool. This is nothing but a dream world, young lady, and don't you forget it.* Just then Darcy winked at her, sending further jolts into her toes and setting her heart racing as she looked away and tried to remember how to breathe.

Twice today she had relied on the muscular arms of sturdy gentlemen and she was forced to admit that it felt completely wonderful doing so. *Okay, yeah. Gentlemen courting like gentlemen, this is the cool part of the Austen world,* she thought to herself. *Love my modern opportunities and cars and flush toilets and all that but ... hey. This part ain't so bad.* She smiled up at Darcy, settled her hand deeper into the crook of his elbow and wrapped her fingers around his pleasantly firm forearm. *Huz-zah, y'all. If this is just a dream, I definitely have had worse ones.*

"Here we are, then, ladies and gentlemen. Home sweet castle," Henry announced from the bottom of the stairs. "Shall we go up?"

Chapter Twelve

The LaGGards reached the bottom of the Northanger stairway and began the careful ascent to their gothic destiny. The ladies clasped the front of their long skirts and proceeded slowly so as not to catch a foot on their hems. With the rock staircase winding through the trees as it did, it was not obvious until one actually mounted it that the flights zigzagged across the side of the hill. So the change in elevation with each step was not particularly steep and the group managed it with relative ease.

At first.

In time, however, the sheer number of steps began to add up and leg muscles made their unhappiness known.

Maggie was the first to speak up. "Say, gang? Can we rest for a sec?" she huffed. "I … uh, I think Catherine's legs are tired."

Catherine looked up in surprise but readily stopped walking. It *was* difficult for her shorter legs to keep up the pace Henry was setting and she was falling behind the group.

"Of course, of course," Henry assented immediately. "Let's all have a rest."

"I would think they have some kind of elevator, for handicapped access or supply delivery or something," Maggie said testily, leaning on a post, unhappy that her lack of outdoor fitness was being exposed for the second time that day.

"They have a golf cart that delivers food twice a day or, I suppose, guests if needed," Catherine contributed, rubbing her tight quadriceps.

"Are you delivering food, Miss Lizzy?" Henry queried

93

mischievously, knowing his bestie's fondness for carrying snacks. "Might qualify you for a ride next time."

"Well, both of her pockets are full of crab rangoons from the buffet if that counts," Jane added helpfully.

Maggie glanced with embarrassment toward Darcy who looked upward discreetly.

"Those were for later," she muttered coldly to Jane. "See if you get any now."

In due time, the group completed their climb and found themselves waiting with other guests in a broad terraced space, the grand gardens at the entrance to the Abbey.

The gothic stone block castle walls, topped with imposing turrets, rose into the starry night. Subtle lighting throughout the Abbey provided some illumination, it is true, for points of interest like gargoyle faces on the castle walls or topiary creatures on the lawn. However, such lighting was also oriented so that it produced long, grotesque shadows and in doing so, managed to create an overall effect of adding to the darkness rather than decreasing it.

"Kind of creepy here at night, isn't it?" Maggie asked, finding her city senses on high alert, as though she were walking down a darkened Chicago alley.

"I believe that's the idea," Darcy added. "Gothic theme and so forth. There's a subset of Janeites that love it."

"Well, Catherine Morland is the character that's supposed to love all things gothic," Jane observed. "What do you say, Catherine? Scary or fun?"

Catherine shrugged and gave a prim smile before answering in her tiny voice. "Both, I guess. I kind of hate it. But …" a broad smile spread across her face, "I kind of love it, too."

"I give you Austen's Catherine Morland in the flesh, my friends!" Henry proclaimed as the group shared a laugh.

"'Though she be but little she is fierce.' And isn't she just!"

"That's Shakespeare, Henry, not Austen! But it does fit our Catherine," Maggie acknowledged. She muttered an aside to Henry as the general conversation continued. "You did a summer rep of *Midsummer Night's Dream* somewhere, didn't you? Let me guess. You were Puck."

"How could you possibly know that?" Henry asked, genuinely surprised.

"Good grief, Henry," Maggie said, shaking her head. "You *embody* puckishness. How could someone *not* know that?"

A familiar couple arrived at the waiting area just then, deep in conversation.

"Welcome! Another country heard from," Henry shouted, beckoning to welcome the newcomers.

Mr. Knightley and Emma from the *Emma* cast appeared in a pool of light near the LaGGards and were greeted warmly all around.

"Is everything all right over at Hartfield, Emma?" Jane asked with some concern, noting that the young woman looked a bit downcast.

"Oh, yes. Everything's fine," Emma answered, unconvincingly. "We've just had some very rich food and I'm not sure it's settling with me very well."

"Oh, my, sorry to hear that," Bingley said kindly. "I didn't see you at the buffet tonight."

"No, no, we have the big librarians' group over at Highbury and they booked a supper with the cast. So we ate there tonight," Emma said reluctantly. She looked toward Knightley who beamed at her innocently. "Jane Fairfax cooked," she added, spitting out the name unhappily.

Maggie pursed her lips and looked at Henry whose eyes

twinkled back at her puckishly. Jane Fairfax, the too-perfect side character who was constantly outshining the original Emma in Austen's book, seemed determined to do so in the role-playing world, too. The staff member playing Miss Fairfax was a dazzling young woman named Sung-mi Park, someone who was not just an overachiever, but in fact, had left "overachiever" status in the dust miles ago.

Mr. Knightley, a mischievous character in his own right, cast in a role as mentor to young Emma for most of the *Emma* storyline (suitor would come later), never tired of pointing out the fine qualities of other people to the proud young lady when the opportunities arose. And with Ms. Park/Fairfax, such opportunities arose frequently.

"My dear Emma, you make it sound like the woman opened a tin and threw it at us," chided the proper British gentleman. "In truth, my friends, it seems that in between semesters at Juilliard, Miss Fairfax has also trained at the *Cordon Bleu* in Paris! The girl takes one's breath away, doesn't she, Emma?"

"Oh, I don't know. *You* always have sufficient wind to talk about her," returned Emma indifferently.

"Well, how can one not effuse, dear girl?" Knightley gushed. "This young woman served us a roast rack of lamb with a jelly made of fresh mint. And she had grown it herself!"

"What, the lamb or the mint?" Maggie asked in an aside to Emma.

"God knows," Emma answered, shaking her head. "Probably both."

"And then came a spinach *au gratin* dish with a type of cheese that she had *invented*, if you can believe it," Knightley raved. "*Fromage de Fairfax*. But she was not done, oh no!"

"Really?" Maggie said to Emma drily. "Once you invent a cheese, you'd think a person would be done."

"You'd think," Emma intoned dully. "But you'd be wrong."

"Then, my friends," Knightley continued, tracing a line along the horizon like a barker hawking patent medicine, "then came dessert. Miss Fairfax wheeled out the dessert cart with our delightful pudding, completely *en flambé!* It was an enormous Baked Alaska, with the meringue sculpted into the shape of a swan! It literally brought tears to the eyes of everyone in the room, didn't it, Emma?"

"Yes, but I think it was mostly from all the smoke," Emma felt obligated to report.

There was barely time for Maggie to give Emma's hands a sympathetic pat before the attention of everyone on the lawn was abruptly diverted. An eerie amplified sound, somewhere between a screech and a moan, was heard, seeming to come from nowhere and everywhere at once. Maggie flinched and grabbed for Darcy's arm reflexively. The visitors looked about in alarm, trying to discern the origin of the sound.

EEEeeee ... eeeeeeeee ... eeEEEeee ... eeeeee ... ee ...

Then, as suddenly as it had begun, it stopped.

"Look there," Henry whispered, pointing at the wooden double doors that formed the entrance to the Abbey. Indeed, where both heavy doors had been closed before, one had now swung open, revealing only a confusion of shadows in the great hallway beyond.

"Was that the door hinges?" Darcy murmured. "Sounded like a wounded animal."

"I've got some WD-40 in my suitcase if they need it," Bingley offered loudly, drawing a nervous laugh from the gathered guests.

The group stood hushed now, staring expectantly at the half-opened front entrance. Then, ever-so-slowly, the second door began to swing open, shrieking throatily in its turn and squeaking back and forth at the end before settling.

Eeeee … eee … oooOOO … ooeeeeeeee … ee … ee … ee … ee …

The guests stood silent and waiting, peering through the gloom to see who or what might appear in the darkened doorway.

"TERROR!" roared an amplified voice from behind the visitors, followed immediately by a crash of thunder and the illumination of a sudden bright light. This prompted startled high-pitched outcries from everyone present though later it would be agreed that Henry's squeal was by far the most shrill.

As one, the gathered company executed a rapid turn to the rear and gazed in wonder at what stood behind them. A bearded and haggard man in caretaker's clothes stood holding aloft a glowing lantern. Another pre-recorded flash of light and ominous roll of thunder echoed from an unseen source in the still evening air.

The sinister man spoke in clear, foreboding tones. "'*Terror of this nature, as it occupies and expands the mind, and elevates it to high expectation, is purely sublime, and leads us, by a kind of fascination, to seek even the object, from which we appear to shrink.*'"

Another crash, another streak of lightning.

"So Mrs. Radcliffe wrote," he continued, "in *The Mysteries of Udolpho,* warning us of our pitiful weakness before our own terror. Miss Austen claimed that such fascination only lived in the overwrought minds of those who read too many gothic novels. But. Is it so?"

Another boom with another sudden flash split the darkness and then retreated with an irritable rumble.

"Be warned, ladies and gentlemen, that tonight in a simple garden maze you shall discover, not terrors that live without, but those that live *WITHIN!*"

This time the noise and light were so intense that the audience's senses were momentarily overwhelmed. Then, when vision returned, the man was gone.

A titter ran through the audience and a few low conversations started.

Henry broke the tension first. "Well, I've certainly had my money's worth. Now who wants ice cream?"

Maggie laughed with relief. "I'll go. Was that the caretaker, that Gary guy?"

"That's the chap," Henry confirmed, nodding. "He's quite different in normal lighting but the whole effect is rather chilling in context, isn't it?"

"Too chilling," Maggie grumped testily. "I am *not* all about this scary stuff."

"I thought you were squealing a bit extra there, Lizzy," Darcy said, rubbing the inside of his elbow where she had been clutching his arm.

"Ha! That's nothing," Maggie said with a wave of the hand. "You should go to a Chucky movie with my Uncle Reggie. He screams so loud, no one will go with him anymore. But, hey, you can't disagree with the man. That doll ain't *right.*"

The orange glow of the caretaker's lantern reappeared inside the garden maze, just before the first turn and the group walked slowly toward it. No sooner had all of them funneled completely into the narrow space between the hedges, however, than they were instantly in darkness again as the caretaker and his lantern vanished around the corner.

Taking a collective deep breath, the pilgrims moved cautiously forward. The gothic Northanger Abbey Night Tour had begun.

Chapter Thirteen

The Night Tour group continued to creep around the first corner of the maze, trying to see what could not be seen, until all had rounded the turn and filed into the section sitting perpendicular to the entranceway corridor. Then, with a sudden simultaneous crash and blinding flash of light, the area in which they stood was suddenly illuminated to reveal an immense topiary dragon, snaking around a white pedestal in the corner, mouth open wide and eyes like giant gemstones suddenly alight and smoldering a fiery red. The gaping maw of this creature with his bulging jaws and great bushy "teeth" was very near Mr. Knightley's head, as it turned out, and the startled gentleman jumped away quickly, yelping and nearly knocking over Emma in the process.

Then the darkness returned abruptly, leaving only a few gasps and murmurings in its wake.

"There, there, Mr. Knightley. Are you all right, dear sir?" This was Emma's voice.

"Yes, fine, of course," he was heard to reply. "Just startled. I was practically in its jaws, did you see?"

"Yes, of course. Nasty old bush, wasn't it? Perhaps Jane Fairfax can make you a soothing tonic later." This, too, was Emma's voice and if, indeed, there was a bit of snark in it, who could blame her?

So it was to be around corner after corner in the dark, leafy labyrinth. The faint flicker from the caretaker's lantern would lead them on, with corridors of the maze sometimes only a few steps long, but sometimes agonizingly far in length as the dread built for the next shocking reveal. Sometimes it might be a stone gargoyle, perched and glaring from above with a monstrous face. Or it might be a rapacious and slavering wolf, carved ingeniously from a bush but with inset eyes aflame, standing on its hind legs and ready to pounce.

Around one corner, the sudden glare revealed a lawn gnome, the harsh lighting set in the ground making his laughing facial expression look hideous and twisted.

"Look! Is that My Little Darcy? The Omaha librarians' mascot?" Maggie whispered to Darcy urgently, tugging on his sleeve and pointing.

"My God, the thing is grotesque," he replied, curling his lip. "I thought at least it would be …"

"What, cute?" Maggie hissed. "Gnomes aren't cute, are they? What *are* gnomes, anyway?"

"I have no idea," Darcy muttered. "Like, leprechauns, I guess or … happy little … gardeners … or something, no?"

"Happy little gardeners?" Maggie giggled. "Did you just say that?" The lights dropped out again and Maggie took her chance to laugh in earnest.

"Oh, zip it," Darcy said, poking her in the ribs with his elbow and gesturing for them to move onward. "You don't know either. We'll google it later."

In time, the group began to grow somewhat accustomed to the routine, as accustomed as one can be, anyway, to sudden loud noises and bursts of light designed to jolt the nervous system. Near the end of the maze the visitors were even a bit jolly, mocking their earlier squeals by giggling and mouthing exaggerated "oooo, aaaa, oh nooo" sounds when the bright flashes and rumbles came and the frightening images, that no longer seemed so frightening, were abruptly illuminated.

Indeed, the final figure was especially unremarkable, a statue of nothing more or less than a gentleman in Regency military dress, a large, imposing bronze man posed on a bronze pedestal with one bronze hand on the sheath of his bronze sword, gazing into the distance. The lights stayed on after this reveal and the guests took this as a signal that the tour was over. Everyone began to chatter a bit and collect themselves before leaving.

"Oh, look," Jane said, pointing to a sign at the foot of the statue. "It's supposed to be General Tilney, Henry's father, the master of Northanger Abbey."

"Boo! I hated that guy in the 2007 movie." Bingley spoke up with emotion. "So mean to poor little Catherine when he found out she wasn't rich."

"Oh, this is dear Papá, is it?" Henry said, jovially springing forward to address the bulky bronze likeness towering over him. "Well, you're a right crabby old fellow, aren't you, General? Sending my beloved Miss Catherine out all alone like you did—for shame! The crust of such a man! If you were here, sir, I might call you out to a duel, truly I might!" He finished with a firm upward shake of his fist to the amusement and cheers of all the Janeites present.

In an instant, however, everything changed. Accompanied by ear-splitting cracks of thunder and moving fast as quicksilver, the bronze man suddenly came to life, pulling his sword from its scabbard and raising it aloft. Fiercely he shouted with a nerve-jangling amplified roar: "ENTER MY WRATH AT YOUR PERIL!"

The lighting began flashing in a dizzying erratic strobe that made each of the man's menacing movements utterly terrifying as he swung his sword about and howled with a terrible war cry. Then, just as quickly as the intense, heart-pounding sights and noises had come, they fled completely away, leaving only the terror of soundless darkness and wild imagination. All thoughts of glee had fled from the petrified company and a profound silence reigned as they stood frozen, afraid to imagine what such a fellow might do with his sword in pitch blackness. No one breathed as the agonizing seconds ticked away.

Then, barely perceptibly, the light began to change, with a soft rekindling of the safety lights and regular pathway illumination. The General was gone, his perch quite empty, to the immense relief of the whole assembly.

Henry, needless to say, had immediately jumped away from his newly-animated father (and his all-too-active sword) requiring only one terrific bound and a profoundly unmanly shriek to cover several feet of distance. He had landed on top of Darcy's feet, as it happened, and clasped his arms around the man's neck to keep from toppling over. At the time of Henry's leap, however, Maggie, similarly galvanized by the General's sudden enlivening, had been screaming and clutching Darcy's waist in a particularly tight embrace of her own.

So it was that the return of ambient light found three players, Darcy, Tilney and their Lizzy, frozen in a peculiar embrace *à trois* that took several long and embarrassing minutes to untangle. Aware of the complex dynamic between these three, none of the LaGGards missed the irony of seeing Maggie sandwiched between two possible suitors. And though the unencumbered players said nothing aloud, they nonetheless exchanged several raised eyebrows as the untripling, so to speak, of their comrades proceeded.

"Henry! Henry, I think my hair is caught on something," came Maggie's muffled voice as she spoke into Darcy's waistcoat. Henry staggered a bit, searching to stand on steady ground alongside rather than on top of Darcy's boots, his efforts hampered by the fact that the buttons on the front of his greatcoat were stuck deep into Maggie's lush hair. Darcy's arms, in turn, were pinned around Maggie's back by the weight of Henry's body but each time he or Henry tried to move back, Maggie yelled in pain. It was clear within seconds that they were all well and truly stuck.

"I say, can one of you lot lend a hand?" Henry implored, turning his head as well as he could toward the LaGGards standing nearby. Bingley helpfully stepped up to grab Henry's feet and guide them one at a time off Darcy's toes. Jane and Catherine, meanwhile, leapt forward and worked on the stuck hairs causing the mashup. It took a bit of wiggling and many requests for Henry to stand still, but in good time the trio was parted, to everyone's great relief.

"Well, that was awkward," Henry said frankly, as he straightened his cuffs. "It was a well done fright tour, though, wasn't it?" he offered as a change of subject.

"I liked it," Catherine said with a quiet giggle. "I think Henry's reactions were the most fun of all."

"High comedy indeed," agreed Maggie as she replaced the lace at her neckline. "Are you making any progress back there?" she asked her new *de facto* hair stylists.

Jane and Catherine were attempting to repair Maggie's undone updo but without much success. "Not really, I'm afraid," Jane confessed. "The ribbon's come loose. I think you'll just have to take it down and start over."

"No worries." Maggie knew her Glorious Mane well. It was best tackled all at once, with a game plan, a sturdy brush and a will to succeed. Trying to tame it by half measures would never do. "Henry, is there a restroom in this place, something with a mirror that I could just run in and use quickly? If you guys will wait, I can tuck it back up in just a couple of minutes."

"Absolutely, my dear. Go inside the double doors at the front, then left through the 'Staff Only' door that leads off the foyer. There's a nice lounge and locker room down there, just before the staff quarters."

Leaving the other LaGGards chatting, Maggie crossed

the lawn and headed into the entrance to the Abbey. The squeaky front doors were rendered innocuous now because the area was illuminated with a friendly golden light. The Abbey foyer, in fact, might have been called welcoming, if one was willing to overlook a few design elements like cold stone walls and mounted metal weaponry at every turn. Maggie found her way past the door marked "Staff Only" and readily found one marked "Staff Lounge" a few steps down the hall.

The lounge was pleasantly well-equipped with makeup mirrors set up along one wall. She quickly seated herself at one of the mirrors and flipped a switch to illuminate the caged light bulbs bordering the glass before scrabbling around in her reticule and pulling out her emergency brush and headband. She had learned a quick routine to pull her mane into submission during her soccer days and quickly put it into practice now. *Be good,* she told her Glorious Mane silently as she pulled out the few stray pins that still dangled limply here and there, *and I'll give you a deep conditioning this weekend.*

"You'd like that, wouldn't you?" she said aloud to her Mane in the mirror as she brushed her curls back firmly, showing them who was boss.

"Like what?" a deep voice asked.

Maggie paused for a moment (as anyone might) to assure herself that her hair had not developed sentience but in fact, it had not.

In the mirror she could see that there was a large man standing directly behind her.

Chapter Fourteen

Maggie saw the middle of him in the mirror, a tall and muscular male figure, wearing a bulging white T-shirt and jeans, holding a costume on a hanger. She turned around hastily and was deeply relieved to behold the rest of him. Above the T-shirt, the General's bronze face was now smiling at her incongruously.

"Oh! Hi!" Maggie said in surprise. "You don't look so scary when you smile."

"Oh, good," said the fellow cheerfully. He hung up his bronze General costume on an open rack and plunked down in front of the mirror next to Maggie. "I'm Enzo. Enzo Pelletucci." He extended a bronze gloved hand. "Oh, wait." He pulled off the costume gloves and re-extended his hand.

"I'm Maggie Argyle. Called Lizzy Bennet here. I'm an essay winner," she said, shaking the man's hand.

"Oh, you're one of the smart people!" he said cheerfully, switching on the lights around his mirror. "I'm totally not. I don't even know who this General guy is. But we're supposed to do Jane Austen next year at my school. Hopefully, they'll just show the movies." He grinned and started pulling at his bronze facial hair. "Ow ow ow. Wow, that does *not* want to come off." He grabbed a bottle of rubbing alcohol and poured a few drops onto one end of a cotton swab. Slowly, he started pushing the thick fuzzy mutton chops off his face as the moistened tip dissolved the spirit gum securing them. "I'm a Pelletucci so you know we're basically all related to Aunt Edith here, right?"

"So I've heard," Maggie acknowledged, returning to her own hair issues. "You're a pretty big guy for a high school kid. Deep voice, too. You made a convincing General."

"Thanks," he continued, poking away with his Q-tip. "I'm a linebacker. That's why I got this job. Aunt Edith needs somebody really big, you know, to fit the costume. She told my Pop that I could work here part time over the summer, at least until football practice starts. It's grunt work mostly, working with the horses down at the Meryton Coach House and doing this thing a few times a week. It's a pretty fun job."

By this time, Maggie had her locks pulled back and secured with her rubber headband. She had tucked her wayward ribbon into her pocket earlier but it was not proving easy to retrieve. She stood to empty her pockets and Enzo watched from the corner of his eye as the rangoons piled up.

Finally, with one mutton chop off and one still on, he paused and turned to her. "Hey, I'm sorry to be nosy but could I get some of those? I skipped dinner to get up here early and I'm starving."

"Sure, no problem," she replied collegially, gesturing toward the pile and grabbing one for herself.

After a minute or two of shared crunching, Maggie spoke up. "Listen, I actually need a hand here, if you could. Just put your finger here," she motioned on top of her head to where the ribbon sat, "and secure it." Pushing a rangoon into his mouth, Enzo rose and readily did so. "I just need to wrap this ribbon over the top of the rubber headband. Gotta look Regency, you know." With the assistance of Enzo's finger, Maggie was able to re-wrap and secure the ribbon relatively quickly.

"Thanks!" she said with a smile. "You're a lifesaver. You can finish those rangoons if you want. I've got plenty back in my room." She grabbed one for the road and left the rest on the makeup table.

"Oh, cool! Thanks."

"I need to run, though." She stood and looked toward the door. "My friends are waiting for me by the maze."

"Hey, there's a shortcut here through the staff quarters that leads directly into the back of the maze. For performers. I could show you."

"That would be great," Maggie agreed.

Still half-mutton-chopped and partially bronzed, Enzo cheerfully rose and directed Maggie out of the lounge door, steering her toward the right in the corridor outside.

"They leave this staff area pretty dark, don't they?" Maggie asked as the door shut behind them and they proceeded slowly down the unlit hallway.

"Yeah, I guess that's true in the evenings. No sunlight through those high windows. The lights by the kitchen are on a motion sensor, though, so they'll come on when we get around that corner. It's not far." Maggie's jangled nerves were on high alert in the dark but the friendly linebacker stayed dutifully by her side as she walked past the staff rooms and toward the promise of light.

As they passed a particular door, however, it opened quietly behind the two players, unobserved by either of them. A pale face above a white nightshirt appeared in the doorway. Suddenly, a bony hand reached out and grabbed Maggie's arm. She yelped and tried to pull away but the talon-like fingers clenched tight.

"You're in the wrong place," a terrible voice croaked from the aged man's wrinkled mouth. In the dim light, he looked a bit like the caretaker, Gary, but this man's head and facial hair was pure white, with twin cowlicks sticking up at crazy angles on both sides of his balding head. He was much older than the caretaker, too, with lines on his wizened face that were clearly drawn by life rather than grease pencil.

109

"What the ... hey! Let go!" Maggie blurted out in alarm. Enzo jumped forward and tried to intervene.

"Hey, buddy, hey, come on now. She's a player, on staff, like us, okay? It's okay for her to be back here. She's Maggie ... something. Maggie, right?"

"Yeah. Yeah, that's right. Maggie," she agreed breathlessly. She had momentarily forgotten the rest of her name but was secure about that much. The man's thin fingers jabbed deeper into her arm and his body leaned unsteadily toward her. "Let go, mister!" Maggie cried in distress. "You're digging in! Stop it!"

"Stop digging!" he echoed, almost wailing. "Yes! Stop! You're in the wrong place!" He pulled his face inches from hers and with all the breath he could muster said distinctly into her ear, "Go to the *cellar*... the cellar ..." His voice trailed off and his grip weakened. Maggie was able to pull her arm away at last and the man stumbled backwards, grabbing at the door jamb.

Just then the door opened fully, throwing light onto the scene at last. Gary the caretaker stood alongside the old man, looking mortified. He was wearing a t-shirt with sweatpants but his shaggy beard made him instantly recognizable. A television could be heard in the background. This was obviously his quarters.

"Dad! Come back in here," he barked impatiently to the older gentleman.

"I'm so sorry," Gary continued to the players, stammering over his words as he took his father's arm. "He's ... he's had a stroke and he's not right in the head. I'm just having him stay for a while. I didn't even know he could walk that far or ... or open the door. I'm just ... sorry. Come on, Dad." He herded his father back inside the apartment, steering him firmly toward a recliner. The older man moaned a few complaints about people being in the

110

wrong place and clutched at his son's firm grip, querulously exclaiming 'stop digging!' as they walked. After settling his father in the chair in front of the television, the caretaker returned to Maggie and Enzo, his face red and discomfited.

"Look, the rest of the staff doesn't know he's here," Gary admitted gruffly, clearly embarrassed by the situation. "I just … I just wanted him out of that rest home and here with me for a little while, you know? The man worked here all his *life*, devoted his *life* to this place. I just wanted him to come home with me, even if it's just for a little while." He looked passionate, almost angry, as he said these words. He exhaled and waited for a response.

"Well, sure," Maggie said, slightly confused. She glanced at Enzo and he nodded compassionately. "That's understandable. Sure." The three stood silent for an awkward moment.

"Could you …" the caretaker paused, averting his eyes downward and trying to compose himself before restarting. "Could you possibly see your way clear not to mention to anyone that he's here?" He looked up from the floor, his gaze landing directly in Maggie's eyes with just a hint of defiance. "Some people wouldn't like it. But *I* need him *here*." It was an uncomfortable stare with an irritable expression that did not quite match the tender pleadings of a man who needed his Dad.

"Sure," Enzo spoke up. "Don't you think we could do that, Maggie?"

"Sure," she agreed, less certainly. It was an odd request that did not quite ring true. *Why would anyone object to his poor old father visiting?* she thought. *There's more story here than he's telling.* However, having no real reason not to accede to the man's wishes, she agreed. As she had learned from Darcy, not every thought needed to be spoken aloud. "Sure. I won't say anything."

111

"Thanks," the caretaker said simply. "Okay, then. Good night." And with that, he shut the door.

"Wow," Enzo said, wide-eyed.

"Yeah, wow is right," Maggie agreed. "Let's *please* get out of here and into some light, okay?"

As soon as they rounded the corner, the motion-activated lights near the kitchen did, in fact, come on and Maggie heaved a sigh of relief.

"Did he hurt you?" Enzo asked, indicating Maggie's forearm.

"I don't think he actually broke the skin," Maggie said, examining the spot. "Just gave me a firm grip, that's all. And a good, old-fashioned gothic scare." She managed a weak grin.

"That's for sure. Kind of sad to see somebody get like that, you know? Devoted his life to this place and look at him now," Enzo said, shaking his head. "Tottering around, babbling nonsense. What did he say to you? Something like 'go to sell it' or 'go to the seller' or something?"

"I think it was 'go to the cellar,' like a wine cellar or something, but sheesh, who knows?" Maggie shrugged. "There's probably more to the story than his son wants to tell, but hey, that is definitely not my business." Maggie exhaled and looked around. "Anyway, thanks for your help, Enzo, but I've got to run. I'm guessing that's the exit that goes out to the back of the maze?" She motioned toward a door with a lighted red "EXIT" sign.

"Yep, that's it."

Maggie pushed the door outward and headed into the night.

Enzo held open the door and called after her. "Tell your brainy essay winner friends, especially that little screamer dude, that the General is coming for 'em in their dreams!"

112

"I will," Maggie giggled, waving back. And so she did.

The message from the spirited General was met with general high spirits by the LaGGards along with a collective sigh of relief that the scary gothic adventure portion of their summer was over.

Or so they thought.

Chapter Fifteen

After an extraordinarily busy Day 2 of the two-week story cycle, the players found that their lives settled into a less frenetic pace in the days that followed. Maggie and Jane managed to stay out of creeks as they understudied the Dashwoods, Darcy assiduously avoided his ardent fangirls as much as possible by locking himself in the Netherfield library and Henry was appropriately charming when he either met up with Catherine at pump room dances or missed her as she flew by in carriages during the wind-up of the first week of the *Northanger Abbey* storyline in Bath.

Maggie and Jane were on understudy duty the day following the stream incident, playing out the fateful outdoor ankle twist where the mysterious Willoughby saves the day by swooping in and carrying Miss Marianne home. This being a favorite bit of Austen canon, with fangirls eager to catch a first glimpse of the handsome villain Willoughby, the *Sense and Sensibility* Nature Walk glade was absolutely packed for Day 3 of the cycle.

"Do you see this turnout, Janie?" Maggie and Jane had positioned themselves in the woods outside of the glade an hour earlier that morning to await their cue to enter. But even then, fangirls had already started to assemble. In fact, the two petite fans named Jen had appeared in the early morning hours, Jen One staking out a front row bench with her sketch pad at sunrise and the red-headed Jen Two keeping her company.

"What's their deal?" Maggie asked Jane, indicating the two Jens.

"It's a great Janeite story," Jane replied eagerly. "Jen One, the little brown-haired one, is a massive Austen lover, comes here every year for vacation. Well, this year, she decided to travel in her Regency clothes."

"Okay, that's quirky," Maggie said, nodding slowly, "but what's the harm, right?"

"Exactly!" Jane agreed. "The girl loves Austen, so who cares, right? Anyway, a couple of obnoxious jocks at the airport baggage claim started giving her a hard time, teasing her, grabbing her bag, that kind of thing. Well, Jen Two comes by right then and she's having none of it. Not only is Jen Two a fellow Janeite who can't stand bullies, get this, she's also a former Marine! Grabs the bully in some kind of judo hold and had him down on his knees before he knew what was happening."

Maggie laughed out loud. "Oh, my word, it's a nerd fantasy! I would have paid money to see that. And she's not even five feet tall!"

"I know, right? But she made him hand that bag back and apologize before she would let him go."

"This is a new classic. Revenge of the Bookworms." Maggie assumed an announcer's voice. "Don't let the A-line dresses and reading glasses fool you. These nerds are here to take some names and kick some butt!"

"I love it!" Jane said, giggling and clapping. "Anyway, they're inseparable now. With Jen One's Austen knowledge and Jen Two's logistical support, they're on track to max out CanonScav this cycle."

Visitors continued to gather as Ferrars, for his part, continued to give his all in the role of Nature Walk guide. He was currently describing a tree fungus about which he obviously felt passionate. But we must truthfully relate that his burgeoning audience heeded but little. Willoughby was coming, and to be utterly frank, whatever attraction fungus might have mustered paled before that knowledge.

From her position offstage in the arboreal wings, Maggie shook her head. "I don't get this fascination with Austen's villains. These are the bad guys!"

Jane laughed. "It's not that complicated, Lizzy. He's cute! Sure, he's a bad boy, but hey, these ladies don't have to live with the guy. Even if they did, I know lots of people who like bad boys better than good ones."

"Yeah, I guess. They'll probably show up in droves for Wickham's arrival in Meryton tomorrow morning, too. Yuck."

Willoughby appeared behind them just then, his cat-like approach unnoticed until he spoke up.

"Hello, ladies." This produced the desired startled reaction from the two women and a gratified smirk from Mr. Willoughby.

"Sheesh, Willoughby!" Maggie exclaimed. "You and Darcy need to stop sneaking up on people in the woods! If my city instincts kick in, I cannot be held responsible for whatever happens to you crazy little white boys."

"Noted," Willoughby said with a solemn nod, though his smirk did not noticeably diminish. "You understand that my actions in this next event, picking you up and so forth, is only because that's the way the part is written. Trust me, I would never dream of touching you otherwise."

"Oh, I understand," Maggie responded with cool congeniality. "And trust *me,* you would never be allowed to touch me if I wasn't *literally* legally obligated to do it. Like with a contract, lawyers, the whole thing."

"Not with a ten-foot pole," Willoughby agreed, his grin stretched taut.

"At gunpoint," Maggie rejoined pleasantly.

"All right, all right, we get it," Jane intervened with an impatient sigh. "You're both very clever but not too thrilled

116

with this part. Hey, I'm not even supposed to *be* here. Austen wrote that Marianne was walking with her *little* sister, not her big one. But Edith decided nobody notices anyway because they're all looking at Willoughby. So, guess what? Here we are. Let's all just do our parts and get this done." She looked disapprovingly at Willoughby. He was in proper gentleman's attire this time but still looked scruffy and unkempt. "What's up with you? You know your tie isn't tied properly, right? Step over here."

Willoughby moved toward her and thrust his neck forward. In fact, his kerchief wasn't tied at all and Jane had to fish the ends of it out of his waistcoat before tying it into a reasonably respectable bow. "Y'all's staff over at *S&S* is failing you badly, letting you out like this," she said, stepping back to observe and tweak her handiwork.

"Whatever," he said sullenly. "I don't think all these girls would care if I showed up in my boxers. Might like it better."

Maggie made a rumbling sound in the back of her throat and Jane thought it best to change the subject.

"So, you're our schedule person, Lizzy. When do we go?"

"When Ferrars says that they will pause a moment because the Dashwood sisters are coming through," Maggie answered. "We thank him, sorry to interrupt, blah blah blah, then proceed like we're heading down the hill, then splat, I go down."

"Which is my cue," Willoughby continued.

"More or less," Maggie concurred.

The offstage players did not have long to wait. Ferrars finished his dissertation with a light joke about fungus (to the effect that one may not like it now but it 'grows on you') and was met with polite applause.

"We will pause now because we see the lovely Dashwood

117

sisters approaching," Ferrars announced loudly.

Maggie and Jane stepped onto the high side of the trail and entered the open glade a few steps later.

"Hello, ladies! How do you find the countryside in this area?" Ferrars inquired, projecting his voice and quieting all in the space.

"Oh, it's lovely, Mr. Ferrars," the ersatz Elinor (Jane) responded with the demure smile one gives to one's crush.

"Yes, delightful," Maggie/Marianne agreed. "I could wander these hills for days!" She then spread her arms and performed a sort of Julie Andrews hills-are-alive twirl to Jane's great dissatisfaction. The elder sister sent a stern look that clearly said *bring it down!* Fortunately, this time Maggie got the message without further need for physical intervention. "But," Maggie continued with a gulp, dropping her arms abruptly, "it looks like there may be rain coming on, Mr. Ferrars. So, we felt we had best turn back to Barton Cottage."

"Oh, my, yes, indeed." Ferrars looked with alarm at the sky, which, for the record, was a bright and cloudless blue, and agreed wholeheartedly with the inclement forecast. "Please, both you and Miss Marianne had best get home, Miss Dashwood, as soon as possible. We shall … speak … another day." He shyly tipped his hat, playing up his Elinor crush by gazing longingly toward her as he received the ladies' farewell curtsies.

The ladies walked away a few steps with every eye following them.

"What a pleasant man Mr. Ferrars is, Elinor," Maggie remarked loudly. "I think he may be partial to you. In fact, … aaaaaaaaaaahhhhhhhhhhh!"

Down went our Maggie, arms flailing ostentatiously with a roll down the hill for good measure. She produced such a tremendous outcry during this display that it echoed off the side of Delaford Ridge and all the way across the lake. (We relate with pride that staff members setting up lunch on the Pemberley terrace heard the piercing yell and were unanimous in the opinion that this Marianne might be the loudest ever.)

Crashing through the woods dramatically, Willoughby emerged from the trees at a full run. "What's happened here? Please, miss, are you all right?" He ran forward and knelt at her side.

His look of concern seemed so sincere that Maggie felt her heart leap in spite of herself. Suddenly, she was an embarrassed Marianne, injured and alarmed but hesitant to admit it to this handsome stranger.

"Oh, I'm sorry to distress you, sir, but I'm sure it's nothing." Maggie took Elinor's hand and tried to stand before falling back with another outcry—"aaaaaaahhhhhh!"—that gave further pause to the wait staff across the lake. "Oh, no, Elinor. I'm afraid I've twisted my foot. Oh, dear. However will I get home?"

"Where are your lodgings, miss?" The gentleman turned to address Elinor.

"We are from Barton Cottage, sir, but you need not trouble yourself," Elinor said. "I'm sure our man Thomas can be fetched to assist my sister."

"Nonsense," said the gallant stranger. "I wouldn't dream of leaving you ladies out here with rain coming in. I can take care of the matter." (This bit of manly chivalry was received with a murmur of feminine approval sounding rather like "*oooooo*" from all sides of the glade.)

Willoughby positioned himself as previously instructed on the downhill side of Maggie, placing one arm behind her back and one arm ready to scoop under her knees. There was a momentary pause as Maggie closed her eyes and waited for the inevitable.

"Marianne." Jane's Elinor voice was urgent and Maggie opened an eye to find her sister's face leaning over her. "Sister, I think you should put your arms around this gentleman's neck. It might assist in the matter."

"Oh! Yes!" Maggie said, instantly remembering Henry's lift training from the day before. She was supposed to grab Willoughby's neck and subtly leap into his arms. She positioned herself thusly and whispered a count to Willoughby. "*On three. One, two, three.*" Up she went into Willoughby's arms to a new round of *oooooooo*'s from every female throat.

It was an uncomfortable ride for both parties. Maggie was trying to think skinny thoughts but Willoughby's build was slight and his struggles were all too real. He had a difficult chore, namely, carrying Maggie's weight *to* the trail then *downhill* in front of dozens of breathless women. To give Willoughby his due, he managed the task with a minimum of grunting though he made up for it with profuse sweating from every conceivable pore.

When he had disappeared down the wooded trail and out of the general line of sight, some of the fangirls thought to follow him all the way to Barton Cottage. "Pray, my friends," Jane said quickly as she saw women starting to leave. "I … I … feel that Mr. Ferrars has something else for us to hear before we leave." Ferrars looked at her goggle-eyed as he definitely did *not* have anything else for the ladies to hear. The shy man had finished up with his best fungus witticism, pulled out his handkerchief, blown his nose and wiped his brow. The talk was distinctly *over* and he was absolutely out of material.

"Mr. Ferrars has … has … recently returned from a visit to his friends in the north and passed through Gretna Green," Jane extemporized. In his real life, Ferrars was, in fact, a Regency wedding reenactor at that Scotland location, well-known to Austen readers as a destination for eloping couples. At the mention of the fascinating wedding town, Janeites froze in their various positions of departure and instead quickly returned to their seats. More than one of them had dreamed of a Regency wedding at Gretna Green.

"I thought you might tell us a bit about what a wedding at Gretna Green was like, here in, you know, the Regency era, Mr. Ferrars," Jane elaborated, waiting for Ferrars to awaken from his fear-induced coma and pick up the narrative.

A moment later, to Jane's immense relief, he found his voice again. "Ah. Yes, yes. Old Gretna Green *is* well-known, isn't it?" The Janeites smiled and nodded eagerly. "Well, yes," he said, gathering strength from this encouragement. "I can do that. You see, since it's just across the border into Scotland, weddings at Gretna Green did not require the weeks-long 'reading of the banns' that the Church of England required back then. Thus, weddings could take place as quickly as one could gallop a coach to Scotland, quite an advantage to an impatient couple!"

Assured that the rapt attention of the ladies in the glade was focused on Ferrars, Jane was content to slip down the hill herself. Just as the gentleman's voice faded, she came upon the bent form of Willoughby, coat off and white shirt soaked through, leaning against a tree and panting.

"You all right?" Jane asked quietly.

"I will be," the man gasped, wiping his brow with a frilly sleeve. "Your girl walked on down the hill."

"Remember, this is just for a short time," Jane reminded him comfortingly. "Soon you'll have the Singh sisters back as your Dashwoods. They're more … small-boned."

"That's what I keep telling myself," Willoughby muttered. "Whatever. Doesn't matter. In a few days, I'll be done with this forever." His face looked very hard during this odd utterance before some vestigial salesman

121

courtesy reasserted itself, almost involuntarily. "But, you know. Thanks."

Jane had no idea how to interpret the statement that "in a few days" he would be done with this forever since a full summer of role-playing still stretched before all of the winners. Had inquisitive Maggie heard this, she might have pursued the issue. But kind Jane decided to let it go. The man was entitled to his own thoughts about whether a summer was many days or few, she reckoned. Instead, she graciously acknowledged his reluctant gratitude and bid him good day before continuing down the hill to meet Maggie.

Chapter Sixteen

Day 4 began with an unexpected JaneyApp message on Maggie's phone.

LadyCatherine: Good morning, Margaret. How is our Elizabeth this morning?

Pausing in front of the bathroom mirror, with only her right arm lotioned, Maggie tilted her head like a confused puppy when she saw the grand lady's name appear. Unconsciously standing a bit straighter and clearing her throat for no reason, she responded immediately.

LizzyB: Very well, Lady Catherine, thank you. And your good self?

LadyCatherine: I am well enough, thank you. I will get directly to the point, my dear. I have been unable to reach our Henry Tilney by text and I thought you might be able to help me. I know you two are close friends.

LizzyB: Yes, I can help you there. Henry is fine but his phone is not. He dropped it in water and I'm afraid it's not been working since then.

LadyCatherine: Oh, dear. How tiresome. And your young Catherine is in Bath this week for the scenes with the Thorpes, isn't she?

LizzyB: Yes, ma'am, for today. She's coming over here later this afternoon. But Henry is still at Northanger. I've got the Wickham Meet Up scene this morning in Meryton but after that I could run over to Northanger and give Henry a message.

LadyCatherine: Yes, that would be very helpful. Please tell him that I would like him to visit me at Rosings for tea this afternoon at 3:00. Catherine, too, if she's available.

LizzyB: Yes, ma'am. I will pass that along.

LadyCatherine: In fact, any of your little band of LaGGards is welcome. I'm afraid I need a bit of quiet help outside of the usual channels again. Discretion is absolutely critical in this regard, Miss Elizabeth.

LizzyB: You know we'll do anything to help the resort, Lady Catherine.

LadyCatherine: Quietly, my dear. Activate your less-Lizzy side.

LizzyB: Yes, ma'am. We'll keep quiet and be there at 3:00 for more instruction. No worries.

LadyCatherine: Thank you. I shall depend on it.

Maggie absently returned to her lotion bottle and pondered the odd conversation. *Why does she want Henry? Something wrong at Northanger, maybe? That place is creepy enough, that's for sure. Old guys springing out of doors, grabbing people.*

"But you promised you wouldn't tell anyone about that," Maggie told her reflection aloud. Her reflection looked back accusingly. *Even Lady Catherine?*

"Oh, good grief. Why would she even care?" she admonished her image sternly.

Realizing in frustration that she had just lotioned her right arm a second time, Maggie made a loud *arrrgh* noise and returned her full attention to her preparations for the Meryton Meet Up with Wickham.

Fangirls and Scavvers alike always turned out in full force for the entrance of the notoriously handsome *Pride and Prejudice* villain in this favorite bit of Austen canon. A particular draw of this event was that most of the main characters of Austen's most popular novel were present in this scene—the Bennet family with their cousin, the silly vicar Mr. Collins, as well as Jane and Lizzy's two suitors, Darcy and Bingley—and they would all meet up together by chance in the Meryton street where Darcy's enemy Wickham had just arrived to join the militia regiment.

Though the other Bennets and Mr. Collins had walked into Meryton on foot, Maggie and Jane had offered to pick up Darcy and Bingley in the golf cart. The gentlemen were more than happy to meet them at the appointed place on the hidden path, just outside the Netherfield carriage house.

"Excellent service, ladies!" Bingley exulted, happily clambering into the back seat. "Thanks so much for the ride."

"Yes, thanks," Darcy echoed in a far more subdued tone as he slumped into the seat behind Maggie and clutched the bar holding the cart roof with both of his hands.

"Okay, what's wrong with Darcy?" Maggie asked, glancing in the rearview mirror as she jerked the cart forward. Darcy's cool eyes met hers in the mirror briefly before her energetic start jostled his face out of her line of sight. For the moment, she could only see his white knuckles gripping the cart.

"Oh, he's just worried about riding a horse," Bingley said, dismissively waving a hand.

"Oh, my, they really put y'all on horses for this?" Jane asked, surprised. "I mean, I know Austen wrote it that way but I wasn't sure they really would have y'all do it."

"Well, they actually told us it was *not* required," Darcy said, sulkily glaring at Bingley. "But Mr. Bingley, Olympic equestrian that he is, wouldn't hear of us coming in on foot. Not such a horseman as him, no indeed!"

Bingley rolled his eyes. "Now look, I only told them that I had ridden before, which they *asked* and which is *TRUE*," he said pointedly toward the back of Darcy's head as the gentleman looked away with a snort, "and I further told

125

them, *when they asked,*" again, toward Darcy's head, "that, yes, I would be happy to help Darcy prepare for it."

"Thanks *so* much, old friend," Darcy said, not sounding grateful at all. "If there's ever anything similarly helpful I can do for you, like perform a root canal with a grapefruit spoon, I'll jump right to it." He pouted and looked glumly at the passing trees.

"Oh, come on!" Bingley whined with uncharacteristic frustration. "It is literally like walking across a room." Bingley leaned forward, appealing his case to the front seat. "It's seventy or eighty yards, tops, ladies, with one of the gentlest old mares I've ever seen. And they've assigned a groom just to walk alongside Darcy. Come on, buddy. It'll be fun." Darcy looked toward him coldly as the golf cart pulled to a stop behind the horse stables.

Maggie set the hand brake and turned around as Jane and Bingley jumped out and waited. Darcy stayed motionless, arms crossed, in the rear seat.

"Go on, guys," Maggie said, gesturing toward the stables. "We'll catch up."

Jane tugged at Bingley's arm and with a couple of backward glances, he walked away with her. Maggie sat quietly for a moment as they left.

"Go ahead. Let me have it," Darcy said testily at last. "I know you're thinking plenty of snarky things about the guy that's afraid of a little horsey ride."

"Maybe. But you're the guy who taught me that not every thought has to be spoken aloud, right?" She smiled invitingly but Darcy was unmoved. "Hey, I'm the girl who was afraid to cross a little stream, remember?"

"Yeah, and you were right, Maggie. You thought you couldn't and guess what? You couldn't."

"Maybe." Maggie shrugged. "But ... maybe I couldn't do

126

it *because* I thought I couldn't."

Darcy considered this for a moment and finally looked Maggie in the eye. "But this isn't theoretical for me. There's no 'maybe.' I really was put on a horse when I was five and truly did take quite a fall. The beast was stung by a bee or something and bucked. Threw me off and I broke my foot. Laid up all summer. There. Satisfied?"

He's truly afraid, Maggie thought with a tingle of compassion behind her eyes. *And he hates feeling that way. And he abhors sympathy, so yeah. Can't go there.*

"Dang, Will. Are we on 'sharing childhood traumas' already?" she asked with faux irritation. "Now you're going to have to hear about my chicken liver debacle from age six."

This, finally, produced a small grin. "You were thrown by a chicken liver, Miss Lizzy? How horrific for you."

"Worse for the chicken liver. I threw *it*. Up. Abruptly. Along with the rest of my lunch. Aunty Gwen said they would taste like chicken McNuggets but … they did not."

"Aunty Gwen should not have deceived you," Darcy said piously.

"Well, she received full recompense for her sins in the back seat of her car, I assure you. Stunk for a month."

They smiled at each other. Maggie leaned toward him and spoke quietly.

"If you don't want to do it, you can just tell them, Will. Nobody will care, even Bingley."

"No, but that's the thing, Maggie. I *do* want to do it. All of my cousins ride and I'm always the only one just … 'standing around in this stupid manner,' like Austen's Darcy, saying I don't *want* to do something when truthfully, I kind of wish I *could* do it, just … better."

"Then do it," Maggie said gently. "Best time for it, right? Not a cousin in sight. And the resort is obviously not going to have you doing something truly unsafe. Lord knows they need their Darcy." She reached out and took his hand. "Do it, Will. Staff here is great. They'll help you. And if you get all stressed out, I'll talk you down afterwards. You know I have a knack for de-stressing you."

"Oh, my," Darcy said, lifting a brow and squeezing her hand. "Are you volunteering to ... debrief me later?"

"You'd like that, wouldn't you?" Maggie said, squeezing back and holding his gaze steadily as her toes spontaneously burst into flames.

Darcy leaned forward and kissed her forehead before exiting the cart. "Later, my dear. It seems I have a horse to ride."

"Huzzah!" she said, noting the red-hot tingle on her forehead that radiated all the way down to her melted toes. She exhaled slowly and wiggled her fingers at Darcy as he looked back over his shoulder and winked.

Horses! her internal voice clucked in dismay. *The man's family has horses. He's* so *out of your league. You know that, right, Lil Miss Argyle? Don't you?* Telling her internal voice to mind its own business, Maggie leapt from the cart. *I am Miss Elizabeth Bennet of Longbourn and I cannot tarry to listen to this folly. I've got business in Meryton with some gentlemen on horses because* that *is, in fact, how I roll.*

And before her internal voice could give her any more guff, she gave her Glorious Mane a toss and walked purposefully to the high street in Meryton.

Chapter Seventeen

When Maggie arrived, the good people of Meryton (played by resort staff) and visitor Janeites of every stripe were stretched out as far as the eye could see. The Nebraska school librarians were out in full force with their leader, Ms. Vranes, sporting a headpiece that resembled a bunch of bananas. Amelia Woodley, Darcy's prime stalker, was being persuaded down from the top rail of the Meryton Coach House fence by two insistent groomsmen, where she had tried to peer into a window and observe Mr. Darcy mounting his horse.

The Two Jens had staked out a spot in front of the Meryton Millinery Shoppe with Jen One, the seasoned Canon-Scavver, pointing toward the street indicating the position that would maximize visibility for purposes of observing Mr. Wickham's arrival. Meanwhile, the fiery-haired Jen Two was keeping a tight perimeter on that square yard of prime real estate by telling potential loiterers to move along because it was a "ribbon unloading zone" for the milliner's shop.

Maggie looked around the packed street for her sisters but instead found Henry, waving a white kerchief to get her attention. She navigated slowly through the roiling sea of people, tacking around numerous human obstacles until at last she hove alongside Henry.

"Ahoy, Miss Elizabeth! Who knew Meryton could draw such a crowd, eh?" Henry said cheerfully.

"True that," Maggie agreed. "Listen, I'm supposed to bring you a message. Lady Catherine wants to see you and the rest of the LaGGards at Rosings at 3 PM. Very mysterious. Can you be there?"

129

"For a command performance for the grand dame herself? Without question!" Henry bowed in assent before changing topics. "I say, old thing, I'm afraid your cousin Collins is on the wrong side of the street. Just there. Perhaps you can assist in gathering him into the family fold?"

"Oh, my," Maggie sighed. "Heading the wrong way, too. Honestly. The man has no sense of direction at all. I better go catch him. See you at Rosings at three, Henry." Taking her leave with the requisite nods, Maggie was off.

Collins proved to be a difficult fox to run down, though inadvertently so.

"Mr. Collins! Mr. Collins!" Maggie called ineffectually to the back of the man's rapidly retreating head. Finally, the gentleman stopped to greet a couple of older ladies and Maggie was able to catch up to him.

The ladies were giggling behind their fans as Maggie approached.

"Mr. Collins, I am here, cousin," she announced loudly, finally seeing the man's head turn toward her. She faced the guests with a smile. "Hello, ladies. I am Elizabeth Bennet from Longbourn, quite near here. Perhaps you have come to know my cousin, Mr. Collins of the Hunsford parsonage in Kent."

"Ah, these dear, dear ladies," Collins' unctuous role player was saying in his musical Jamaican tones. He displayed his toothy smile before bending to kiss the hands of the delighted visitors. "They have been so kind in assisting a newcomer, Miss Elizabeth. Even my patroness, Lady Catherine de Bourgh, would be so impressed by the good manners of these fine women. Pray, are all of the ladies of Meryton so agreeable and handsome as these two?" This set the ladies' fans a-flutter as they tittered breathlessly behind them.

Collins inhaled, preparing to unspool another lengthy compliment, but Maggie cut him short.

"Pray, forgive us, ladies, but we must join our family now," she interjected quickly. "We must make haste, Mr. Collins." He stood looking disappointed for a moment. "I beg you, sir, we *must make haste.*" She gave him a grimace, jerking her head up the street pointedly.

Bowing with an extended front leg, Collins doffed his hat and swept it so grandly that it rendered him slightly off balance and he leaned heavily into Maggie. Subtly righting him with a hand to his elbow, Maggie smiled at the ladies and took her opportunity to pull the vicar up the street by employing a pincer grip that she did not relinquish quite as soon as Collins might have preferred.

Heeding not his protestations, Maggie doggedly steered him back toward the meeting place assigned to the Bennet family for this event. "Hang on, Mr. Collins. We're heading for the apothecary shop at the top of the street."

"Oh, I suppose we must, my dear," the man puffed. "But I wonder if we could slow the pace a trifle."

Maggie settled into a slower gear and released her grip on the man's arm as they passed the Meryton militia bunkhouse. She caught a glimpse of the staffer playing "Denny," the militiaman who would present Mr. Wickham, standing in the doorway. In fact, Maggie began to notice that several bright red militiamen's coats dotted the street in this area.

We can confirm for the record that the dapper military uniforms are, indeed, one of the favorite period costumes purchased by male visitors at the resort's custom clothing shop. In the spirit of full disclosure, however, we must inform the reader that the battle medallions and sashes on the visitor's costumes will not bear the close scrutiny of a historian. Present among the militiamen today, for example, were sashes for three different centuries of the Princes of Wales, a red ribbon for a Salt Lake City 5K Fun Run "finisher" and the winner of a silver medal from an eighth-grade oboe competition held in Fond du Lac, Wisconsin. These flaws are generally overlooked by most Janeites, however, in light of the great fun that these faux militiamen, many of them supportive Janeites-by-marriage-only, experience when wearing their "regimentals."

"Miss Elizabeth, my dear," Mr. Collins began as he gazed ahead toward the top of the street. "I ... hesitate to ask but ... have ... the new staff members proved satisfactory in the roles of Mary and Kitty?"

Maggie looked toward the man with compassion. Clearly, it was still a sensitive subject.[5]

"Yes, the new ladies are working out quite well," Maggie answered carefully. "Rather young staffers. First time they've been out of the kitchens to play characters, I think. But having fun. You can get to know them at the Cards and Supper event at Aunt Phillips' house tomorrow."

"Yes. Looking forward to it," Collins said with a wan smile.

In short order, the family was united at the top of the street and introductions of New Mary and New Kitty were made all around. Shortly thereafter, at the appointed time, the family began their official promenade. New Kitty soon ran off with Lydia toward a hat shop window and New Mary peered through her spectacles in properly Austenesque disapproval.

"Such a lack of propriety is found in young ladies nowadays," Mr. Collins ventured toward his newly-minted cousin Mary. "Don't you find them sorely in need of a few sermons from Mr. Fordyce?"

New Mary put a gloved hand to her mouth to hide her smile. "I think you are probably quite correct, cousin, though I'm sure you would know better than I do."

5   For the backstory of why the resort replaced the previous Mary and Kitty players, please see Book One.

Collins, who never met a conversational opening he would not cheerfully plunge into, took a breath and began the education of New Mary about Fordyce and a great many other things, too.

Jane, meanwhile, walked alongside Maggie and quietly posed a question. "How did it end up with Darcy? Is he riding the horse?"

"Yeah, I think so," Maggie answered, looking around nervously before commenting again in a lower tone. "I guess he got thrown from a horse as a child."

"Did he get back on afterward?" Jane asked with alarm.

"Well, no, I'm guessing not," Maggie replied, looking a bit bewildered. "I mean, he broke his foot so he probably had to go to the hospital or something instead of, you know, finishing the ride."

"That's not good." Jane shook her head. "If someone ever gets thrown off, especially if a *kid* falls off, you're supposed to put them right back on the horse, or some other horse if it's safer, to keep them from being afraid for life."

"But ... huh." Maggie paused, realizing that she was deeply out of her depth in the equine world. "Isn't that just a saying? Like, 'If the horse throws you, you have to get back on again.' I mean, that's not a literal thing, is it?"

"It kind of is, though," Jane stated firmly. "The horse has to be trained that throwing people off doesn't work. So somebody has to ride that horse even if it's somebody else after a rider comes off. But it's also about training the rider's brain, too, with a safe ride so the rider gets his confidence back. Otherwise the fear can just build up more and more over the years."

"Well, I'm pretty sure they *never* put little Darcy back on a horse." *And the poor guy's been scared ever since,* Maggie thought empathetically. *Sometimes those old wives' tales are right.* Maggie looked out into the street just as Lydia and Kitty were seen meeting up with Denny and Wickham in front of the milliner's shop just ahead. "Oh, hey, we're on."

Since this was the day before he would obtain his red militia uniform, Wickham was still in his civilian clothing. Nonetheless, his handsome face and incandescent smile still made him strikingly attractive. In fact, his dazzling smile rather mesmerized New Mary and New Kitty when he flashed it in their direction. Lydia, however, had been immunized by exposure and readily found her voice to demand an introduction to Wickham from Mr. Denny. For her part, Maggie added an introduction to Mr. Collins. True to his role, Wickham was all affability as the greetings progressed.

And progressed some more. And then some more.

CanonScavvers on both sides of the street stood, pencils poised, ready to mark off this event as the pause in the action stretched out longer than expected. Scavvers were a patient lot, however, and no one budged.

Jane slid worried eyes toward Maggie and both stole surreptitious glances toward the Coach House. But horses came there none.

For her part, Lydia had no problem filling the long minutes rattling on about hats and flirting with the militiamen. And to her credit, New Kitty was able to chime in with a cough or two whenever Lydia had to take a breath. But even Wickham's smile was beginning to dim as it became increasingly clear that the equestrian denouement of this event was overdue.

"I wonder if we should be getting along," Maggie *ad libbed* tentatively. Mr. Denny, who was played by an experienced resort staffer, shook his head.

"Oh, no need to rush, Miss Elizabeth," he said congenially. "Sometimes the pace here in Meryton is a bit slow this

134

time of year, *especially* near the stables." He looked at her pointedly and continued the merry conversation. "Wickham here was just telling me about the wonderful meal he enjoyed in London yesterday. Pray tell the ladies about the size of the goose, Wickham."

So he's saying that early in the season like this, Maggie interpreted, *there are often delays with the role-players getting out of the stables on their horses. Well, I don't wonder. Bunch of bookworms on horseback. What could go wrong there?* She looked up the street again, biting her lip and hoping that the universe would give Darcy just this one break. *He tries so hard, really he does. He wants to be a fun guy. He's just so … not. Come on, Will. Come on.*

Just at that moment, the two men appeared on horseback, a most glorious sight to Maggie's eyes.

"Woo-hoo!" Maggie exclaimed, extending her arms over her head in a cheer that turned all eyes her way. Momentarily frozen with her arms signaling a touchdown, Maggie's thoughts raced for cover. "Yes, indeed!" she said loudly. "That was … one huge goose, Mr. Wickham. This big, was it?" she asked, bringing down both hands to demonstrate a two-foot gap.

"More or less, yes, Miss Elizabeth," Wickham said coolly. If he rolled his eyes, Maggie didn't care. The horses were approaching. Darcy had conquered his fear.

Well, sort of.

To Maggie's admittedly unpracticed eye, the horses seemed to be unusually close to each other with Bingley's horse slightly ahead and to the right of Darcy's horse. In fact, as they rode closer, it became clear that Darcy's horse actually was being led by Bingley himself. Darcy, meanwhile, from atop his slow-moving mare, was leaned over with the horn of the saddle clenched in a death grip, both of his eyes firmly closed.

As the mounted men approached, Maggie caught a glimpse of a large groomsman keeping pace with the horses as they progressed along the street. It was, in fact, young Enzo Pelletucci, aka The General, this time looking not-at-all bronzed and in fact, rather pale and worried. He glanced frequently up at Darcy's face and never veered more than two feet from the man's left boot.

In time, the unhurried horsemen reached the Bennet family cluster and came to a stop. Groomsman Enzo moved forward and took the reins of Darcy's horse, murmuring something to Darcy. Darcy, in turn, opened one eye into a wary squint, peering downward and looking miserable. Maggie caught his eye and gave him an encouraging smile and a tiny golf clap. He managed to raise his head a few inches and open both eyes, barely, but his facial expression was still that of a man with acute nausea.

As in Austen's original, Bingley took the lead in speaking, greeting his dear Jane and inquiring after her health in the wake of her recent illness at Netherfield. Cousin Collins was introduced, and nods and curtsies were successfully exchanged all around. Then came the critical moment that the CanonScavvers had waited to see: Darcy sees his old enemy Wickham in a nonverbal moment where Darcy 'turns red' and Wickham 'turns white,' reflecting the unpleasant history between the men.

On this particular morning, Wickham turned to greet the men on horseback as they were introduced and did a fine job of displaying shock upon seeing Darcy. He recovered, however, and doffed his hat wearing a sly Wickham grin. Now it only remained for Darcy to touch his own hat in a disdainful return of the greeting. Enzo nudged Darcy's leg to indicate his cue and the party stood waiting.

In a great display of effort, Darcy pried his right hand free of the saddle. Then, though his elbow remained glued to his ribcage, he managed to raise his trembling white fin-

136

gers to his hat brim before quickly re-gripping the saddle horn and heaving an audible sigh. His look of abject terror during this exercise was apparently close enough to pass for disdain and the CanonScavvers were satisfied. Pencils scratched and the event was over.

"What happens next?" Maggie whispered to Enzo.

"I'm leading his horse up to the apothecary then we'll dismount him out of sight behind the shop. It's not going to be pretty. I've got a few guys waiting."

"Well, whatever you people did to get him on that horse, it's a miracle," Maggie continued, looking up at Darcy admiringly. "He looks great. You did a good thing for that man."

Enzo looked at her uncertainly. "If you say so. Felt like we were killing the poor guy but he kept saying, 'no, no, come on, I've got to do this.'"

Maggie felt a huge *ping*, actually more of a *clannnnnggg*, of real affection in her heart. *Darcy's not just handsome; he's actually kind of lovable.* This was new. Maggie had long acknowledged, with some distinct irritation, that Darcy's good looks tingled her toes. More recently, she had come to admire his loyal efforts to assist his friends, too. But this dogged determination to overcome his *own* myriad social shortcomings, this was ... different. *He's kind of lovable.* She found her breath coming faster which was very irksome to her internal rational self. *Okay, okay, he's adorable just ... pull yourself together, chica. Score one huge* ping *for Mr. Horsey Man. Fine. Sheesh.*

She gulped and nodded a smiling farewell to Darcy as Enzo took his lead position in front of the horse. Darcy managed a slight nod in return before his horse jerked forward again and his eyes clamped shut involuntarily. He doubled over once more, issuing a keening moan. Bingley smoothly urged his horse into a slow walk beside him and cooed soothing words in Darcy's direction. The two men proceeded thusly up the street and finally went mercifully out of sight behind the apothecary's shop.

The Bennets, meanwhile, walked to the nearby Meryton location designated as the house of their Aunt Phillips. They were escorted to the door by the militiamen where a noisy invitation for cards and supper the following evening was issued to all by Mrs. Phillips. After that, Maggie and her resort family could finally enter the Phillips' door for an offstage celebration of the day's event.

"Huz to the ZAH for Darcy, you guys!" said Maggie, exuberantly offering a high five to Jane. "I cannot *believe* he got on that horse!"

"I know!" Jane concurred, happily slapping Maggie's palm. "He looked like death but maybe nobody noticed."

"I thought he was going to throw up," Lydia shared candidly.

Aunt Phillips, an experienced staffer, spoke up reassuringly. "He did great. I've seen a lot of Darcy players and believe me, many of them don't even try to get on the horse. Darcy's sort of a grim character anyway so his expression looked just like he should."

As the chatter in the room continued, Maggie drifted toward the window and gazed out. The older woman stepped to the window, too, after a time and spoke quietly alongside Maggie as she looked out into the street. "Took a lot of courage for him to do that, I think. Seems like a good guy."

Maggie grinned shyly as she replied. "Seems like it."

The two women looked at each other knowingly and returned their gaze to the street without speaking because at that moment, nothing more needed to be said aloud.

Chapter Eighteen

After lunch, Maggie and Jane were cheered to discover that their understudy duties were likely drawing to a close as they met up with the Dashwood sisters at Barton Cottage. The patches of poison ivy rash on the Singh sisters' limbs looked significantly less inflamed than when they had last seen them.

"Look, ladies," Elinor said eagerly, pulling up her hem and directing attention toward her bare feet as the ladies chatted with Maggie and Jane in the sitting room. Obviously starved for company, Elinor had called for a tea tray and seemed eager to talk. Meanwhile, Marianne had nodded off on the couch but even as she slept, it was clear that more of her scalp was restored to its natural color. And indeed, the blotches on Elinor's feet had faded considerably in the last two days as well.

"Much better," Maggie acknowledged. "What does Miss Judith say about shoes?"

"Miss Judith says I can use soft shoes by tomorrow so I can do the "Walk with Lucy Steele" event tomorrow afternoon if I promise not to walk too far." Elinor was clearly radiant at the prospect of returning to duty even if it meant leaving her twin behind.

Marianne snorted out of her doze looking dejected. "I can't wear shoes until next week," she said mournfully. "But Miss Judith says I can go to the London dance on Tuesday. Big rejection by Willoughby ... most popular scene of our storyline and ... " she interrupted herself with a huge yawn and completed her sentence with garbled sounds that vaguely resembled the speech of a Star Wars Wookie.

"You'll be there, you'll be there," Elinor said soothingly,

139

apparently fluent in Wookie. "Colonel Brandon has been carrying her around. He brought her downstairs today and offered to carry her to the lake for the bathing event on Saturday." The ladies murmured their appreciation of the man's gallantry.

Maggie spoke up. "Brandon is a great guy and knows how to carry a lady. He carried me across a stream the other day with no problem."

Elinor spoke up delicately. "I heard that Mr. Willoughby struggled a bit carrying you after the ankle twist, Lizzy."

Maggie shrugged her shoulders. "He's such a bony little thing, you know? He did what he had to but … that guy's just different. Honestly, I'm glad you two are in his cast, not me. I hate playing swoony swoon with him. But Brandon's your man if you need carrying."

"Well, if I'm hearing y'all correctly," Jane clarified, "it sounds like Willoughby's poetry reading today is the last event we'll need to understudy. Is that right?"

Elinor thought about it for a moment. "Well," she said slowly, "if we allow Colonel Brandon to carry my sister to and from the lake on Saturday, then I suppose that is true."

"Oh, thank goodness!" Maggie exclaimed. "I mean, no offense to *Sense and Sensibility* or Austen or *whatever* but I am *dying* for us to get back to being plain old Jane and Lizzy Bennet. Honestly, Jane and I get into a fight almost every time we have to be Dashwood sisters. Not sure how you two do it."

"Years of practice," Elinor said with a wise nod. "And it turns out that high-dose antihistamines can be extremely helpful, too." She looked at Maggie and winked.

The ladies burst out laughing and Marianne woke up long enough to join in the merriment, briefly, before drifting off again.

The afternoon event with Willoughby was awkward. Maggie would have cheerfully tap-danced on the man's spleen in order to wipe the smirk off his face but instead she had to act like she loved the guy. *Meryl Streep herself couldn't act a love scene with this numbskull,* Maggie thought to herself testily. *The man is a buffoon.*

Willoughby emoted through the requisite sonnets while Jane and Maggie sat on a blanket nearby and tried to act Dashwoody. Jane in her Elinor role could roll her eyes in disapproval of Willoughby whenever she wished, which was often. But Maggie had to "be all swoony swoon" over Willoughby and each time she spoke up in her "Marianne" voice, it got more and more difficult.

"Oh, Mr. Willoughby," she said, trying to muster a loving tone as women around the glade dabbed at teary eyes in response to his reading of Shakespeare's Sonnet 116. "How effortlessly you evoke the words of the Bard. It's as if you carry around a book of sonnets just for the purpose of pleasing women. It's as though you read poetry to, oh, I don't know, achieve some *goal* with women. Excepting the obvious, of course, because you would never seduce anyone and leave them with … "

"Beautiful indeed, Mr. Willoughby," Jane interrupted smoothly. "Do have another piece of this delightful bread, Marianne." Jane pulled a six-inch wad of bread out of the basket and shoved it at her sister. Maggie began chewing and was, to Jane's great relief, rendered speechless by the doughy mass for two more sonnets.

Finally, the event came to a close. By this time, Maggie was gnawing on the three-pound loaf of salami that Jane had handed her when Willoughby had started reciting his original poems. As soon as he had uttered the first two lines—*"You can be my song, my lady fair, That I'll play all night long, my little bear …"*—Jane had reached into the basket for her emergency sausage.

141

Maggie glanced accusingly at the sun a few times as she chewed, convinced that time was standing still while Willoughby droned on—*"And I will be your little lute, And you can pluck me like a fruit ..."*—but to her great relief, the sun did not disappoint. Time moved in its accustomed forward direction and the ladies were finally free to go to tea at Rosings.

Lady Catherine's staff had set a fine tea for everyone in the library and the LaGGards waxed nostalgic remembering their first tea upon arrival at the resort.

"We had our first argument about the *Pride & Prejudice* screen adaptations in this very room, remember?" Henry said wistfully.

"You provoked it, as I recall," Maggie said pointedly to Henry. "You knew Bingley would be a 2005er."

"Still am!" piped up Bingley from his armchair. "Fight me, you 95ers!"

A noisy discussion followed while Henry looked around the room grinning, hands folded across his belly like a silent movie sultan watching his harem dance.

"You are a bad man, Henry," observed Maggie above the resulting din.

"I am, my dear. I am. But how dismal life would be without me, eh?" he replied with a naughty grin and a *que será será* shrug.

Ping, went Maggie's heart as she shook her head and chuckled at Henry's mischief. *I'm just never going to hate this guy like I should,* Maggie thought. *He makes me laugh. Just like my dad. Maybe that's enough and you can settle for that. Or maybe that's not settling, it's the core. How does anyone ever know?*

At last, the library door opened. Lady Catherine entered briskly and immediately the room fell silent. To everyone's surprise, Thaddeus Blackwell, the elderly writing instructor and particular friend of the grand lady, accompanied her. Maggie was extremely glad to see her favorite instructor.

"How are you doing, Mr. Blackwell?" she asked, eagerly rising to give him an unexpected hug that made the gentleman giggle. Maggie dislodged a white tuft of his hair in her exuberance, rendering it ridiculously perpendicular to his balding head. She then tenderly smoothed the wayward hairs back against the man's pink scalp while they exchanged a few words of greeting.

When all in the room were seated comfortably once more, Lady C took the floor with her customary down-to-business approach.

"Well, something has come to my attention, dear friends, that involves a painful episode from the past. Even though it was many years ago, loyalties still stand very divided in my family. So, I've come to the difficult conclusion that I must seek help outside my family. This is where you come in, dear LaGGards. Obviously, I must, once again, count on you to show the utmost discretion."

"Of course, Lady Catherine," Maggie said quite seriously. All heads nodded in solemn agreement. "What's happened?"

"It seems all very petty," she said, clearly annoyed. "Started with some vandalism at Northanger, someone digging up some of the statuaries and trees in the garden maze a number of days ago."

Darcy and Maggie exchanged a look. "Could it be the librarians?" Maggie asked cautiously. "They have a reputation. Stole a gnome. That kind of thing."

Bingley turned to Darcy in confusion. "They did what?" he whispered.

"Stole… a … gnome," Darcy hissed. "I'll tell you later."

143

"Well, they were my first thought, too," Lady Catherine agreed. "But no. The first incident happened last week, before the tourist season started. Our full-time people are the only staffers on the premises during the training week for essay winners. So it leads back to staff, I'm afraid." She sighed deeply.

Jane spoke up. "We were at Northanger for the Night Tour just a few days ago, Lady Catherine, and everything seemed fine. There was no damage in the garden area, at least nothing we could see."

"No, our groundskeeper Gary is very efficient and tidied everything up before the guests arrived. Wouldn't even have known anything was wrong except the cook here at Rosings ran up to Northanger for some supplies last week and saw the poor fellow working overtime, putting things to rights, bless his soul. I wouldn't even have reported anything to the sheriff if it hadn't been for the wine."

Lady Catherine indulged in another sip of tea as the group waited breathlessly, all eyes following her cup. Then she took another sip, apparently forgetting that she had left a cliffhanger. The group looked toward Mr. Blackwell hopefully but he only offered a pleasant smile and a shrug.

"The wine, Lady Catherine?" Maggie prompted finally.

"Hmm? Oh, yes. The wine." Lady Catherine continued. "This is odd, too. The cellar at Northanger is quite extensive and the sommelier from Pemberley went to get a particular vintage there a few days ago. Well, he found that two bottles of wine were missing. That is to say, one was missing and the other was just there on the floor, broken."

"Valuable vintages, Lady Catherine?" Darcy leaned forward with concern. Stealing wine was sacrilege to a vintner.

"No, that's the peculiar thing. Rather ordinary, in fact. We keep the expensive vintages locked up in wine safes that are built into the walls and they were untouched. These were just inexpensive bottles, sitting on the racks in the center of the room."

"It seems your thief has an undiscerning palate," Henry offered.

"Doesn't narrow it down much among thieves," harrumphed Darcy to whom drinking cheap wine was practically criminal anyway.

"Well, again," Lady Catherine continued wearily, "It's all quite petty. It's certainly not the first time that someone has nipped a bottle from one of our wine cellars. Ordinarily I wouldn't even report it. But the sommelier said that other bottles on the rack had been … rearranged. Malbecs put in with the merlots, a shiraz in with the syrahs, that kind of thing."

"Dear God," uttered Darcy.

"Animals!" murmured Henry, amused. Maggie gave him a look and he pursed his lips in dutiful silence.

"But that's not the worst of it," the good lady said with her most profound sigh yet. "Larry's back."

Henry's lips burst apart again. "Not *Larry!* Well, that's us doomed then."

Maggie thwacked Henry on the knee with a teaspoon before turning to Edith. "I'm so sorry, Lady Catherine. We'll send the children out if necessary. Please continue."

"No, no, it's all right," Edith replied, raising her hand. "I know I'm doing a poor job of narration here. It's just difficult to bring all this back up again."

"Take your time, Edith dear," Mr. Blackwell said soothingly. "You're among friends here, I believe."

The grand dame straightened her posture and returned to her customary take-charge manner. If the problem was to be solved, the story must be told.

145

"Larry Tedesco was my father's accountant for over thirty years. He was my dear friend. He married my cousin Violet. His son grew up here alongside all my nieces and nephews. The man was like a brother to the Pelletucci family."

She paused and took a deep breath.

"And then one day we discovered that Larry had been embezzling money for over thirty years."

And at this, even Henry was too gob-smacked to speak.

Chapter Nineteen

Larry Tedesco's story was obviously going to require the serving of something stronger than tea. Edith called for staff to serve a round of sherries and Henry selflessly offered to consume the ones declined by Catherine and Mr. Blackwell. Edith poured two in succession for herself without apology.

Properly braced, then, the good lady began the strange story of Larry Tedesco which we shall supplement as the need arises.

"Larry's father, Barry Tedesco, had worked for my great-grandfather Nicky Pelletucci in his business ventures down in the city since the 1920's. Helped my father get this place built, too. But when the Bellissimo Resort opened here in 1950, it was on such a small scale, just the main lodge and two guest houses, my father and mother kept the books themselves back then. I remember my father showing me his big ledger books."

Benny Pelletucci was always proud to share and explain the smudged ledgers in his office—"ya gotta get *two* pens, kiddo, see, a blue one *and* a red one." Eventually, Edith grew old enough to discern that it was her *mother* who kept the place afloat in those halcyon early days, but her father's simple exuberance was still a pleasant memory.

"Then in 1962, Papa decided to expand the resort. Everything got more complicated. That's when he hired Larry Tedesco to help out with the bookkeeping."

Well, yes. As previously discussed, when laundry bags filled with cash courtesy of Grandpa Nicky come into the picture, things get more complicated. The expertise of young Larry Tedesco, fresh out of NYU, was needed at that

147

point. And though Benny Pelletucci never quite trusted the catlike fellow with the thin fingers and even thinner mustache, his expertise with numbers was undeniable.

"Whatever anyone says about Larry, he saw the resort through some very lean times financially in the '70s and '80s when business slowed down. Larry made the hard cuts, told my father what he didn't want to hear when we had to close up a guest house or cut back staff. Plenty of people resented Larry. But the facts speak for themselves. We stayed open when many resorts in our area closed. That's what I never understood. Why would this man work so hard to keep the resort solvent and then steal money from it?"

It's complicated, as we shall soon see.

"Anyway, Larry came in the summer that year but Thaddeus already had come in the spring, didn't you? Tell them a bit of your story, my dear."

Mr. Blackwell picked up the thread of the tale.

"Well, I was delivered on one of Mr. Nicky's trucks directly from New York City like a load of laundry, in April of 1962. Still wet behind the ears, wasn't I, Edith?"

The good lady, who had heard this little jest many times, nodded and smiled.

And for those keeping score, yes. That was the same truck with the laundry bags full of cash.

"I had worked for Mr. Carlo, Mr. Benny's father, at his Arthur Murray dance studio in the city. Mum and I had come over from London after the war, me just a tyke, my mum a young war widow with nothing to her name but an old steamer trunk with a few family mementos."

Those mementos would later find their way to the cabinet in Mr. Blackwell's classroom and play a key role in the most recent intrigue at Camp Jane.[6]

"Mr. Carlo was kind enough to give my mum a job as a dance instructor, then me as well when I got old enough. He let us stay in a little apartment off the studio. He was a widower, Mr. Carlo was, and became right fond of my mum. Courted her for years though she never would marry him. When mum died, well, that's when I moved up here to the resort. Mr. Carlo closed the dance studio, you see. Couldn't dance without his 'Bella Rose,' he said. The youngsters don't remember Bella Rose, do they, Edith?"

Probably not. Bella Rose was the heroine of the wildly popular series of post-war Stella Carlotta romances whose glamorous and improbable adventures relieved the daily tedium for decades of homemakers. Unlike her slipper-wearing readers, however, the stiletto-heeled Bella Rose spent her days in exotic locales thwarting legions of Nazis, communists, and mad scientists while romancing shirtless men and keeping her own "abundant" and often "heaving" breasts mostly inside her bodice, if the book covers were to be believed. But we can assure the reader that any physical resemblance between Rose Blackwell, weary British taxi dancer, and Bella Rose, exotic crime-fighter, was something only Mr. Carlo could see.

"No, I imagine they don't remember Bella Rose," Edith said, patting Blackwell's hand kindly.

But indeed, Grandfather Carlo loved a good romance, both in life and in literature. He even read Jane Austen, despite merciless teasing from his male family members, and courted Miss Rose with Austen quotes, along with his original poetry, of course.

---

6   For the full story of Mr. Blackwell's mementos, please see Book One. Have you really not read Book One yet? Honestly, you should. We can't keep doing these footnotes.

In fact, Carlo Pelletucci poured his artist's soul into numerous artistic endeavors over the years. His failed paintings and sculptures rested peacefully in Barry Tedesco's storage unit along with a number of unsingable songs and unfinished symphonies, all works that were far better the day they were still un-begun. Never had a man loved the arts more. But just like his love for Miss Rose, the arts, alas, did not seem to love Mr. Carlo back.

"Anyway, my grandfather Carlo dearly loved Rose Blackwell and promised her that he would take care of her son. So, after she died, my father Benny generously welcomed her son Thaddeus here as a dance instructor."

Yes, well. Generosity takes many forms. Sometimes it wells up from a benevolent heart. Sometimes it grows slowly over time.

Sometimes it only fully blooms with the arrival of a truck full of cash.

Benny always figured the British kid was a package deal with the dough and that Thaddeus was the 'gift from his father' that Grandpa Nicky had mentioned. Like a suddenly reformed Scrooge, Benny found generosity within moments of the truck's arrival, opening wide his arms to young Thaddeus *and* the bags he rode in on.

Back in the present time, the Rosings library had grown silent. Miss Edith had paused in her narrative and was looking tenderly at Mr. Blackwell, recalling his arrival. She squeezed his hand and he returned her gaze with a smile.

Well, there's a story there, that's for sure, Maggie thought to herself. Her eyes slid toward Jane who nodded her head in agreement. *It's obvious. Whole lot of* pinging *going on there.*

Unable to contain herself any longer, Maggie burst forth. "So what *happened*, Miss Edith? Mr. Blackwell is here teaching dance and Larry Tedesco is keeping the books, the resort is expanding, making money and everything seems

150

fine. So what in the world happened to Larry?"

"I honestly don't know," said Edith quietly. She shook her head sorrowfully and bit her lip before resuming the story.

"The three of us were all great pals for a long time. But Larry … changed. After a couple of years, there was something in his eyes that was different. I saw it. I didn't want to … but I did. People started to say he had turned against the family. But how could that be? Larry <u>was</u> family! He married my cousin, right out there on the big dock! I was in her wedding party, for heaven's sake, wore a big pink hat. Very 1970s." She shrugged and shook her head again.

"Anyway, after the wedding, I didn't see Larry much. He had a son, life went on. The years passed. Then one day, out of the clear blue sky, my Uncle Vinny finds a second set of ledgers that Larry has been hiding. Brings it to my father. A lot of it's encrypted, columns using numerical codes that no one could decipher. People did that kind of thing back then for security. But one column had Larry's own bank account number! The bank confirmed every transaction. Somehow, Larry had been funneling money to his own private account for thirty years! Something had changed in that man. But I don't know what, children. I really don't."

She paused and teared up. Kindly, Bingley reached for his handkerchief and handed it to the good lady whereupon she thanked him and dabbed her eyes and nostrils. Bereft of his hankie, then, Bingley could only wipe his own moist features on his sleeve, which he did copiously until Darcy finally rolled his eyes and handed his own kerchief to his tender-hearted friend.

So ends the story of Larry Tedesco, as least as much as Edith knows of it, thought Maggie, sympathetically looking at Edith's distraught face. *She's never understood it.* Maggie's

151

eyes moved to Mr. Blackwell's face but she was startled to see something entirely different there. The man was looking at Edith in obvious distress, it was true, but he was *not* confused. He was torn, deeply torn, by some internal dilemma.

He knows! thought Maggie suddenly. *He knows exactly what went wrong with old Larry. He just doesn't want to tell Edith.*

"Mr. Blackwell," Maggie said quietly, leaning forward. "Do you think, perhaps, it's time to tell Miss Edith what happened? With Larry." The little man looked at her forlornly as all eyes in the room turned first toward Maggie, then toward him in stunned surprise.

Edith whispered toward him. "Thaddeus? Do you know something? About Larry?" She picked up his hand again. "We all had such good times, didn't we?"

This made him smile. "Oh, my, yes. We did." He took a breath and looked at her again.

"Do you remember that night when we danced on the terrace, Edith?"

Edith's eyes sparkled. "How could I ever forget? I was seventeen that summer. But still so terribly shy."

"Your father made you dance with Larry that night, didn't he?"

She looked surprised. "He did. My father always made me dance with him when Larry's father was there."

"And old Mr. Barry *was* there that night, entertaining clients. And oh, Larry looked so proud, going around the floor with you. Such a pretty girl you were, with all of that hair put up on the top of your head."

"My bouffant," she laughed. The LaGGards sat mesmerized, trying to picture Edith's gray hair teased upward into a bouffant. "I can't believe the things you remember,

152

Thaddeus. But those dances, oh, they made me so nervous. Do you remember how you convinced me to dance on the terrace after everyone had gone?"

"I do. I made you close your eyes and told you all of Aunt Jane's characters were out there dancing with us, didn't I? Bingley and his Jane, Wentworth and his Anne, Tilney and his Catherine, they were all there with us, dancing easy as you please at a neighborhood ball. They were there alongside you and me, on the terrace there in the moonlight, weren't they, Edith?"

This was the first dance Edith had ever enjoyed, the first time she had danced alongside Jane Austen's characters, the first time she had known what it was to share her love of all things Janeite with another human being. It would be many years before she would re-shape the resort into an Austen wonderland and many years beyond that before she would know about her dance partner's special relationship with Jane Austen's family. But the fact that she was able to share her beloved fictional world with young Thaddeus was enough. She fell for him that very night.

Edith spoke dreamily. "Children, this dear man said to me, in his proper British voice, too, 'You *are* handsome enough to tempt me after all, Miss Elizabeth. Please do me the honor of dancing with Mr. Fitzwilliam Darcy this evening.' What could I do? I went to the floor with this lovely man and twirled round and round in his arms. How could I not, children? How could I not?"

The two older folks smiled at one another for a long, long moment. Bingley broke the silence with a sob and a loud blow into Darcy's handkerchief. "This is so touching. They're killing me," he managed to burble. Jane rubbed his back and murmured comfort.

Edith leaned forward. "What made you think of that night, Thaddeus?"

He looked at her guiltily. "Larry saw us. Dancing out there. I saw the look on his face from the library window. So angry, he was, Edith. So angry. So jealous. That's the night he started to change. He … he told your father … about us."

Edith looked stunned. "Told my father *what*, exactly? There was nothing to tell. I was dancing with you, just like I had been dancing with Larry and three other boys an hour earlier. I just enjoyed it more with you."

"Well, I'm quite sure Larry told him something bad. Your father came to my room, talked to me very loudly, you know how loud his voice could get, Edith, and he was so loud that night. He told me that I was just a hired worker without a penny to his name and that I was never to dance with his daughter again unless people were around. He said that I was never to think of kissing you or, or, dating you or, or being with you. I was, just … never to think of you again." He hung his head. "He was so angry, Edith. And I owed your father everything. When I saw Larry at breakfast the next day, he had that smug face, that cat grin. You know the one I mean. And when you came down, he, he looked at you so strangely."

"I remember," Edith said, her eyes focused on another time. "Bold as brass, Larry walked up to me that morning and told me that I was only to dance with him from now on. And of course, I sassed him, told him I would do as I pleased. I expected him to joke with me about it. But you're right. His eyes were different that morning. He had changed."

"He loved you, Edith." The words suddenly tumbled forth like a moan from the dear man, the dreadful ache of a lifetime that had never found a remedy. "And he was just so jealous. I tried to obey your father, I tried not to love you, truly I did, Edith, you know that. But Larry could see it then, he could see what was between us after that night,

154

and he watched us every day, every day, Edith. That's what changed him. I saw it in his eyes that very night. Larry loved you so." Tears formed in his eyes.

"No, Thaddeus, no," she said, gently taking his hand in hers and rubbing it. "He may have thought so. But whatever that look was in Larry's eyes, it wasn't love. I know what love looks like. That wasn't it."

She kissed the palm of the gentle man's hand and his soft smile returned.

We can confirm that Bingley wept the loudest of anyone, though it would be folly to pretend that the eyes of anyone in that room were bone dry. But there, finally, was the star-crossed love story of Edith Pelletucci and Thaddeus Blackwell exposed not only to the world but to the lovers themselves. And there, finally, was Larry Tedesco revealed as the worst kind of villain, one who stole not only money but the happiness of two 'most beloved' people with his infernal interference.

Indeed, not everything works out like an Austen novel in real life, though there are, as we see, similarities.

Chapter Twenty

Edith poured herself another sherry from the carafe on the tray and sipped it pensively.

"After Larry was found out as an embezzler, my cousin divorced him. Larry was fired, of course, though my father didn't prosecute him. He didn't want the publicity and the money was long gone, anyway. My father kept Violet and her son on staff for a while because they had nothing to do with it and they were family, after all. But it was hard on them. Some family members just couldn't get past it and those two heard plenty of nasty comments directed their way, I'm afraid. To this day, most of the family is still bitter. Anyway, in time Violet remarried to a nice man named Johnson from the Midwest who visited the resort one summer. She and her son moved out there and everyone did quite well. The boy took his stepfather's name and grew up to be the head groundskeeper at the College of the Ozarks. Raised his own family, lovely wife, twin boys. Violet doted on her grandsons, used to dress them up in little Regency outfits for their Christmas cards every year. After Violet died, though, I lost track of all of them. Until six months ago."

Edith set her sherry glass back on the tray with a sigh.

"Larry's son showed up here, desperate for work, looking terrible. He'd gotten laid off from the university in a round of budget cuts, lost his house, started drinking too much. His wife had left him and his grown sons hadn't talked to him in years. He was a mess, gaunt and scraggly, I could barely recognize him. I felt sorry for him. I knew personally what a tough start that boy had in this world."

She sighed. "I had a job opening up at Northanger because the caretaker was retiring. But we both knew that all my family members would oppose hiring him simply because he was Larry's son. So he begged me to take him on quietly, during the low season. He promised he'd stay up at Northanger and not attract attention. So, that's what I did. And for months, it worked! Sure, a few people knew there was a new groundskeeper named Gary at Northanger, some skinny guy with a beard. But no one knew him under his stepfather's name of Johnson."

"Now hang on, wait just a tick here," Henry said, holding his hand up for silence. "For clarity here, Gary Johnson, the groundskeeper of Northanger Abbey, with whom I have chatted with many times, is the *son* of the infamous Larry Tedesco?"

Edith nodded solemnly. "That's right."

"Gary??" Maggie exclaimed. "Barry Tedesco has Larry, then Larry has *Gary?* Oh, come on, Miss Edith. They gotta stop with that rhyming name foolishness."

"I know, I know," Edith agreed with a wave of her hand. "I tried to talk my cousin out of it when poor Gary was born. Then, Gary had twins, so *they* had to have rhyming names, too! Now, we can only hope one of *them* breaks the cycle." She shrugged hopelessly. "Anyway, certain members of my family would be furious enough if they knew I had hired Gary here. But that's not the worst of it."

"Right!" Maggie exclaimed as she jolted upright, eyes wide. "Because caretaker Gary brought his embezzler father onsite here with him! Larry Tedesco's back and he's staying with his son at Northanger!" The rest of the group looked at her incredulously.

"Well, yes. That's right." Edith looked at Maggie strangely.

"You mentioned it. That, you know, that Larry was back," Maggie added. She cleared her throat. "Before."

"Yes, I suppose I did," Edith murmured, rising and walking behind the couch in agitation. "Larry has been at an upstate rest home for years. But two weeks ago, Gary brought Larry *back here*! Moved him into his staff quarters at Northanger!"

Instantly cold, Maggie shivered from head to toe. She suddenly felt the steely claws of the old man digging into her forearm in the dark hallway. *That was the infamous embezzler Larry Tedesco! No wonder his son didn't want people knowing his father was living with him! At least I don't have to be the one to spill the beans to Edith,* Maggie realized gratefully. *She already knows.*

"Wow, Miss Edith," Maggie said innocently. "Um, how did you find out?"

"One of the Northanger cooks recognized Larry!" she exclaimed with exasperation. "Saw him wandering around the hall. I begged the woman not to say anything. I sent her to visit her daughter in Florida, actually. Might have been the coward's way out but it was all I could think of at the time." She shrugged miserably.

"Sometimes discretion is the better part of valor, Miss Edith," Darcy observed and the LaGGards murmured their agreement.

"But it's just a question of time before someone *else* figures it out," she stated sadly, seating herself heavily on the couch again. "No one knew what Gary looks like because he was just a kid when he left here. We could make that work. But *everybody* knew Larry! He has a very distinctive look. My father called him the Cat Man. Said he looks just like a cat."

Maggie guffawed. "Ha! He does!" All eyes turned toward Maggie. "I mean, probably. Probably looks like, you know, a cat. Cuz your father said so." She coughed. Henry squinted at her suspiciously.

"So … um … what do you need from us, Miss Edith?" Maggie asked, leaning forward and ignoring Henry.

"Your eyes, children. Your ears. Especially yours, Henry and Catherine, up at Northanger. All of you, really, because I don't know the *origin* of the trouble. I cannot simply order Larry off the property for no reason, that would be cruel to poor Gary. But these small incidents at Northanger, holes dug in the garden maze, wine bottles shifted around, occurring just as Larry returns, this does not feel like a coincidence. Nonetheless, I *cannot* bring these concerns to my family yet, especially Angela. You remember my niece, Angela, the chief operating officer?"

They remembered. How could they forget? Angela was the intimidating businesswoman who had nearly killed Collins when she found out his role in the adventure last week.[7] Henry, for one, was convinced that sitting next to Angela at dinner the previous week had shrunk a couple of his favorite body parts. "She gives off *rays,*" was all he would say. Maggie was skeptical but Darcy and Bingley had assured her that this was, in fact, a thing that some women could do. Yes, they remembered Angela, they assured Edith. Henry nodded vigorously and crossed his legs as the men looked at each other pointedly.

"Well, if Angela *ever* found out I had hired Larry's son, believe me, before sundown she would have me committed to that sanitarium right alongside Larry! Maybe she'd be right to do it, too. I probably *am* losing it." She rolled her head on the back of the couch unhappily.

Mr. Blackwell moved his hand toward the sherry decanter. "A drop more, my dear? You look distressed." She declined with a wave of the hand and he continued. "Well, *I* don't think you're ridiculous, Edith. Aunt Jane would be proud of how you have protected her legacy here. Your

---

7   Honestly, just read Book One. You can thank us later.

instincts are marvelous. If *you* say something is wrong at one of Aunt Jane's houses, well, people should listen."

A moment passed as this truth sunk in. He was right.

"Well, something is *wrong* at Northanger!" Edith exclaimed, sitting up and pounding on the armrest of the sofa. "I feel it in my bones. Logically, I know that Larry is too old and senile to do any real harm. And it makes no sense that Gary would do anything to put his job at risk. But *somebody* is doing *something* and I want to know what it is!"

The LaGGards all agreed, of course, to keep on the watch for their dear Lady Catherine. They filed out of the library as though they had just been inducted into a society of spies, literally stopping to synchronize their pocket watches, and vowing to keep their eyes and ears open wide and remaining on high alert.

And, of course, for days they saw absolutely nothing suspicious at all.

Not for lack of trying. Sunday afternoon, for example, with Maggie and Jane finally relieved of their understudy duties, the LaGGards took an outing to Bath for the dedication of the new quarters for the *Persuasion* cast. Shy Captain Wentworth stood on the dais wearing a painfully frozen smile (or possibly, a death rictus mask, it was hard to tell) as Lady Catherine made a little speech and handed him the key to the newly repurposed *Persuasion* row houses in front of a cheering crowd.

Ever vigilant, the LaGGards scanned the crowd for suspicious activity like the private security team they imagined themselves to be, Henry whispering into his cufflinks and Maggie with her bonnet pulled down over her eyes to conceal which direction she was gazing. But the day stayed stubbornly unremarkable.

Monday morning's report to the LaGGards' group text

was an even deeper dive into a pool of intrigue that seemed to have gone dry.

JaneB: Noises in attic at Longbourn. Resolution: Squirrels.

CatherineM: Noises downstairs at Northanger. Resolution: Henry in wine cellar. "Parched."

CatherineM: This is Henry. Maintenance shed lads said my phone part came in. Resolution: You will once again have my witty commentary as of tomorrow morning. You're welcome.

Darcy: Return of Henry to chat makes me slightly nauseous. Resolution: Antacids.

Bingley: Netherfield out of corn flakes this morning. Resolution: Froot Loops.

You get the idea.

Rather like a car that won't make the weird noise in front of the mechanic, the mystery afoot at Camp Jane lay stubbornly dormant while the LaGGards' attention wandered to the quotidian realities of life at the resort.

Unlike them, however, we have the option of skipping ahead to the good part. And so we shall.

The second Tuesday of the two-week story cycle was an unusually busy day. *Pride and Prejudice* was at Rosings during that part of the cycle and Darcy would be observed delivering a key explanatory letter to Lizzy as she took her morning walk. *Persuasion* had an afternoon tea at Bath and *Emma* had the mixed doubles Scrabble championship. *Northanger Abbey* was hosting a reading by Henry Tilney from the gothic novel *Udolpho* at a sunset bonfire.

Sense and Sensibility took center stage on the second Tuesday, however, with a late evening ballroom dance in London. This was an immensely popular event with the Janeites because, after all, who doesn't love a London ball? Moreover, in a dramatic bit of Austen canon, Marianne would be rejected by Willoughby at this event. Noting the *location* of this rejection was one of the most challenging items of the entire Canon Scavenger Hunt since the venue was very large and the room of the rejection scene, which had to be recorded on the list, was changed each cycle. For many reasons, then, the *S&S* London ball was one of the resort's most popular events with huge crowds expected.

For her part, Maggie was dutifully walking around the grounds at Rosings by 8:00 AM that Tuesday morning, meandering through the trees on the Rosings lot, while early-rising Scavvers set up camp on benches and tree stumps along her route. (The ever-attentive Miss Amelia Woodley, Darcy's most faithful stalker, had crawled out on a tree limb, determined to miss nothing.)

Not so many people this morning, thought Maggie to herself, observing the sparse and yawning crowd. *Regency mornings aren't so fun without a vente cup of Starbucks in your hand, are they kids?*

She chuckled to herself as she brushed a thin stick along a fence. *In the storyline, I just turned down Darcy's proposal of marriage yesterday. Imagine. Turned down Darcy. If Will did go for you, against all odds, Miss Thang, could you ever turn down a Darcy? For a Henry, no less?*

She snorted at the idea. That just seemed ridiculous. Sure, she had to admit that Henry *was* quietly racking up quite a few heart *pings* being clever and witty and helpful. *He might even be ahead on* pings *if it comes to that,* she noted, biting her lip. *But Darcy? Oh, lawd.* Darcy set her toes on fire, melted her knees and shut down her higher cognitive functioning. *And he's becoming quite lovable,* she explained to her inner voice. Her inner voice was very skeptical, however, being pretty convinced that Maggie only cared for the exterior of the man. *No, really,* Maggie insisted. *He's improving himself. And he ... you know. Likes me.*

The involuntary grin that came to her face at this thought

spoke volumes. But her musings were suddenly interrupted by a booming voice.

"Miss Elizabeth!" Darcy had approached quietly and was standing directly in front of her on the path. She started like a scared rabbit.

"Dear God, Darcy, I've warned you about sneaking up on people in the woods!" she exclaimed, far more Maggie than Lizzy in that moment.

"My apologies, Miss Elizabeth," Darcy said with a suppressed grin, obviously pleased to have startled her out of character. "I have been walking this area with the hope of meeting you this morning. I hope you will be good enough to read this letter. I can assure you that it does not contain a repetition of the sentiments you found so disgusting yesterday." He handed her the letter abruptly and gave her a surreptitious wink. Just like Austen's Lizzy, she took the letter wordlessly, frankly unable to think of anything snotty to say, or indeed, any words at all, what with the tall man winking at her and all.

Darcy bowed, turned on his heel and walked off toward Rosings while Maggie sank down onto a bench and broke the seal on her letter. *Check!* The CanonScavvers' pencils ticked off another item and they began to drift away.

As she rattled open her letter, however, Maggie was distracted by raised voices nearby. Miss Woodley seemed to be stuck in her tree. An older female guest had noticed the young woman's predicament and insisted that her tall grandson help the distressed damsel. After a significant bit of micromanaging from the ground by Grandma—"Kevin! She's falling! Kevin! Grab her! Well, don't grab her *there*, Kevin, honestly!"—Miss Woodley was finally returned to the ground by the helpful and scarlet-faced Kevin. If the shy man *could* have died of embarrassment, he would have fallen to the turf at once, grateful for the exit strategy.

But alas, he lived. Furthermore, Miss Amelia fluttered her eyes so appreciatively and curtsied so prettily that Kevin's steely-eyed grandmother suddenly felt faint and required the support of *both* of them for an immediate cup of tea at Pemberley.

Respect, Grandma. Maggie lifted her chin in greeting to the good woman as she pretended to hobble past and the older lady returned the greeting with a knowing nod. *Grandma may have said she needed your company on her little Austen vacation for her mobility issues, Shy Kevin, but that woman had a whole nuther game in mind. Stick with her and you will not die alone.*

Returning her attention to the letter in her hand, Maggie was surprised to discover that it was not simply a prop but an actual message from Will, though his style was quite Darcy-esque.

My dear Miss Elizabeth,

Be not alarmed that I'm going to hit on you again though I think you would probably like it if I did, you brazen minx.

The real question is what are you doing tonight? Bingley, Jane and I are going to the S&S ball in London. Thought you might like to lift a hoof there, too. I know you wanted to support Henry at his bonfire reading but maybe all three of you could come over to London afterward? They have late carriages scheduled. I was going to text Tilney about it but Catherine said his phone is still down. So perhaps you could posit the idea when you see him.

Or perhaps you could come along with Jane and Bingley and me earlier. You're not joined at the hip with Tilney, you know. Though he seems to think you are. (Insert rolled eyes here.)

Thoughts? Especially about me? Or ... well, no. Mostly me.

Your obt servant,

F. Darcy

Maggie sat back on the bench and smiled lazily. *This man could not possibly be jealous of Henry, could he? Oh, that's hilarious. A Darcy jealous of a Tilney. That's fourteen kinds of Austen wrong.*

She liked the idea of catching a late carriage to London for the ball, though. She hadn't danced with Darcy since the winners' training week and the idea did not sound horrible. *Not horrible at all,* she told herself. *I could wear my green ball dress. Darcy liked that one.*

Her Rational Self piped up at this point to remind her that Henry would be there, too. *Right. Good old Henry. Sure, I could dance with him, too,* Maggie told herself as a distracted afterthought, her toes still bubbly from thoughts of dancing with Darcy. Her Rational Self sighed and retreated to her usual perch on the back of Maggie's psyche. She had tried. Her Rational Self always tried. But this was an uphill battle. Maggie's taste in men ran heavily toward the toe-melters and the heart *pingers* like Henry could barely get any play at all.

Henry! Maggie sat up straight, suddenly remembering that she had agreed to hike with Henry to the forest chapel today. She had made the firm demand that no streams be forded in the attempt, a stipulation that Henry had eagerly embraced. Firmly confident of a dry activity, then, Maggie eagerly turned her steps toward Northanger.

Chapter Twenty-one

Twenty minutes later, Maggie was noisily striking the iron door knockers on Northanger Abbey's front doors but finding no response. "Henry?" she called out, cautiously pushing open one squeaky door and stepping into the foyer. "Catherine? Anyone around?" The place seemed deserted. She shivered thinking of creepy Larry Tedesco just down the hallway behind the door marked "Staff Only." *I really do* not *want to run into that guy again,* she thought anxiously, shuddering and feeling his cold, steely grip on her arm again.

Just then the phone in her pocket buzzed, causing a momentarily jumbled perception that Larry Tedesco was biting her on the leg. A panicky downward look, however, proved that neither Larry nor his teeth (presumably two separate entities at this stage of his life) were present.

CatherineM: Hey, Lizzy. Henry said he would wait for you in the staff room at Northanger. He says you're going hiking or something? Janie and I are getting our hair done at Rosings. Come on over and join us instead!

JaneB: We're getting hot iron curls with these amazing old-school irons! You have to see this.

LizzyB: Awww, how girly. Nah, I'm good. I promised Henry I'd go hiking with him today. Where are the other boys?

Bingley: Hello, girls. I'm at Delaford and Darcy's walking over. Brandon said he would teach me how to beat Darcy at billiards if I could teach him how to dance a quadrille. Marianne's back in shoes and I think he wants to up his dancing game.

LizzyB: Ha! Tell the old guy not to pull any muscles tryna hang with the young folk.

Bingley: Lol! I'll tell him. He's cool though.

LizzyB: He is. But don't tell him I said that. Don't want him getting the big head. Catherine, I'll see you tonight at Udolpho but I'm heading over on a late coach to London afterward. Wanna come, chica? Por favor!! *begging hands*

CatherineM: Oh, I'm coming, chica! Love that rejection scene. We'll bring Henry along, too. Hey, my irons are hot. Gotta go. Have fun, Lizzy.

JaneB: Don't get wet, sis!

LizzyB: Haha. Don't get your hair burned off! See you tonight!

Bracing herself and cautiously pushing open the "Staff Only" door, Maggie was deeply relieved to see morning light streaming through the high windows, brightening the gray stone walls of the corridor. *Well, well,* she thought with relief. *Downright cheery in a Better-Homes-and-Dungeons kind of way. Much better than it was that night, anyway.* She stepped more confidently into the hallway and strode down to the dressing room, preparing her saltiest comments for Henry as she burst through the door.

"Say! Any raggedy old bums hiding in here? I know my *friend* Henry would have answered the front door, but raggedy bums might ..." Her voice trailed off as she realized that the room was empty.

"Henry?" She poked around behind the racks of costumes and carefully knocked on the restroom door before checking inside, but the facts remained unchanged. Maggie was alone in the dressing room.

What's going on? She decided to wait for a few minutes. Five minutes passed. Then ten. She stepped out into the silent hallway and pondered her next move. *Just get your phone fixed, Henry, would you?* she thought irritably. *So hard without text. How did Regency people ever find each other?*

Her attention was diverted by a series of metallic clanging noises, faint scraping sounds and muffled voices coming from the direction of the kitchen. *Well, at least there are humans here.* She walked purposefully toward that end of the hallway, biting her lip as she passed Gary Johnson's door, relieved to note that on this day no spooky people leapt out at her and none of her body parts were grabbed.

She speedily rounded the corner, passed the back exit and peered through the round windows in the swinging kitchen doors. No one was there.

"Hello?" she called, stepping into the kitchen. The gleaming modern appliances and cook stations stood silent and empty but as she was turning to leave, she noticed a yellow legal pad on the counter. Approaching it with stealth, for some reason, she peered forward to read the scribbled note.

"FOOD SERVICE/HOUSEKEEPING STAFF— Water leak. No water at Abbey for 24 hours. Guests moved to Bath apartments. Pls report there for your shift. Check JaneyApp for today's schedule."

What is this? Catherine just said Henry was waiting for me here. Maggie furrowed her brow and tried to make sense of the perplexing scenario. Suddenly, the outside door slammed and two men carrying tools passed by the kitchen windows, conversing loudly. The man farther from Maggie was carrying a shovel and the nearer one was Caretaker Gary, laboring under the weight of a pickaxe propped on one gaunt shoulder.

Beyond curious now, Maggie tiptoed out into the corridor after they passed. The cellar door stood open a few steps further down the hall, the obvious origin of the noises and conversation. A moment of decision had come. We regret to inform the reader that our Maggie decided, as ever inquisitive people in creepy castles must, that the only reasonable thing to do at this juncture was go down into the cellar. Thus, heart pounding, she cautiously headed downstairs.

Henry is probably down there, heckling the workmen, she thought, irrationally. The men's voices were quite audible and Henry's distinctive dialect was not among them. *These guys will be grateful if I take him away,* she thought, trying to stay light-hearted, a difficult feat when one's heart has turned into a thumping cantaloupe cowering behind one's tonsils.

She lifted her long skirt and crept down the wooden stairs slowly, trying not to make them creak. More of the cellar became visible with each step and it turned out to be a rather large room by wine cellar standards. A bank of padlocked wine coolers was built into the north wall, directly facing Maggie. A second bank of locked coolers was built across from it into the south wall. The south coolers, however, were currently obscured by a tall and heavy wooden storage rack, almost as long and as tall as the room itself and filled with wine bottles. It was sitting at a peculiar angle over the top of a rectangular hole in the stone floor. The rack was the subject of heated discussion by the four men in the room.

"No, you idiot! Take the bottles *off* before you move it any more!" Gary was saying angrily to one of the workmen. Maggie froze on the stairway, reluctant to intrude in such a volatile moment. "And remember where you got them this time so you can put each one back in the same slot."

"Now, look!" Gary's shovel-carrying buddy spoke up testily. "I thought you said we only had twenty-four hours on this thing. It could take two hours just moving these stupid bottles back and forth!"

"Well, I guess you'll just have to work faster, then, won't you?" the caretaker snapped back. "This all could have been done by now if anyone on your brain-dead crew could tell north from south."

The men all started mumbling complaints at once.

169

However, Gary shouted back a few select words and told them to remember who was, in fact, the boss. Since this seemed to shut everyone up, it is fair to assume that the boss was him. As further verification, the glum but now obedient workers began to remove the bottles from the rack and set them in exactly the order Gary directed.

This seemed mundane enough, almost comic, and Maggie's heart began to migrate back to its accustomed niche behind her sternum. *This is probably the brilliant crew responsible for breaking and rearranging Edith's wine bottles in the first place,* Maggie realized with a smug smile. *Not exactly Rhodes Scholars, but harmless enough, seen in context. Hopefully, they can fix a pipe.*

She gazed toward the rectangular hole on the floor, partially visible underneath the rack, where several of the gray stones had been removed and stood stacked against the wall. (There was a similar rectangular shape where stones had recently been *replaced* along the north wall. *Resolution: Geniuses dug wrong hole,* Maggie thought with a grin.) Where the stones had been removed under the rack currently, solidly packed earth was visible below, likely due for a smiting by Gary's mighty pickaxe if the thin man could manage to lift it over his head.

Maggie stood, wiped the dust from the back of her dress and opened her mouth to ask the workmen if they had seen Henry. Suddenly, however, she heard a quiet voice directly behind her.

"Don't say a word," the voice whispered. "It's not safe."

"Henry?" she whispered back, turning around quickly. The wiry figure stood crouched on the stairs just above her, his finger to his lips urging silence. But it was not Henry.

She was standing face-to-face with Willoughby.

"What is your *deal*, Willoughby? Are you *everywhere?*" Maggie hissed to the man with supreme irritation.

He placed a finger to his lips and continued to beckon urgently for her to follow him up the stairs. Reluctantly, she followed the man up to the kitchen corridor.

Deciding she would go no further with the annoyingly ubiquitous fellow until she had some answers, Maggie stopped and crossed her arms in a display of intransigence. "Where's Henry?"

"Please, just keep your voice down," Willoughby muttered urgently, motioning with his palms downward. "Let's step outside. I'll explain what I can."

"Well, you had better, mister," Maggie said, channeling her mother's huffiest voice as she stepped outside. Once there, she recrossed her arms and looked expectantly at Willoughby.

"Okay, listen," he said nervously. "Do you know who Larry Tedesco is?"

This being the last thing on earth Maggie expected to hear from Willoughby's mouth, for a moment she could only gape at him and form incoherent syllables.

"Wha ... waa ... how ...," She frantically tried to gather her confused wits. *How could this guy possibly know anything about Larry Tedesco? He's a car salesman from Kansas City!* "Why do you ask?" Maggie managed to say with a slightly imperious edge to her voice.

"Okay, I'll take that as a yes," Willoughby said with a distracted wave of the hand. "I guess a lot of people know about him. Anyway, he's back here at the resort and that Gary guy is his *son!*"

This was the oldest of news. "So?" Maggie rejoined sharply. "I don't care if his father was Genghis Khan! What makes you think skinny Gary is so dangerous?"

"Because your precious Henry Tilney was talking to him this morning and now the man is *gone!*" he blurted. "I saw

171

them myself, chatting in the staff lounge this morning after breakfast. Then they left out of here together in a great big hurry, walking on the path to the maintenance shed."

"Well, again, Willoughby, *so what?*" Maggie was losing patience. None of this was consequential. She put hands on her hips and explained the obvious. "Of *course* he's going to the maintenance shed. He's supposed to pick up his phone this morning. Maybe Gary had business there, too. Anyway, Henry's coming back to meet me here and we're hiking up to the chapel."

"Yeah, so where is he?" Willoughby extended his palms skyward and mimed looking around before extending two fingers toward her. "That was two hours ago. Two hours. Have you gotten a text? Or seen him here?"

A slow beat passed. Maggie's eyes narrowed and she bit her lip, considering.

"Okay, yeah, that's weird," she finally conceded, exhaling and shaking her head.

Willoughby raised his hands heavenward. "Thank you! Yes, it's officially weird. Two guys go off in the woods but only one comes back? And the missing guy, one of the gabbiest guys at this whole place, supposedly gets his phone back this morning but no one's gotten a text yet?" He shrugged. "Weird, right?"

"Yeah," Maggie agreed. *The weirdest part of the whole thing is not hearing from Henry on group chat. He lives for that stuff.* She pulled out her phone for an updated check. Henry was still conspicuously absent. "Well, I guess we can't exactly go ask dear old Gary until we know more about what happened."

"God, no," Willoughby said, forcefully shaking his head. "We can't tell anyone yet."

"Hey! The guys in the maintenance shed will know if

Henry made it there, at least," Maggie suggested. "Do you have a JaneyApp number for them?"

Willoughby shook his head. "No, but it's a short walk from here." He motioned toward the path that led into the woods. "I can take you over there. Just to make sure you don't fall into any streams." His lips curled into a toothy smile. Unamused, Maggie shrugged and motioned for him to lead.

The path from the kitchen door led alongside the tall hedge row of the garden maze and directly into the woods. As they got closer, it became obvious that this was a well-traveled dirt road through the trees. *Probably Northanger's golf cart path for supplies and maintenance,* Maggie thought. *I don't need Willoughby for this. And what if Henry shows up while I'm gone?* She hesitated near the end of the hedgerow.

"I think I should wait here for Henry," Maggie said aloud. "He's probably fine, lost track of time and is standing around yukking it up somewhere."

"Oh, come on, Lizzy. It's five minutes to the shed. Maybe he's already there, like you said, yukking it up with the techie guys," Willoughby urged. "Five minutes. And no swimming this time, promise." The teeth appeared again.

Ick, Maggie thought with distaste. *Probably sold a lot of extended warranties with that smirk. Wonder what he's selling me, being all nice like this?*

Maggie conceded grumpily. "Okay, okay. Fine. Whatever. Let's just go." She moved forward, muttering to herself, "What a tool."

Just then, Maggie heard something, perhaps a rustling, and had the prickly sensation that someone was watching her. She wondered if Henry was having a prank.

"Henry?" she called out tentatively toward the tall hedges

of the garden maze. No one answered. The rustling sound stopped. She shrugged at the puzzled Willoughby and resumed her trek into the woods.

Chapter Twenty-two

The walk to the shed was, as advertised, a brief and easy jaunt. The path from Northanger to the maintenance building cut laterally across the wooded ridge and was obviously in frequent use by staff, though unmarked on maps given to guests.

"How did you know about this trail, Willoughby?" This was only one of *many* questions that Maggie had for this guy. "You seem to know way more about the resort than the other essay winners. Did you come here before for vacations or something?"

"I did, actually. With my grandma. She grew up around here, used to come here to dances back when it was the Bellissimo. Knew some of the old staff. Took me and my brother here on vacation when we were kids. Dressed us in little sailor suits with short pants. She loved this place."

"So, I guess it had changed over to the Regency theme by the time you came around?" Maggie asked.

"Right. Gran was really proud of Edith for keeping the resort open, for the jobs and stuff. Because so many Catskill resorts closed back then, you know." They walked a few more steps. "My brother really hated all the Regency stuff, though, the dressing up and bowing. All of that, you know? So he wouldn't come after the first couple of times. But me, yeah. I just lovvvvved me some Jane Austen. So those last few times, Gran only took me. I think she liked me better." He looked down at the trail without expression. *What's that look?* Maggie wondered to herself. *Is he guilty about being the favorite?*

"So, I guess your Grandma knew about the whole Larry Tedesco thing because she lived around here when it all came down?" Maggie asked.

"Yeah," Willoughby said quietly. They walked a few wordless paces before the man spoke up again. "I mean, it was in all the papers. Of course she knew. Right?"

"Sure," Maggie said carefully. "That makes sense." *That makes no sense at all,* she screamed internally. *Edith's father didn't press charges because he didn't want the publicity! It wouldn't have been in the papers. No one would have known. I do not believe one dang word coming out of this man's mouth!*

The yellow paint on the metal-sided maintenance shed became visible through the trees just ahead.

"Okay, I'll go in and check with them," Willoughby said, walking forward quickly. "You wait here. These I.T. guys can be squirrelly."

Maggie shook her head as Willoughby quickly entered the building and closed the door behind him. *See, even that's wrong. The guys here can fix Henry's phone but are too 'squirrelly' to say whether or not he picked it up?*

She considered barging in behind him but opted to peep through the dusty window on the side of the building instead. Two men were seated on either side of a T-shaped workstation illuminated by dropped fluorescent lights and strewn with electronic parts. Multiple monitors sat on the table that formed the top of the "T" and there were yards of heavy cable running everywhere.

There was, however, no Henry at all.

One of the workers picked up a phone plugged into a power strip at the workstation and Maggie recognized Henry's flashy gold case. Willoughby said something and the three of them shared a laugh. The fellow with the case called Willoughby over and turned the screen on. Whatever he showed him produced another group chuckle. Willoughby patted the man on the shoulder and motioned toward the door.

Maggie hurried back to the front of the building and leaned against a tree nonchalantly as Willoughby reappeared. "Well? What did they say?"

"Strangest thing. They've got his phone but he never picked it up." Willoughby shrugged, looking puzzled.

"Well, I'll take it with me," Maggie reasoned. "When Henry shows up again, I can just give it to him then, save him a trip."

Somehow, this idea did not sit well with Willoughby. "No, it's not … well, yeah, it's *here* but it's … it's not ready. We can't take it yet."

"It's not ready?" Maggie asked skeptically. *I just watched the guy turn the screen on.*

"Nope. Not ready. Can't take it yet." Willoughby tried another ingratiating smile but this one failed to charm. Maggie huffed and leaned back against her tree.

"This is just so not Henry," she said, gazing up and shaking her head. "I really expected him to be in there. He's *always* in the middle of a big group of people, not hiding out somewhere." She reached into her pocket for her phone. "I'm going to tell my friends that he's missing."

"Oh, say, wait though," Willoughby interjected quickly. "It would be a shame, you know, to worry them if he's really just up the path or something. Listen, you guys were going to the chapel today, right?" he asked brightly. It didn't come off as breezily conversational as he was trying to make it, but it seemed a harmless enough topic.

"Yeah. Henry's been kind of obsessed with it ever since he heard about it from skinny Gary."

"There's that Gary guy's influence again," he muttered looking at her significantly. "That's suspicious. Look, we're almost *at* the chapel. Do you suppose he could be waiting for you there?" He pointed up the hill toward the trailhead. "See? It's right through there. Let's check that one last place and if he's not there, then we'll know he's really missing and you can, you know, alert everybody."

"Okay, whatever. But let's get going, okay?"

Maggie's unease in the woods was magnified tenfold by having Willoughby as a trail guide. She found herself really missing Henry as they ascended and took the forest path. *Henry's no outdoorsman but he's reliable. I need reliable.* She registered a tiny heart *ping* as she pictured Henry's helpful face. But there was no time for such nonsense and she tramped forward with renewed energy.

It was not as near as Willoughby had tried to describe it but after a steady ten-minute hike, they did, in fact, arrive at the chapel. It was quite lovely, too, an open brick pavilion with rough wood trim and long eaves, accessed with a few steps at the back. It had simple natural wood benches and a slightly raised platform with a wooden lectern at the front. But otherwise, it held no other adornment or religious artwork. *No need to represent something that's already on full display,* Maggie thought to herself as she did a slow 360-degree turn, observing tall evergreen trees soaring majestically into the sky on all sides.

Returning to the matter at hand, however, none of those three hundred and sixty degrees contained a single Henry. It was time to call the cavalry. She reached for her phone.

"Wait!" shouted Willoughby. "Do you hear somebody?" He ran down the steps and jogged around to the uphill side of the building. Maggie chased after him, pausing in surprise as she came to the rear of the chapel.

She seemed to have stumbled across a junkyard of toys discarded by the neglectful children of giants. Besides broken benches, piles of bricks and garden rocks strewn everywhere, the most eye-catching items were figures from the

Northanger gothic garden. Here was a large chicken-wire dragon's head with only busted bulbs where his fearsome red eyes should be. There was a headless lunging wolf body and next to it, the wolf's head was now incongruously settled on the body of a centaur. Maggie found that the creatures were utterly robbed of their fear factor as they sat ridiculous and jumbled in the sunny glade.

"Good grief," Maggie exclaimed. She lifted the bare-chested torso of the ceramic centaur and shook it at Willoughby. "Those Nebraska librarians would have a field day up here, right? They stole a gnome, you know."

"They did *what?*" the man asked, profoundly confused.

"They stole … a … gnome. Oh, never mind." She set down the centaur's torso and proceeded to where Willoughby was standing. "What did you hear?"

They were standing on the back side of the chapel near a large metal door, covered in brush and limbs. The door was apparently an entrance to an underground cellar, set at a slanted angle a few inches above the ground. Someone with a sense of humor had set two five-foot-tall cement gargoyles standing watch, as it were, squatting against the chapel wall on either side of the metal door, one still wearing a weathered workman's cap. From the brush accumulated on the top and around the sides of the door, it appeared that the cement sentries had successfully driven off intruders for a great many years.

Willoughby motioned for quiet. "Do you hear something?"

Maggie listened intently. Sure enough, muffled sounds were coming from beneath the metal door.

"Henry?? Henry, is that you?" Maggie cried out frantically. A muffled voice was saying something with two syllables, possibly "it's me." Then a vague metallic "tap tap tap" sound came from beneath their feet.

179

"Henry! Henry! Hang on! It's me, Maggie! We'll get you out buddy, we'll get you out." She started clawing at the branches on top of the doors, stabbing herself fiercely with pine needles in the process and discovering a small metal ventilation turbine under the pile. Oddly, there seemed to be pine straw stuffed into the tube that served to muffle sounds coming up the pipe from below. The brush pile on the door concealed the much larger problem, however, a long and bristly tree limb with a fourteen-inch circumference lying across the door.

"We're going to need help," cried Willoughby, pulling out his phone. He shouted an epithet almost immediately and put his phone back in his pocket. "This stupid phone! Lizzy, do you have service? Quick, give me your phone. See if you can get Henry to answer you back."

Maggie handed over her phone and tried tapping on the metal ventilation pipe with her shoe. "Henry! If it's you tap one time for yes." A single tap responded.

"Oh! It's him, Willoughby, it's him!" She tried to lift the heavy limb but couldn't get it to budge.

"Ask him if he's all right," Willoughby said, wandering around the glade, lifting Maggie's phone to look for a signal.

Maggie placed her face down near the top of the ventilation pipe. "Henry, are you okay?" Another single tap was heard along with a muffled voice that seemed to verify his well-being. "He's okay, Willoughby. He's okay." She smiled in relief.

"Keep talking to him," Willoughby urged, continuing to wander.

"Henry, we're going to get you out of there, okay? Willoughby is here and he's calling for more people to get you out." Suddenly, the metal pipe came alive like a snare drum line playing a Sousa march. The muffled voice, too, found new vigor, seeming for all the world to be chanting the same syllable over and over again.

"Can he be saying 'No?'" Maggie asked desperately. "Oh, come on Willoughby. He's losing it in there! Don't you think we can budge this thing if we lift together?"

"Maybe," Willoughby said, bending to make the attempt. "Look, all we have to do is lift the branch as high as the gargoyle's lap, see?" He pointed to the protruding knees of the ugly squatting sentry. "If it can rest there, we can get the door open a little bit."

"Yes! Great!" Maggie ran to the same side as Willoughby and on the count of three, both lifted with all their might. It nearly worked. Another count and another lift brought them even closer. Finally, the third count and the third lift found success. The limb was resting on the gargoyle's knees leaving about twelve inches of space for the door to open. The latch had long ago rusted away so the squeaky hinges opened as soon as Maggie pulled on the handle.

"Henry? It's me, Maggie," she called into the dark. "Are you okay?" She wiggled into the space, feeling rough cement stairs beneath her hands and called again. "Henry?"

"Yes! It's me and I'm fine! But don't come down here, Maggie! Run for help!"

"Help is coming already," Willoughby said urgently, behind Maggie. "Go tell him. He must be out of his head."

"Help is coming, Henry. They're already coming." She wiggled further into the dark stairway, failing for the second time that day to realize that one has *many* other options besides descending when a dark and creepy cellar presents itself.

"Maggie, for once in your life, listen to me! Run!" Henry screamed from the bottom of the stairwell, presenting the better option as forcefully as ever one might.

But of course, she did *not* run. She pulled her feet into the stairwell, crouched her way down the stairs and fell into Henry's arms.

"I'd never run away from you, Henry," she murmured into his shoulder.

"Oh, Maggie," Henry sighed, stroking her hair and looking up to see Willoughby's face in the doorway. "But this time you should have done."

With a tremendous crash over their heads, the metal door slammed shut and the two friends found themselves embracing in pitch dark.

"You really, truly should have done, my dear."

Chapter Twenty-three

"Hey, did you see this?" Bingley set aside his billiards cue and looked at his phone with sudden intensity.

"What, another picture of Jane's new hairdo?" Darcy asked with a sardonic look across the billiards table towards Brandon and Ferrars. "Oh joy. How have we lived without it?"

Ferrars snickered behind his hand and Brandon gave Darcy a look. "Now, now," he reprimanded mildly. "Don't be bitter, Darcy. I'm sure your Lizzy will send you all *kinds* of photos eventually."

"No, guys," Bingley said, gesturing with urgency toward his phone. "It's Henry. He's back on the LaGGards' group chat."

"Oh, well, that *is* good news then," Darcy said with no diminishment of sarcasm. "I have been so eager to hear his thoughts on absolutely everything."

"Yeah, well, I don't think you're going to like this thought very much," Bingley said, looking toward Darcy anxiously.

Darcy glanced up sharply and saw trepidation in his friend's face. With a tiny knot in his stomach, he set aside his cue and pulled out his own phone, scrolling to the LaGGards' JaneyApp chat to read two very odd postings.

Tilney: Hi, people. I have my phone back. So that's a golly good show. I'm going to the city with Margaret to see a Broadway show. So don't worry about us. We can't answer our phones in the city. Or in Broadway. Haha. But we are fine. Just going on a normal date with my girlfriend. So don't worry. Pip pip horay!

Tilney: Don't worry about how we are getting there. We have a car that someone let me use. A Broadway person, my friend, that you don't know. But I know lots of Broadway people. So that's how we are going to the city. So don't worry even if you don't hear from us for a while. Cheerios.

Darcy looked up from his phone with an expression of such profound confusion that he could not even speak. Brandon and Ferrars immediately laid down their cues and crowded around the other men's phones.

They read. Then read again. The four men looked at each other, then bent their heads to read a third time. But clarity did not come.

"'A *golly* good show?'" Brandon finally managed to say aloud. "'Pip pip horay?'"

"Good Lord. Did they turn off Tilney's Autocorrect?" Ferrars queried, bewildered.

"Cheerios is a cereal," Bingley declared, firm in his conviction but trying not to sound haughty.

"'I'm going on a *date* with my *girlfriend?!*'" Darcy finally exclaimed, unequivocally pointing out the elephant in the room.

"Yes. That really is the meat of this story, isn't it?" Brandon said mildly, glancing around the room to the other men's worried faces. "What did Lizzy say she would be doing today, gentlemen? Anybody know?"

"Um, we had a morning event at Rosings," Darcy responded distractedly. "Receiving the letter from me. She was definitely there for that. About 8:30. It's a short event."

"I know she chatted with the other girls afterward," Bingley continued, scrolling through the group chat. "Ah! She said she was going to *Udolpho* at Northanger tonight and then coming over later to the *S&S* ball in London. Yeah, right here. She's definitely planning on attending those two events at the resort tonight. Oh." He paused. "Apparently, she was meeting Henry to do something this morning. Hiking." He looked up at the other men and shrugged.

"Oh, that doesn't signify at all," Ferrars said, lightly. "Those two are always tramping about the place, poking their extroverted noses into something or other. But surely they wouldn't leave the property without letting someone know."

"That's true," Darcy mused. "I can't speak for Tilney but Maggie's very responsible, especially about fulfilling our obligations here."

"Why don't you text her, then, Darcy?" Ferrars asked gently. "Not in a demanding way, of course, just ask her what she's up to. Light as air, you know."

Darcy shook his head. "No matter what I say, she won't like it if I sound jealous of Tilney."

"But you are jealous of him, aren't you?" Bingley asked guilelessly. The other gentlemen smiled and looked downward. "Well, he is. Aren't you?" he appealed to Darcy.

"I'll have to get back to you on that one," Darcy said diplomatically. "Difficult social question."

"Well, there's no reason *I* can't text her," Brandon said, pulling out his own phone. He paused and addressed Darcy. "Just for the record, friend, in my book, our Miss Elizabeth is a free moral agent. If she wants to take her day off to go down to the city for a matinée with a friend, that's her right. My only problem is that a grown woman needs to speak up for *herself* about her plans so her people don't worry. Are we on the same page, Darcy?"

"Absolutely," Darcy agreed soberly. "She can do as she pleases. But this note from Tilney is just … odd. Doesn't even sound like him. What actor says '*in* Broadway?' And at the same time, Lizzy is suddenly absent from chat altogether? Also, extremely odd. I'd just feel much better if I heard something directly from her. That's all."

"All right then," Brandon agreed. "I'll give her the big brother treatment, let her know to stop worrying folks."

"Yes, that's the stuff," Ferrars said, nodding in approval. "Give her what for, Brandon."

Over the next few hours, various texts were sent to the two parties in question, initially quite breezy in tone but growing progressively more insistent as the day wore on. Jane and Catherine were recruited to the effort and they tried a variety of techniques, too, from celebration ("Heard you got a hot date with Henry! Spill, girl!") to guilt ("I can't believe you are ignoring your own sister.")

But as we already know, no answer would come.

Maggie gripped Henry tighter after the lights went out in the chapel cellar. "Henry!! The limb must have fallen across the door again! I don't think Willoughby can lift it by himself."

"No, I imagine not," Henry said calmly. "I … I don't suppose you've got your phone, do you, my dear?"

Maggie reached toward her pocket then realized it wasn't there. "No. Willoughby's got it. So he can call for help."

"Right." Henry sighed deeply. A long moment passed.

"He's not calling for help, is he, Henry?"

"No, my dear. I expect not."

"Oh, God! Why did I believe that guy?" Maggie blurted. "I'm so *sorry*, Henry. I should have run when you told me to. I'm so sorry." She devolved into a weeping, moaning mess, burying her face in his shoulder and pounding him with her fist.

"There, there," Henry said kindly, patting her on the back and absorbing her blows. "I'm quite glad of your company. I was blasted lonely in here, believe me. Rather hopeless, truth be told. Glad to know I was missed, though. Especially by you."

Several minutes passed tearfully. Finally, Maggie inhaled a great snotty snuffle that seemed to echo in the dark room.

"Henry, is there any kind of light down here?" she asked tentatively. "It sounds like a big room."

"Yes, of course, my dear. Stupid of me. I've got a little torch right here and some candles and matches on a table." He pulled a small flashlight out of his jacket and illuminated it. "Huzzah! Let there be light!" Even distorted by the shadows around the tiny glare of yellow light, Henry's smile made her feel instantly better. "How nice of you to visit, Miss Elizabeth," he quipped with a formal bow. "Step on in and I'll show you the whole lair."

She took his hand and advanced a few paces as the tour commenced.

"Just to the right of the stairs, along the north wall, shelves … in a cellar!" Henry announced with an overdone flourish, mimicking one of Austen's favorite toadies, Mr. Collins.

"Happy thought indeed!" Maggie responded with a half-smile.

"That's my girl," Henry commended, patting her hand. "Even trapped in a cellar by miscreants, our Lizzy can still return the proper Janeite line."

Henry shone the light on the metal industrial shelves. They were stacked with bulk-quantity dry goods, the largest ones in sealed white buckets marked "FLOUR," "OATS" and "POWDERED MILK" alongside many smaller containers with similar block print labels.

"Well, there's the kitchen, I guess," Maggie observed.

"So it seems. There's a rather good supply of drinking water along the west wall, just perpendicular to the kitchen there. Not sure if it's comforting or worrisome, but they're rather well kitted out to keep guests here for quite some time, it seems." He then shone the light around the large, open center of the room, displaying a few folding chairs and card tables.

"Now over there, I suppose that's the east wall, stacks of canvas cots. Might be where the mildew smell is coming from, not sure. And I haven't even gotten down there to the south wall. Stacks and stacks of junk down there, God knows what." He shone his beam in that direction, but the distance was too great for the small pocket light.

"You said there were candles and matches? Should we use those for a while to save the batteries on our light?"

"Oh, clever girl." He shone his light toward a table near the "kitchen" area. "Look, I've been collecting my treasures on a table just there. Can't offer tea but I do have a cup of water there, for what it's worth."

"Sounds wonderful," Maggie said gratefully.

Henry's faithful little beam guided them to a rickety table that had, to its credit, four usable legs unlike many of its fellows, and a couple of rusty folding chairs that did, with significant pressure from Henry, reluctantly condescend to unfold and support human weight. Once seated, Maggie seized Henry's proffered plastic tumbler of stale water like a camel at an oasis, draining the whole cup and giving a satisfied burp as she thumped the empty tumbler on the table. Henry offered to pour more from a gallon plastic jug reassuringly marked "DRINKING WATER" but Maggie waved it away.

"No thanks. I really wasn't thirsty. I just … needed to do something normal for a second, I guess. Just drink a cup of water to reset my brain or something. If that makes sense."

Henry nodded. "Perfectly reasonable. I should do the same. My brain hasn't functioned properly for hours." He poured himself a few swallows of water in the glass and savored each sip like fine wine. "Mmm. A tepid little vintage. Notes of dust and despair. But pairs wonderfully with a friend." He smiled at Maggie and downed a hefty swallow.

Maggie found the candles and matches among Henry's treasures and felt triumphant when she managed to light the damp wick using only two matches.

"Huzzah!" she celebrated. "Okay, Henry. Let's talk."

"Oh, good. My favorite thing. Let's."

Henry's eager smile across the candle flame was enormously comforting. She smiled back at him reflexively and took a deep breath. *Ping,* she thought looking at the man's kind eyes. *If it was just about pings, Henry would be ahead by a mile. Which won't matter at all if we don't get out of here,* her Rational Self interrupted urgently. *Come on, Maggie! Focus!* Maggie clapped her hands together and turned to the matter at hand.

"Okay, then. First things first. Did Willoughby bring you over here this morning? He told me Gary the caretaker walked out with you. But that was a lie, wasn't it?"

"Oh, absolutely. It was Willoughby himself. You see, the Northanger cast was told at breakfast to pack up and go to our apartments in Bath since they were working on a water leak in the Abbey wine cellar. So good little Catherine and the others packed up as instructed, put their overnight bags downstairs for pick up. I asked Catherine to text you that I'd be waiting for you at the Abbey for our hike. Did she do it?"

"She did. She's a good kid."

"She is. Anyway, I didn't like the idea of leaving my own wee bed, especially when Miss Edith was so keen on us watching out for mischief at the Abbey, so I popped downstairs to make my own assessment, of course. I found only

189

a lone worker removing stones from the floor down there."

"Invading your sanctuary, the wine cellar? Sacrilege!" Maggie said impishly.

"Well, it was, rather. And they don't even have a wine cellar over at the Bath apartments, I'm pained to say. So it's rather inconvenient for a gentleman who prefers unfettered access to products of the vine, you know."

"Poor, poor you," Maggie intoned drily.

"Indeed. Tragic. Well, the workman said they said they'd be done in twenty-four hours, no question about it. And I knew I'd be out hiking and doing events until the wee hours anyway. And one cherishes a tiny dram at the end of a long day, you know."

"So you decided not to leave Northanger …," Maggie said, cutting to the chase and motioning for him to get on with it.

"Only reasonable conclusion, really. Well, I took a seat in the Abbey staff room to wait for you. Then *Willoughby*, of all people, springs in on me not two minutes later, as though he had been hiding behind a potted plant. And oh, the man is bright as a new penny, chatting me up with that ghastly smile of his, trying to convince me, oh, my, it's not *safe* to stay and the *noise* will be horrific. Ridiculous arguments, really. So, I politely take my leave, anxious to get my phone from the shed, you know, before you arrive for our hike. And the cheeky fellow actually follows me!"

"The nerve! So, did you actually get to talk to the guys in the shed?"

"Well, yes, briefly. But they just kept saying the phone wasn't ready, needed more time, that kind of thing, over and over. Seemed a bit odd when they had told me so specifically to come that morning, but there was nothing I could do except come back later. So Willoughby says, 'Oh,

I've an idea, let's stroll over to the little chapel while you're waiting. I can show you exactly how to get there.' I mean, didn't sound like a bad idea at the time. I'd done a rather bad job of finding it initially as you know. So, I walk over with the chap. We knock around a bit in that odd little rubbish heap out back, and what do you think? Willough-by 'discovers' a cellar door."

"Of course. Was it just … open when you saw it?"

"Well, the door was closed but it had no lock on it. Swung open immediately. Now, mind you, there was a great thick limb standing upright next to it. Seemed like someone had put it there to be funny, made it look as though the gar-goyle was holding it like a weapon or something. I even joked about it. 'Oh, the Queen's Guards need that size of pike, mate,' that kind of thing. Had Willoughby take a selfie of us next to the gargoyle. I know how you love my gargoyle shots."

Maggie rolled her eyes and motioned again for Henry to continue.

"Anyway, he pops down into the cellar, then comes back out and says, 'Oh my, you *must* go down and see this, it's *so* amazing.' Even hands me the little torch. So, innocent as a lamb, I head down there and look around a bit. Then suddenly, *bam!* I'm standing there alone, the door is closed tight and I can't lift it so much as an inch. Willoughby shouts down the air duct. 'Oh, no, Tilney! The branch has fallen! We'll need help to lift it! Hang in there, buddy, and I'll run for help!' Initially, I wasn't concerned, you know. Grabbed my little torch and poked around a bit looking for another exit, but of course, there is no other exit. Time passed and passed and passed. Eventually, it dawned on me that the man was not coming back and that I was jolly well stuck."

"And now I'm jolly well stuck with you," Maggie added

ruefully. "But *why*, Henry, *why?* What are they planning to do with us?"

"That's what we only have our wits to discover, my dear." Henry chewed his lip for a moment. "And it seems rather important that we do. Edith was right, something odd *is* happening at Northanger. You know the big water problem, no water for 24 hours, all of that? Not true. I checked the tap in the dressing room lavatory before I left. The water is still *on* at Northanger."

"They just wanted people out of there, obviously, including us," Maggie said, nodding solemnly. "And Willoughby is right in the middle of it somehow. That guy spends more time at Northanger than his own location. Oh! And guess what? He knows all about Larry Tedesco."

"Indeed! Curiouser and curiouser," Henry murmured. "All right. Tell me everything you know about the irritating little weasel and let's figure this thing out. Let's do it for Edith! No, let's do it for Jane Austen!"

"Hey, let's do it for US, Henry!" Maggie placed her hand into the center of the table next to the candle. "One, two, three, Camp Jane?"

He placed his hand on hers and the Janeite call rang out.

"ONE, TWO, THREE, CAMP JANE!"

Chapter Twenty-four

Dinner at the LaGGards' table on the Pemberley terrace was a grim affair that evening. The *S&S* cast, except for the chronically unsociable Willoughby, joined the diminished LaGGards' group and contributed what they could to keep the table chat positive. But it was uphill sledding with Darcy deep into a silent brood.

"Whatever it takes, I am definitely going to spend some time in New York City this summer," Marianne Dashwood declared passionately. "It is so alive, with *so* many museums and concert halls!"

"*So* many department stores!" Jane observed.

"*So* many subway rats," Elinor said glumly, receiving a pointed look from Brandon that prompted her to try again. "Of course," she amended, erasing her comment by waving a butter knife, "you cannot take my opinion too seriously since I am not a fan of large cities. But, yes, so many adventures to be had there. What fun." She stared back at Brandon to indicate that was the best she could do.

"Yes," Ferrars agreed with forced merriment. "What a lark the two scamps must be having. What adventures they shall have to tell us about when they return!"

Everyone nodded, smiling wanly. Then the table fell silent, the clank of cutlery suddenly deafening in the void. No one really believed that. The two missing friends were people who shared their every thought via talk, text or sky-writing, if necessary. Even if Maggie and Henry *had* run off together on a sudden adventure, it was *impossible* to think that they would do so without live-streaming it.

"Maybe, Lizzy's cell phone plan doesn't work in the city?" Catherine posited uncertainly.

"When we were in the city a couple of weeks ago, her phone worked fine," Jane said quietly, involuntarily glancing toward Darcy. "This just doesn't seem like a phone problem."

"And Henry, well, even when he didn't have a phone at all, that man found a way to talk," Bingley said emphatically. "I mean, he *borrowed* phones from everyone, me, Catherine, even guests, just to text his ideas about the weather or the dessert tray at Pemberley. He'd find a way to talk if he had to use tin cans and a string."

No one tried to dispute these facts.

Brandon cleared his throat. "Has anyone mentioned this to Miss Edith? I know they're not technically due back for another couple of hours but is there a point at which she should be told?"

Catherine spoke up, her tiny voice sounding particularly strained. "Henry and I are supposed to be at the bonfire location at Northanger by 7:30." She glanced around the table as everyone did the math. It was almost six o'clock.

Darcy suddenly came to life and spoke up unexpectedly. "Look, there are only a handful of afternoon shows playing on Broadway on a Tuesday and all of those are over by now. The *only* reason they would not have called by now, at least to let us know where they were, is ... well, if they didn't *want* anyone to know where they were, frankly."

"What now?" Brandon asked, puzzled.

"We found out a couple of weeks ago that JaneyApp comes with a default security tracker," Darcy explained. "Only Edith and another admin have access to it, but the tracker can display every place the phone has been. The only way to deactivate it is to shut the phone off completely."

"So, you're saying ..." Brandon hesitated, then continued. "They could be maintaining this radio silence so they *couldn't* be found?"

"Yes," Darcy said without elaboration, leaving the fertile imaginations of the Janeites around the table to run amok.

"A secret lovers' tryst. So romantic," Marianne sighed before immediately crying out in pain and turning to her sister. "Ow! Why are you kicking me?" Marianne's many days in a haze of antihistamines and Willoughby infatuation had left her seriously out of date *in re* the ongoing Darcy vs. Tilney drama with Lizzy.

"Oh, I beg pardon, sister," Elinor replied smoothly. "But now that we are on to other topics, the buffet is offering trifle for dessert, my dear. Could you be a dear and fetch me a tiny serving?" After Marianne had left on her assignment, Elinor turned her pragmatic attention to Brandon's question.

"This is my thought about notifying resort staff, Colonel. It is not our place to interfere with Elizabeth or Tilney's *private* business. However, if they have to miss a resort event, that is different. There are protocols in place for that sort of thing, understudies come into play, as we had occasion to learn firsthand last week."

"Catherine, do you know who understudies for *Northanger?*" Jane asked.

"Our staff said that the *Emma* cast understudies for us. So, it's Frank Churchill for Henry and Harriet Smith for me."

"Not bad casting," Jane murmured. "One smooth talker, one shy innocent. Edith knows her stuff." The table contemplated the similarities of the Austen characters chosen as understudies and nodded their approval.

"But when do we, you know, pull the trigger on this and tell someone that Henry's missing?" Brandon persisted.

"It's tricky. I mean, what if Henry walks in ready to go at 7:30, no problem, and we've reported him as AWOL to Edith and dragged poor Frank Churchill over from *Emma* for no reason?"

"Or what if he's already made *other* arrangements to have someone fill in for him tonight?" Jane suggested.

"I think Henry might be very hurt if we didn't trust him to take care of his responsibilities," Catherine said slowly, gazing downward. "He plays the fool a lot but Henry is actually pretty serious about his acting. I'm always running late for events but *he's* the one hurrying us along, saying 'can't miss the curtain, old girl' or 'the show must go on' and that kind of thing."

She looked up at the other players and spoke with firm resolve. "I think we trust Henry. He's our friend and I think we should trust that no matter what happens tonight, *we* should have confidence that Henry's done his very best to do the right thing for Camp Jane. And for us." There was a moment of contemplative silence before anyone spoke.

"Well, huzzah, then," said Darcy finally. Everyone smiled, missing Henry acutely at that moment. "As long as you're prepared to read *Udolpho* yourself, Catherine, we shall go about our usual business tonight, confident that Tilney has a plan in place."

"Oh, dear," shy Catherine murmured with a gulp and a slight tremor in her voice. "I hope it doesn't come to that. But I'll do whatever it takes."

"We all stand ready if it turns out help is needed, Miss Catherine," said Brandon kindly. All the others nodded their agreement, too.

"As usual, Janeites rock, y'all," said Jane. "This is usually Lizzy's thing but …," she put her hand into the center of the table. "Is it 'One, two, three, Camp Jane' time?" The others eagerly leaned in.

196

"ONE, TWO, THREE, CAMP JANE!" came the cheer, drawing applause from all the guests on the Pemberley terrace and strengthening the friends' resolve for whatever lay ahead.

"It's official. I'm hungry."

Maggie stood up from the little folding chair and stretched. There had been no thought of lunch, of course, in the early hours after the door had shut and Maggie's adrenaline had been running high. But it was well and truly dinner time now according to Maggie's pocket watch and her stomach had seconded the idea noisily.

"I'm a bit peckish myself, truth be told," Henry agreed, also rising. "Shall I hunt and gather or are you keen to confirm gender stereotypes and take the lead in the kitchen?"

"Well, maybe you can hunt up more utensils from wherever you got that cup. Bring me a couple of bowls or cups, if you can find them. Maybe spoons or something. I've been staring at that bucket of oats and powdered milk for an hour and now I'm obsessed with them. I think I can put them together with some water and make enormous bowls of oatmeal."

"Oh, yum," Henry enthused. "Gruel for our first meal. Emma's Mr. Woodhouse would be proud."

"Well, it may taste horrible and cold but it's all I can think about right now. Find me something bowl-shaped and we'll go from there, okay?" Each took a flashlight from the table of treasures and headed to their tasks.

Soon, Maggie had opened the sealed buckets of oats and powdered milk and declared both to be bug-free and fit for human consumption. Henry, unfortunately, found neither bowls nor cups, only plates. However, he did find a small camp stove and a kit of utensils that included nested cook pots along with a variety of metal cutlery. Lighting the stove was a tense business since Maggie kept shrieking

197

"Henry! Stop! I smell gas!" every time he tried to ignite the burner by turning on the gas jet from the little tank. In time, however, Henry was able to convince Maggie that the screaming was not, in fact, helping and she agreed to clamp her hand over her mouth. Shortly thereafter, the burner was lit, the water with oats put on to boil and the mood in the room significantly lighter.

"Henry, look!" Maggie exclaimed from her spot investigating a lower shelf. "Sugar!" She gleefully pulled out the bucket. "Yippee! And ... oh, Henry! There's tea! You can have your tea!"

"Really?" Henry said, immediately interested. "Oh, we've two burners here, Lizzy. Can a chap put a kettle on for tea?"

"Righto, guvnor. I'll even join ya for a cuppa tay," Maggie said cheerfully in a vaguely Artful-Dodger-inspired accent that she, along with many other Americans, erroneously thought of as typically "British."

In time, Maggie stirred a bit of powdered milk and sugar into the oatmeal (that had been boiled to within an inch of its life by the two amateur cooks if we're honest) and declared that dinner was served. Each hungry diner took a generous portion in one of the metal cook pots, dug in with a large aluminum spoon and proclaimed the mushy porridge the best food they had ever eaten.

Maggie glowed with pride as she served tea after dinner to Henry with the smallest cookpot she could find standing in as his teacup.

"Black or white tea, sir?" Maggie asked poshly, holding her spoon above the powdered milk bucket with her pinky finger extended.

"Oh, black, please, miss, thanks just the same. Might take a bit of sugar, though," he answered, ever the pleasant customer.

She dipped her spoon cordially into the sugar bucket and stirred it into his rather-too-literal "pot" of tea, pinky still aloft. Then, giggling, she served herself in the plastic tumbler, stirred in a massive amount of both milk and sugar, and sipped alongside Henry, exhaling deeply. Maggie lit another candle and they turned off their flashlights. For a moment, even trapped *under* Camp Jane, the two found the rest that always comes to Janeites with a shared cup of tea.

"Almost 7:30," Henry said, consulting his pocket watch. "Even if no one's missed us yet, Catherine is sure to sound the alarm when I don't show up for *Udolpho* at Northanger. She knows I would never miss a performance."

"That's true," Maggie acknowledged hopefully. "We just don't know if the Northanger people, Gary and the diggers, especially, are bad guys or good guys. I mean, clearly Willoughby and the techie guys are bad guys. But Willoughby kept saying Gary was a *bad* guy, taking you out in the woods and so forth, which turned out to be a complete lie. So if a bad guy lies and says *another* guy is bad, does that make the other guy good?"

"Well, I don't know, my dear, but it certainly makes one's head hurt thinking about it," Henry responded, wrinkling his nose. "So, if I'm following here, your thought is that Gary might be a good guy? And Willoughby ..."

"A known bad guy ..." Maggie interjected.

"Yes. Is trying to keep us away from *good guy* Gary?" Maggie nodded solemnly. "Well, we can't rule it out, I suppose, my dear. But isn't Gary the son of the most infamous Bad Guy in resort history, Larry Tedesco? *And,* riddle me this, Lizzy! If dear Gary is such a *good* guy, why would he suddenly be moving everyone offsite and digging up the cellar at Northanger under cover of a fictional water leak, eh?"

199

"Because I think his father told him to," Maggie said simply. Henry tilted his head like a puzzled spaniel.

"Listen, Henry, there's something I haven't mentioned. I actually met Larry Tedesco, that night I was in Northanger after the Night Tour."

"I knew it!" Henry sat straight up and pointed at Maggie. "Edith said he looked like a cat but *you* already knew that!"

"I did," she admitted. "And he does. Weird whisker mustache, hair that stands up like little cat ears, just creepy. Dude jumped out at me, grabbed me on the arm." Maggie briefly related her encounter with Larry and Gary Tedesco in the staff quarters of the Abbey.

"Sounds awful, my dear," said Henry sympathetically. "I'm glad that great hulking Enzo fellow was with you. Might have had a different outcome if you'd been alone."

"Well, I think ultimately I could hold my own in a fair fight with Larry Tedesco, but yeah. I was glad Enzo was there, too. Anyway, I'm *telling* you this, Henry, because I keep thinking of what Larry said to me that night. At first, I thought it was just, you know, nonsense. Just the dementia talking. But now, I'm not so sure."

"What did he say?" Henry leaned forward curiously.

"He whispered to me, very clearly, 'go to the cellar.' Just like that. 'Go to the cellar.' And where does his son start digging? In the cellar! So I think he must have told his son the same thing, 'go to the cellar.' Look, Larry Tedesco was here when Northanger was built, right? Did he *put* something underground, back when that cellar was built? Something he wants back now?"

"Could he have buried the embezzled money there?" Henry said, lifting a brow. "Hmm. Did the man say anything else while you were there?"

Maggie shrugged. "Not really. He jumped out at me first

200

thing saying, 'you're in the wrong place' but Enzo explained that it was okay because, you know, I was with staff. And, let's see. I said, 'hey, stop digging on me' or something because those nails were digging in pretty deep and he kind of echoed that, 'stop digging,' over and over. I don't know. He just kept saying some version of those three things to me or to his son, repeatedly, the whole time."

"'You're in the wrong place,'" Henry repeated to himself. "'Stop digging.' Lizzy ... didn't you say that the men in the cellar had dug *in the wrong place?*"

"Yeah," she said, suddenly catching the idea. "Hey! Yeah! So, they *go to the cellar* and start digging two weeks ago. But they were *in the wrong place*. So they had to *stop digging*. That's what old Larry Tedesco was trying to tell *me!* I say 'stop digging' and he thinks 'hey, finally someone's listening to me.' So he tells me, hey, 'go to the cellar' and get them to 'stop digging' because they are digging 'in the wrong place.' He told his son, too, over and over. That's got to be it! They're trying to dig up something Larry buried, maybe the money from the resort, but they were digging in the wrong place! That's genius, Henry!"

"Perhaps," Henry acknowledged, with a modest bow. "But I think there's another possibility. You mentioned that Willoughby's gran knew all about the resort, showed him the path here to the chapel, even knew about Larry Tedesco, right?"

"Right. I actually wondered if maybe she had been an employee at one time."

"Hmm. Now, this chapel building with its well-stocked cellar, another bit of resort trivia that Willoughby's dear old gran knew about, is obviously from the old days, too. And Willoughby stuck *us* here in gran's secret hidey hole to keep us *away* from that very important digging at Northanger, agreed?"

"Absolutely," Maggie concurred. "So he *must* be connected to the digging at Northanger, too!"

"It seems he must. But …" Henry said, raising a finger and pausing for effect.

"Buuut?" Maggie queried indulgently, waiting for the showman's dramatic reveal.

"What if they're all *wrong?*"

Henry leaned over until he was directly over the candle, sending eerie shadows flickering across his face.

"What if Larry Tedesco was trying to tell you to *go to the cellar* because he knew they were *all* digging *in the wrong place*, not just in the *wrong* hole, but *in the wrong cellar?*"

Henry gestured around the dark cellar.

"Perhaps, with the accidental help of Willoughby's gran, you're the first person to follow Larry Tedesco's instructions accurately. *You're in the wrong place, stop digging,* he says. Just *go to the cellar.* And *you*, Maggie dear, have finally gone to *the right cellar.*"

Maggie sat for a long moment staring at the shadows on Henry's face as the truth of his words sank in.

"Well, then," she said at last. "*We*, Henry dear, need to find out what everybody's looking for. Grab your torch, old bean, and let's get to it."

Chapter Twenty-five

Catherine Morland paced the Northanger Abbey bonfire site nervously, glancing up every few seconds toward the stair-top entrance to the garden. If wishing Henry to appear could have made it happen, the man would have come ages ago. Her wishes were now just an echo chamber of the same words on repeat, *please come, please come, please come, Henry.*

But wishing wasn't working. And Henry wasn't coming.

Gary the caretaker stacked the last cord of wood into the bonfire pit and walked toward Catherine. He, too, had begun glancing around several minutes earlier, apparently also looking for the missing player.

The only people at the site who seemed carefree were the guests who had come for the event. They were seated on benches arranged in a circle around the bonfire pit. This particular event was not taken directly from an Austen novel, so there were not many CanonScavvers present. However, the bonfire reading seemed to be quite popular with couples. There was much more giggling than usual among the merry attendees as the potential for scary gothic stories in the dark also meant an opportunity to comfort one's lady friend in a protective hug and the gentlemen were eagerly practicing for this eventuality even before the sun had set. There were lanterns hung on posts at intervals around the circle but they provided only muted lighting, again, to the delight of all present.

The exception was the lantern behind Henry and Catherine's bench. This one had a proper light so that the reader could easily see and read from the book *Udolpho,* made famous in Austen's Northanger Abbey as the gothic novel that prompted young ladies like Catherine Morland to let their imaginations run wild.

"Time to light the bonfire, Miss Catherine." The caretaker's gruff voice from behind her startled Catherine involuntarily. She turned, clutching the large *Udolpho* book to her chest, looking into the man's angular face. "No sign of Mr. Tilney, then, eh?"

"No," Catherine said sadly. "I'm afraid not."

"Well, he don't start reading until 8:30. Maybe he'll come yet." He considered a moment, then decided to speak up. "Miss Edith don't like people missing their events, miss. If I'd known earlier, I woulda got that understudy guy over here from *Emma*. But it's kind of late now. If Mr. Tilney don't come … are you just going to read it out yourself?"

"Yes," Catherine said, mustering a bright voice. "That's the plan. I can read it."

"Oh, I'm quite sure you can *read* it, miss," Gary said cautiously. "Miss Edith gets some clever folks in here for her winners." He looked around the circle a bit uncertainly. "It's just that, well, you've got a very soft voice, miss. See, the fire makes quite a crackle with the wood burning and with an outdoor venue like this, the sound just drifts off. I'm not sure anyone will hear you. Sorry, miss. No offense."

"No, I understand," she responded nervously. He was probably right. She moaned the word *Henrrryyyy* internally but still his smiling face still did not appear at the top of the stairs.

"Look, miss, if we're going on with this, I've got to get this fire started. It's time." He walked toward the center of the woodpile and all eyes were on him as he carefully used pieces of kindling and matches to coax the flame to life.

Meanwhile, Catherine continued to pace and elevated her wishes into desperate silent prayers for Henry to appear. Earnest petitions went aloft along with wisps of bonfire smoke as Catherine clutched *Udolpho* tighter and visualized Henry at the top of the stairs with all her might. Afraid to look but knowing she must, she opened her eyes and looked toward the entrance. Her heart skipped a beat. The figure of a dark-haired man wearing a top hat at a jaunty angle, short of stature and wiry of build, was just topping the stairway and striding toward her. Could it be? As he came closer, she gasped and cried out his name.

"Willoughby??"

In the cellar, Maggie was gasping, too, having a small coughing fit. It had been triggered as she tugged a heavy three-ring binder off a high shelf, stirring up a cloud of dust. It was thick with moldy papers and the rings had rusted closed.

"I say, old girl. Are you all right over there?"

"I will be, Henry. No worries. I found something."

"Bank ledgers?" Henry asked hopefully.

"I don't think so. Smells old, though. Phew!" Maggie jerked her head away from the musty item.

"Well, it will be in good company with the rest of this reeking lot. Bring it over."

Henry had set up a new treasure collection on a ping-pong table as the pair worked their way down the shelves that ran along the long wall to the right of the stairwell. Henry had found a large bulky flashlight that he was able to upend on the table to provide general illumination. This improvement had made their search work much more efficient since it eliminated the need to communicate while holding a flashlight in one's mouth. However, none of the items they had found, mostly playing cards, poker chips and a few checkerboards, seemed particularly valuable.

Maggie plunked the binder down on the table and dust

205

particles floated through the beam of light from Henry's upward-facing torch. She sat on a stool and opened the cover, immediately causing the first page to fly out onto the table.

It was the cover page of a sort of handbook which purported to teach no less a skill than "Enjoying Your New Fallout Shelter—1962 Edition." Beneath this bold title was a quaint Dick-and-Jane style illustration of a stereotypical 1960's family, visible in their shelter by the magic of a transparent roof, apparently unfazed by the above-ground cataclysm since a smiling Mom was cooking supper in a dress and pearls while the kids played cards. Dad, meanwhile, was wearing a tie, smoking a pipe and improbably reading a blank newspaper.

"Ha! This is a fallout shelter, Henry! People built a lot of these back in the early 60s. Mystery solved!"

"Huzzah!" He walked to Lizzy's side of the table and looked at the artwork. "I say, Lizzy! We're doing something wrong because we look a fright, and these people look immaculate! Mum is full of post-apocalyptic cheer, cute little bow in sister's hair, ruddy cheeks on brother. Pity, though. Poor Papa seems to have gone mad, reading his blank paper over and over, poor sod."

"Well, he's a white man from the 1960s who can't go out and sell insurance anymore. I mean, of course he's going to have issues." She shrugged and winked at Henry.

"Now, now, I understand your father is quite white-ish. What does Mr. Argyle do, pray tell?" Henry asked, seating himself across from Maggie.

"Sells insurance," Maggie said drily.

"He doesn't!" Henry exclaimed gleefully. He paused and pointed at Maggie. "He doesn't, does he?"

"Nope," she said, pointing back to her banter-worthy

friend with a grin. "Nah, he works for a non-profit. Provides counseling for homeless kids in shelters all over Chicago."

"Ah, so he would be a valuable man here in the fallout shelter. Not going daft like the father in the picture, but rallying the rest of us, keeping *us* sane."

"He would. He's great in a crisis. I wish I could be more like him that way. But I'm useless." Unexpectedly, the stress of the day suddenly caught up with poor Maggie and tears pooled in her eyes. "Why haven't they come, Henry?" she asked aloud. She looked across the table pitiably as tears slid down her cheeks. "They have to know we're missing by now. Why haven't they come?"

"Oh, my sweet girl," Henry gazed at Maggie compassionately and quickly pulled his stool next to hers. He gathered her into an embrace and Maggie laid her head on his shoulder and wept in frustration. "Oh, no, sweet girl, no," he cooed. "They don't know where we are, do they? No. But they're looking madly for us, I'm sure. Scouring every inch of the place, even as we speak. And we're safe and snug here, aren't we? Of course, we are. Enough tea and porridge to last an age."

"I don't *want* to be here an age! And I *hate* that bucket thingee!" she cried out petulantly, giving Henry's chest a couple of thumps for emphasis.

"Oh, now," Henry remonstrated softly. "You were so pleased to find our little loo, weren't you? Has a proper toilet seat on it, doesn't it? Tidy little disposable bags?"

"It's still a *bucket* and I *hate* it!" she declared, devolving into wracking sobs.

"Well, that just shows your impeccably good sense, my dear. Shh, now, shh." He rocked her until her weeping subsided, stroking her lush curls and murmuring soothingly. "You are an amazing woman, Maggie, such resourcefulness and pluck. Wonderful in a crisis. Your father would be so proud of you right now."

He placed his hands gently on each side of her head and leaned back to look in her eyes, now frightened and sad, but nonetheless quite fine. "*I'm* proud of you, Maggie."

He's such a kind man, Maggie thought to herself, looking back into Henry's dear eyes. Her heart registered yet another Henry *ping* though her toes remained steady and cool. *He's so cheerful and supportive. Just like … just like …*

Henry tilted her head, ever so gently, upward toward his. It was a question, one that needed an answer. Maggie searched his eyes to know what was in his heart and, more to the point, what was in hers.

And then in a moment, they both knew.

Just like my father.

Henry smiled to see it written there in her eyes. He nodded and tapped his chest to let her know he had discovered it in his heart, too. Then, he tilted her head downward just a bit, kissed her tenderly on her forehead and clasped her close again.

"I think that's just where that was supposed to go, don't you think, Maggie Argyle?" he asked softly.

"Exactly right, Ian Henry Tidball," Maggie answered. With a profoundly relaxing sigh, she snuggled into his embrace. *Just like my Dad, my best friend ever. Henry's so like him. No more than a friend, I guess, but thank God, no less. Thank God. Like the brother I never had. Finally.*

"Maggie," Henry said absently, stroking her hair, "did you know, me mum's mum is from Jamaica? Mum says that's where we get 'the wave in our hair and the wit on our lips.' This amazing mane of yours makes me think of mum every time I see you. She used to let me braid it up for her at bedtimes when I was a lad. I could have a go with yours if you like."

"Maybe later. This explains so much about you, Henry," Maggie said, smiling into his chest.

"Great influence in my life, my mum. Wicked sense of humor and speaks her truth aloud, believe me. You'd love her."

"I'm quite sure I would, my friend. Quite sure indeed."

Chapter Twenty-six

Nothing Willoughby says makes any sense at all.

Catherine bit her fingernails and stared at the dark trees whizzing past as she bounced in the open carriage on the way to the *S&S* ball in London. She was still wearing her smoky bonfire clothes because Gary hadn't allowed her to enter Northanger to change ("water's still out, miss") but it wasn't the fact that she smelled like a charcoal briquette that was bothering her. It was Willoughby. *Something is off with that guy,* she thought to herself, attacking another nail and mentally reviewing the event.

Willoughby had galloped up to her in a tearing hurry, beckoning her to join him in the lengthening shadows behind the garden maze hedgerow several paces from the bonfire.

"What are you doing here?" Catherine had asked. "Aren't you supposed to be over in London for the ball?"

"I'm on my way," he assured her breathlessly. "But I've got a message from Tilney and …" he gulped for air and bent over, propping himself up with his hands on his thighs. "I'm supposed to come over here and do something for him first."

"Is Henry okay?" Catherine asked, her heart suddenly pounding.

"Yeah, he's fine," Willoughby said with a wave of his hand. "He's just staying overnight in the City with his girl-friend, that Lizzy chick."

"What? Like, in a hotel? With … Lizzy?" *Ouch,* she thought, not wanting to admit how much that idea stung. *Gee. Henry said they were just friends,* she thought before immediately directing her wayward thoughts back on track.

"I don't know where they're staying but … here. Look at it for yourself." He scrolled to the proper place on his JaneyApp before handing it to her and bending over again, still gasping for air.

Tilney: Hi, chap. I'm staying in New York City tonight so don't expect me back any time soon. Lizzie is staying, too, so no one should worry about us. Can you please go do my event for me at Northanger, lad? I don't want Edith to be mad so please don't tell her, okay? Just do the event and don't let anyone tell Edith. Especially don't let the small girl at Northanger tell people because they will be really mad at her for no reason even though the event will be fine. Thanks, old dude, and cheerios, then.

Catherine looked up, mystified. *Hi, chap? Old dude? Again with the Cheerios? This is absolutely **not** from Henry.* She pulled out her own phone but there was nothing new from Henry. Impulsively, she glanced at the bent and still-winded form of Willoughby and quickly took a photo of the "Henry" text before handing his phone back to him.

"So, see, that's about you especially," he said, pointing at his phone. "Henry *especially* doesn't want you telling people that he's missing, Connie."

"It's Katie," she said tersely. "And yeah, I see that. I guess I'm 'the small girl at Northanger.' So, how did you actually get this?"

"JaneyApp message, just a bit ago," he responded, finally catching his breath and standing to look around. "We should get going, right? JaneyApp cast call schedule says the event starts at 7:30. So, if we get started here quickly, I can do it then head over to London and do my event over there. I'll be a bit late but it will be fine."

"No, 7:30 is the call time for the cast to report," Catherine corrected, shaking her head. "The reading won't start until 8:30. Takes a while to get the fire burning, sun's not down yet. See? Can't start until then."

"Oh," Willoughby said, obviously thwarted. "I didn't know that. I mean, Henry, must not … know that. About the schedule and whatnot."

*Sure. A guy who's been reading cast call schedules all his life forgot how they work. This guy isn't even very **good** at lying,* she thought bitterly. "Well, anyway," she said addressing Willoughby aloud, "you obviously should get over to London, like, *now.* There's no use in wrecking two events. I'll talk to the caretaker. Maybe they can mic me or something."

"Yeah. Hey, that guy's got a mic on," Willoughby pointed toward the General Tilney character striding out of the front door of Northanger. It was young Enzo, intimidating as ever in his great bulk and white mutton chops, but not quite so frightening when he was costumed as a country gentleman rather than a bronze statue come to life. "Isn't that guy in this event? I saw his name on the call sheet."

"Yeah, briefly," Catherine acknowledged. "He comes up to me at the end when I'm all scared and invites me inside for a cup of tea. This is the part of the story before he finds out I'm not rich, so he's still being extra nice to me."

"Well, maybe you can borrow his mic," Willoughby said with a shrug. "Or maybe he can read to you instead of Henry."

It actually wasn't a horrible idea. The General's voice was huge. And it would be reasonably in character for the man to read to his little guest during his nice guy phase. Catherine stepped into view of Gary and Enzo, eagerly waving to them. Enzo cheerfully approached her and greeted her in character, more or less.

"Hello, my fair Miss Morland. How are you this fine and, um, fiery evening?" He bowed low and she bobbed a curtsy.

"I'm not so great, actually, and I need a huge favor. Step over here for a second and Willoughby can explain the problem." She grabbed Enzo's arm and stepped again to the dark side of the hedge.

But Willoughby would explain nothing. He was gone.

Catherine alone was left to explain the issue. Fortunately, Enzo was an amiable fellow and after a brief explanation to Caretaker Gary, the reading actually began on time.

Even better, it didn't turn out too badly. Enzo proved to be an enthusiastic reader and his amplified voice did not fail to entertain. What he lacked in correct pronunciation, he made up for in volume and what he called the "spookification" factor by shaking his fist and issuing savage war cries whenever he lost his place. Between these fear-inspiring actions and Catherine fake swooning whenever puzzling big words came up in Enzo's text, couples in the audience had many opportunities to clutch their sweeties tightly and they applauded enthusiastically at the end. Even Gary conceded gruffly that things had worked out all right and that he saw no reason to call Edith.

But something is definitely off, about Willoughby, about Henry's message, about Lizzy, about Northanger, about everything, Catherine reiterated to herself back in the bumpy carriage. *Something is just off.*

"Are you doing all right, Miss Morland?" Enzo shouted from the driver's box.

The young man's thoughtful words were no longer amplified to spookify volume but his natural voice was loud enough to pierce her thoughts. Enzo had kindly offered to drive her personally to the *S&S* ball in London and she had gratefully accepted.

"Yes, I'm fine, General! Thanks for asking," Catherine replied loudly, leaning forward to make herself heard. "I really appreciate the ride."

"Call me Enzo. I had to bring this carriage over to London anyway for an event tomorrow morning," Enzo shouted over his shoulder. "Glad I could help."

"Well, it's really nice of you, Enzo," she shouted back, gripping her bonnet against the whistling wind. "What's the event tomorrow?"

"Lydia's wedding to Wickham. Brand new venue. It's an Austen Canon event, too. First time in the cycle. I'll be driving their wedding carriage afterward."

Enzo slowed the horses as they entered the city limits and stopped at the London Coach House. "I'm supposed to leave the carriage here for decorating but the venue for the ball is just up the street, see?" He extended a gloved hand toward a pristine white building just ahead. Late coaches arriving from other events on the main property were lined up outside the door of an imposing two-story stone edifice with light spilling from every window. Dancers were visible through the second-floor windows and strains of music drifted on the cool evening breeze. Enzo handed off the reins to a livery man and walked back to help Catherine out of the high coach.

He opened the small half-door and let down the stairs for her to descend, but even on the last rung it was obvious that the last step was still too high for her diminutive legs to reach the ground.

"I don't mean to be pushy, Miss Catherine, but ... may I help?" Enzo asked delicately. "I'd have to lift you."

"It's fine," she said with a smile. "My little brother is your size and he picks me up all the time without even asking. So thanks for that and yes, please. Let's do this."

Enzo carefully grasped her around the waist and lowered her toward the ground. At the last moment, however, he swerved to place her a few feet further away from the carriage than expected.

"Whoa! Sorry," he apologized. "The horses just left an unexpected obstacle right over there." She noticed the pile of obstacle to which he referred and offered her thanks for the sudden move.

"Hey, you've seen me through all kinds of ... obstacle tonight, Enzo. It's been a tough night with Henry missing, but I thank you for all your help."

"Listen, I've got a sister, too. And if some guy stood her up, he'd have to answer to me." He thumped his thumb on his chest. "I'll help you any way I can."

"Thanks. For the record, though, I don't think Henry stood me up on purpose. I just don't." She shook her head with firm conviction. "There's no way he sent that text. I think Willoughby's wrong or lying or something. There's just no way Henry wouldn't show up for a performance. I think he's missing. I think he's in trouble."

"What do you think happened to him?" Enzo asked with sincere concern.

"I honestly don't know," she said helplessly. "But my friends are awesome at figuring things out when we all put our heads together. They're meeting me over at the dance. They will probably think I'm crazy for worrying but they usually listen and try to help anyway. I've just *got* to make them listen this time. Anyway, thanks for everything." She waved and started to leave.

"Catherine, wait." She turned to see the young man's face looking deadly serious. "I don't think you're crazy."

"Really?" she asked hopefully, taking a step back toward him.

"Really. In fact, I think you may be right. That Willoughby dude is squirrelly as Central Park in May. I keep seeing him over at Northanger like he lives there. Twice I've seen him up on the third floor where *nobody* lives."

"Maggie was right!" Catherine said breathlessly. "She said she saw a man up in that third-floor window."

"He was up there, all right. And there's a creepy old dude wandering around the first floor and some guys digging down in the wine cellar! Dang it, *everything* is off at Northanger. I probably should have spoken up a while ago but, hey. I'm speaking up now. Henry is in *my* cast, and so are you. It's Northanger staff's job to look after you guys. So, yeah. If you'll let me, I want to help. We'll make 'em listen, okay?"

"That sounds awesome, Enzo," she said, relief evident in every quarter of her ear-to-ear grin. "Come on. They're waiting."

Indeed they were. Everyone had amused themselves for a time with Regency business as usual, Jane and Bingley dancing, Brandon and Ferrars chatting up the Dashwood sisters and Darcy hiding out in the gentlemen's billiards room due to the abundant presence of Nebraska librarians at the venue.

But when Maggie had failed to show up for the London dance to surprise Darcy, as he had secretly hoped she would, and Catherine had texted that Henry was a no show at Northanger, it was hard to pretend that nothing was wrong. Though Darcy stayed closeted in the billiards room, Bingley and Jane and their *S&S* friends had drifted down to the foyer of the grand house to await Catherine's arrival.

"Well, this is really upsetting," Marianne exclaimed, twisting her hankie, "and it's getting quite strange, I mean, *strange* strange, don't you think, Elinor?"

"Yes, my dear, with your usual flair for the obvious I think you've captured it," Elinor deadpanned. "Jane, for your sake, I wish we could be more helpful in solving this mystery since you and Lizzy were so helpful to us in our time of need. But Marianne and I are required to stay here at the venue until after the rejection scene."

Jane moved a bit closer and lowered her voice. "So, when is that coming? And where?"

Marianne spoke up with an animated giggle. "We don't know! It's so top secret that they won't even tell *us!*"

"Apparently, if you can believe it, past Mariannes have had difficulty not blurting out secret information," Elinor intoned, looking steadily at Ferrars.

"Indeed," Ferrars replied with a solemn wink for his crush. "Staggers the imagination."

"Secrets only keep us all further from the bracing fresh waters of truth, don't you agree, Miss Marianne?" Brandon asked with a poet's wistfulness.

"So true, Colonel Brandon," Marianne said, smiling politely and sparing Brandon a tiny crumb of recognition upon which the besotted man would feast for days.

"Anyway," Elinor continued, "no one at all knows the specific location, not even the event managers. Some time tonight, we will get a text to rotate randomly between three separate locations. Willoughby will get a set of three locations, also, only one of which is the same as ours. Then, whenever we all find ourselves in the same room, which will be a true surprise, even to us, we are to proceed just as Austen wrote it. Marianne calls out Willoughby's name, he acts cool toward her in front of his fiancée, Marianne gets hurt and shocked."

"Dramatically hurt and shocked," Marianne added happily. "And almost faints."

"Yes, yes. Dramatically hurt and shocked and almost faints," Elinor repeated. "It is amazing how often Marianne has to be carried in this story. I wonder if Austen was having a little fun with all of Marianne's swooning. I never noticed it before, but the woman hardly moves without tumbling over."

Elinor looked toward the rear of the entrance hall and sighed deeply. The Two Jens and a smattering of librarians were already beginning to gather. "Well, we shall have to go now. We are supposed to keep circulating, to keep the CanonScavvers from piling up in one room." She jerked her head toward the back wall where the Scavvers immediately looked away, pretending to ignore the Dashwood sisters. "Please give us a quick text if Elizabeth and Henry turn up," Elinor requested, patting Jane on the hand.

When the Dashwoods had cleared the room, Jen Two gave a sharp whistle to gather the attention of the other Scavvers before issuing the enigmatic order, "Cloak room, top of the hour, for assignments. Scatter." Catherine and General Tilney entered the door a moment later and were nearly trampled during the Scavvers' hasty exit, though on the plus side, the new arrivals had no trouble finding their waiting friends in the newly-emptied foyer.

The young Miss Morland accepted welcoming hugs and her helpful friend Enzo was warmly greeted by all. But Catherine was in no mood to delay and came quickly down to business after these salutations were exchanged, glancing around the hallway. "Listen, is there somewhere private where I can pull out my phone? I want to share this text."

"Well," Colonel Brandon offered, pointing to the Cloak Room door, "I don't think anyone will be in there, not until the top of the hour, anyway. As long as we're out of there before the Scavvers come in for their briefing, I think we'll be alone." All shrugged in agreement and Brandon opened the anteroom door.

"Boy, this isn't like any closet we have in Indiana," Bingley said, gazing about the well-appointed room in wonder. "It's got chairs and everything!"

"Might have held cloaks in the Regency era but was much more than a closet even then, to be sure," Ferrars explained. "Nowadays, it's a term for a rest room in the UK or a private meeting room in the US. Your Capitol building in Washington D.C. has one for each political party, I believe, but there's nary a cloak in sight nowadays."

"Hey, Catherine," Bingley said, pulling out his phone, "go ahead and start, but I'm texting Darcy to come down here. He needs to hear this. He's been pretending all day that he's fine but that guy is really worried about Lizzy."

"Yeah, well, I think we should all be worried about both of them," Catherine said firmly. "And we need to decide what we're going to do." She turned to Enzo. "What are you listed under on JaneyApp? I can't find you."

"I'm listed under VincenzoP3. You are looking at a proud third generation Pelletucci right here, folks, Vincenzo Pelletucci, the Third."

He proudly pulled himself up to his full height and smiled.

"My gramps was Benny Pelletucci's brother, Vincenzo One, the guy that built Northanger and brought down Larry Tedesco. If somebody's up to no good at the Abbey, believe me, I'm the guy you want on the case."

Chapter Twenty-seven

Maggie stretched and yawned like a drowsy jungle cat. "Getting hard to stay awake here, Henry." She rubbed her eyes and looked at the treasure table glumly. "Lot of games but not much else. I guess we'll never be bored here."

"True enough," Henry agreed. "It's an odd mix, really. A few cheerful family games but it seems they were counting heavily on gambling their way through the nuclear apocalypse." Three roulette wheels and several canvas bags of poker chips and cards now rested on or near the treasure table.

"I don't see much of real value except maybe this vintage Monopoly game." Maggie picked up the brightly colored play money. "You know, I don't think I ever finished one Monopoly game in my life. We'd play for days sometimes."

"Oh my. Sounds rather like cricket," Henry observed.

"We would run the bank out of money after a while. But did you know, you can use anything for money if you run out in Monopoly? It's in the rules. Robbed my cousin's pretend grocery store cash register, used cash from other games, even tried gutting my mom's wallet once. But that didn't go well."

"Monopoly is quite an American game, isn't it? The goal is literally and nakedly to obtain all of the money, isn't it?"

Maggie laughed. "Yeah, raised some of us to be good little capitalists, I suppose. With top hats and cigars and literal 'get out of jail free' cards." *Darcy probably played it day and night,* she thought with a grin as she reached for her phone to ask him when he was fitted for his first top hat as a child. In a flash her grin faded, of course, as the truth flooded back when she felt her empty pocket. *Can't*

220

believe how many times a day I think of that guy, she thought gloomily. *Is Will thinking of me? And what can he possibly be thinking with Henry gone, too, and Willoughby probably telling all kinds of lies about us?*

She sighed deeply and another yawn followed in its wake. "Have we found any bedding yet, sheets, blankets, that kind of thing? I'm honestly going to have to lie down before too long."

"Really?" Henry pulled out his pocket watch. "Oh, my. Later than I thought. We'd both be up and dancing if we were over at the *S&S* ball, though, wouldn't we?"

"Yeah, probably," she said, smiling wanly. "Willoughby had to show up for that one. I just want to scream, 'sit on him, people, don't let him go! He's locked two people in a cellar!'"

"We've got to trust the LaGGards to keep looking for us, old girl," Henry said resolutely. "They know we're not the sort to leave everyone in the lurch. It may take them a bit of time to find us, though, so we need to be patient. But at the end of the day, I trust Janeites, don't you?"

"I do!" she acknowledged. "And that's the core problem I keep having with Willoughby! Supposedly, he's a Janeite, like us! This guy actually *won* the top Austen essay contest just like you and I did, submitted an essay, a video reading, two personality tests. It's a lot of work, as you know very well. He did all that to come here to do what, lock people in cellars?"

"What do we know about this fellow, anyway?" Henry asked. "Apart from the fact that no one, except Marianne, seems to like him very much."

Maggie tilted her head back to visualize the man. "Well, let's see. He's a short and bony white guy, cheesy smile, writes bad poetry."

"Has a grandmother originally from this area," added Henry, "but sells cars in Kansas City. Quite far from here, it is, Kansas City?"

"Definitely," Maggie confirmed. "See, we are in the *eastern* US now, but that city is in the *Midwest*, like my city, Chicago. Both cities are just east of the geographical center of the US."

Henry squinted. "*East* of the center is in … the middle … of the *West*, then?"

"What? No." Maggie looked confused. "Well, yeah. Sort of. Look, the West is big, okay? Never mind that."

"Right. Sorry. Anyway, the man lives quite far away but grandmama grew up here in New York."

"Yes. And she brought the grandkids, including Willoughby, back here to visit the resort," Maggie mentioned. "So Willoughby has some kind of an attachment to this place and a lot of insider info, too. I wonder if his grandma worked here at some point. If so, she might even be part of the Pelletucci family."

"Interesting thought," Henry acknowledged. "It's always been a family-run business. What's Willoughby's real name, anyway? They announced it at the Winners' Welcome Dinner."

"Geez, what was it?" Maggie said, biting her lip. "I think we would have noticed if it was Pelletucci or DeStefano or Tedesco, any of the colorful local names."

"Yes, had a rather bland sound like Wilson or Jackson," Henry mused.

"Johnson!" Maggie shouted. "'Jerry Johnson of Johnson Motors, Kansas City, MO!' That's how he introduced himself. Like that 'Bob Vance, Vance Refrigeration' guy on 'The Office.' A walking advertisement for himself. Classic Willoughby."

"Indeed!" Henry agreed with a chuckle. "I say, Lizzy, side-bar here, but *Kansas* City. Not actually *in Kansas*, then?"

"Not all of it, just … oh, just *go* with it, Henry," Maggie said in exasperation. "We're trying to connect Willoughby here. We know Mr. Willoughby Fancy Pants Johnson of Johnson Motors has a local connection, maybe even a Pelletucci connection, *here* at the resort." She raised her index finger. "Also, he seems to be in league with the techie guys from the shed since he got them to withhold your phone." She raised a second finger.

"Likely, likely," Henry agreed, nodding.

"And," Maggie continued, "he's probably in league with skinny Gary the caretaker, too, and the diggers," a third and a fourth finger were raised, "because skinny Gary and his crew both want Northanger cleared out for their little digging project, something Willoughby clearly wants, too. And they are *all* looking for something in that cellar, probably the *wrong* cellar, because Larry Tedesco"—finger number five—"told them to!" She closed the five-finger conspiracy mob into a fist and thumped it on the table. "And here we sit, helpless, not even able to figure out what they're looking for!"

Maggie let loose with another leonine yawn, this one with a tiny roar attached.

"Poor Lizzy," Henry sympathized. "Have a lie down, my dear. I think there may be linens in that tall cupboard on the south wall."

This particular cabinet was in the farthest and darkest corner of the cellar so Maggie grabbed a flashlight for her investigation. She was pleased to notice that empty white laundry bags were strewn all over the floor in that area, a sign that boded well for the presence of linens. The tall metal cabinet, however, had a sturdy padlock joining the two metal doors in the center.

"Henry, it's padlocked."

"Ah, yes! But the screws on the hinges are rusted out on the left door. Just pull, my dear, and the door should come right out."

And so it did. One heartfelt tug and the left door came away in Maggie's hand, still attached to the other door by the padlock. The connected doors swung open awkwardly on the remaining hinges of the right door and the beam from Maggie's flashlight picked up neat stacks of folded linens and blankets on the higher shelves. She let out a victory cry.

"Huzzah, Henry! We've got sheets and blankets!"

"Wonderful, old girl. Not too mildewed like the cots, then?" The bundled canvas cots had not stood up well to the passage of time. The ones they had tried to unfold had pulled apart at the stitches or were covered in black mold.

"Nope. I mean, it smells like the closet of a thousand-year-old grandma, but I think everything will air out." She shook out a few sheets and some rough camp blankets and spread them out over nearby tables. "It's hilarious that they locked up the sheets but not the food."

"Yes," Henry murmured thoughtfully. "Odd. I say, Lizzy, anything else in there that might have a bit of value?"

"Doubt it," she said, eyeing the lumpy laundry bags on the lower shelves. "More canvas bags. Darker color bags. Maybe from a different laundry service?"

"Well, let's give them the old butcher's hook, shall we?" Henry brought a second torch over to the cabinet while Maggie pulled one of the bags out onto the floor. The drawstring had uncooperatively mildewed into an impenetrable knot.

"You know, I don't think this can be laundry," Maggie observed. "At least not laundry from *this* century. Did we find a pair of scissors anywhere?"

"No, but there's a fair-sized knife in the kitchen." Henry ran to retrieve it. With a bit of sawing, the stiffened string was severed and the reluctant bag was forced at last to reveal its contents. Both heads eagerly aimed their flashlights downward.

"What am I looking at, Lizzy?" Henry asked. "Is that currency? Good old US cash?"

"I ..." said Maggie, but that was as far as she got. There were clumps of bills, that was true enough. Some of it was in stacks held by adhesive paper bands but many of the bills were loose where the glue on the bands had failed over time. Maggie picked up a loose bill and held it under her light, examining it curiously. "A five-hundred-dollar bill?"

Henry reached into the bag and found another with the same odd denomination. "I rather thought the orange five-hundred-dollar bill in Monopoly was just a whimsical idea, not something based on legal tender. Can these be real, Lizzy?"

"I doubt it," she answered skeptically. "My Uncle Reggie showed me a hundred-dollar bill once and told me it was the highest possible bill you could get in the US."

"I see," Henry said pensively. "Uncle Reggie a bit of a bill collector, is he?"

"Sort of," Maggie answered carefully. *Not like you're thinking. But Uncle Reggie knows cash, I'll give him that.* "Whose picture is on these bills, Henry? Parker Brothers? Milton Bradley?"

Henry peered closely at his. "McKinley? Is that a famous American?"

"Probably. It's the name of my cousin's elementary school," Maggie answered with a shrug. She rooted deeper into the canvas bag and came up with a bill that looked a bit different than the five-hundreds. After peering at it closely, Maggie started to chuckle.

"Henry, these are fake! Look at this." She extended the bill toward Henry who examined it carefully under his torch.

"Oh, my!" he exclaimed with a smile. "A one-*thousand*-dollar bill? Yes, that looks decidedly off. You Yanks love playing games with the old ready, don't you?"

"I know, right?" Maggie shook her head. "I had a boss once that brought in some fake thousands like this for an employee incentive program. They had *his* ugly face on it, but other than that, it looked pretty similar. Well, hey, if we ever run out of Monopoly money in our many years together down here, no worries, mate. We've got bank!"

"Huzzah!" he celebrated. Relieved to see Maggie joke about their situation rather than worry, Henry cheerfully helped her replace the bag in the cabinet and close the squeaky door.

Though the cots were not usable, Henry had found an old exercise mat and once it was laid flat and layered with sheets and blankets, it made a passable pallet. After all flashlights were extinguished, Maggie removed and bundled her petticoat into a decent pillow while Henry did the same with his waistcoat. The front of Maggie's dress was stiff with dried milk where there had been an unfortunate spill during the cooking process. Now, she bit her lip and pondered the idea of removing her dress and sleeping in her underclothes.

"Henry?" Maggie said tentatively. "It's pretty stuffy in here. I might peel off a bit." There was a pause. "Just don't shine that flashlight over here if you get up in the night."

"Of course, my dear. Listen, I've got an idea," he suggested. "This shirt of mine would make quite a modest nightshirt for you. Full coverage, eh? I've still got my coat so I won't miss it." Maggie agreed and after quickly removing the stained dress, shuffled into Henry's blousy shirt. There was something cozy about wearing a man's shirt and she smiled as she wrapped it around her.

"Okay, little bairnie," Henry soothed, "under the covers you go." Maggie snuggled down underneath a sheet and Henry layered her with a blanket before sitting down cross-legged beside her. "I'll keep the first watch."

"Aren't you going to sleep, Henry?" Maggie asked, suppressing a yawn. "I'm fine if we share a mat." She patted his knee. "I think we know what we're about now."

"I'll join you in a minute, Maggie. You just cuddle doon." He tucked her hand under the covers and sat beside her.

"Cuddle doon," she murmured, smiling into the darkness. "My Dad read that poem to me when I was little. For years I wouldn't go to sleep without it."

On his side of the mat, Henry smiled, too. "I won a prize at school with that poem when I was just a wee fellow. Wore a kilt me mum made and I performed it in a grand, old Scotsman's voice, I did. Brought the house down."

Suddenly, he was six years old again, standing on the stage in front of the school assembly in his tiny kilt and sporran. The memory of his mum's smile and her voice from the front row—"that's our Henry, he's got a gift, he has"—made him smile nostalgically as he began his recitation now. "Cuddle Doon, by Alexander Anderson," he began.

"The bairnies cuddle doon at nicht

We muckle faught and din

'Oh, try an' sleep, ye waukrife rogues,

Your faither's comin' in.'

They niver heed a word I speak
I try tae gie a froon,
But aye I hap' them up an' cry
'Oh, bairnies, cuddle doon!'"

As Maggie dozed beside him, Henry laid down and continued each verse, describing the bedtime antics of wee Jaimie and Rab and Tam, in the Scottish rhythms that soothed both players like the sound of familial heartbeats. And like the poet Anderson's naughty siblings, who shared a taste for shenanigans until they finally found rest together, two of our most mischievous Austen characters found their peace in sibling kinship, too, that night, drifting off together as Henry whispered the final lines.

"The bairnies cuddle doon at nicht
Wi' mirth that's dear tae me
But soon the big warl's cark an' care
Will quaten doon their glee
Yet come what will to ilka ane,
May He who rules aboon,
Aye, whisper, though their pows be bald,
'Oh, bairnies, cuddle doon!'"

Chapter Twenty-eight

Catherine did not intend for anyone to overhear. But, as we all know, things happen.

The Cloak Room was proving to be a surprisingly comfortable sitting room for the guests since the actual cloaks and hats were relegated to an adjacent space in the back of the room. So finally, though Darcy would only agree to leave the billiards room with Enzo acting as bodyguard, Catherine managed to gather everyone in said Cloak Room—Jane, Bingley, Ferrars, Brandon and Enzo himself grasping Darcy firmly by the elbow—to present her evidence.

"All right everyone, I'll get right to it. I think our friends are in trouble. All day we've only been talking about Henry and Lizzy going to the City together because that's what we were told, supposedly by Henry himself. But now I don't think that ever happened. Who thinks it's not like Lizzy to go off without telling anyone?"

Jane's hand shot up along with Catherine's and in a moment all of the gentlemen except Darcy followed suit, even Enzo. "I don't know her as well as you guys do," Enzo explained to the group, "but I don't think she would go off on some overnight date with that Henry guy when she's so stuck on Darcy here."

Darcy blushed scarlet and stared at the floor while all other eyes stared at Enzo. "What, you guys didn't know that?" Enzo said, looking around in confusion. "Darcy, man, come on. I wish somebody looked at me the way she looked at you when you were on that horse, dude. Seriously."

This took a moment for the group to absorb. However,

after a few side glances and raised eyebrows, no one could disagree.

Bingley finally spoke up. "Look, Tilney is kinda spontaneous, I guess, and maybe he would do this kind of thing, but this just isn't like Lizzy. Lizzy is a read-the-packet, follow-the-schedule person. Good grief, she gets on me all the time for *not* following the schedule! And besides, there's no way she runs off like this without at *least* telling Janie. They're real close and there is just no way."

"I agree," said Jane quietly. "I've gotten texts from Lizzy every day I've known her, until today. Something's wrong."

Brandon chose his words carefully. "And we don't think that perhaps our Lizzy was *influenced* by Tilney to be a bit spontaneous? They *are* good friends."

Darcy spoke up forcefully. "Our Lizzy, aka Miss Margaret Argyle, is one of the most stubborn humans on this or any other planet. You could not influence that woman to put butter on toast if it wasn't her idea *first*. Trust me."

"Well, can we agree that it's *unlikely* that Lizzy came up with this particular plan?" Catherine queried the room. Darcy shrugged noncommittally while the other heads in the room nodded vigorously.

"So, most of us think it wasn't *Lizzy's* idea to go anywhere. And *I'm* saying, there is *no way* Henry intentionally missed his performance here," Catherine insisted. "I forwarded y'all that text he supposedly sent Willoughby. But that is *not* Henry talking. No way." A few people pulled out their phones to check the forwarded message. Affirmative mumbling followed.

"Catherine, do you think Willoughby knew this text was fake?" Bingley asked.

"Worse! I think he *sent* that text," Catherine asserted, tossing her head back. "I mean, whoever sent it misread the cast call sheet times and Willoughby misread the call sheet, too. Coincidence? I doubt it."

"Which means Willoughby may have sent us fake 'Henry' messages this morning, too," mused Jane, mental wheels turning. "Fake account or hack or something."

"But if Willoughby is trying to catfish all of us, *why*, dear girl?" Ferrars asked, throwing up his hands. "What purpose does it serve?"

"Well, that's fairly clear, I think," Brandon chimed in. "He wants everyone to ignore the fact that Lizzy and Tilney are *missing*."

"Yes, but this little ruse only works for one night, doesn't it?" Ferrars said, shaking his head. "We're all sure to raise the alarm after that. What good does one night do for him?"

"Maybe he only needs one night," Jane said. All eyes turned toward her.

"Willoughby said something a few days ago, after an event," she continued. "He wasn't happy at all and he said something like, 'oh, well, doesn't matter, it's *only for a few days.*' It sounded like he was saying that he would only be here for a few days. So maybe *tonight* he finishes whatever he's doing and then, after that, he's *gone*."

"Northanger is shut down for only one night," Catherine mused. "And Enzo said he had seen Willoughby hanging around over at Northanger."

Enzo affirmed this report. "He's been staying in that third-floor bedroom, for no good reason since he already has a room at Delaford."

"Lizzy was right! She knew someone was up there!" Jane exclaimed with increasing intensity. "And now Lizzy's gone!" She turned to Bingley, suddenly near tears. "We've got to tell somebody! Resort security or the sheriff or Miss Edith or somebody. We've got to report them missing, and

… and … have Willoughby, like, arrested or something." A tear slid down her face and she fumbled around in her reticule for a handkerchief.

"Oh, Janie, come on now, don't cry. Come on. We'll find them." Bingley, cut to the quick by Jane's emotion, put an arm around her while trying to control his own distress. "Of course, we'll let security know. Of course we will. They can look for them, can't they, Enzo?"

"Sure," the young man assured the group. "No problem. One of my cousins works in security up by Rosings. They've got video footage of anyone who comes in or out of that front gate. I'll call him right now, have him check the video. That way at least we'll know if they're onsite or off." Enzo stepped into an alcove and pulled out his phone.

"But what about Willoughby?" Jane sobbed. "He might be the only one that knows where they are! If he's planning to leave … we can't let him!"

"I know what you're saying," Brandon reasoned calmly. "But what proof do we have that he's done anything wrong? This is just speculation. You can't detain a man because he prefers a different guest room. And *we* believe the texts are fakes but he could just say they are *real*. They can question him, but it's a 'he said, we said' situation right now, I'm afraid."

"Willoughby will just lie," Jane muttered miserably. "You know how he is."

"Now, look!" Darcy said sharply. "Let's keep some perspective here. For all we know right *now,* Willoughby is just a role player from Iowa City or wherever he's from, dressed up like an Austen villain. Now, if he's a *real* villain disguising himself as a *pretend* villain, yes, we need to find that out. But he *might* just be an eccentric guy. And that doesn't make him particularly unique here, people! Look around this room—all of us standing here in 19th century clothing, waiting for a fictional character to be rejected at a ball! If you started locking people up for being *eccentric*, my God, there would hardly be a Janeite at this resort left to hold the key!" He crossed his arms peevishly and the others stood silent in the wake of this outburst.

"Well, I might have said it differently," Brandon said, giving Darcy a displeased look, "But I'm afraid he's right about detaining Willoughby without proof. Regardless of what he may or may *not* know about Lizzy and Henry's whereabouts, without some kind of *evidence* of wrongdoing, public or private security may question the man but ultimately, they cannot detain him."

"But we can."

All heads turned in surprise as a voice was heard from behind them. Unobserved during the preceding conversation, the Two Jens and several librarians had entered through the rear servants' entrance to the Cloak Room and were now standing among the coats, waiting for their turn in the main sitting area.

The head librarian, Laura Vranes, stepped forward and stood in front of the group of ladies with her hands on her hips. Her formal ball gown was striking, a deep teal-colored velvet covered in sparkling beads. Most spectacular, however, was this evening's headdress which was no less than a peacock replica, its tail feathers fully opened into a dramatic halo and the bird's head tilted downward at an imperious angle as if challenging all comers to prove their worth.

"Ladies," Brandon said in greeting, "we seem to have stayed past the top of the hour but we will depart in a moment." The Colonel gave a courteous bow which prompted similar reciprocal greetings around the room.

"It seems you're having a bit of trouble with Willoughby," Ms. Vranes continued, stepping forward. "Perhaps you are all aware, we're on the hunt for Mr. Willoughby ourselves tonight, for purposes of CanonScav."

"Yes, we gathered as much," Brandon returned pleasantly. "Perhaps we should join forces. Your plan is to combine personnel with other Scavvers to surveil the man, it seems?"

Jen Two stepped forward. "Yes! Exactly!" she said, happy to be understood by the military man. "We don't know where the engagement will take place. But I've got diagrams and if we deploy our teams into each possible room, we can provide surveillance coverage over the whole venue." She cleared a tea table and unrolled a blueprint across it to explain her plan in more detail. The librarians gathered around for their instructions and the gentlemen listened in fascination.

Meanwhile, Jen One stepped forward to speak to Jane and Catherine. "The scoundrel Willoughby is at it again, it seems."

"We think he has done something odious with Miss Elizabeth Bennet and Mr. Henry Tilney," Jane explained in the Austen-influenced English that Jen One seemed to prefer. "But we, um, we needs must gather proof of his misdeeds. We shall be about that this very night."

"Yeah, I mean, yes, this fine evening," Catherine chimed in. "Before the cock crows ... um, thrice." Jane frowned at her but she rattled on nonetheless. "Or before ten of the, um, you know, the clock since that is when everyone returneth to Northanger Abbey. We thinks Willoughby might be done with his nefarious mischief and escape before he can be discovered if we do not detain him until that hour."

"We shall not let that happen, my friends," Miss One said gravely. "I know you must worry terribly about your sister, Miss Bennet and her lively friend Mr. Tilney. If Willoughby disturbs a hair on either of those dear heads, we shall all be most seriously displeased!" Miss One declared with Austenian indignation. "I shall speak my thoughts to Mr. Willoughby most sternly, most sternly indeed, when we find the miscreant. But I shall hold my tongue for the moment, lest I be thought to be another Miss Bates." She broke character for one small wink to the ladies before returning to her dignified Regency demeanor and joining her CanonScav colleagues at the table.

"Willoughby needs to be afraid of these women," Jane said to Catherine with an admiring smile.

"Very afraid," Catherine replied as the ladies exchanged a surreptitious fist bump. "Darcy's terrified and they're not even after him."

Indeed, Darcy had disappeared when the librarians entered the room. Enzo was standing in an alcove speaking on the phone but he had soon found himself joined in the tiny space by Mr. Darcy. Even though Darcy was not a small man, he seemed determined to position himself behind the larger man's armpit. Only Darcy's head was visible at times as he peered out from behind a bicep to assure himself that the librarians were still occupied.

Enzo muted his phone and peered over his shoulder at Darcy. "Dude, are you okay?"

"Fine, thank you. Just ... these are the women I was telling you about. The librarians. They stole a gnome, you know."

"They did what?" Enzo asked, genuinely perplexed.

"Stole ... a ... gnome," Darcy replied testily. "Why does no one see this as a problem?"

"No, it's not that. I just didn't quite ... oh, hang on. Yes. I'm here, Pauly." Unmuting his phone and lifting his index finger toward Darcy, Enzo returned to his phone call.

"Nevermind," Darcy muttered, taking a last look around the room before ducking for cover again.

The surveillance plan was elegantly simple. The Scavvers would be assigned to various rooms throughout the venue. If anyone spotted Willoughby, they were to send the location using one text buzz to all of the other Scavvers. When all three potential locations were revealed, the Scavvers were to tighten the circle by moving to those three rooms. If at any moment, Willoughby was seen in the same room with Marianne Dashwood, the Scavver on duty was to send out two buzz texts. The others would converge, Scavvers would be present for the coveted moment of Austen canon and Willoughby would be, unbeknownst to him, under surveillance for his possible crimes.

"After the rejection scene when the Dashwoods leave," Brandon added, "Willoughby's role requires him to stay at the ball with his new love interest, Miss Grey. But we are concerned that he might slip away after the dance ends. It's a lot to ask, Ms. Vranes, but could your group keep an eye on him *after* the ball?"

"Say no more, Colonel Brandon," the dear lady said, shaking her peacock feathers and calmly raising a palm. "Do not forget that the women you see before you are not just librarians, but *school* librarians. There is nothing more heinous in our eyes than a bully, especially a bully who attempts to harm lovers of books."

"Yes!" shouted Jen Two, raising a fist in solidarity.

"If Willoughby intends to harm two of our Janeites," Ms. Vranes continued, her voice steadily rising, "two of our finest essay winners, well, he has messed with the wrong people." There were a few cheers. "That gentleman doesn't know it, but this will be the most memorable night of his life. Tonight, he will know the true power of literature, my friends. Tonight, the bully loses and the readers *WIN!*"

In the chorus of cheers that followed, Jane jumped forward and placed her fist in the center of the group, over the table. "One, two, three, Camp Jane, y'all!"

"ONE, TWO, THREE, CAMP JANE!" rose from every throat, loudly enough to cause a perplexed footman to open the door and peep into the room. Assured that all was well, however, he stood aside in the doorway to allow the determined ladies to leave for their assignments.

The plan to catch Willoughby was on its feet, shod in delicate dancing slippers, it is true, but marching inexorably forward nonetheless.

Chapter Twenty-nine

The *Sense & Sensibility* London Ball was not without surprises. But we will not trifle with the reader's good sense and pretend that anyone robbed the Two Jens and their librarian co-conspirators of the CanonScav prize that night. Colonel Brandon was frank in saying later that he had participated in international field exercises with companies of trained soldiers that did not equal the preparation of the Janeite women determined to stalk and bring down Willoughby.

By midnight the Dashwood sisters had received their texted instructions and were dutifully rotating between the Music Room, the Ballroom and the Library, waiting to be surprised by the appearance of Willoughby with his wealthy new fiancée, the odious Miss Grey. Marianne had her hankies ready for her public rejection and Elinor had a bottle of lavender water in her reticule so she could revive her sister to sentience and walk her out of the venue. The Two Jens and their librarian helpers had identified and gathered in the three rooms where the Dashwoods were now limiting their activities. The trap around Willoughby was closing.

The difficult meeting was made particularly awkward this evening, however, by the inadvertent interference of a guest. The Dashwood sisters were obediently lingering in the Music Room when the occasionally uncivil Pamela Engelvardt entered, chanced upon a rather bawdy piece of Regency sheet music entitled "The Irishman" sitting open at the pianoforte and impulsively decided to play it. And not only did she play, friends, nay, she sang, too, at a volume that jet engines would envy. Neither the three glasses of wine she had enjoyed with dinner nor the ear-splitting decibel level she had chosen, however, enhanced her ability to stay on pitch. In short, one might liken the atmosphere in the Music Room to the sound of a yowling cat accompanied by a smoke alarm, if not for the disservice this would do both to cats and alarms.

"The Dutch Mynheer, so full of pride

The Russian, Prussian, Swede beside

They all may do whate'er they can,

But they'll never love like an I-I-Irishman!"

As Willoughby and his paramour, Miss Grey, who was dressed in an exquisite gown and dripping with jewelry, glided into the Music Room arm and arm, they were both clearly taken aback by the impromptu concert. Miss Grey, played by a young resort staffer who was thrilled to be assigned to play a character role after spending two summers in the Pemberley kitchen, was particularly confused. She could be heard shouting into Willoughby's ear, "Was this in the book?" to which the gentleman replied at similar volume, "I don't know. Just go with it. Marianne may not be in this room."

But of course, Marianne *was* in that room. However, rather than leaping forward to play her impulsive role when she saw Willoughby appear, she turned to her sister in confusion.

"Who is that?" she whispered urgently.

"That is Willoughby, of course," Elinor said as quietly as she could, given the noise in the room.

"He looks like him but isn't he ... fatter than he was two weeks ago?" Marianne said, unconvinced.

"Listen!" Elinor hissed crossly. "Thanks to the Pemberley dessert tray, we are *all* fatter than we were two weeks ago! But I don't care if he looks like a piggy in pantaloons to you, I am *not* being sent back home because you couldn't

239

play the role of a hysterical woman. I would literally die from the irony!" She stared into her sister's eyes. "*That* is Willoughby. *This* is an order. Do what we came to do."

With that, her younger woman nodded, gulped and leapt to her feet in full-blown Marianne mode. "Good heavens, sister!" she exclaimed loudly. "He is there, he is there! Oh! Why does he not look at me?" Elinor caught her sister by the arm and encouraged her to show more composure. But this was Marianne Dashwood and composure was not in her limited repertoire of emotions.

"Willoughby! It's me, Marianne!" she burst out, running indecorously across the room and extending her hand to him. Jen One nodded toward the three librarians assigned to the Music Room and one of them stepped behind a curtain to send the double buzz notification to the others. The critical scene had begun, despite its incongruous soundtrack.

"…Like an I-I-Irishman, an I-I-Irishman

But they'll never love like an I-I-Irishman!"

Over the noise, Willoughby gamely went on with his role. As instructed, he ignored Marianne's hand, turned to Elinor instead and made polite small talk. "How pleasant to see you, Miss Dashwood. I trust your mother is, you know, healthy and whatnot? How long have you girls, er, I mean, you ladies been in London?"

Elinor, for her role, was supposed to be too shocked by Willoughby's slight of Marianne to speak. So there was a slight scripted pause at this point. Mrs. Engelvardt, however, leapt into the breach and filled the moment with song. Thus it was that as Jen Two, Laura Vranes and her peacock, as well as the many other librarians continued to stream into the room as summoned, they arrived to find the critical Austen dialogue paused for a time and then nearly buried under the incongruous screeching of the good lady Engelvardt extolling the superiority of an Irishman's lovemaking.

"Now the London folks themselves beguile

And think they please in a capital stile

Yet let them ask as they cross the street

Of any young virgin they happen to meet

And I know she'll say from behind her fan

That none can love like an I-I-Irishman!

"Good God, Willoughby, what is the meaning of this?" Marianne finally blurted out, her distressed shrieks rivaling the vocalist for shrillness. "Have you not received my letters? Will you not shake hands with me?"

At this point, Willoughby looked confused for a moment and stood staring at her re-extended hand. Looking quite confused, he peered wide-eyed around the room, seeking instruction. Jen One murmured to Jen Two in disbelief, "How is a Janeite essay winner not familiar with this? Surely any nabob might have viewed the Emma Thompson movie." Jen Two could only shrug and agree.

Elinor spoke up energetically to make herself heard to Willoughby. "I'm sure you *will* take my sister's hand, won't you?" She waved her sister's hand at him limply and nodded to urge him forward. Receiving this cue, he reached out and took Marianne's hand briefly.

Marianne continued to entreat him. "But have you not received my notes? Here is some dreadful mistake, I'm sure. What can be the meaning of it? Tell me, Willoughby, for heaven's sake, tell me, what is the matter?"

"Yes, I got your notes, I think," Willoughby stammered awkwardly. Elinor nodded in agreement. "Right. I got 'em. So, you know, thanks for that. Er, them. The notes. Well, um, I've got this lady waiting for me." He jerked a thumb toward Miss Grey. "So, gotta go." He bowed and turned his attention back to his bejeweled escort.

Marianne staggered, moaned and looked near to swooning. Elinor quickly led her to a chair and produced the lavender water to recall her to her senses. Meanwhile, the songstress added a few furbelows on the keys and screeched the final climactic notes.

"Like an I-I-Irishman, an I-I-Irishman,

None can love like an I-I-Irishman!

Not a one, not a one, not a single one can l-o-o-o-ve

Like an I-I-I-I-I-I-I...ri-i-i-ish ... ma-a-a-a-a-an!"

The song ended with a flourish amid scattered applause. As the non-librarian CanonScavvers ticked off their cards and began to drift out of the room, Willoughby took Miss Grey's arm and began looking toward the exit door, too. Elinor, in the middle of rubbing a moaning Marianne's wrists, sent a pointed look across the room to the head librarian, jolting the feathered woman into action.

"Wonderful, my good woman, wonderful!" Mrs. Vranes proclaimed, applauding enthusiastically and moving to the side of the piano. "I don't believe this dear lady has delighted us nearly enough, don't you agree ladies?" She motioned to her fellow librarians, by now standing in all the corners of the room, to gather round at the pianoforte. "Shall we have a round of 'Slumber Dear Maiden?' Or is it late enough in the evening for 'Knees Up Mother Brown,' ladies?"

"Oh, Knees Up, Knees Up, please!" the librarians clamored, circling round the grand piano and trapping Willoughby neatly in the curve of the instrument. One of the librarians energetically took Miss Grey by the hand and led her through the crowd and out of the room, all the while forcefully engaging her in conversation about her new gown which she was only too happy to discuss.

"Do you know 'Knees Up, Mother Brown,' Mrs. Engelvardt?" Laura Vranes asked, the peacock on her head gazing down at the pianist, poised to pass judgment if the answer was negative.

"I am a Kindergarten teacher," Mrs. E declared proudly. "I played the kids' exercise version in my classes."

"Well, you'd be welcome at my school any day, good lady!" said Ms. Vranes warmly. "Play away. But I think we'll stick to the original lyrics." With a saucy toss of the peacock's feathers, the Janeites impromptu group singing began.

"Knees up, Mother Brown

Knees up, Mother Brown

Under the table you must go

Ee-aye, Ee-aye, Ee-aye-oh ... "

Jen Two leaned toward Jen One. "This can't be Regency era, can it?"

Jen One shook her head. "Probably Victorian. But it's definitely immobilized Willoughby."

This was certainly true. The man was the lone male in the room now and was completely surrounded by the librarians who were vigorously using the space around him to lift their knees as the song demanded. "It has a nice bounce, doesn't it?" Jen One said with a grin as she swayed to the music. Jen Two laughed and gave her a fist bump as the two joined their voices on the chorus.

"Oohhh, my, what a rotten song

What a rotten song

What a rotten song

Oohhh, my, what a rotten song

And what a rotten singer too-oo-oo!"

Elinor leaned toward Marianne. "I think Willoughby will be well-supervised tonight. But our assignment requires us to leave the building. I can text the others once we are in the carriage. Are you ready?" Realizing that she was no longer the center of attention, Marianne sat up and immediately regained her senses.

"Certainly," she said with sudden calm, rising and walking out of the room. "That scene did not go as I had anticipated it in my head," she commented to her sister.

"Agreed, my dear," Elinor concurred. "And I'm sure it will be quite different the next cycle and different again the one after that. But that is the interesting thing about life, isn't it?"

Marianne giggled and took her sister's arm. "I'm so glad you and I got to come together, *badi*."

"Me too, *choti*." Elinor patted her sister's hand as they paused at the top of the stairs leading to the foyer. "Now, remember to wobble a bit as we call for the carriage. You are still very shaken as we leave." Marianne immediately fell into near-swoon mode, groaning and leaning heavily on her sister.

Elinor shook her head and smiled as the Dashwoods began their descent. "You do this all too well, sister. Altogether too well."

As the sisters passed the Cloak Room door in the foyer, the LaGGards and their helpers were inside waiting to receive Enzo's report. It was well after one o'clock in the morning by now and everyone except Darcy had sagged into chairs or loveseats, yawning and leaning on the armrests. Darcy, meanwhile, paced alongside the back wall like a caged tiger, periodically stopping to glance at his pocket watch and sigh in annoyance. Bedeviled by the orchid arrangements in glass vases throughout the venue, Ferrars had taken an allergy pill and dozed in his chair for the last hour.

Brandon shook him awake when Enzo began speaking.

"Okay, folks, here it is," young Vincenzo III said tensely. "Elinor just texted that Willoughby is contained by the librarians and the Two Jens. My cousin at the front gate alerted the Security Chief. They've contacted staff at each guesthouse, and no one has seen them. They are still checking through the security footage from the gate which will take a few hours so he'll let me know in the morning. But so far, there's no sign of anyone unaccounted for entering or leaving. And guys, I don't think he's going to find any sign of them leaving."

"Why's that?" Jane asked, suddenly alarmed.

"Because I don't think they ever left. When I told my cousin about Tilney sending weird messages, he said he had heard about that from a techie at the I.T. shack. Says it was supposedly a prank. This techie dude named Harris was bragging about some promise of big bucks from Willoughby for helping him send fake texts from Tilney's account. Said the Willoughby guy wanted to make it sound like Tilney had run off with Darcy's girlfriend, talked like it was some big Jane Austen prank or something. Said everybody would love it."

"It *was* a hack," Catherine said triumphantly. "I *knew* that wasn't Henry."

"Right," agreed Enzo. "I actually know that Harris dude. He's awake all night on Minecraft anyway so, hey, I texted him just now. And the guy acted all surprised, like, hey, the whole thing was supposed to be over by lunch. The Tilney dude was supposed to come back for his phone in an hour, everybody has a big laugh, no biggie. But Tilney never came back. His phone's still sitting there at the shack." Enzo took a breath. "Willoughby got him to send one more message at about 7:30 tonight but Harris says that's all. And nobody's heard from Lizzy at all, right?"

"Not since this morning when she was going to meet Henry at Northanger," Catherine said forlornly.

"Yeah," Enzo agreed glumly. "I actually guilted that Harris guy into checking Lizzy's JaneyApp account. That was the last text she sent. No activity at all since then."

This was foreboding news and the weary players felt the weight of it. Even Darcy sat down to absorb this information.

Jane's eyes filled with tears and she turned to Bingley. "Where is she?" The compassionate man's eyes moistened, too, as he reached to hand her his handkerchief. He murmured comforting words that he did not believe and enfolded Jane in an embrace.

"Oh, come on now, come on. It'll be all right," he said softly. "Listen, can't we call somebody, like the sheriff?" Bingley looked around at the group.

Enzo responded quickly. "My cousin said the county sheriff's office won't take any action about a missing adult until they've been gone twenty-four hours. But Resort Security is out searching the grounds right now. Also interviewing coach drivers to see if anybody remembers driving the two of them over to the London or Bath properties today. My cousin is still checking the security footage from the gate. So, they're doing everything they can."

Darcy spoke up slowly. "You know, Tilney and Lizzy got lost before, didn't they? Got all muddy last week. Hiking around off the marked trails?"

Brandon looked embarrassed. "That's true. Miss Jane Bennet and I were with them. My land navigation skills have diminished since my retirement, I'm afraid. But Miss Lizzy and Tilney do seem to have a taste for adventure hiking."

"Listen, Brandon," Darcy asked, warming to the idea,

"can you tell Security approximately where you got lost the first time? Maybe they got lost again."

"Oh, that's a good idea!" Jane said, sitting up and wiping her nose with Bingley's kerchief. "Lizzy always said she wanted to try that hike again. Didn't she say that she and Henry were going hiking today, Catherine?"

"She did!" Catherine confirmed excitedly. "Oh, do you think that's what happened? They got lost in the woods again? Maybe Lizzy dropped her phone or something?"

"But that would mean they've been out there all day and all night," Jane said anxiously. She stood and addressed Brandon. "Come on, Colonel. Let's go show them where we got lost."

Brandon spoke to her gently but firmly. "Miss Bennet, I promise I will do exactly that. But I'm going to ask you to let me go with some of these gentlemen here. I believe we discovered last time that those woods are not friendly to ladies' Regency dresses or footwear and I'm not going to risk you going out there at night."

"But what do *we* do?" Jane asked, pushing a wisp of hair out of her reddened eyes.

"Sleep," Bingley said, standing up and speaking with more force than usual. "I'm going to insist here."

"That's right," Brandon agreed. "We'll take the first watch tonight. But if we don't find them tonight, we are going to need you ladies at full strength to take over for us tomorrow morning. Bingley, can you assist the ladies in getting home?"

"Absolutely," Bingley agreed, taking Jane's arm. "I'm taking you ladies back to Longbourn. Catherine, since you're kicked out of Northanger tonight, will you stay over at Longbourn in Lizzy's room until they find her? It's right next door to Janie and we need you to keep her company, okay? Can you do that for me?"

"Sure," said Catherine, warmly looking at Jane. "Even if she does cheer for Oklahoma football."

Jane spared a tiny smile. "And I can overlook the fact that you root for Texas. For one night, anyway."

"All right, then, gentlemen, let's get to work while the truce holds," Brandon declared. "Ferrars, you know your way around the woods above Delaford so let's start there. Enzo, you look like a guy that can handle himself on a hike."

"Righto, Colonel," Ferrars said, hopping up to 'attention' as well as his belly would permit. "The birch pollen is murderous up there but anything for our Janeites," he added, checking his pocket for his requisite handkerchiefs.

"Hey, I'm in," Enzo assured the group. "I'll text Security to meet us at Delaford with some flashlights and then I'll round up a carriage to take us over there. Sorry I can't take you back in Wickham's wedding carriage, Catherine. The livery stable crew is decorating it tonight."

"Wickham's wedding!" Darcy exclaimed, jumping to his feet, and beginning to pace again. "I completely forgot! I have a Canon event here in London first thing in the morning. It's the first time they're doing the Lydia/Wickham wedding at the new venue. The Gardiners invited me to stay with them in London tonight since they're in it, too. They've got my costume! The Resort is having a little inaugural celebration in ..." He checked his watch. "Dear God, four hours. Taking some publicity photos with the players at the new chapel site before it starts."

"Stay here, get some sleep and by all means, change clothes before your event, Darcy," Brandon said, wrinkling his nose. "You still smell of cigars from the billiards room." Heads around the room nodded in agreement. "Look, Darcy," Brandon continued. "Hopefully, this will all be over in the morning but if it's not ... well, we will need a strong second shift tomorrow." The Colonel looked pointedly at the ladies and then steadily back at Darcy. The message received, Darcy finally agreed with a resigned nod of his head.

"Understood, Brandon. Do what you must. Keep in touch, especially if you turn them up, regardless of the time." The two gentlemen shook hands without speaking. Nothing more needed to be said aloud about the grim possibilities of what the morrow might bring. So, the two discrete men remained silent and instead, to their credit, simply went about their tasks as ever true gentlemen do.

"Huzzah, then, Janeites," said Brandon, heading for the door. "Let's get to it."

Chapter Thirty

Dawn was one of Jessi Lowery's favorite times of day. Even on her dream vacation to Camp Jane, where the days stretched out before her at the leisurely pace of the pre-technology era and no troubled children needing therapy were on her appointment calendar, she still liked to get up early. At the resort, she had formed the habit of enjoying an early cup of chai tea and a few pages of Austen on the lakeside bench outside of the Netherfield guesthouse where she was staying.

The morning after the *S&S* London Ball was particularly quiet for reasons that were not hard to discern when she tiptoed past the front parlor with her cup of tea and book in hand. Spread out upon blankets on the floor, were a dozen of her librarian housemates, all sleeping soundly. (No wonder. She had been awakened less than two hours earlier when they had all stumbled home from the Meryton Distillery, where they had obviously been overserved since their vigorous singing of "99 Bottles of Beer on the Wall" was hampered by repeated disagreements about which bottle number they were on.) Oddly, a lone gentlemen, who had clearly been overserved along with them, was fast asleep in the very center of the slumber party, with ladies closely packed on all sides of his supine form. He was swaddled tightly in a blanket with only his head, mouth agape and snoring, showing above his wrappings and a fully-plumed peacock standing sentry on top of his belly.

After Miss Jessi quietly closed the front door of Netherfield behind her and walked to her accustomed bench, she discovered that she was not alone. Young Dora Engelvardt from Longbourn, the guesthouse next door, was *not* usually an early riser. Preferring to read late into the night with a flashlight under her covers, she was, in fact, often difficult to rouse in the mornings when it was time for school. Nevertheless, on this *particular* morning, Dora could be observed sitting on a rock near the water's edge, quite close to Jessi Lowery's favorite bench, glumly tossing pebbles, shortly after dawn as the mist was still rising from the lake.

It was an unusual sight, a young girl, alone so early in the morning and so obviously unhappy. It raised enough red flags for Miss Jessi to set aside her book.

"Hi, there."

"Hello," the young lady intoned dully. Obviously well-trained, she rose from her seated position and offered a curtsy. "I hope that you and your family are well."

Jessi nodded graciously. "We are all well, thank you. I am from a distant land called Missouri, and the young people of my acquaintance call me Miss Jessi. Whom do I have the privilege of addressing?"

"I'm Dora Engelvardt, ma'am. We're from around here. The village of New Rochelle in the shire of Westchester." She curtsied again, deeper this time, just to make sure that it took.

"You are a very well-spoken young woman, Miss Dora," Jessi acknowledged. "Do you enjoy Jane Austen?"

"Yes ma'am, I do." Dora sighed deeply. "It's one of my special interests. I'm a pro-gi-dy. I remember things." This explanatory statement obviously gave her no pleasure this day, however, and her gaze wandered back out to the lake.

"Miss Dora," Jessi said, leaning forward, "I work with kids at my job and I have pretty good instincts about how kids feel. So I can just kind of tell that you're not happy today. I'm sorry if that's nosy but I thought I should be honest about it."

Dora squinted at the woman. "Are you a therapist?" she

asked in frank distaste.

"Yes, but I only do it if a *kid* wants me to be their therapist," she answered truthfully.

Dora sighed again. "My mom took me to a therapist a couple times. But it didn't work. Getting therapy is a problem for pro-gi-dies."

"Because of you being smarter than the therapist sometimes?" Miss Jessi asked pleasantly.

Dora smiled wryly. "Okay, that was a pretty good instinct. So, do your instincts tell you *why* I'm not happy?"

"Not really." Miss Jessi shrugged. "But my guess would be that it's about something a grown-up did. Or maybe didn't do."

"Yeah," Dora said, her despondency visibly burning off as the fire of anger ignited. "Yeah! They don't listen," she spat out. "I mean, I know important stuff, Miss Jessi. But they *don't listen.*"

"Gotta be frustrating," Miss Jessi agreed. "I mean, what kind of stuff are we talking about here?"

"Like, this guy and this lady go for a walk in the woods, right? But only *he* comes back!"

"That happened here?" Miss Jessi said, furrowing her brow.

"Yeah, right up there at Northanger." Dora motioned upward toward the castle. "Yesterday morning. My mom took me up there during the day so I could see the animal statues in the maze. They show them during a Night Tour but it's very creepy and I don't do creepy. So she took me during the day."

"Sounds interesting."

"Yeah, it was pretty cool. I wanted to see it because Mr. Darcy told me there was this one place where these librarians stole a gnome."

Miss Jessi was caught off guard. "I'm sorry, the librarians did what?"

"Stole … a … oh, nevermind. Doesn't matter." She dismissed it with a wave of the hand. "Anyway, my mom let me walk the maze by myself. So I was right in the first part, by the turn to the first dragon shrub thingee. But I could see through the bushes when Mr. Willoughby and Miss Elizabeth Bennet came out of the back door of Northanger. They took off walking down this little path into the woods. Then later on right before we left, I saw Mr. Willoughby come back by himself."

"Well, maybe Miss Elizabeth took a different path home or she came back after you left," Miss Jessi suggested reasonably.

"My mom said the same thing." She looked at Miss Jessi accusingly. "Nobody listens."

"I'm sorry," Miss Jessi said. "What are we missing?"

"Miss Elizabeth doesn't like that Willoughby guy at *all*," Dora said impatiently. "When they were leaving I heard her say 'what a tool' about him. It made me laugh a little bit and I think maybe she heard me so I hid down in the bushes. But I could tell she didn't really want to go with him."

"I see. But he wasn't … dragging her or anything?"

"No, not like that," she said impatiently. "He's skinny and Miss Elizabeth could probably whip his butt if he tried that. Sorry." She curtsied in apology for her language. "But she didn't come back, Miss Jessi," she continued, pleading her case. "Not all day. I kept asking people *all day* and nobody knew where she was. This morning, I knocked on her door at Longbourn and there's some other lady in her room, one of Miss Elizabeth's friends. She didn't know where she was, either." Dora disconsolately threw more rocks into the lake. "I don't care what my mom says, Miss Elizabeth is *not okay.*"

The only sound for a very long minute was the rapid-fire *splish splish splish* made by the pebbles as Dora threw them, one after the other, *not-o-kay, not-o-kay, not-o-kay.* After that, her anger and her ammunition spent, there was only the silence of futility.

Miss Jessi zeroed in. "Can you tell me what makes you *sure,* absolutely *sure,* that something is wrong, Dora? I really want to hear."

"Her phone," she said softly. "When Mr. Willoughby came back, he had a cell phone in his hand. My mom and I passed him as we were leaving. He was kind of embarrassed because guests aren't supposed to see staff with their phones. He put it in his pocket but I already saw it. It was Miss Elizabeth's phone."

"Hmm. You know, you're right; we hardly ever see staff with their phones," Jessi said carefully. "How can you be sure that it was Miss Elizabeth's?"

"Because I saw her with *that exact phone* last week," she said, raising her head to look the therapist in the eye. "I lost my ball during croquet at Netherfield and when I went into the woods to look for it, Miss Elizabeth was with Mr. Darcy, trying to text her sister. She put the phone away fast but I saw it, really clear. I remember the cover design because it looked exactly like the dress my teacher wore for Kwanzaa last year. It's called African kente cloth. It's really pretty. I want a dress like that, too, but my mom just keeps saying 'we'll see.'"

"And Miss Elizabeth's kente design, that's the design you saw on the phone Mr. Willoughby had when he came back from the woods?" Jessi asked, her heart beating faster in genuine alarm.

"Yes! And I'm not 'mistaken' or 'being nosy' and there *is* no 'logical explanation' no matter what my parents say," Dora answered bitterly. "*That's her phone!* Who walks into the woods, hands their phone over to some guy they don't even like and then *disappears? From the woods? And doesn't even tell her friends?*" She shook her head. "No way. She is *not* okay."

There was a pause as Jessi centered herself with a deep cleansing breath. Then, she rose resolutely, collecting her book and teacup. "Okay. You convinced me," she said simply. "I'll put these things back in the house and we'll go tell someone. Who should we tell first?"

"It *should* be Mr. Darcy," Dora said urgently, rising immediately. "He's sort of her boyfriend, I think. But he's at an event. So, maybe her sister Jane? At Longbourn?"

"Sounds good. We'll just keep telling different people until somebody listens."

"Okay. But … seriously, that could take a while, Miss Jessi," Dora warned kindly. "Grown-ups can be pretty bad at listening."

"Don't I know it, kiddo," Miss Jessi agreed, following the intrepid youngster as they headed toward Longbourn together.

Chapter Thirty-one

The first notification buzz from Jane came through on Darcy's phone during Lydia and Wickham's wedding.

Darcy's usually grim temperament had been made even worse that morning by a lack of sleep and an unfortunately-timed bad hair day. The photographers wanted him in almost all of the publicity shots for the new venue, of course, since Darcy was one of the most recognizable *P&P* characters in the scene. However, in a cruel twist of fate, the handsome man had awakened from his brief few hours of sleep at the Gardiners' house with his hair in a peculiar windswept shape. His hairs reached skyward on one side of his head while compacting into an immovable bump resembling a recalcitrant camel on the other. The hair stylist assigned to the photo shoot was reduced to standing on a chair between shots to spackle gel into Darcy's hair with a small putty knife while uttering sibilant curses under his breath, neither of which improved the dour mood of Pemberley's master.

So, when the notifications started arriving during the ceremony, Mr. Darcy's expression could only go further downhill, devolving into a full-out glower by the time the couple swept up the aisle and out of the church.

CanonScavvers were delighted and commented that the gentleman playing Darcy had the "perfect scowl" for his role.

Unconcerned with these accolades, however, Darcy followed the vicar into a side room off the front of the nave and hastily pulled out his phone.

JaneB: Darcy, there's a little girl here at Longbourn, that little Dora girl. She told a guest, a lady therapist, that she saw

Lizzy go into the woods yesterday morning with Willoughby. Then she says he came back alone but with Lizzy's phone in his hand. She described her phone cover perfectly, Darcy, that African cloth design. I think the little girl really did see it. The therapist lady believes her, too.

JaneB: OK, you're probably in the wedding now but please, contact me as soon as you can.

Darcy's heart was suddenly pounding as he read these words. He found himself furious at the idea that Willoughby, *Willoughby*, that irritating, unctuous little man, might have touched something of Maggie's. Just the notion of him holding Maggie's colorful phone, her "heritage phone" she called it, in his grubby hand made Darcy flush hot with anger. He quickly returned Jane's message.

Darcy: I'm free now, Jane. How are you doing?

JaneB: Scared. Enzo just texted and there were no unknown cars in or out of the front gate yesterday. So they HAVE to be in here but no one knows where. Poor Enzo was up with Ferrars and Brandon on Delaford Ridge all night with security, bless their hearts. Brandon finally texted me before he went to sleep about thirty minutes ago but there was no sign of Henry or Lizzy anywhere. Security is expanding the search to the adjacent properties today.

This was disheartening. Darcy had convinced himself that they would probably be found somewhere in the woods where they had gotten lost the first time, hunkered down for the night and embarrassed at being lost. He had played out in his mind the humorous accusations he might make about what those two might have been up to all night. But now it all seemed hollow and nothing was funny in the least. He had actually hoped she *was* with Tilney so she wouldn't be alone.

"I hope she's *not* alone," he murmured aloud. "She would hate that."

"Sorry?" The erstwhile clergyman, who had removed his vestments and changed back into his shopkeeper garb by now, had stopped with his hand on the door handle when he heard Darcy's voice. "Need something, my friend?"

"No, um, nothing," Darcy said quickly. "Sorry." He returned quickly to his phone as the man shrugged and left.

Darcy: Where's Bingley now?

JaneB: Bingley's on his way over here but he needs you, Darcy. Lord help us, we all need LIZZY to plan what we should do. Ironic, right?

Darcy: It is.

Darcy had no real answer for this. He needed Lizzy, too, he realized. His breath caught in his chest and he stood helpless for a moment. His phone buzzed again.

JaneB: Darcy, what should we do? We need to get this right. That's our Maggie and she needs us to get this right. She needs us to step up. She needs us.

Maggie.

Darcy's head snapped up with sudden clarity when he saw her real name. It was true that Lizzy needed them, the Janeites, her LaGGards, her friends. But more to the point, *Maggie* who embodied Lizzy Bennet in her own inimitable way, with her incredibly fine eyes and tumbling auburn hair and tendency to eat too many rangoons and overshare her thoughts, Maggie, the Maggie he woke up thinking about every day now, the one that could be his Maggie, if he could just get his act together long enough to be worthy of her, the Maggie that he was starting to need alongside him all the time, that Maggie, now, incredibly enough, needed *him*.

Dawn had come for our Will. Action followed straightaway.

Darcy: Text security everything the girl said. Take Dora up to Northanger. I'll meet you there. Let's walk through whatever she saw, whatever she heard, put our heads together and see where it leads us. I'll be there as quickly as I can.

JaneB: OK. Come quick. I'm really scared.

Me, too, Darcy thought, his breath coming fast as he tapped out his last message and ran out of the church.

Darcy: Don't be scared. Be strong for Lizzy. On my way.

The open wedding carriage, now festooned with floral garlands, was still standing in the street outside the church when Darcy burst out of the front door. Lydia and Wickham were seated in the open coach chatting with the guests clustered around them. Enzo, short on sleep from the previous night, was sitting on the driver's box holding the reins and yawning cavernously. Darcy approached him quietly.

"Pssst. Enzo!"

The young man looked down and smiled in recognition. "Hey, bud. Sorry to say, no sign of them up in those woods last night. Security is going to try again in the daylight, spread out a bit, too. No strange cars on the videos from the gate either. It's weird, man. Like they just disappeared into thin air." He shook his head and stifled another yawn.

"Listen, someone saw Lizzy yesterday morning leaving Northanger with Willoughby," Darcy said urgently. "Then, he came back *alone*, carrying *her phone.*"

Enzo sat upright, suddenly alert. "Seriously?"

"Seriously. I need to get over there. We're going to walk that route where she was last seen. Where are you going from here?"

"Nowhere, really. I just take them down the main London street here and we're done. I told those two they could ride along when I take the carriage back to Meryton afterward. You can come too if you want."

"Perfect," said Darcy. "How much longer will this take?"

"Whenever she tosses that bouquet, we can leave," he said, glancing over his shoulder. "*IF* she ever tosses it. The fangirls are pretty distracted by Wickham, I think." Indeed, Lydia was trying to get the gaggle of ladies to her side of the carriage but they seemed disinclined to leave the smiling Wickham.

"Wickham," Darcy muttered with distaste. "Holding up the works, as usual, by dazzling the ladies."

"But his charms are nothing compared to yours, Mr. Darcy, if only you used them, sir." Darcy turned around to see the ubiquitous Two Jens. It was Jen One, the Austen expert, who had spoken and she greeted the gentleman with a smile. "Mr. Wickham has a fine address and manner, it is true. But ladies want a man of true character. Women will see that character shine through if one can rouse themselves to show just a *bit* of charm, Mr. Darcy. Surely one can do that."

"She's right, Mr. Darcy," Jen Two agreed. "Just a bit of charm and ladies will see the true man underneath. At the end of the day, ladies want a Darcy, not a Wickham."

"Perhaps you are right, ladies. I shall take that under advisement." Darcy tipped his hat in thanks and the two ladies returned two curtsies. "Did you ladies stay the night in London? I saw you just a few hours ago, as I recall, at the *S&S* ball."

"We did," Jen Two responded. She moved closer and whispered the rest. "We stayed right here in the church, actually. That lady over there, Amelia Woodley? Standing with her gentleman friend, Kevin. The four of us walked here together at about 4 AM after the *S&S* ball, climbed in a back window and slept in the pews upstairs until the other guests arrived. The four of us will always be the first guests to attend Lydia's wedding, sitting right in the front pews," she said proudly.

"There's justice done, then," Darcy said kindly. "Do something for me, please, before you leave? The four of you go back upstairs and take a photo of yourselves there in the front pews, will you? Send it to this address." He pulled out the card of the publicist and handed it to the ladies. "Tell them you were the first ones in. I'll vouch for you. Tell them Darcy wanted it included in the souvenir brochure for this venue, all right?"

"Oh, thank you, Mr. Darcy! We'll go right now!"

The ladies thanked him profusely and ran to tell Amelia Woodley and Kevin of their good fortune. Darcy waved as the Two Jens ran off for their photo shoot. Miss Woodley paused at the church door and gave a farewell wave to Darcy before joining hands and racing inside with Kevin, her new and completely human love interest.

"So. Just a bit of charm from a Darcy will have more appeal than all of Wickham's simpering, eh?" Darcy's eyes narrowed to steely slits as he stretched both of his arms to shoot his cuffs and settled his morning coat with a determined jerk. "Let's find out." He lifted his head, formed his face into something approaching a smile and advanced into the fray.

"Ladies, what a morning we have had, haven't we?" Darcy spoke up loudly as he bravely swam into the midst of the crowd of women. "One more bachelor is off the market. Mr. Wickham can only attend to Mrs. Wickham now. So, no point speaking to that old family man now. Not all of us can be free and single men like me, Mr. Fitzwilliam Darcy, free to take an eager look at whoever catches that bouquet." With some difficulty, he broadened his smile to include visible teeth.

"I say, up there! Miss Lydia," he continued, "oh, beg pardon, ladies, beg pardon. *MRS.* Wickham!" He forced a chuckle that sounded nearly lifelike, and a number of the ladies giggled appreciatively. "Let's get that bouquet thrown so I can discover who is the most eligible maiden here today! Avert your eyes, Mr. Wickham, you married fossil! This is all for me, Mr. Fitzwilliam Darcy!"

Darcy quickly opened the coach door and leapt up into the carriage, something that definitely got the ladies' attention. "Who will be next? Who will be the young women picked to marry next, observed here by me, Mr. Fitzwilliam Darcy?"

It would be unkind to use words like "stampede" to describe what the fangirls did next. However, it would not be incorrect to say that the young ladies made haste *away* from Mr. Wickham's side of the coach and into position near Lydia with remarkable alacrity after Mr. Darcy's enticing invitation.

"Geez, Darcy, proud of yourself much?" Lydia said to the gentleman standing next to her. Wickham leaned back in the seat, rolled his eyes and muttered "Pathetic." Darcy stood over him unapologetically.

"Just throw it," Darcy said through gritted teeth.

"All right, ladies," Lydia called out. "I'm going to let it fly!" She turned her back and on a count of three, tossed her bouquet rather farther than she had intended. It flew over the crowd of ladies and ended up in a nearby cluster of staff members who had come over for the inaugural event and were waiting for a special coach to take them back to the main property. Emerging from the clutch of laughing employees came a confused Thaddeus Blackwell, a posy caught in his white hair and the rest of the bouquet in his hand.

"You shall be the next to wed, Mr. Blackwell," Darcy called out to the older man.

"Oh, my," said the gentleman sweetly. "You shall be my

best man, Darcy! Aunt Jane would love that."

Darcy gave Mr. Blackwell a salute and sat abruptly, shouting toward Enzo. "Let's see how fast this thing can move, my good man. There's a lady in distress."

Chapter Thirty-two

"Right here," Dora indicated, pointing at the back door of Northanger. "Miss Elizabeth and Mr. Willoughby came out right there, together."

"All right, then," Darcy said, definitively taking charge. "That's where we start. Please show us just what you saw." Dora led off with Jane by her side and Bingley, Catherine and Darcy following closely.

Darcy's ride back to the main property had taken surprisingly little time. While Lydia had dreamed of a merry post-wedding carriage ride at a *clip-clop* pace as she waved to visitors on the streets of London, the trip this day had flown by at a speedy *galumph-galumph* if we're honest. Enzo did not spare the horses as he raced down the London street and he truly stretched the team out once he hit the open countryside. Lydia leaned toward the driver several times to shout complaints. But each time the carriage seemed to surge forward faster at *just* that moment and her message was interrupted as she was thrown back against the bolsters. Perhaps it was coincidence. Perhaps not.

In any event, they were under the shade of the Meryton Coach House *porte cochére* far sooner than Darcy had expected. He hopped down from the coach quickly, leaving Wickham to assist his complaining bride, as Enzo descended and handed the reins to a stable boy.

"Thanks, Enzo," Darcy said, gratefully shaking the young man's hand. "Listen, I've gotten a text from Laura Vranes, the head librarian, and Willoughby is still unconscious and under their supervision. If he tries to get away today, they'll know it. But I have to ask one more favor. Sorry. I know you've been up all night."

"Nah, it's all right," Enzo said with a wave of his hand. "I got my second wind with that ride. What do you need?"

"Someone's got to tell your Aunt Edith about Willoughby. One of her hand-picked essay winners is probably a very bad guy. I would rather she would hear that from you, from family, before this gets out of hand, gets to the sheriff or, God forbid, the media."

"Oh, wow. I hadn't thought of that," Enzo said uneasily. "Aunt Edith is a very protective person. And she can't stand it if someone is trying to harm the resort."

"How well we know," Darcy agreed. "Lizzy's phone in Willoughby's hand definitely connects him to her disappearance, at least in our minds. But we may need to build a case legally to make sure Willoughby doesn't get away. Edith has access to Willoughby's essay and his background application. Maybe you can find some motive this guy might have for coming here and harming people."

"Yeah, that's good," Enzo said, warming to the idea. "I'm on it. Keep me posted with whatever you find out at Northanger."

Catherine had not been idle at Longbourn, seeking out the bleary-eyed Mrs. Engelvardt for permission to take Dora on an educational hike with some of the essay winners. Permission was given readily while Dora's mother leaned in the doorway, holding her aching head, before returning immediately to bed.

Meanwhile, Jane had filled her reticule with breakfast scones for Dora and the others, *just as Lizzy would have done,* she had thought with a pang. Jane had also seated Miss Jessi at the Longbourn dining table, informing staff that her guest would be taking breakfast there today. She encouraged Miss Jessi to inform Mr. and Mrs. Bennet and every other person at Longbourn, for that matter, about Lizzy's disappearance and find out if anyone had any idea where she might be.

Fortuitously, then, all the LaGGards arrived at Northanger nearly simultaneously and Miss Dora went to work immediately. "This is where I first saw them," she was saying now. Dora stood on the stone path about eight feet from the kitchen door of Northanger. "I think Miss Lizzy was mad at him. I couldn't hear what she was saying but she was standing like this." She mimicked Maggie's arm-crossed and hands-on-hips gestures while rolling her eyes and giving exaggerated sighs.

"Yeah, that's her mad look all right," Bingley confirmed. He had been on the receiving end of Maggie's ire after running late on more than one occasion.

"And then she came over here …" Dora walked to the spot near the hedge where Lizzy had paused. "And she basically said she didn't want to go. But he was like, 'oh, come on, it's only five minutes to the shed.' He pointed at that path right there."

"That's the maintenance shed," Catherine said. "Henry's been over there a lot while the tech people were working on his phone."

"Anyway, Willoughby says he will take her over there, I think to find Mr. Henry, and Willoughby says 'no swimming this time.' Then he smiles like that's funny."

"So not only is she not with Henry, she doesn't know where he is, at least at this point," Darcy murmured. "What's that about swimming?"

"He's teasing her about our botched hike," Jane interpreted.

"Yeah, well, she didn't like it," Dora asserted firmly. "When Willoughby walked away, she said, 'what a tool,' just like that. 'What a tool.' My Dad said that's not a very nice word and I'm not supposed to say it." She smiled. "It made me laugh a little bit, though."

"Understandable reaction, at least to all of us who know Miss Elizabeth," Darcy responded, side-eyeing the adults as all tried not to smile.

"But I think she heard me laughing so I crouched down behind the hedge, like this." She demonstrated squatting low. "Miss Elizabeth turned around and said, 'Henry?' But then she turned back around and left. I didn't see her again. Just Mr. Willoughby, kind of a long time later, looking at her phone."

"Can you guess how long it was before Mr. Willoughby came back?" Darcy asked.

"I walked the whole maze," she mused. "Then I walked backwards through it and that's when he was coming back."

"Okay," Darcy said, calculating the time. "Walking the maze is, let's say, twenty minutes each way. So, forty minutes elapse before Willoughby comes back. I say, let's walk down this path for half that time, say, twenty minutes, and see where we're at. That's where Willoughby would have had to turn around and come back."

All agreed and they set out immediately. The caboose of the LaGGard train, Catherine of the tiny limbs, had barely walked for two minutes before the long-legged engine in the front, Darcy, shouted back that he could see the maintenance shed through the trees. Another few minutes and they were there.

"Let's ask these guys if they saw anybody," Jane proposed brightly, walking toward the door.

"Do we have to?" Darcy said testily. "This is definitely not far enough."

"No, but these guys might know something," Jane answered reasonably, arranging the neckline of her dress in a subtly lowered position. "Why don't men ever want to stop for directions?"

"Because we know where we're going and this isn't *it,*" Darcy rejoined sullenly.

With a roll of her eyes and a toss of her lush hair, Jane walked forward into the dark lair of the tech shed calling out "Hello?"

Back outside, Bingley spoke up confidently. "If they know something, those guys will tell Janie."

"And why is that?" Darcy snapped.

Bingley looked at his friend in disbelief. So did the others, even Dora. "Darcy. Buddy. Have you actually looked at Janie lately?"

"What, because she is an attractive woman? Female beauty mysteriously loosens men's tongues somehow?" Darcy said, intimating that this was ridiculous.

"Yes," his companions answered in unison. It was a truth universally acknowledged but somehow the universe had left Darcy behind on this point.

"I'm afraid so, Mr. Darcy," Dora added. "Pretty women get out of traffic tickets, too, especially if they cry. My Dad told me."

"Ergo, it must be so," the gentleman muttered with a petulant sigh.

Jane swished out of the front door just then, smiling radiantly and wiggling her fingers toward the gentlemen in the shed. "Bye Harris," she sang out. "If you're ever in Oklahoma, look me up!" Dropping her smile as soon as she closed the door, Jane moved purposefully toward the group.

"Okay. Lizzy came by with Willoughby at approximately ten o'clock, left with him about five minutes later." she reported matter-of-factly.

"See what I mean?" Bingley said, jabbing Darcy in the

arm.

"Not now, Bingley," Darcy said, batting him away like an insect. "Sorry, Jane. Go on, please."

"Willoughby came in alone, joked around a little about the prank they were playing on Henry's phone, sending fake texts, ha ha, all that. The tech guy only saw Lizzy later through the window when the two of them left. He said they walked uphill to the trail that goes to the chapel." Jane stepped to the side of the shed and pointed up the hill to the trailhead. "He also said that Henry had walked the same way with Willoughby *earlier*, saying they were going to the chapel."

"The chapel! That's it!" Catherine said excitedly. "That's where Henry and Lizzy wanted to go hiking yesterday."

"Let's go," Darcy said, leading the way without further commentary, his thoughts reeling. *Did she get a fake text telling her to meet Tilney there? Then what? How does someone immobilize two strong people? Were they threatened that the other might be harmed? Were they restrained, tied up … or … were they …* Darcy snapped himself back to reality. Some things were too horrible to contemplate. "This trail is a little rougher," Darcy called back to his companions. "Follow me carefully, everyone. Watch your step. Assist Miss Dora please, Bingley."

Even moving quickly, it took almost fifteen minutes for the group to walk to their destination. Once they could hear gurgling water, Jane called out that the building must be nearby. When they crossed over the stream on the rustic bridge and the structure of the chapel was visible through the trees, Darcy confirmed the time on his pocket watch. It was almost exactly twenty minutes since they left Northanger. This had to be the right location. Everyone rushed forward, shouting their friends' names, looking on all sides of the chapel.

269

But of course, it was futile. The junkyard yielded nothing, the open chapel was empty. The place seemed deserted.

"This has to be the right place," Darcy insisted. "If they walked further, Willoughby wouldn't have had time to turn around and make it back to Northanger in the right time frame. I guess the only thing left is to confront Willoughby and make him admit whatever he's done."

"He'll probably just lie, though, Mr. Darcy," Dora said realistically. "Tools lie a lot."

Darcy sighed. "They do, Miss Dora."

Catherine gazed over the railing at the gothic junk. "If we were in a gothic-themed resort, like *Udolpho,* every church would have a catacomb, every castle a dungeon. But in Austen's world, not so much. No dungeons to speak of."

"Northanger has a wine cellar," Bingley said absently, picking burrs off his sleeve. "Henry was down there all the time, treated it like his personal wine stash. And I can definitely picture Henry poking his nose down into somebody else's cellar if he thought there was wine down there." This idea evoked faint smiles and nods all around. "No basement in this church, though. No stairs." He gestured around the chapel and shrugged.

"Well, now, in Oklahoma, we put access to a storm cellar *outside* the house," Jane said, sitting up more alertly. "Like a door in the ground with stairs going down. Keeps you from being trapped inside your shelter if the house falls over."

Darcy spoke up. "Did we check for *outside* stairs?" The group exchanged glances and then rose in unison, hastily exiting the chapel.

"Might have an air duct sticking up," Jane shouted as the group searched the area again. "Watch for that."

Darcy noted a large debris pile banked up along the side of the chapel with a long and very thick log lying underneath the pile. Two concrete gargoyle statues, one wearing a worn cap, squatted on either side of the pile about six feet apart, almost as if guarding the pile against all intruders.

Sentries, Darcy mused. *Like sentries guarding a doorway.* His heart beat faster as he approached and saw something that might be a rusted exhaust pipe sticking up out of the brush.

"Over here!" he called out excitedly.

In short order the group dispatched enough brush from the top of the pile to establish that this was, in fact, a metal cellar door, blocked by the massive branch. Darcy and Bingley wrestled with it mightily to budge it even a few inches.

Jane found the air duct and tried shouting down. But the sound was deadened, likely stuffed full with something. Even knocking on it with a stick produced only a muffled *clunk.* "Come on, ladies," she urged instead. "Let's help the gentlemen."

Even little Dora took a hand at tugging on the enormous limb. Darcy lifted with all his might and wondered, briefly, what a hernia actually felt like because something definitely felt very near to popping. The huge branch did not go gently but in the end it was not equal to the determination of bookworms who will not, *will not,* let the tools win in this world and will move heaven, earth and gigantic tree limbs if necessary, to defeat them.

So, with a great *oomph* the door was cleared of its obstacle and our eager Darcy, heart pounding, threw open the metal door and was the first man down the stairs.

"Maggie?" he called out into the pitch darkness, an edge of desperation in his voice. "Tilney? Anyone down here?"

"Will?" He thought he heard a sleepy voice, soft and barely there.

"Maggie? It's Will! I'm here! Where are you?" Darcy felt around in his morning coat for his phone and finally managed to find it and turn on his flashlight. He shone it around wildly, seeing flashes of a large room with tables and chairs scattered around.

"Is it really you?" Maggie called out, a bit louder this time. Darcy swung the light in the direction of her voice. There on the floor, in the tiny circle of light, Maggie and Tilney were side by side on a palette of sheets and blankets, half-dressed and surrounded by various pieces of their clothing, sitting up and shading their eyes from the light.

"Dear God! It's Darcy!" Tilney burst out.

"Will, it's *you!*" Maggie screamed ecstatically, gathering her clothing around herself and trying to rise.

Darcy's light swung wildly as he pushed aside random obstacles to clear a path to Maggie. He heard footsteps in the darkness running his way. Then, suddenly, he felt a tight embrace around his neck and a leap into his arms as his phone went clattering to the floor.

"Thank God you've come!"

"Are they here, Darcy??" Bingley appeared on the stairs at that moment, just in time to shine his own phone on the scene of a striking *tableau*, namely, Darcy holding a shirtless Tilney in his arms and Maggie, hair wildly askew, standing behind them wearing Henry's shirt and very little else.

"They're here, Bingley," Darcy said. "Tell the ladies we've found them."

"The girls are here, too?" Henry cried out. "Huzzah!" He leapt down from Darcy's arms and headed for the stairs. "Oh, sweet, sweet freedom! Dear God, Bingley, is it really you?" He embraced the man warmly and Bingley burst into tears. "I'm blind as a bat, old man, sorry. Is Catherine here?"

"Yep, she wouldn't rest until we came for you, Henry. Janie, too. Come on, let me help you out," Bingley said, leading him carefully up the stairs.

Darcy picked up his phone and turned toward Maggie, shining his light to identify a pathway before pocketing it and heading toward her. "Are you okay? Are you really okay?" he asked breathlessly.

"Yes, I'm fine," she answered, feeling her way toward him. "A little embarrassed. It's not what it looks like, Will. It was stuffy down here and I spilled food on my dress and Henry lent me his shirt. And … nothing happened with Henry, really."

"Maggie, I don't care about that. I don't. I'm glad you had someone with you."

She had reached him at last and she threw herself into his arms, tears springing to her eyes. "I missed you so much, Will. All the time, I just kept thinking of you and reaching for my phone and … you weren't there. And it was terrible being apart from you, just terrible. I didn't think it would be this bad. But it was terrible!" She wept in earnest and nestled deeper into Will's embrace. "It's crazy how much I hated being apart from you," she sobbed. "It's crazy that I like you this much."

"It's completely crazy," Will agreed, rocking her gently in the darkness and burying his face in her incredible, wonderful, fully Maggie hair. He spoke into her ear. "But let's not be apart anymore, okay?"

"Okay," she agreed, looking up at him and sniffling as she leaned into the crook of his elbow.

Darcy caressed her face, her hair, her ears, her wonderful shoulders, but still unable to get quite enough of her Maggie-ness, he bent to kiss her right then and there, deeply, profoundly, and with every ounce of his handsome, awkward, imperfect Darcy soul poured into a long breathless moment in time.

And since Maggie reached up and kissed him back, and not by half measures either, but rather until her eyes rolled back in her head, she finally felt what it was to have not only her toes but also the wall around her stubborn Lizzy heart melt away, too. It was just for those few priceless ticks, mind you, but melt it did, friends, gloriously so. And while this may be commonplace in fiction, it is truly precious in real life for it can only happen when one flawed person dares to risk imperfectly loving, and more to the point, being imperfectly loved *by*, another exquisitely nonfictional human soul.

Chapter Thirty-three

When Lady Catherine de Bourgh rose and tapped the side of her glass with a teaspoon, the many voices in the Rosings Dining Hall were immediately hushed.

The audience invited for supper this Friday at the home of Miss Edith, aka Lady Catherine de Bourgh, two days after Maggie and Henry were rescued, included a varied cross section of resort personalities. All six LaGGards were reunited along with their youthful new friends, Enzo Pelletucci and little Dora Engelvardt. Edward Ferrars, Colonel Brandon and their lady loves, Elinor and Marianne Dashwood were present from the *Sense & Sensibility* cast, too. From the resort staff, Miss Edith's favorite, Mr. Thaddeus Blackwell and her manager of operations, the intimidating Angela Pelletucci, were also at the table.

"Friends, I'd like to welcome all to our special meal this evening," Miss Edith began. "We are particularly pleased that two of our favorite players join us today in good health. Please join me in a warm welcome for those individuals, Miss Elizabeth Bennet and Mr. Henry Tilney."

Maggie and Henry had been seated in a position of honor directly to the right of Lady Catherine and they nodded to acknowledge the applause of the room.

"Right posh treatment, this, isn't it, Lizzy?" said Henry, quite pleased with the event.

"Better than oatmeal any day," Maggie agreed.

From across the table, seated at Edith's left hand, Darcy gave a wink in Maggie's direction as he applauded. Maggie felt it ripple in her toes and immediately her smile broadened in spite of herself. *Crazy man,* she thought reflexively, *don't make it so obvious.* Then again, she rethought, *at this point, who cares?* She winked back and Darcy felt a ripple of his own.

Miss Edith continued. "The last forty-eight hours have brought unprecedented revelations to light about the Regency Resort. The people gathered here have been instrumental in making this happen and we wanted to celebrate your contributions to keeping the resort strong. We will ask one indulgence: the things we tell you here must never leave this room. Can we all agree to those terms?"

The group all solemnly murmured their assent. Young Dora urgently whispered something in Catherine Morland's ear and was reassured that her "yes" was sufficient to seal her oath of secrecy and that no curtsy was necessary.

"Very well," Miss Edith acknowledged. "Recently, you have come to know the history of Larry Tedesco, a former accountant accused of embezzlement who left the resort in disgrace before my time as manager. Some of you know that Larry, though much diminished by age and illness, recently returned to the property in the company of his son Gary, our caretaker of Northanger Abbey. When everything came to light two days ago, I asked my manager of resort operations, Angela Pelletucci, to re-investigate Larry's crimes and report them to me so that I can know, not by rumor but by fact, exactly what happened. Angela has uncovered some surprising results and I'd like you to hear them." She motioned for Angela to take the floor.

"One more thing, I believe, Aunt Edith," Angela said crisply.

"Oh, yes, my dear," the good lady agreed. "I have invited Larry's son, Gary, here tonight. He deserves as much as anyone to know the truth about his father so I've asked him to join us. I hope you will join me in welcoming him." She gestured toward the rear door of the Dining Room and a servant opened the door and beckoned for Gary to walk in. The caretaker, wearing what might have been church clothes for a Regency-era workman, entered shyly and sat quickly where he was directed, his eyes on the table.

"Hello, Gary. You are welcome here," Edith said to him warmly. He looked up briefly and nodded before immediately casting his eyes downward again. The *grande dame* turned her attention once more to her assistant. "All right, Angela. You have the floor."

Angela reached into a satchel sitting on the floor next to her chair and pulled out a brown, old-fashioned, ledger book, quite weathered. As she placed it on the table, a fine mist of dust rose up from it.

"First off, I'd like to thank one of our newest staff members, Mr. Enzo Pelletucci, for finding these ledgers for us. His grandfather Vinny, Mr. Benny's brother, kept them in storage all these years and we appreciate Enzo digging them out. Without these books the whole affair would still be a mystery to us so we are indebted to you for helping us sort this out." Enzo looked embarrassed and acknowledged the applause of the room with a small head bob.

Angela continued. "I have reviewed the books kept by Larry Tedesco during the thirty-two-year period that he was the accountant for the resort. After examining them, I can say three things with absolute certainty: Number one: Larry Tedesco was a gifted accountant. As some bookkeepers did back then, he kept his books in a numerical code, so it was a bit challenging to unravel. But in the end, his books proved to be very precise, his calculations virtually flawless. However, fact Number two is also true: Larry Tedesco diverted money that was not his to his private account."

Maggie couldn't help but glance toward Gary's chair. The man seemed to grow thinner and shrink even further into his seat. *Poor guy,* thought Maggie. *I hope Edith doesn't hold him responsible for the sins of his father.*

"Number three, however, is equally important for everyone to know," Angela continued, looking a bit harassed. "Larry Tedesco never stole one penny from the Regency Resort."

"What, now? You just said he diverted funds!" Maggie burst out loudly.

"Nice to have you back, Miss Elizabeth," Lady Catherine said evenly, calmly placing her hand on Maggie's forearm. "Angela, please continue."

"Larry, and before him his father Barry Tedesco, in addition to managing finances for the resort, kept the books for several private accounts of early employees, too. This was more common back then, especially in family-owned businesses. The money that Larry diverted actually came from one of those private accounts. In fact, every cent that Larry Tedesco stole came from the account of one person: Mr. Thaddeus Blackwell."

"Jealousy," Jane murmured into Bingley's ear as he nodded solemnly.

Eyes around the table turned toward Mr. Blackwell. He smiled wanly and looked around at his tablemates with a gentle shrug before speaking.

"Well, I don't know what Larry got up to, but I always had a roof over my head and a bit of money in my pocket, thanks to Edith's family. I was never shorted for one day of my wages, Edith, not for one day," he said fervently to his beloved lady friend at the head of the table.

Angela cleared her throat. "Indeed, it seems Mr. Blackwell received all of his wages on schedule. But there was other money that was supposed to come to Mr. Blackwell as an inheritance and this is the money that Larry diverted for himself. Aunt Edith, I'm sorry, I haven't even had time to discuss this part with you because we've just confirmed it, but Mr. Blackwell's inheritance came from your grandfather, Mr. Carlo."

"Grandpa Carlo?" Edith said, puzzled. "Carlo Pelletucci, owner of a failed dance studio and very little else in this world? What inheritance could he have left besides used bunion pads and stretched-out leotards?"

Angela took a deep breath. "Your Grandpa Carlo deposited money for years into an account for Rose Blackwell from which he paid her salary. After her death in 1962, Mr. Carlo continued to deposit money into the account, as a trust to support her son Thaddeus who, of course, was a minor when he came to live here. Larry Tedesco had oversight of that account from the time he took over as resort accountant in 1962. Unfortunately, starting in 1964 and for thirty years thereafter, aside from Mr. Blackwell's salary, the bulk of his trust money was diverted into Larry Tedesco's private account. There is only a partial accounting of what he did with all of the stolen funds, but there is evidence that Tedesco paid some of the bills for the resort during those years out of this illicit account. To some extent, these stolen funds were used to keep the resort open during the lean decades."

"My God, Mr. Blackwell's money saved Camp Jane!" Maggie murmured, echoing the stunned sentiments of all in the room.

"Well, in a manner of speaking, there is some truth to that," Angela acknowledged reluctantly. "There is also a notation that a substantial upfront cash payout was given to young Thaddeus when he moved here to the resort but we do not know what happened to that cash. Aside from the upfront cash and the money for Mr. Blackwell's salary each month, however, all of the rest of this sizable inheritance went directly to Larry Tedesco's private slush fund for over thirty years."

"Oh, this is ridiculous," Edith exclaimed, giving the table

an irritated slap. "My grandfather Carlo was a dear man and great lover of the arts. But he was never interested in business. Grandpa Carlo just wanted to spend his time with his 'muses,' he used to say, dancing or painting or writing, always pounding out something on that old Royal typewriter. But to my knowledge, aside from scratching out a living with the dance studio, he never made a dime."

"And, apparently, that is exactly what he wanted everyone in the family to think," Angela continued, "due to the *way* he made his money."

Edith was suddenly on alert. "Angela, if there is some unsavory aspect to this, perhaps we should speak in private."

Angela shook her head. "No, Aunt Edith. Nothing like that. All of the money was completely legitimate and earned by his own hard work. It's just, well, it was unconventional for the time your grandfather lived. Mr. Blackwell, do you remember what Mr. Carlo used to call your mother?"

"Oh, yes, indeed," said Mr. Blackwell with a nostalgic smile. "He called her his Bella Rose, after the heroine in the Stella Carlotta romance novels."

"Actually, it was the other way around, Mr. Blackwell," Angela said evenly. "The character was named after *her*. You see, Mr. Carlo *did* successfully publish, but to his great embarrassment, it was only under a female pen name. Stella Carlotta, author of the Bella Rose adventures and one of the most prolific writers of romance novels in the twentieth century, *was*, in real life, Carlo Pelletucci."

This set the crowd chattering. Edith looked pale from shock and immediately called for a servant to bring in a restorative sherry and leave the bottle nearby. As Miss Edith took these measures, it became clear that the Stella Carlotta name was known to many, even internationally.

"We found boxes of those when we cleaned out my grandmother's attic," Brandon said dreamily, seeing them in memory. "Literally. Boxes. Goodwill wouldn't take any more. Said they already had shelves of Stella Carlottas."

"Come to think of it, my grandmother always had a stack of Stella Carlotta paperbacks on her bedside table," Maggie recalled. "Geez, there was a fortune just in what *she* spent on those at the local Rexall."

"*Your* grandmother was nothing to mine, Lizzy," Ferrars contributed from his spot down the table. "Gram kept those books out of my reach, though. Seems she thought they were a bit steamy."

"My *abuela* said I couldn't read them until after I was married because they had *secretos del matrimonio,*" Catherine whispered to Henry shyly.

"They were quite educational," Henry acknowledged. "I used to steal them from my grandmother when I would visit. I discovered many things from dear Bella Rose. For example, it is, apparently, dashed hard for women to keep their bosoms covered in the normal course of a day of fighting mad scientists. No end of ways one's clothes can be ripped off, it seems."

"Why am I not stunned to learn that a *man* wrote these fantasies?" Maggie commented acerbically to Henry.

Once Edith was sufficiently recovered, she tapped her glass for attention again. "Well, this is rather a shock for us in the family but a tragedy indeed for our dear Thaddeus."

"If it helped the resort, I cannot think of a better use for it, Edith," Mr. Blackwell said eagerly. "It's my duty to help Aunt Jane's legacy, anyway."

"That's very kind, of course, Thaddeus, but still," Edith continued, shaking her head in dismay. "To learn of and lose a fortune in one day is hard indeed."

"But it's not all lost, Aunt Edith," Angela interjected. "Some of the Stella Carlotta books are still in print and the royalties, at least at a small rate, have continued to accrue undisturbed in Mr. Blackwell's account since Larry was fired in 1994. Also, the publisher is planning to re-issue a number of them in e-book format as Cold War-era historical romances for a new generation of readers. So your grandfather's gift to Mr. Blackwell will likely provide for him very well heading into the future."

This brought a shy smile to Mr. Blackwell's face and a round of applause from the crowd. Even Gary joined in, looking relieved.

Edith leaned forward in her chair at this point and addressed her next remarks toward that gentleman. "Gary, I believe it is time for you to tell your story. Has he arrived?"

"Yes, ma'am. He's waiting just outside."

"Very good. I encourage everyone to listen with an open mind," Edith admonished the crowd. "Gary, tell your story as you wish."

The man rose to address the crowd, literally hat in hand, like a defendant at the bar in an old movie.

"Yes, it's true, I'm Larry Tedesco's son. My mom, rest her soul, was Violet Pelletucci, one of Aunt Edith's cousins. I was born here and spent some of the happiest years of my life growing up here. Then my father, well, you heard what he did. My mom and me, believe me, never knew anything about it, certainly never saw a dime of that money," he said earnestly, shaking his head.

"No one here holds you responsible for your father's errors, Gary," Edith stated firmly, looking especially at Angela, who pursed her lips tightly but did not deign to argue with the good lady.

"Anyway, you know my story. I had a good life as plain old Gary Johnson of Kansas City. Grew up and got a good job, married a great woman and had twin sons, cutest little things you ever saw. I thought I was done with the shame of being Larry Tedesco's son. But I guess the past always haunted me."

He sighed deeply and shifted his weight, fidgeting with the brim of the hat in his hand. "Sometimes I'd think that people were looking at me, thinking, 'oh, there goes the son of a thief.' Then, when I got laid off and we lost the house, it got worse. I started feeling like people were accusing me of things I didn't do. Started drinking too much, taking out my feelings on my wife, on my boys. She left me and, well, it was the right thing to do. I wasn't a fit husband or father in those days."

Edith interjected. "I'm pleased to say, however, that last autumn, Gary showed up here a changed man. He's been through recovery, worked hard to rehabilitate himself and wanted very much to return to the place he once called home. So. We thank you for your honest assessment, Gary, but the past is quite gone and we no longer need to concern ourselves with it. Please let our friends know what has happened to you recently."

"Right." He shifted his feet again. "Once Aunt Edith took me on here, I felt like more of a man again. I got in touch with my ex-wife and my grown sons a few months ago, started getting to know them again. One of the boys, Jerry, was real excited that I was working here because he used to come out here all the time with his Grandma Violet, Aunt Edith's cousin. That boy loved the whole Jane Austen thing. He had entered the Camp Jane essay contest and won a spot before we reconnected. I was so excited that he would be coming here. Even his brother said he would come out and visit while Jerry was playing his role."

"Jerry!" Maggie exclaimed, suddenly. "Jerry Johnson of Johnson Motors, Kansas City, MO!" She leapt up and pointed at Gary. "Your son is the guy that locked us up! Your son is *Willoughby!*"

Darcy and Brandon both stood up and everyone started speaking at once. Henry tried to calm Maggie and urge her to sit down again. Brandon, for his part, blocked Darcy and held the man's elbow firmly to keep him from advancing toward the frightened caretaker. Finally, a piercing whistle sliced through the cacophony, freezing everyone in their tracks. It came from young Dora Engelvardt who was standing on an ottoman and glaring at the noisy adults.

"People, look," young Dora began, her patience with non-listening adults clearly exhausted. "Miss Edith just said we can't blame a son for things his father did. So logically, we can't blame Mr. Gary for things his grown-up son did, right?" No one spoke. Gary's eyes shifted nervously from face to face, waiting to hear the verdict.

"Right?" Miss Dora said again, more forcefully.

"Right!" Edith said, raising her sherry glass to young Dora and downing the contents quickly. Everyone relaxed and returned to their seats, muttering to the effect that of course they hadn't *personally* meant any harm to Mr. Gary and that it was just an awkward situation and of course they would hear the man out.

"And the little child shall lead them all," said Henry piously as he threw a wink Dora's way. "But I would begin your story in haste, dear sir," he added as a warning in Gary's direction. "I can only hold our Lizzy back for so long." Maggie looked daggers at Gary and crossed her arms.

Glancing nervously at Maggie, the man continued.

Chapter Thirty-four

"Well, Miss Lizzy is partly right," Gary continued, clearly uncomfortable. "My son who won the essay contest is Jerry Johnson, a car salesman from Kansas City. You all met him when you first got here, right in this very room, when he was assigned to play Willoughby. But he's not the guy who locked you up, Miss Lizzy and Mr. Henry. I promise you. Jerry's waiting outside so he can tell you what happened."

He stepped to the door and called for his son. Willoughby, dressed in a particularly meticulous way this evening, looked like the trim and smooth dandy that Maggie remembered from the Winners' Welcome Dinner. She recalled that he had charmed Marianne intensely during the training week at Camp Jane, much to Elinor's chagrin. Oddly, however, when Willoughby looked at Marianne directly tonight, they both blushed mightily and looked away immediately.

Elinor leaned toward her sister, instantly suspicious. "What have you done?" Marianne said nothing, waving her hand and putting her finger to her lips instead.

"Good evening, all," Willoughby said nervously before flashing a subdued, less-toothy version of his salesman smile. "I understand I have a lot of explaining to do. But I want you to know, I am exactly the guy you all met here at the Welcome Dinner three weeks ago, Jerry Johnson of Johnson Motors in Kansas City, MO. I love Jane Austen and I love this resort. So when my dad called to say that he was working here, I was thrilled. I had won a role in the resort essay contest so I could spend the whole summer here with him! I even convinced my brother to come out here and stay with dad for a couple of weeks. But that turned out to be a very bad idea."

285

"Your brother?" Maggie asked snarkily. "Who's he, Hairy Johnson? Contrary Johnson, the oppositional one? Your real estate brother, Glengarry Johnson?" Henry tapped on her arm but she pulled away. "No, I mean it, Henry. This is four generations of these rhyming names. People get on my nerves with this foolishness."

Willoughby looked confused. "Actually, he's Terry Johnson. We're twins, see, and …" Maggie screamed a loud *arrrggh* but Henry quickly poured her a sherry and motioned for the man to continue.

"Go on, please, Willoughby," he said courteously. "She'll be fine. You've come here, you've had a lovely reunion with your father, even your brother's come along, everyone is happy. Then what happened?"

"Well, we were all getting on so well, so I suggested we go out to see Grandpa Larry at the facility. He's not well, you know. But all he could talk about is how he wanted to come back to the resort to make everything up to Edith."

"To me?" Edith said in surprise. "Bit late for that."

Willoughby continued. "He kept saying he needed to give you the cash he took, Miss Edith. He wanted to 'give Edith the greenbacks,' you know, the cash, said it over and over. He promised he would help us find the cash he took if we would just take him back to the resort. My Dad didn't want to do it but my brother talked him into it. We brought Gramps over to Dad's apartment at Northanger, Terry moved to the empty bedroom on the third floor upstairs. It was kind of funny, whenever people saw Terry around, they just called him Willoughby, which obviously happens all the time with us. That's how I got the idea to have him play the Willoughby part when I couldn't. Except for the first day of the story cycle, you've all been interacting with Terry, not me."

"*I* knew the difference," Marianne said triumphantly.

"Right away. When I first saw him at the London Ball."

"*You* don't even know how to put on shoes when you go out of doors," Elinor snapped irritably, "and if you did, perhaps you might have caught this deception many days earlier. But, yes. You got one thing right in this mess, sister. I will note it in your permanent record. Anyway, let the man talk."

Gary sadly picked up the narrative where his son had left off. "We started looking for the cash but my dad has dementia and wasn't very helpful. He'd say 'ya gotta get down by the roots' so, you know, we thought he'd buried it outside. Tore up the gardens. Nothing. Then he was like, 'no, you have to go down by the root *cellar*. South wall of the *cellar*.' We figure he means the wine cellar. Had some trouble telling south from north but it didn't matter. Dug all over that Northanger cellar and it just wasn't there. Bottom line, we never found any cash."

He shook his head and worried his hat brim again. "And while I'm digging this useless hole, my son gets incapacitated and sends his brother Terry out to play his Willoughby role. Terry, who barely cracked a book in high school, much less won a Jane Austen essay contest! You'll have to tell this part, Jerry, because I never knew any of this. Go on. Tell 'em what happened, genius."

"Well, I met a girl," Willoughby said, clutching his heart and gazing at Marianne Dashwood with a ridiculous smile. "Some of you noticed during the training week that Miss Marianne stole my affections immediately. We were having a wonderful time in this lovely resort. Anyway, we met in the glorious woods one afternoon … then …" he looked at Marianne, asking for permission with open palms.

"Oh, God, I don't want to hear this," Brandon murmured, hiding his eyes with his hand.

"Steady on, now, old chap, steady on," Ferrars soothed,

patting the Colonel's arm.

"Oh, all right, Willoughby. Fine. Tell them," Marianne said, immediately hiding her face behind her napkin.

"I got poison ivy, too," Willoughby said while turning a shade of bright purple, "in a rather delicate area."

Looking ill, Brandon reached his long arm across the table, commandeered Miss Edith's sherry and drank the last dram directly from the carafe. Wordlessly, Miss Edith motioned for the server to bring another bottle for her and a round for the whole table.

"Don't misunderstand. It wasn't quite what you're thinking," Willoughby pleaded. "When her sister called out to Marianne, I hid in the bushes until both of them had left. I actually got the worst of it then when I was … relieving myself *after* Miss Marianne left. Unfortunately, I chose badly at that time and … well, it was not just that I couldn't wear shoes for a few days. I couldn't wear … pants."

"You were out there in the woods with *him!*" Elinor said, turning to Marianne in outrage. "When I was tramping all over, searching, and you were rolling around out there with *this man!*"

Marianne, of course, began to weep. "He said I was his so-o-o-ul mate, that he loved me and that we were meant to be together for-e-e-everrrrr," she sobbed. Elinor rolled her eyes and the sobbing continued.

Maggie spoke up sharply. "Okay, okay, Willoughby, you went for a roll in the ivy and it didn't work out too well. But why didn't the resort just call in your understudy? That's what they did with us."

"I didn't *tell* anyone at the resort," Willoughby said miserably. "The Tedescos are outcasts here and I was terrified Aunt Edith would send me home or maybe even fire my father. Plus, I had a built-in understudy, my twin brother, sitting in a room at Northanger. All I had to do was put him in some of my costumes, walk him through a few simple events and give him some of my original poetry to read. Then after a few days, I'm back in pants and no one is the wiser. I didn't even tell my dad."

"He didn't, Edith, I promise you," Gary said, clearly exasperated with his sons. "So, the Pantsless Wonder here was stuck in his Delaford room for days on end. And I guess Terry was either bringing him food or skin cream or out doing the character events. So I hardly saw either of 'em. *They* were the ones that were so hot to find this money and then they both disappeared! I had to call in guys from other crews and work overnight up there, feeling like an idiot the whole time. And Dad just kept going on about the *greenbacks*. Grandpa Barry told him there were *greenbacks* on the truck with Blackwell sixty years ago. Gotta find the *greenbacks*. Whatever. Just an old guy out of his head, I guess."

"Well, they were green, that's quite true," Mr. Blackwell spoke up kindly, "so Larry wasn't wrong about that."

No one knew quite what to say. Curious, Maggie leaned forward. "What was green, Mr. Blackwell?"

"The bags," he clarified with a smile. "Of money. Well, *my* bags of money. *They* were the green bags. Mr. Carlo was quite clear when I got on the truck. The white bags were for Mr. Benny. Those weren't mine and oh, my, there were ever so many of those. But the green bags, those were for *me*. Mr. Benny, your dear father, Edith, hugged me as soon as I got out of the truck, bless him, and he told his men, 'now you put all those bags away in a safe place.' And off they marched straight away like little ants they were, carrying bag after bag after bag. Took 'em to quite a safe place. Never quite found out where but I know your father kept them safe, my green bags and his white ones, because I never saw any of those bags, ever again."

Maggie and Henry turned toward each other, suddenly struck by the same thought. "I say, old thing," Henry began, "the bags of play money that we found in the bottom of that locked cabinet, were those laundry bags …?"

"Yep," she answered, with a broad smile. "As green as the Chicago River on St. Patty's Day, my friend."

"That's what I thought," Henry said. "The empty ones were all white, I think. But the ones they had locked away, those were quite green, weren't they?"

"Absolutely green," Maggie said, smiling broadly. "Two bags at least, maybe three. Wow. Can't wait to tell him." She offered a delighted fist bump to Henry.

"Huzzah, old girl. You spread joy wherever you go. It was almost a pleasure being imprisoned with you." He returned the bump, both gleefully adding their customary dorky fireworks flourish at the end.

"The pleasure was all yours, Henry, I assure you." They giggled like schoolkids and returned their attention to the adult conversation. Jerry and Gary had been seated at Edith's invitation and provided beverages. Willoughby, the Jerry version, was speaking.

"I'm just so sorry, Aunt Edith," he was saying. "I just had one dumb idea after another, trying to set everything right, for my dad, for my gramps, for you. But I'm so stupid! I had no idea that Terry was only helping out so he could get the money for himself. *He* had the idea to clear everybody out of Northanger. And *he's* the one who panicked when these two wouldn't leave and got Harris to send those fake texts."

Willoughby looked forlornly at Maggie and Henry. "My brother and I used to play in that fallout shelter when we were kids. But I never dreamed he could do something like that. All Terry wanted was to grab the money and skip town. Would have done it, too, if there had been any mon-

290

ey to take and if the librarians hadn't slowed him down until security could get him. My brother's the real Willoughby, I think, the real villain. Or maybe I am, the guy that loved too quickly and too much." He looked remorsefully at his erstwhile Dashwood love interest who shrugged and turned her face away indifferently. Marianne's ardor for Willoughby had clearly cooled during her convalescence, something that may have saddened her a bit in the moment but brightened Colonel Brandon's spirits immensely.

Eventually, the room sat silent as the servers, answering Edith's request, refilled glasses of sherry or other beverages around the table. Edith savored a sip from her glass and encouraged those at the table to do the same. A thoughtful smile came to Edith's face as the contemplative quiet filled the room and in time, she spoke her thoughts aloud.

"You know, Willoughby is one of Austen's most intriguing characters because he is two things at once," she observed slowly. "I have always believed that Willoughby truly loved Marianne, at least as much as a cad can love. Not all scholars agree, but *I* believe Willoughby loved Marianne. But it was too fast, too much, wasn't it? Then again, Willoughby also loved her too little. He wanted money so intensely that he caused terrible pain, even to the ones he loved. He is a dichotomy, double trouble, if you will, on both ends of the spectrum as he loves both too much *and* too little. Maybe Willoughby should always henceforth be played by twins here at the resort to truly capture the duality of the man."

Edith poured herself another sip and swirled it around in the glass slowly as the Janeites in the room contemplated the intricate Austen character, relatable, even likable, in many ways, and yet so villainous.

"Is Willoughby a true villain," Edith queried the Janeites, "or is he simply a darker version of an Everyman? Can a *good* man be two seemingly opposite things at once? What do you say, Darcy?"

Darcy looked across the table at young Dora. "Can one be proud *and* socially awkward at the same time?" Dora nodded solemnly. "I believe one can."

His glance shifted to Maggie. Her fine eyes, crackling with intelligence and spirit, moved him deeply. "Can one be valued too highly by the world but at the same time, barely worthy?" Darcy asked quietly. Her warm smile and the flush of color on her neck told him all he needed to know. "I would have to say yes, Miss Edith," he said, turning his attention to his questioner. "I believe any of us can be two seemingly opposite things at once."

Maggie lifted her glass and took a sip in his honor, afterward exhaling raggedly as her toes melted down like gummy worms on a summer dashboard. *So, if this guy is the real deal, what are you, Margaret Nichelle Argyle?* she challenged herself. *Are you the real deal? Sassy for shore nuff, but ready to love a worthy man?* She felt again the press of his lips on hers as she had leaned backwards in the arms of her rescuer, standing there in the cellar. The memory was almost unbearably wonderful. *Well, if you're not, it's time to* **get** *ready, girl. Whatever this is that I feel for that man, it's so big, it makes me feel bigger and smaller, both at the same time. Double trouble at both ends. Is that what love feels like after all?*

"Miss Edith, I think any of us, at any given time, are probably too much *and* too little, simultaneously," Maggie said, giving her opinion freely, as ever Lizzies must. "We're all too giving but also too selfish, too open to love but also too reserved. We're all double trouble, like Willoughby. All day, every day, but just to a lesser degree. Hopefully."

"Hopefully, yes, to a lesser degree," Edith laughed, lifting her glass. "One, two, three, Camp Jane, everyone!"

And in the end, as the joyful cry rang out, that was

enough, simultaneously a deeply important belonging and a delightfully silly pastime, to get everyone through until tomorrow, because at Camp Jane, the weddings will always come tomorrow and that's how every story should end anyway.

Epilogue

The *Pride and Prejudice* double wedding ending the story cycle did not fail to delight guests and cast members alike the next day, both by following Austen's script and adding a real life surprise twist.

Both of the brides looked radiant, of course. The buttons down the back of Lizzy Bennet's charming wedding dress cinched the garment into a flattering shape with a proper empire waist that embraced Maggie just as a woman might like to be hugged, tightly where necessary with plenty of freedom otherwise. The bridal gown necklines ran a bit higher than the women's other dresses, showing less of what Maggie called her "sample bosom," since these garments were designed to be particularly modest. However, this obviated the need for bosom lace covering and left Maggie's long neck and smooth caramel shoulders quite open to admiration. With her Glorious Mane swept up into a high cascade, we can assure the reader that Maggie's full loveliness was appropriately admired by all, particularly by her groom, as she moved forward to meet him.

As the younger sister, she was the first bride down the aisle, walking directly behind the flower girl who was, by special request of Maggie and Will, played by Dora Engelvardt. The youngster was quite serious about her task, counting out an exact number of rose petals for each handful to ensure that she had enough to last and was quite pleased when her final toss coincided precisely with reaching the end of the aisle.

Maggie could not help shyly finding Darcy's eyes as she slowly processed, clasping a simple bouquet, toward the front of the Pemberley ballroom, set up today to resemble a chapel. Darcy kept his stiff demeanor, of course, but with a softness in his eyes that immediately made her blush and look away as she felt the blood rising in her neck. *He sees me,* she thought to herself as a glowing smile came to her lips. *He sees the real me, the ridiculous me, and still likes what he sees.* She raised her eyes toward Will and sent a wink his way, managing to make him blush in his turn and raise a corner of his mouth into a tiny grin.

He stepped forward and extended his arm toward her when she reached the front of the room and she took her place beside him. Then, everyone in the room, including Darcy and Maggie, made a quarter turn rearward to wait for Jane's entrance.

"Your shoulders are exposed, Miss Elizabeth," Darcy muttered into Maggie's upstage ear. "Brazenly."

"You love it," Maggie murmured over her shoulder in reply.

"I do," Darcy admitted. Unobserved, he placed his palm flat against the small of her back creating an electric tingle along her entire spine. "And I don't think you mind at all."

Not at all, she thought impishly. She subtly stepped the heel of her shoe on his boot, however. "Maybe. But this is not the venue, crazy white boy. Behave yourself."

"At your service, Miss Elizabeth," he whispered, squeezing her back one last time before returning his hand to his side.

Jane was at the doorway, looking transcendent. Sunlight streaming in from the high windows found new contours in her face to set aglow as she walked forward, her countenance such a mesmerizing study in calm that one could almost forget she was moving. Bingley had stepped forward toward the aisle and had immediately been overcome, tears dripping out of his eyes as he watched her approach.

"Steady on, Bingley," Darcy murmured, handing his friend a handkerchief as he had done many times before.

"Oh, Darcy, look at her," Bingley gushed, literally, flooding new runoff onto his face even as he tried to swipe it dry. "She's an angel, Darcy, an angel." He pocketed Darcy's moist handkerchief and stepped toward Jane, extending his arm to escort her to the front of the chapel.

"Let's all try to keep it together, people," Maggie muttered to all her compatriots as the two came alongside and straightened into a line before the vicar. "The summer's young and we're doing Austen. Lots more weddings to come."

And this was truer than she knew at the time.

Of course, all the other venues had their day to wish their players joy. too. For example, the entire town of Bath, including the *Persuasion* cast, attended Captain Wentworth and Anne's wedding and subsequent dance at the Grand Pump Room. Emma and her Knightley wed upon the gazebo on the lake near the *Emma* Highbury setting with Laura Vranes, in a stunning swan headpiece, and more than four dozen librarians cheering them on a bit more raucously than Austen might have imagined. Henry and Catherine were tasked with an adorable post-wedding carriage ride, as their driver, Enzo, rode them through all the venues in their matrimonial attire. Henry was in his element, insisting that the carriage stop wherever a few people were gathered so that he could stand and declare his love for Catherine and recreate the Austen scene where he asked for her hand.

The *Sense and Sensibility* site hosted a huge afternoon banquet late in the day for their part in the wedding day celebrations. Both Dashwood sisters and their suitors-turned-husbands, Edward Ferrars and Colonel Brandon, were smartly dressed in their nuptial finery for this reception, allowing everyone to forget that Austen wrote their two weddings on very separate days. But since two weddings were clearly necessary to tie up the story, Edith was happy to make a double wedding feast at Delaford to close the *S&S* storyline in perpetuity at Camp Jane.

Every second Saturday, therefore, Ferrars and Brandon got to marry the lovely Singh/Dashwood sisters and we can assure the reader that never had two men stood taller and happier alongside their secret crushes. However, many, *many* days would pass before the shy fellows could even consider saying anything aloud about their feelings to the Singh sisters themselves. But that story will have to wait for another day.

After all the storylines wrapped up, all the guests and wedding parties were invited to Pemberley for the final scheduled event, the Saturday evening Cake and Punch Receiving Line at the Pemberley ballroom. All resort guests were invited as the personal guests of Lady Catherine de Bourgh to go through the line and greet the grand lady herself, along with all twenty of the main players in the storylines. The event served as a celebratory final event before the guests had to travel home to the twenty-first century the following day.

Though our Maggie was a bit cranky and hungry by the time the receiving line was dismissed, we can report that she was able to try all the flavors of cake in short order and her good humor soon returned. She had barely had time to wrap a slice of red velvet wedding cake in a napkin and stuff it into her reticule, however, before the evening revealed its surprise.

Lady Catherine de Bourgh called for attention, but this was not the surprise. This usually occurred at the close of the storylines, where the *grande dame* of the Regency Resort personally thanked the guests for their kind attendance and bid them return again for another delightful summer of Austen adventure. This speech was clearly supposed to be the end of the festivities and Lady Catherine was heading into the final round of her well-rehearsed address when Thaddeus Blackwell stood and approached the good lady, standing just behind her left shoulder.

We must inform the reader that in the few days since Mr. Blackwell had caught Lydia's bouquet, a great deal had changed in the man's life. No longer a penniless fellow, Mr. Blackwell's green bags had proven to be the highest possible quality of green indeed.

As was often the case with Maggie's Uncle Reggie, you see, he had been only partially correct when he had told Maggie that one-hundred-dollar bills were the largest denomination of US currency. This was true during the current era. However, at the time that Carlo Pelletucci, aka romance author Stella Carlotta, had drawn money out of his delightfully legitimate account for young Thaddeus in 1962, five-hundred and even one-thousand-dollar bills in US currency *did,* in fact, exist. Mr. Carlo had generously withdrawn a great many of these denominations for young Thaddeus when he had prepared the green-bagged cash portion of the inheritance for his protégé.

Perhaps it will not surprise the reader to know that shortly after this era, the US government put an end to printing these large denominations due to concerns that they were ripe for misuse by persons wishing to launder money such as, oh, say, racketeers and mobsters. (*Apropos* of nothing, we will mention that all of Mr. Benny's white laundry bags from his Grandpa Nicky's truck were emptied during the expansion work of the resort and not a single bill from all that cache was ever seen, found or thought of again. Indeed, Grandpa Nicky died not long after the delivery was made. However, it is said that in the days before his passing, a spring had returned to the old man's step and his gin rummy game had never been sharper.)

Despite discontinuing the printing of those large bills, the US government did, and to this day, in fact, still does continue to recognize those denominations as legal tender. More to the point, however, only a small number were known to exist in the world before Mr. Blackwell's bags were retrieved from the resort's fallout shelter. Therefore, when Mr. Blackwell, accompanied by Maggie and her LaGGard friends, had emptied the contents of one of his green bags on the counter of a paper currency collector in New York City, the numismatic expert was so overcome that he had to sit down and send his grandson upstairs to find his medication. *That's* how rich Mr. Blackwell had become, heart-clutching, fetch-my-pills rich, in the days since his green bags had been discovered. The bills as legal tender alone were worth six figures. But as rare, uncirculated, discontinued bills, their value was so much more that it was hard to calculate. The gentleman with the heart medication was still in consultation with his colleagues across the country to produce a final figure but it was going to have a great many zeroes attached to it when it came, a great many zeroes indeed.

So now, when the gentle Mr. Blackwell rose to bring a new chapter to his own storyline, it was as a very wealthy man indeed, a Darcy-rich man. And just like Mr. Bennet could not refuse to give his daughter's hand to a man like Fitzwilliam Darcy, Thaddeus Blackwell now felt confident that Mr. Benny surely would never refuse him the most ardent desire of *his* heart, his daughter Edith's hand.

Edith finished her expressions of gratitude and accepted the applause of the assembled guests before Mr. Blackwell spoke up.

"My dear, I wonder if I might have the floor for a moment," Mr. Blackwell said quietly, stepping forward to Edith's side.

Edith looked at the man in surprise. "Of course,

299

Thaddeus," she responded, mystified.

Blackwell addressed the crowd first. "Hello, dear friends. How wonderful to be among friends of my dear Aunt Jane, the most loyal friends a family ever had. My aunt was a woman who valued family deeply, even with all our many faults, you know, and she wrote about families with a certain wry touch but also with love. I know she would view all of you as part of our family, just as I do." Touched, the guests applauded and murmured their approval.

"But just as neither Aunt Jane nor Aunt Cassandra ever married, I, too, have never married. I cannot say whether my Aunt Jane ever knew true love, but I believe she must have done in order to write about it so perfectly. I certainly intend to ask her when I see her. Or perhaps I'll ask Aunt Cassandra as Aunt Jane's answer might be a bit sharp-tongued." This sent a titter through the crowd and Mr. Blackwell hid his grin behind his hand for a moment before continuing.

"As for me, however, I can speak with confidence. I found my love. Indeed, I found my beautiful complement many, many years ago and it has been the work of my life to be worthy of asking for her hand. But I shall need a bit of help from some of Aunt Jane's favorites. Mr. Darcy? Colonel Brandon? May I have your assistance?"

The two gentlemen stepped forward, smiling a bit smugly as though they were privy to a great secret. In the meantime, Mr. Blackwell pulled a small throw pillow off a nearby couch and stood before Edith clutching it. Edith began to smile, staring deeply into the eyes of her beloved. Surrounded as she was in this moment, by Austen's characters, in the Pemberley ballroom, she found herself floating just off the floor, her breath coming in short bursts, as deeply in love with Thaddeus as the night they had danced on the terrace just outside.

Mr. Blackwell tossed the pillow to the floor and asked for the assistance of Darcy and Brandon, one on each elbow, as he was gently lowered down onto one knee. The audience began to weep as they watched this, including Jane Bennet who kindly wiped both her own and Bingley's tears with her embroidered hankie.

Lowered onto his knee, he thanked the gentlemen and indicated that they might step back. Then, as Mr. Blackwell began to speak, the characters of all Austen's suitors stepped forward from the crowd, a flash mob of handsome men in wedding attire, and formed a half circle around the back of the dear kneeling man.

"Edith Pelletucci," Blackwell began, "you are the finest friend that the Austen family has ever known. You are the finest friend that *I* have ever known. Like Wentworth here, I have loved none but you and I promise to love you steadfastly forever more."

Wentworth stepped forward and lifted Edith's hand to kiss it before returning to his place behind Blackwell. Tears began to pool in the good lady's eyes as one by one each one of the beloved characters stepped forward to kiss her hand as Blackwell called them forward.

"Edith, I have loved you since your youth like Knightley loved his Emma and I shall love you ever after, too. Reprieved now by fate from the consequences of my youthful dithering, I promise to love you henceforth from the depth of my foolish heart like dear Edward Ferrars loved his Elinor. But I shall also love you with all the passion and loyalty of Colonel Brandon toward his Marianne as well." Each in their turn, the gentlemen named stepped forward and bestowed their kiss before returning to their place behind Blackwell.

It was Henry's turn to step forward now. "Like Henry Tilney loved his Catherine," Blackwell continued, "I shall love you in perfect felicity forever more." Henry bent to bestow his kiss and gave a mischievous wink as he added his own stage whisper to Edith, "Even if a bit of disobedience is called for now and again." Edith thumped him lovingly on his head and shooed him back to his place behind Blackwell.

"I promise to love you with a love as pure as Bingley's," the gentleman went on as Bingley stepped forward, "and to see you every day as the angel that you truly are." After kissing Edith's hand, Bingley tenderly placed it against his forehead for a moment to add his own gesture of affection before returning to his station, quite overcome.

"And finally, my dear, precious Edith," Blackwell continued, "I must speak as I spoke to you that night we danced together, as Darcy spoke to his Elizabeth. All these years since, Edith, in vain I have struggled, out of some sense of loyalty to your father's wishes for you to marry well, rather than marrying a penniless beggar like me. But it will not do, my dear, no indeed. My feelings will no longer be repressed." Darcy stepped forward solemnly and bent low to bestow his kiss affectionately before resuming his place in the supportive circle.

Blackwell extended his hands and took both of Edith's hands in his before continuing. "You must, Edith, now at last you *must*, allow me to tell you how ardently I admire and love you." He kissed her hands fervently and pressed her fingers to his cheek tenderly while he looked up at her. "My feelings have not changed, have never changed, in all these years. I am half agony, half hope to hear your answer, my dear. Will you now, at long last, do me the honor of consenting to be my wife?"

Edith was not a woman given to strong emotion but this, finally, was a day of unmitigated joy for her. Tears welled over and ran down her cheeks as she placed the dear man's hand on her own cheek and gave him her answer.

"With all that I am, you silly, wonderful man, I consent to be, truthfully, what I have always been in my heart, your loving and most beloved wife."

A cheer erupted from the ballroom, loud and sustained with much applause and chatter. The gentleman in Blackwell's circle sprang forth to help him rise to his feet.

"Kiss her, old man. I'd say it's overdue!" Henry encouraged him with a slap on his back.

"Oh, right you are!" Blackwell agreed, stepping forward to embrace his love and plant a surprisingly passionate kiss on her lips. This, too, made the room burst forth into even more raptures.

"Is there a ring, old boy?" Henry shouted as he and Blackwell's other wing men returned to their places in the ballroom.

"Oh, no indeed," Blackwell assured him. "Edith must pick her own decorations. She would prefer that very much. Won't you, my dear?"

Edith laughed as she gazed at him. "He knows me very well," she conceded to the room, provoking a gentle chuckle.

"You must arrange it all, my dear. You shall do so much better than I would," Blackwell said with true admiration. "I do have one request, though." The crowd hushed in anticipation.

"What is it, Thaddeus?" Edith asked with some curiosity. "You ask for so little in life, my dear. Name it and it shall be yours."

"This place has always been our family home," he began. "You have had your wonderful Pelletucci family all around you. And with Aunt Jane's characters here, too, *they* have been like having *my* side of the family in residence. So I would like our wedding party to be with your family, of course, but with Aunt Jane's *characters* also. Could we do that, Edith?"

She smiled. "I can't picture anything more perfect, Thaddeus," the good lady replied.

"Oh, wonderful," Blackwell said, clearly relieved. "And these particular friends, the essay winners this year, have been of such extraordinary service to the resort in recent weeks, my dear. Perhaps we could treat them by bringing *their* families to the resort for the occasion, too? What do you think?"

"Marvelous idea," Edith agreed, ready to consent to anything at this moment. They hugged and this provoked another round of cheering and excited conversation in the ballroom.

Maggie turned to Darcy and spoke quietly. "So, does that mean that our families are coming *here* for the wedding? Like, my mom and dad are going to meet up with *your* mom and dad?"

Darcy looked a bit green. "Oh, my. I suppose so."

"Well," Maggie said with some trepidation, "that's going to be quite a parTAY."

"Or quite a disaster," Darcy said ominously.

"Or probably both at the very same time," Maggie said, confidently hugging Darcy around the waist and gazing at the true romance that stood before them, one made more beautiful with every wrinkle that real life had brought.